Readers love the Chronicles of the Riftlands by ROWAN MCALLISTER

The Wanderer

"…an excellent action/adventure in an exotic setting, and I enjoyed it from beginning to end."

—Rainbow Book Reviews

"*The Wanderer* takes us on the beginning of a journey into a world we have never experienced before. It is a beautiful beginning to a series I eagerly await to see unfold."

—The Novel Approach

"It was an absolutely lovely fantasy story and if we are lucky a wonderful indicator of what we will have in store as the story progresses."

—Love Bytes

The Priest

"Full of fascinating fantasy world-building, engaging characters, and a new plot twist to the overall arc, it was everything I could have hoped for from a sequel."

—*Divine Magazine*

"*The Priest* is another excellent addition to the Chronicles of the Riftlands. It has the same fantastic character development and riveting story arc that made *The Wanderer* so amazing."

—Joyfully Jay

By Rowan McAllister

Cherries on Top
Danny Doormat
Feels Like Home
Green the Whole Year 'Round
Hot Mess
Lost in the Outcome
My Only Sunshine
Power Bottom?
A Promise of Tomorrow
The Second Time Around
We Met in Dreams

CHRONICLES OF THE RIFTLANDS
The Wanderer
The Priest
The Seer

A DEVIL'S OWN LUCK
A Devil's Own Luck
Never a Road Without a Turning

ELEMENTAL HARMONY
Air and Earth
Water and Fire

Published by Dreamspinner Press
www.dreamspinnerpress.com

The Seer

Rowan McAllister

DREAMSPINNER PRESS

Published by
Dreamspinner Press

5032 Capital Circle SW, Suite 2, PMB# 279, Tallahassee, FL 32305-7886 USA
www.dreamspinnerpress.com

This is a work of fiction. Names, characters, places, and incidents either are the product of author imagination or are used fictitiously, and any resemblance to actual persons, living or dead, business establishments, events, or locales is entirely coincidental.

The Seer
© 2021 Rowan McAllister

Cover Art
© 2021 Paul Richmond
http://www.paulrichmondstudio.com
Cover content is for illustrative purposes only and any person depicted on the cover is a model.

All rights reserved. This book is licensed to the original purchaser only. Duplication or distribution via any means is illegal and a violation of international copyright law, subject to criminal prosecution and upon conviction, fines, and/or imprisonment. Any eBook format cannot be legally loaned or given to others. No part of this book may be reproduced or transmitted in any form or by any means, electronic or mechanical, including photocopying, recording, or by any information storage and retrieval system, without the written permission of the Publisher, except where permitted by law. To request permission and all other inquiries, contact Dreamspinner Press, 5032 Capital Circle SW, Suite 2, PMB# 279, Tallahassee, FL 32305-7886, USA, or www.dreamspinnerpress.com.

Trade Paperback ISBN: 978-1-64405-908-1
Digital ISBN: 978-1-64405-907-4
Trade Paperback published March 2021
v. 1.0

Printed in the United States of America
∞
This paper meets the requirements of
ANSI/NISO Z39.48-1992 (Permanence of Paper).

To all those who feel like being different is a curse.

Remember, no discovery, invention, or innovation was ever made by someone who wanted to be like everyone else.

Cherish and nurture what makes you different, because a rainbow needs every color to make it whole.

Chapter One

Dakso Kavalyan swaggered down the gangplank and onto the dock, swallowing against the thickness in his throat. As he gave anyone who eyed him too closely a hard stare, he surreptitiously wiped his sweaty palms on the supple worn brown leather of his breeches and licked the beads of salt and sweat from his upper lip.

"I swear that gets worse every time," he grumbled only loud enough for his partner to hear.

Shura gave him a friendly shove from behind to get him moving out of the way of the other disembarking passengers, and when Daks threw her a disgruntled scowl, she smirked up at him. Her dusky cheeks had flushed darker in the wind off the water, and even though she'd braided her thick black hair, stray strands whipped wildly around her face.

"Guess it's a good thing this will probably be our last trip, then, isn't it?"

Her words were quickly snatched away on the wind, while gulls screeched overhead and the general chaos of the docks tried to drown her out.

"Yeah, maybe," he grunted.

As they made their slow progress with the rest of the crowd toward the gates to the city, he warily scanned their surroundings, taking note of any red cloaks of the Brotherhood or blue tabards of the King's Guard in the bustling mass of humanity.

A blast of warm, salty air caught his own heavy brown cloak, and he reluctantly pulled the damp wool tighter around him as he cast a sour look at the threatening clouds blanketing the sky. Spring had been unusually warm this year, and that wasn't exactly a boon. This far south, a good long winter kept many things at bay¾ contagious fevers, pirate raids from the Southern Isles, and war, to name just a few. It was the latter that worried him most. From all the reports and portents he'd overheard that winter, too much of the three kingdoms of Kita was unsettled these days, and the weather seemed to be mirroring that unrest.

Another shove from behind had him reaching for the dagger sheath hidden at the small of his back, but Shura only rolled her eyes at him and made shooing motions with her hands when he glared over his shoulder.

"Move, you great lump. I would be somewhere with a roof over my head before Tomok Skygod decides to relieve himself all over us," she hissed.

He shot an anxious glance at the men and women in their immediate vicinity before frowning at her. "I'd watch that kind of talk, if I were you."

She only rolled her eyes again and pushed past him. "How many trips does this one make? I am not an idiot. And, in case you've forgotten, *you're* the one who usually gets us into the most trouble, not me."

He allowed his lips to curve in a slight smirk before pulling them into a forbidding scowl again.

She had a point.

Even with his much longer legs, he hurried to keep up with her as the crowd shuffling toward the gates seemed to part effortlessly before her determined stride. He had to hide another smile as he swelled a little with affection and pride. Sometimes being exotic—and a little scary—had its advantages. Shura might be a foot shorter than him, but she could be just as intimidating.

The blue-tabarded soldiers of the King's Guard posted on either side of the great iron gate above the docks eyed them suspiciously as they approached, but obviously decided they weren't enough of a threat to interrupt the flow of traffic to question. When the gate and guards were successfully behind them at last, Daks cracked his neck and rolled his shoulders, trying to ease the tension that had built there. He needed to relax or he'd start to draw attention they didn't want.

They wove their way in hurried silence through the familiar warren of streets from Rassat's seedier harbor and warehouse districts toward their usual lodgings in the slightly safer merchant area that bordered them. Shura's Cigani skygod, Tomok, had apparently decided he'd held it long enough, because he released his burden on them in a heavy downpour several blocks from the Dog and Duck, and they had to run the last bit or be drenched to the skin.

Breathless and dripping all over the rough plank floor, they crowded into the dimly lit common room as more people ducked in out of the rain behind them, forcing them farther inside before Daks's eyes had time to adjust. He threw a glare over his shoulder, and the people closest to him stumbled a step back, throwing up their hands in a combination of fear and apology.

"Come in. Come in."

Faret, the portly proprietor, waved cheerfully at the growing crowd from his place behind the long wooden bar that dominated one side of the room.

When Shura pulled back the hood of her cloak, revealing her face, Faret's eyes widened briefly and his smile tightened. His gaze swept the people behind them before he waved again. "Come. I have a table for you," he called, switching to common tongue as he rushed around the bar.

After more than ten years of missions, both Daks and Shura were quite fluent in Rassan, but no one else needed to know that, so they never corrected him.

The two men seated at the table Faret led them to in the far back corner of the room moved off without comment after he whispered in the ear of one of them. And once Shura and Daks were seated, he said, "I'll bring food and drink," and hurried off to tend to the other newcomers.

They tucked their heavy, sodden packs safely under the table and draped their cloaks over the backs of their chairs to dry out as much as possible. The common room was crowded, noisy, and overly warm. The odors of unwashed bodies, wet wool, fish, ale, and pipe smoke were heavy and overwhelming after the gusting salt-and-sea air of their crossing from Samet. Shura's small round nose scrunched and her scowl deepened, but since her face seemed set in a perpetual scowl, only someone who knew her well would be able to tell the difference.

"The smell never gets any better either," Daks groused under his breath, and her full downturned lips twitched.

Though from vastly different backgrounds, both of them preferred the open air, fields, and forests of their childhoods to the tightly packed press of humanity and buildings of a city, but duty and conscience called… at least one more time anyway.

Feeling his mood sour even further at the thought, Daks expelled a breath and tried not to let his face show the seething anger that had churned inside him since their last meeting with the powers that be in Scholoveld. A small, forbidding scowl was enough for the role he played; anything more than that and he risked having the guard called on him by some nervous local.

One of Faret's daughters—Ilia, if he remembered correctly—arrived with a tray of stew, coarse bread, and tankards of ale, and Daks handed over a small pile of coins. Though he'd paid much more than the meal was worth, the girl pocketed the money with a solemn nod and hurried off to see to the other patrons.

"You better be careful with that," Shura murmured behind her tankard. "Those cheap bastards didn't give us much to work with this time. We can't afford to be quite as generous as before."

He reluctantly set his tankard back down after a taking a big, much-needed gulp. "I know," he replied, wiping his mouth on the back of his hand. "But it may be a while before we're back, if ever, and Faret and his family have been kind to us. They do a lot of good here when they can."

Her perpetual scowl softened as she threw him a concerned glance. "I know it's killing you that we won't be able to hit the market, that we only have enough to pay for information and leave, but we're still doing good here and back home too."

Daks grunted and took up his tankard again, as he scanned the room while trying not to make it *look* like he was scanning the room. He'd been in the spy business for more than twelve years now, and the mantle still didn't sit comfortably on his shoulders. It itched like the cheap, low-grade wool Rassan merchants sold to travelers too stupid or greedy to know the difference.

"Your heart's always been too big for this," she continued quietly, startling him with both her sudden loquaciousness and the uncharacteristic sentimentality.

He snorted and shot her a look before turning his eyes back to the room. "I think you might need to slow down a little on that ale. Heartless scoundrel happens to be my middle name. Just ask anyone."

He threw her his best cocky grin, and she sniffed. "Only for someone who doesn't know you."

This time he set his tankard down and focused all his attention on her, their cover be damned. The wisps of black hair the rain had plastered to her face had dried a bit, so they framed her high cheekbones and firm jaw rather than clinging to them. Her straight black brows had drawn down enough they almost touched the bridge of her nose, and her dark brown eyes studied him right back, more somber than their usual wary sharpness.

"Maybe I was wrong," he said. "Maybe you should drink more. Don't get sentimental on me now, Shur. You'll scare the shit out of me."

Her answering scowl was all he needed to settle the small tremor of unease in his belly. "Ass," she growled under her breath. "All I'm saying is that it might be a good thing we're being forced to move on to something else, because this is sucking the life out of you. I see it every time you set foot in this city. You can't save them all."

The "*and Josel is long past saving*" hung in the air between them, but thankfully she didn't say it out loud. They both couldn't get all weepy and emotional. They still had work to do.

When he only grunted, she angled her body away from him again, and they drank and ate together in silence for a while, trying to catch snippets of the conversations around them.

The heavy wood door to the inn opened and closed. People came and went. Luckily, no one seemed to be paying them much attention beyond the usual amount Shura's unusual looks garnered. The noise and bustle seemed much as it always had been, but Daks didn't think he imagined the new undercurrent of tension, a tightness around the eyes of everyone in the room, a brittleness to the laughter.

Rassans were a fairly tense people as a rule. Who could blame them with a religious order that was part loving embrace, part iron fist dominating their lives and hovering over their shoulders all the time? But things had changed in the capital city of Rassat in the three cold winter months since their last mission. He could see it for himself now. He could feel it along his skin.

All the rumblings coming out of Rassa and the portents of the Seers at the Scholomagi said Rassa was hurrying toward civil war—or at the very least, a rebellion. As soon as winter had released its icy grip on Scholoveld, Daks and Shura had been dispatched by the High Council, along with others, to confirm.

The king of Samebar had his own spies, but he rarely saw fit to inform the High Council of the Scholomagi of their findings, so the High Council employed a few of their less talented magic wielders, like Daks, to gather their own intelligence. He'd never given a damn about the politics and seesaw of power between the mages in the north and the king in his southern capital. All he'd ever cared about was finally having something useful to do with the pathetic "gift" he'd been given. And if he got to drink free ale, save a few lives, and bash a few evil bastards' heads along the way, he was a happy man... mostly. Now, though, even that was being taken away from him.

Shura shifted in her seat, and her sudden tension snagged his wandering thoughts. He followed her gaze to Faret as he approached their table and ducked his balding head.

"Pardon, travelers, but we are busy this day. Would you share your table with a fellow traveler?"

"Of course," Shura said, nodding to the slight figure hunched beneath a dripping brown cloak at Faret's elbow.

Daks had been expecting their usual contact, as arranged, so when the newcomer drew her hood back to reveal a stranger, he and Shura both sat up.

"I'm Dagma," the young girl said hurriedly as she cast nervous glances to either side before focusing on them again. She took the seat across from them, with her back to the room, and leaned over the table. "Maran couldn't make it. I'm her daughter. She sends her apologies," she hissed far too conspiratorially in trade tongue.

Both Daks and Shura eyed her skeptically, still tensed for possible fight or flight, but when Daks shot a questioning glance to Faret, the innkeeper gave an almost imperceptible nod before hurrying back to his bar.

"Sit back in your seat, *bebe*. You don't want people to think you're up to something," Shura murmured¾ almost gently for her. The use of the Cigani pet name was new too.

Daks quirked an eyebrow at her, but she only scowled back at him and returned her attention to the girl.

Dagma hurriedly sat back with an almost yelped "Sorry" and flushed cheeks as she undid the ties of her cloak and let it fall over the back of her chair. The girl had her mother's wheat-colored hair, pert nose, and soft brown eyes, which helped reassure Daks that she was who she said she was. The change to the plan still made him uneasy, but it wasn't as if Maran was a key contact. As a highly sought-after dressmaker for many of the wealthy families whose social circles reached as high as the king's court, she'd been a useful enough informant. She had a steady flow of gossip and had always been willing to pass it along for good coin. But nothing she sold to them was worthy of this much drama.

"Is your mother all right?" Daks asked, bored with the situation already but trying not to sound it.

"Yes. It's just—" She shot another nervous glance around her. "—things are happening faster these days, and she had to meet some… *others*. The rain meant certain… *things* were canceled, and the others had time to meet with her. Plus, her face is becoming more recognizable, and it's harder for her to move about... *unnoticed*."

The girl was enjoying playing spy far too much. Her exaggerated stops and starts and emphasis on vague words were pushing him from bored to irritated. But for some reason Shura continued to nod indulgently and make little encouraging sounds, while Daks blinked at her in disbelief. Shura was practically cooing. If the girl hadn't been far too young, Daks might have wondered if Shura was hoping to get her into bed later.

Where was Shura the irascible, Shura the Cigani scourge of villains, Shura of the barbed tongue who did not suffer fools lightly? *His* Shura?

She kicked him under the table.

There she is.

"I'm sorry, what?" he asked as he surreptitiously rubbed his shin.

"She was saying her mother will be able to meet with us tomorrow, somewhere a little less public, and will hopefully have more news than she would have had today. But Dagma can answer some questions for us now," Shura hissed irritably.

"Oh."

Does that mean we have to pay both of them? He palmed the small pile of coins in his purse.

Any lingering softness in Shura's expression soured as she stared at him, and Daks forced himself to focus on the young woman across from them. "Where does she want us to meet? I don't think going to her shop would be a good idea, even after dark," he said, trying to sound helpful and involved.

Dagma frowned as her glance shifted to Shura and back to Daks. "You don't know?"

A niggle of foreboding tingled along his skin. "Know what?"

Dagma licked her lips and leaned in. In a hushed whisper she said, "Mama has joined the *rebels*. She closed her shop two months ago after the brothers took Val."

"Who's Val?" Shura asked, shooting Daks a worried look.

Dagma's eyes glistened in the dim light. "My little brother," she replied, suddenly sounding very young. "Mama fought and screamed. Val cried. The neighbors had to drag her away before the brothers could call the guard. It was—it was horrible." Her lips trembled.

"What rebels?"

Daks hadn't meant to growl the question, but the anger he'd carried inside him for years threatened to break the stranglehold he kept on it at the mention of the Brotherhood.

He received another kick from Shura that made him grit his teeth. He threw her a wounded look before clamping his lips closed and huffing out a breath. Their primary contacts were *all* rebels in one way or another, but Dagma made it sound like this was something more organized, and that was information they needed to have.

Dagma's unshed tears dried as she looked at him like she was beginning to wonder if he was a little dense. "The *rebels*," she hissed, casting her gaze nervously about the room again as if she suddenly remembered where she was.

Daks gritted his teeth, clenched his fist around his tankard, and took a calming breath. Hoping to avoid another bruising kick to his shin, he softened his expression and his tone. "Perhaps we should wait and talk to Maran. It might be safer for you if we cut this conversation short."

He should've known better than to attempt subtlety. He'd been chosen for his gift, his skill in a fight, and his ability to impersonate a ruthless black marketeer, not because he was a charmer.

Dagma stiffened and her eyes narrowed. She ran a hand over her demurely plaited hair as she drew back her shoulders and lifted her chin. "I'm with the rebels now too," she huffed quietly. "We all share the risk, for Val and everyone else who's lost someone they love."

"You're very brave. And we're so sorry to hear about your brother," Shura cut in before Daks could open his mouth again. She pushed forward, grinding an elbow into his ribs in the process. "But this conversation sounds like more than our usual trade with Maran. So, for all our sakes, perhaps it is best kept to that more private location you mentioned, where we may all talk at length and you can tell us everything you've been up to."

Dagma's eyes softened and her cheeks pinked as her attention riveted on Shura again. That was fine with Daks, especially if it meant no more physical attacks on his person. Of the two of them, Shura was the better-looking anyway, and Dagma obviously agreed.

Cigani were rare in Rassa. Since the Brotherhood had taken over hundreds of years ago and made life hell for anyone who didn't share their fanatical beliefs, Shura's people had eventually all been pushed out of the lands they used to roam freely. Her skin color and slightly catlike dark eyes sometimes made missions there challenging, but her looks and shapely figure came in handy with starry-eyed boys and girls—and many men and women too. If Shura was disposed to being charming and gentle today, Daks was fine with being the dumb brute who sat quietly while the grownups talked.

As he took a pull from his refreshed tankard, he glanced at his partner and a small smile curved his lips, edging out some of the anger still seething inside him. When Shura was being soft like this, he sometimes regretted that neither of them swung in the other's direction. But then he'd remember what a horrible idea that was and how terrible they would be together in any relationship other than the one they had, and sanity would return… or sobriety, whichever came first.

After another furtive scan of the room, he set his tankard down and forced himself to listen to the conversation again before Shura gave him yet one more bruise somewhere more sensitive than she'd hit already. Except when he focused on Dagma, she was already rising to leave.

"Good day, traveler," Shura said, nodding to the girl.

"Good day."

Dagma bobbed her head before pulling on her cloak and whipping the hood up with a little too much enthusiasm as she scurried toward the door.

"What'd I miss?" Daks asked after scooting his chair out of Shura's reach.

She narrowed her eyes at him and pinched her lips.

"What? You obviously had her handled," he protested.

"Are you done?" she asked, nodding toward his plate.

"Yeah."

"Then let's go to our room."

Without waiting for a reply, Shura donned her damp cloak, shouldered her pack, and made her way to Faret's bar. After exchanging a few words with her, Faret waved to another one of his four daughters, and she led them up the stairs toward their usual room at the end of the hall above the kitchens. The heat rising from the great hearth below wasn't ideal after the closeness of the common room, even if it did chase away some of the damp, but it was the room nearest to a second set of stairs only the family used—which also afforded Daks and Shura a means of coming and going from the inn without being seen.

Daks hung his cloak on a hook by the door, tossed his pack in a corner, and slumped into one of the two plain wooden chairs set up next to a small table by the only window. He took a sip from the almost empty tankard he'd carried up with him and frowned. He'd have to go back down for a refill soon.

"Comfy?" Shura asked.

She stood over him with her hands on her hips and her teeth bared in what only an idiot would think was a smile.

"It's a little warm in here and the chair is hard, but, eh, you take what you can get."

When she continued to glare at him, he sighed and set his tankard down. "What? You were the one telling me the job was sucking the life out of me and that it was a good thing this would be our last. You got the girl's information. We'll know more tomorrow, right? First part of our mission accomplished. Yay us."

She glared at him for a few seconds more before she huffed out a breath and dropped into the chair opposite him. "I need to know you're here and focused before we head into an unknown and potentially dangerous situation tomorrow. You've been off since they told us this was the last of the funding for our missions."

It was his turn to narrow his eyes at her. "You know I've got your back. Always."

"I know. And there's no one I'd rather have there than you."

When she didn't say anything else, Daks grimaced and sat forward in his chair. "Look. You know better than anyone this intrigue shit isn't why I signed on. There are other teams much better at that than we are, much less, uh, *noticeable*. That wasn't why I took the job. Now it looks like this last trip is only going to get us deeper into it… and that's *if* the girl wasn't exaggerating. Plus—" He clenched his jaw before he could say the rest, grabbed his tankard again, and downed the last of its lukewarm contents in one swallow.

Shura's frown softened and she nodded. "I know. Maran's boy, Val. But we don't know why the Brotherhood took him yet. He might not have been gifted. Or he might have been gifted in a way they'd find useful."

His lips twisted sourly. "Great. So instead of mysteriously disappearing off the face of Kita, never to be seen or heard from again, he can look forward to a lifetime of forced servitude to the bastards. That's so much better."

"There are many brothers who seem to truly enjoy their positions," she offered with little enthusiasm.

"But what percentage of the ones who are taken? And if you mean the Thirty-Six, those sick bastards only get off on the pain and power. They'd twist him into someone his mother wouldn't even recognize. If only I'd ever *seen* the boy, touched him. I would have sensed if he had any gifts and spared them that. We could've gotten him away."

"We don't know if he had any. They could have chosen him for some other reason, known only to them. This could have been political. Or they could have found out what she's been doing and this was punishment."

"This is supposed to make me feel better?" He closed his eyes and twisted his neck from side to side. "I'm sorry," he said finally, giving her a pained smile. "I know you're trying to help, and I also know you feel the same way I do about them." He blew out a breath and rubbed his forehead. "Maybe you're right. Maybe it's time I take a break and do something else, instead of bashing my head against this wall over and over. I mean, let's look on the bright side. From all we've heard, things seem to be escalating here just fine without us. Perhaps we won't have to do anything at all and the Brotherhood will crumble from its rotten foundations up, all on its own. Maybe a break where we simply stay home and give aid to those fleeing the coming troubles is the best we can do."

"Maybe a bit of rest for you too," she added quietly.

"Hey, we had the winter," he said with a chuckle and a wry smile.

"Being at the Scholomagi with all its politics and division, and then at your family's holdings, with all that drama and tension, was nothing like a rest," she shot back.

He shrugged. "You were there too. If you don't need a rest, then neither do I. I'm as tough as you are... mostly." He said that last with another smile and a wink, and her lips quirked as she shook her head.

"You take it more personally than I do, which is why you find it more draining," she replied more seriously, pouring a bucket of cold water on his attempt to deflect. "I'm here because of you, *Vaida*. This is my fight only because it is yours. The oaths were sworn. I am bound. That doesn't mean my heart breaks as yours does."

Daks shifted uncomfortably and turned to look out the small round rain-streaked window to the lovely view of the dirty side of the neighboring building. It wasn't that Shura didn't care for the plight of the Rassans or the Sambarans, but her people faced enough hardship and prejudice that they couldn't afford to take on anyone else's troubles. He felt guilty sometimes for keeping her away from them, but he had his own demons to fight, and her being oathbound to him hadn't exactly been his decision.

Still, the subject—and that damned Cigani title she'd given him—always made him uneasy. *Vaida*—chief, leader, boss.

He grimaced. He was no leader, even if he'd spent the first half of his life being trained to become one before his gift was discovered and his life turned upside down. There was a reason his younger sister was heir to the family hold and not him, and it wasn't only because of the laws regarding the gifted in Samebar. He didn't want to be anyone's boss, ever.

After all their years together, he'd like to believe Shura stuck with him because of their friendship, not because of the oaths she'd sworn after he'd saved her entire family from certain death. But the Cigani were a proud and mysterious people, and they took their oaths very seriously. She would stay regardless of whether she liked him, and regardless of whether he wanted her to. She would be his right arm until the day he died… and he would have been lost a long time ago without her.

When he turned his gaze back to her, he found her staring pensively out the window into the gloom, mirroring him.

"The sun will go down soon," she murmured before clapping her hands together and meeting his gaze again. "Grayla is expecting me tonight after the guard change," she continued more briskly. "Can I trust you to stay out of trouble until my return?"

He fought a grin that would probably only earn him another bruise.

Grayla was Shura's contact in the stables at the King's Guard barracks. Ostensibly, the reason Shura always went alone was because it was easier for only one of them to sneak in and out of the barracks without being spotted. Shura was by far the smaller and nimbler of the two of them—and better at lying her way out of sticky situations if she was caught—so of course, she was the better choice. It had nothing to do with the fact that Grayla was lithe and toothsome and happened to think Shura hung the moon.

He never knew exactly what went on during their "meetings." He probably didn't want to know. But Shura always returned with straw in her hair, a smile on her face, and information on troop movements, so who was he to question it?

"Of course. I'll be fine," he replied with mock cheer. "I'm tucked up all cozy in the inn, no reason to go out on this miserable night, right? Faret's ale is as good as ever. I'll have a couple more to keep me company until your return. Maybe I'll go back to the common room for a while, get a feel for the atmosphere and see what I can overhear over a game of dice or cards."

She narrowed her eyes at him. "We have no money for the slavers' market."

He put a hand to his chest and widened his eyes. "Who said anything about the slavers' market?"

"There is no reason to go there," she continued sternly. "We get our information tonight and tomorrow, perhaps one day more for our other contacts. Then we go home, report, and possibly try to help those fleeing to Samebar in the coming weeks and months, which is a very worthy endeavor." She paused, but when he didn't say anything, she leaned forward, holding his gaze. "One more gifted won't make any difference to the Scholomagi, and we have no money for their passage back with us anyway. Right?"

He lifted his tankard in salute and shoved the bitterness welling in his stomach down. "Right," he replied firmly before tilting his cup against his lips, only to find it disappointingly empty.

When she continued to glare at him, he rolled his eyes. "I'll be a good boy. I'll catch up on some of that rest you've been going on about. If you're not back by dawn, I'll go to our meeting place and track backwards from there. I'm not a complete idiot, you know. I've done this a few times myself."

"You are no kind of idiot," she replied somberly. "You are only yourself, and I know that man well. We cannot save them all, and we cannot save any of them if we are dead or captured for no reason."

"This is true," he agreed.

She studied him for a few seconds more before shaking her head. "You will do as you always do, no matter what I say. But remember, if you are caught, I must try to rescue you. I am oathbound. I will not leave without you. It is my life you hold in your hands as well as yours."

He flinched. She certainly knew how to make a hit count. He placed a dramatic hand to his chest. "You wound me. I will be good. I promise."

One corner of her lips lifted. "I'll never ask that. Just don't get caught, and don't take any pointless risks."

"It's a deal."

She eyed him skeptically for a little longer before letting out an exaggerated sigh, rising, and collecting her cloak.

"Hey," he called before she could step through the door. "You don't get caught either. You're the one doing the dangerous bit tonight. Don't think you distracted me from that fact with your nagging."

"We follow the plan as always. I am the careful one, remember? I do not let my passion lead me as you do."

"Be sure to tell Grayla that during your 'meeting,' okay?" he replied, smirking.

Another glare and a cluck of her tongue were the only response he received before she pulled the door closed behind her, leaving him alone to stew in his thoughts.

AFTER LESS than an hour, he just couldn't take it anymore. The swirling mess in his head drove him down to the common room, in hopes of finding some distraction. He scanned the late-evening crowd, searching for a likely game to try to join, but the atmosphere had turned from tense to somber. People sat huddled over their tables in quiet conversation, seemingly uninterested in encouraging newcomers to join them.

For the briefest of moments, he considered trying to find more private companionship for the night, but he abandoned the idea fairly quickly after another scan of the room. Pursing his lips, he leaned against Faret's bar and drank deeply from the tankard he'd ordered. He'd known Faret a long time now, but the man discouraged too much open interaction with the people he "helped" so as not to draw suspicion. Daks couldn't blame him, but the man was a good conversationalist in private, and Daks could have used some of that right now.

With another heavy sigh, he eyed the door to the street and pursed his lips. He could always take a walk down toward the docks and probably find someone along the way to take the edge off for a few coin instead... but as Shura had pointed out repeatedly, they didn't have much coin to spare, and that sort of transaction wouldn't really give him the distraction he was hoping for anyway.

Trying to be the good boy he'd promised he would be, he had Faret refill his drink and morosely returned to their room. After brooding for a while, he stretched out on one of the narrow beds and forced his eyes closed. Perhaps he'd finally had enough of Faret's fine ale to numb some of the turmoil inside him so he could fall asleep.

Their informant, Maran, writhed in the arms of shadowy men, screaming as monsters in bloodred robes dragged a terrified, faceless little tow-haired boy away. Daks was close enough to reach them if he ran, but some invisible force held him paralyzed, and all he could do was watch. He shouted over and over, but no one seemed to hear. As the terrible scene played out in front of him, the little boy began to change. He grew to a man's height. His hair darkened to an all-too-familiar auburn, and Josel's heartbreakingly beautiful face now stared back at him, contorted in fear and sadness.

"I have to go, love. Can't you understand that?" Josel cried.

Daks bolted upright, sweating and gasping. Throwing off the smothering wool blanket, he stumbled out of bed and braced his arms on the table by the window. Images from the dream swirled through his head but slowly faded to mist as he struggled to calm his breathing.

"Seven Hells."

He clenched his jaw and slumped into the chair next to him before his shaking limbs could fold and dump him on his ass. The rain had finally passed, and a full moon shone through the window, barely visible above the tiled roof of the neighboring building.

Once his breathing had returned to something approaching normal, he glanced at the rumpled bed he'd recently vacated before turning his back on it. He needed to get out.

Just for a little while, he promised himself and the absent Shura guiltily as he pulled on his boots.

He'd only go for a short walk. He'd avoid dark alleys and stick to the main streets, like any other honest merchant or laborer heading home after a night at his favorite pub.

What trouble could he possibly get into?

For all its problems, Rassat was one of the safest cities in Kita, and not because of the King's Guard. The guard could only put you in a cell or set you to hard labor, but the Brotherhood's pain priests and their mysterious magics could take you as ritual fodder for the common good—they called it redeeming yourself through pain or something equally revolting. Even worse, they could make you disappear completely, to face unknown holy horrors and eternal damnation, falling through the Seven Hells forever. They had the gods on their side, after all... at least that's what they claimed.

To be fair, Rassa still had its fair share of criminals. He was technically one of them, after all. But the less-than-law-abiding had to be smarter and more secretive than your average smash-and-grab back-alley thug if they wished to escape the Brotherhood and the forced piety of the rest of Rassa's upright citizens. Safer or not, it wasn't a bargain Daks would ever be willing to make. Better the demon you know? Not hardly.

After grabbing his cloak, he crept out of his room and locked the door behind him. Shura could get an extra key from Faret if she returned before him, but he highly doubted she would. He'd just get some fresh air, use up a little nervous energy, and work out the tightness in his muscles. He'd return before she was any the wiser.

From the back stairs, he could still hear the quiet hum of conversation rising up from the common room. Most of the crowd had probably gone home or found other lodgings for the night, but there were usually a few poor souls who'd stay until Faret either kicked them out or forced them to pay for a spot by the fire.

Faret's wife, Jana, and Ilia were still in the kitchen cleaning up as he stepped into the room, and he nodded to them on his way through. Jana's scowl in return wasn't particularly friendly, but it wasn't new either. Faret wanted a better Rassa for everyone, including his wife and daughters, so he gave safe haven to anyone he thought furthered that hope. But Jana didn't have to be happy about it. Daks couldn't blame her for that. He only had to worry about himself and Shura, and that was more than he could handle most of the time.

Outside, he took a deep breath of slightly fresher and significantly cooler air. Like its twin capital in Samebar, Rassat had been built at the mouth of the great Matna River, where fresh water met the sea. The air was damp and tinged with cook fires, fish, and the usual unpleasant smells of too many people crammed into too small a space, but at least the salty winds off the ocean helped break up some of the worst of it. Right now anything was better than inside the inn, where the walls and memories closed in on him.

He didn't consciously choose a direction to walk. It might have been safer for him to head uphill toward the inner wall that marked the old city and served as a divider between the wealthy and the rest of Rassat, but the wind took him in the opposite direction—at least that's what he told himself.

He'd been walking for some time, trying not to think about much of anything, when his surroundings became significantly more familiar in the moonlight. At that point he couldn't exactly lie to himself anymore and say he was surprised at where he'd ended up. If Shura found out, she wouldn't believe him, but this hadn't been his goal; really it hadn't.

After checking to make sure the shadows were uninhabited by man and rodent alike, he stepped off the tan-brick-lined street and slipped into an alley between two large warehouses before scanning the buildings around him for any signs of life.

The warehouse district began just inside the gates to the docks and ran along the southwestern wall of the city until it hit Arcadia— an ironic nickname given to the slums where the Unnamed and other unfortunates were allowed to scrape out a meager existence. The location was perfect for the temporary storage of goods going out and coming in from the ships, but it also had the added benefit of blocking the view to Arcadia—and some of the smell—from the sensitive eyes and noses of Rassa's elite making their way up from the docks.

As usual, the place was deserted after dark. King's Guards manned the towers along the wall and patrolled the main streets but largely stayed out of the district's side streets at night. Anyone with goods of any value hired their own guards to watch the buildings after dark, and everyone else just took their chances. Isolated and sparsely populated, it was the perfect location for more illegal pursuits, including the uglier side to Rassat's labor market—aptly nicknamed the Slavers' Market by the common folk.

It could be argued that there was no such thing as a pretty side to a slavers' market, but there was, at least, a more presentable one. During the day, the people who ran them were merely recruiters for outgoing vessels. The contracts they offered were simple. A man or woman agreed to a certain length of indentured servitude in exchange for transport out of Rassa and the promise of paid work after their debts had been discharged at their new home. What they didn't tell their recruits was the jobs promised were rarely what they got or where they expected to go, and their treatment once they arrived hinged entirely on the whims of their new masters. Some got lucky, most didn't. And anyone who left on such vessels was rarely heard from again. Still, to some, it remained preferable to what awaited them back home, and more and more might be seeking this way out as the unrest in Rassa grew. But the night markets were another, even uglier story.

On an ordinary mission, Daks would have sent out notes to his various contacts before he and Shura even left the docks, and he would have received word back within a few hours on where the next night market would be held. His money was always good, and his purchases never returned to tell the tale, so the lowlifes he dealt with thought him an excellent, if picky, client, as trustworthy as any of the other scoundrels who frequented such places.

With the coin they were typically given, he couldn't afford more than one or two "contracts" each mission, and his instructions were clear: find only the gifted and send them on to the Scholomagi before the Brotherhood got to them. If no one appeared who had a gift, he had to walk away empty-handed, with the haunted, desperate, frightened faces of the rest following him out the door and into his nightmares.

Shura wasn't wrong. He did lose a little more of his soul every time he went, and the people he saved only brought a little of that soul back. So why did he do it? Because he couldn't live with himself if he didn't at least try, for his own sake and for Josel's.

He grimaced. He shouldn't be here. He had no money to help anyone. Even if he happened on a market, he'd only be torturing himself with what he couldn't do. And yet here he stood, searching the shadowed buildings and opening his Sensitivity as wide as possible, hunting for even the slightest tingle of magic from a gifted desperate enough to take the risk.

One advantage Rassa had over anywhere else was the distinct lack of magical "noise" he needed to filter out. At the Scholomagi, the hum of magic was almost overwhelming. Between the raw talent centralized in one city, the bespelled objects and magical amulets, the ancient relics in the vaults below the school, and even the very wall surrounding Scholoveld, a Sensitive was bombarded day and night with it and had to keep his shields up or he'd go insane. The rest of Samebar was better, but still noisy. Any Sambaran who could afford it bought and relied on magical items in their daily lives, and the hum was quieter but nearly as constant along his skin and at the back of his mind even in the remotest villages.

In Rassa, however, the Brotherhood had outlawed any magic beyond that which the sacred Thirty-Six wielded long ago. They'd also spent the intervening centuries culling those with talent out of the population, whether for their own ranks or to simply make them disappear. His trips to Rassat should actually be a relief, if it weren't for the toll it took on his soul and the very real possibility of being discovered and imprisoned. Luckily, Sensitivity was only a receptive magic. Not even another Sensitive could sense him using it.

Knowing it was probably a mistake, he pushed his gift to its limits but still encountered nothing beyond the usual gentle, almost imperceptible hum of the earth beneath his feet. If there were any magic users nearby, they weren't active right now.

A wave of guilt immediately followed his surge of relief. Apparently he'd only come out here to soothe his conscience. No gifted meant he wasn't missing out on saving anyone… but he was. There were still plenty of nonmagical souls who would be shipped off to parts unknown this night, as they were every night, and he wouldn't be helping any of them.

"You can't save them all."

He clenched his jaw and closed his eyes. He shouldn't have left the inn. He could almost hear Shura's "duh" in his mind, and it brought a grim smile to his lips. He should go back now, like a good boy, and hopefully Shura would never know he'd left.

As he forced himself away from the rough plank wall he'd been leaning against to head back the way he'd come, the sounds of booted footsteps and hushed voices echoing off nearby buildings made him freeze in his tracks. His rueful smile vanished, and he withdrew into the shadows again, straining to listen past his quickening heartbeat. He recognized one of those voices. And as the two men passed his hiding place and continued down the street, his feet took off to follow before his brain had a chance to catch up—not that his brain was going to be of much use. Its urgent whispers of caution and safety were being shouted down by a decent amount of ale, painful memories, old guilt, and that anger and helplessness that had been boiling inside him since he'd left Scholoveld.

Politics. Infighting. Budget cuts. Bunch of stuffed robes in their safe little towers, playing with their potions, tomes, relics, and people's lives, never really doing anything to make the world a better place. No care for the lives they could save if they just tightened their belts a little.

His fists clenched and unclenched at his sides as he strode silently but purposefully after the two men in the dark. The voice he'd recognized belonged to Tarek, a slaver of the worst kind. The bastard didn't care where the desperate people who came to him went. He dealt with buyers most of the others wouldn't touch, and he wasn't above snatching the unwilling if the opportunity presented itself—women, children, what they'd be used for didn't matter to Tarek.

Daks had been itching to take a piece out of the man for years, but he'd never found an excuse that wouldn't jeopardize his cover and future missions.

Guess what, Tarek? We have no future missions.

Nothing he did tonight would change much, of course. He could put Tarek out of commission for a while, but someone would always come along to take his place. Still, using his fists on a piece of garbage like Tarek might slow the man's operation for a few days at least, and help Daks sleep better tonight. He had to take his victories where he could find them.

Tensing his body in anticipation, he followed the two men around a corner into a small square and was just about to pounce when movement off to his right caught his eye. Acting solely on instinct, he spun on his heel and dove into the shadows between two buildings, crouching low. A second later, he blew out a breath and whispered a fervent thanks to gods he didn't even believe in as a new man stepped into the square wearing a very distinctive set of robes. Moonlight might mask the bloody color, but no one would ever mistake the cut for anything else.

Tarek and his companion continued on, oblivious to the newcomer, and Daks gritted his teeth at the lost opportunity even as he broke out in a sweat. What was a member of the Brotherhood doing slinking around the warehouse district at this time of night? And why didn't he announce himself to Tarek?

Daks closed his eyes to calm his heartbeat and focus his gift. He let his senses expand outward to touch the brother, but nothing more than an odd little tingle of something dormant played along his nerves, and he relaxed slightly. At least it wasn't a member of the Thirty-Six. Their holy relics put off enough energy he probably could have felt it at that distance without even trying. The gods were being kind to him tonight despite his stupidity. He could just keep quiet. As soon as the brother moved along, he could scurry back to the Dog and Duck and forget he'd ever been dumb enough to venture out in the first place.

That would be the smart thing to do.

But no one had ever accused him of being particularly smart—except Shura, and she was biased. The mystery of a brother wandering around the warehouse district alone in the dark seemed too much of a temptation to walk away from.

Shahul, Protector of Fools, smile on me, he thought, sending up a plea to one of Shura's gods just in case.

When the brother headed in the direction Tarek and his companion had gone, Daks followed at what he hoped was a discreet enough distance. He couldn't hear Tarek or his friend anymore, but the brother continued his journey without any hesitation, making Daks wonder if the man had incredibly good night vision or wasn't following the slavers at all.

This is a bad idea. This is a very bad idea.

His nerves started getting the better of his curiosity the longer their trip progressed and the more of Faret's ale he sweated out. Instead of relying on his other senses, he dropped a little farther back and sent his gift out. Being a Sensitive wasn't exactly every child's dream as far as magical power went, and it certainly wasn't prized and coveted at the Scholomagi. But at least Daks's gift wasn't weak. If he really worked at it, he could sense more than just magic. He could sense groups of nonmagical people too, provided enough of them crowded together. If the brother was going to a meeting somewhere or there was an ambush waiting, Daks would hopefully be able to sense it in time. Anything smaller than a large group and he should be able to fight his way out either way, but at least he wouldn't be blindly walking into a mob.

At first he sensed nothing. Then he nearly tripped over his own feet as something latched on to his gift and dragged his focus off to the left somewhere.

Magic.

Not the magic of the Thirty-Six, though. Something different.

He shook his head, trying to get a read on what he'd sensed, but the sound of running footsteps jarred his consciousness back to his body. The brother had taken off at a run in the direction the magical energy had come from. That couldn't be a coincidence.

Fuck me to the Seven Hells!

Daks started running too.

The brother had to be another Sensitive—what the Rassans called Finders. Daks couldnt think of any other explanation for why the man had taken off just when Daks felt the magic. He threw his senses outward again as he ran, but the strong pulse of magical energy had vanished. He slowed and clamped his eyes shut, straining, searching. The sound of the brothers pounding feet had disappeared too, but Daks wasnt sure if the man had stopped or just gotten too far ahead of him. His hands shook and his temples pounded with the effort, but he finally caught the merest ghost of residual energy a few streets away.

Praying the brother had gone in the opposite direction, Daks took off, clinging to that tingle of energy like a lifeline.

Are you really racing a brother toward a gifted? Are you insane?

These questions rang through his head in Shura's voice, but he didn't slow his pace. Sometimes he just had to lead with his gut, and his gut told him to run toward the problem, not away from it. In that moment, he felt more alive and less defeated than he had in weeks.

He fixed things when they were broken. He freed people when they were chained. He bashed heads when they needed bashing. That was his nature. That was the only thing keeping him going on dark nights when pain and regret closed in. All that other crap he'd had to deal with at the Scholomagi and back on his family's holding was complicated bullshit he couldn't change anyway. Here he could make a difference.

He ducked through alleys and skirted darkened buildings in as straight a line toward the source of the magic as he could manage. At last he skidded to a halt, his eyes riveted on a shadowy figure in an alley across another open square. Whoever it was, they weren't using any magic now, but the last tendrils of it clung to them like smoke; otherwise he never would have spotted them. Breathing heavily, he propped a hand against the rough wood of the building next to him and took a moment to get some air and decide how to approach. The brother could still be out there. Daks didn't have much time for social niceties, even if that had been his forte.

He could just sneak up and give the stranger a little tap on the temple or the back of the head and apologize later. That would probably be more effective than relying on his charm in the limited time he had… but that might make establishing a rapport later a bit challenging.

A sudden sliver of light where there shouldn't be any caught his eye, and he froze. A door had opened across the square, spilling enough light to illuminate Tarek's ugly face as he and his companion stepped hurriedly inside a warehouse. He'd been so distracted, he hadn't heard them approach. The door closed, and all became dark and quiet again as Daks ground his teeth in frustration.

He'd apparently found the market he wasn't supposed to be looking for. Now that he wasn't straining to follow the last wisps of magical energy, he could sense the press of bodies in the building. Out of the corner of his eye, he saw the gifted take a few paces out of the shadows toward that door, then stop. From that distance and with the layers of clothing and bulky bag swung across his or her chest, Daks couldn't discern any features, but whoever it was hugged themselves before they took another, more determined stride forward, forcing Daks into action. He couldn't let them go through that door. Nothing good would happen to them there.

"Hey!" he hissed as loudly as he dared, rushing out of his hiding place. "Don't do it. Come with me and I'll find you a safer way out."

The figure's hood fell back as he whirled in Daks's direction, and Daks caught a glimpse of a fine-featured young man, probably only a couple inches shorter than his own six feet, in the moonlight. But instead of Daks's urgently hissed offer stalling him long enough for Daks to get close, the man's eyes widened in apparent horror and he threw a hand out in front of him.

"Stay away!" he shouted before turning and bolting.

Shit!

Daks took off after him. "Wait! I'm trying to help. I can help you."

"No!" the man yelled in seeming panic over his shoulder. "Stay back! Get away from me!"

His voice had gone up a couple of octaves from the first "Stay away," but why? Daks could be a little scary-looking sometimes, he guessed, but this seemed like a bit of an overreaction. After all, he was only offering to help.

He'd chased the man all the way across the square before the tingling along his skin registered and Daks realized what that meant. Unfortunately for both of them, Daks's brain kicked in too late as the man made a strangled noise and crumpled to the ground. Magic radiated from him in waves, unmistakable to any Sensitives in the area. Daks spit out another curse and rushed to the prone form.

"Hey, push it back," he ordered, as if he was one of the professors at the Scholomagi.

The young man flailed at him, groaning. "Get away. Don't touch me. Please don't touch me."

Daks hesitated. How was he supposed to get both of them to safety without touching him? They needed to leave. Now.

Whatever the man's gift was, he just had to take the chance it wouldn't lash out at him once he made contact. He grabbed the man's wrist and ducked under his arm to drag him to his feet as the magic rolled over him, tingling along every nerve. "We have to get out of here!"

"No," the man groaned weakly a second before another, stronger surge of energy erupted through him.

This close, the magic was almost overwhelming, but Daks wasn't blinded so much that he missed the brother stepping into the road ahead of them.

Seven Hells! If not for Rift-blighted luck, I'd have none at all.

Daks tried to spin them in the opposite direction, but the brother shouted, and the man in his arms suddenly stiffened and collapsed again, his weight dragging Daks down with him. Daks slowed his descent, but only marginally, because the next wave of energy blasted him to his knees. He wasn't the only one to feel it either. The brother, who'd closed the distance between them, suddenly gasped and rocked backward like he'd been hit by something.

"The many will be one again, one and gone.
One will fall. The ring broken. The doors opened.
Keep free.
Repent, oh Tanagers, a new song is made, an old song renewed."

The voice coming out of the man on the ground was very different from the one that had been yelling at Daks only a few seconds before. It almost sounded like two voices overlapping. If all the hairs on Daks's body hadn't already been standing on end from the magic, they would have been now.

Prophecy. Gods, he hated prophecies.

He struggled to retain consciousness, and his ears were left ringing in the sudden silence after the words stopped. All three of them remained frozen until the man on the ground's eyes rolled up and his head lolled to the side. That seemed to break whatever spell they were in because the brother surged forward, flapping his hands, his face flushed and glistening with sweat in the moonlight.

"By order of the Brotherhood of Harot, I demand you back away and identify yourself," he croaked at Daks, sounding just as shaken as Daks felt.

Daks slowly rose from the crouched position he'd held since the gifted had gone down and lifted his hands in a placating gesture as his head cleared. He took a single step back and sucked in a breath.

"Evening, Brother. I am Tarek Vastan. This young man appears to be in need of a healer. Do you know of one nearby?" Daks asked in his best Rassan, thinking quickly.

"I said step back," the brother replied with growing confidence.

"I did," Daks replied innocently.

"Well… step back again," he hissed, appearing nonplussed.

Daks took another single step backward.

The brother narrowed his beady little eyes as he squared his shoulders. "Are you defying me, citizen—?"

"Tarek," Daks enunciated clearly. "Tarek Vastan."

"Well, Tarek, if you do not wish to be collected by the King's Guard for your insolence, you should do as you are told."

"Of course, Brother."

"Well?" the brother asked, glaring.

"Well, what?" Daks replied, blinking innocently.

The brother's lips tightened, and his round cheeks darkened further. "Be gone with you, before I change my mind and have you detained!" he blustered, flapping his right hand at Daks again while he drew something out of his robes with his left.

Daks took another wary step back at the move and braced himself for an attack, since he couldn't quite see what the brother held. A moment later, his gift told him exactly what it was, but the knowledge only made him marginally less uneasy—especially since Rassans were, by their own laws, not supposed to use enchanted objects beyond the thirty-six stones of Harot.

Daks's heartbeat sped as he tried to decide his next move. From the feel of it, the brother had used some sort of message or summoning stone. It would key an answering response in another stone somewhere else, and Daks was pretty sure he didn't want to meet whoever was on the other end. When the brother cast an impatient glance in his direction, Daks bowed and made to look as if he was leaving, and the brother turned his attention back to the man on the ground.

"Get up. By order of the Brotherhood, I demand you get up," the brother said peevishly. But when he received no response, he kicked the prone body in the side. "Get up. Identify yourself."

Daks was still trying to convince himself to do the smart thing when the brother apparently grew impatient and landed another hard kick. The defenseless man moaned, and Daks sighed inwardly.

Shura's going to kill me.

"Hey, uh, Brother? How about I help you get this poor guy to a healer. He looks pretty heavy. Uh, let me be of service to you, or whatever," he offered stiltedly as he began to edge closer again.

Daks knew the correct words he was supposed to use, the formal ritual phrasing all Rassans had beaten into them for addressing members of the Brotherhood, but some perverse part of him just couldn't bring himself to say them. He was still too pissed off and keyed up.

The brother gaped at him like he couldn't quite believe Daks hadn't just evaporated because he waved his limp little hand. "Are you a simpleton? By the power of the Holy Order of Harot, and Quanna, Moc, and Chytel themselves, I order you to leave. What happens here does not concern you. You have heard my command. Obey or face the consequences of your insolence."

"I'm only trying to help," Daks stalled while he struggled to come up with some sort of plan.

The brother inflated himself to his full height—which was still several inches shorter than Daks—and declared, "Not another word or you shall be remanded to the guard."

Daks glanced down at the still unmoving man on the ground. He looked so vulnerable, so helpless. He'd obviously been desperate enough to escape the brothers that he was willing to chance the night market... and Daks had chased him right into one.

"Did you hear me? Or are you too simple to understand?" the brother hissed snidely.

A muscle in Daks's jaw ticked a second before he closed his eyes, took two steps forward, and sent his fist into brother's round face. Before the man could do more than yelp in shock and pain, Daks hit him again with all the frustration and anger he'd built up over the last several months—Hells, *years*—laying him out.

He did say "not another word."

The impact on his knuckles felt way too good as he grinned at his own joke, but reality crashed closely behind his little act of rebellion.

Cursing himself for the fool the brother had called him, Daks quickly bent and hefted the Seer onto his shoulders. The tromp of many booted feet in the distance goaded him into motion quicker than anything else could have, and he lumbered away as fast as his overburdened body would carry him, the man's lumpy bag thumping him in the ass with each labored step. Whatever was in that bag was hard, sharp-edged, and heavy, and he wished he'd had time to untangle it so he could leave it behind, but too late now.

He'd just reached the shadowed alley he'd come through earlier when flickering torchlight wavered across the buildings on the far side of the square. He cast one quick glance behind him to gauge the level of threat and nearly stumbled in surprise at what he saw. The men who had come to the brother's call were definitely armed, but they weren't wearing the blue of the King's Guard, nor were they wearing the red robes of the Brotherhood. They weren't in any kind of uniform at all.

What the...?

Whoever they were, he couldn't afford to be caught by them. Grunting with the strain, he adjusted his heavy burden and huffed and puffed back the way he'd come, swearing at every bruise that damned bag made on his rump. Shouts rang out in the night behind him, orders made, but they echoed strangely through the empty streets. He had no way of knowing if the others had found his trail or not, so he simply plowed on while his legs, back, and shoulders screamed in protest.

Eventually, he ran out of strength and had to stop to catch his breath and think. He couldn't go back to the Dog and Duck. Even if he could make it that far, it was too dangerous to Faret and his family. Plus, someone was bound to see him carrying a body across his shoulders eventually, and report him to the guard.

He let out a low groan as he set his burden down and slid to the ground next to him. Judging from the signs of neglect and disrepair of the neighborhood, he'd taken a wrong turn somewhere. From the smell alone, he figured he'd somehow looped back toward Arcadia.

Seven Hells.

At least he'd lost his pursuers. That was something.

With a hiss of pain, he climbed to his feet before his muscles could seize up and began to search for somewhere to hide. Near the end of a small street lined with run-down, rotting buildings, he found a little hovel that looked like it hadn't been inhabited by anyone but rats in a long time. It would have to do for now. The old latch on the door had rusted shut in the salty damp, and Daks had to force it open, but he took that as another good sign no one would happen by and discover them.

Slinging that heavy body over his shoulders again wasn't the worst thing he'd ever had to do, but it certainly wasn't the best. He'd been tempted to drag the still-unconscious man the last bit, but he didn't want to leave any telltale ruts in the muddy ground. Plus, the muck under his boots smelled pretty awful, and he certainly didn't want to bring any more of that in with them than he had to.

Once he'd dumped his burden inside, closed the door, and slumped onto the dirt floor next to the inert body, he finally let himself acknowledge just how royally he'd fucked up.

Shura's not only gonna kill me, but she's going to take great pleasure in making it as slow and painful as possible.

Chapter Two

Ravi jolted awake, his heart pounding. Every muscle in his body complained at the sudden movement, and he clamped his eyes shut again as he stifled a moan. He tried cracking one experimental eye, only to close it again as an all-too-familiar knife of pain stabbed through his skull—a Vision hangover, a big one. Fear quickly replaced shame as he realized he wasn't home, and he also wasn't alone.

"Are you finally awake?" a gruff male voice asked peevishly in trade tongue.

Ravi squinted through his pain at the gloomy interior of the room. The voice seemed vaguely familiar, but he couldn't place it past the throbbing in his head. A large body moved in the shadows, but thankfully didn't come any closer. Still, Ravi quickly made another scan of his surroundings, noting the window and door to his right and the shabby, abandoned feel to the place.

Once he'd identified the only exit, he swung his wary gaze back to the man in the shadows. The guy sat far enough away that Ravi could probably make a run for it. Hard to tell under the thick wool of his cloak, but he looked too bulky to be fast, especially if Ravi caught him by surprise.

Biting his lip, Ravi surreptitiously tested his limbs as he strained to remember what had happened. He'd been in the warehouse district, because Vic had finally come through with a time and place for one of the night markets. He'd packed his bag and taken off as soon as the others had gone to sleep and the mighty bells of Blavod Keep had rung the correct hour.

By the time he'd reached the square, his knees had been shaking so badly he could barely stand, and then a Vision had hit him out of the blue—an embarrassingly intimate one that left him sweating and confused. The Visions were coming too often now, but this one had happened without any provocation at all. He'd been *alone*, for gods' sakes. It was only a matter of time before the Brotherhood caught up to him. No matter how scared he was, he had no choice but to leave.

That first step toward the door after the Vision had cleared was hard, but he'd taken courage from it and forced himself to take another… only to stop again as someone started yelling at him.

Ravi's heart sped, his face flushed, and his hands curled into fists as the memories began coming through much more clearly. A small, distressed sound escaped his throat before he could call it back, and the shadowy figure sharing the hovel with him moved closer. He loomed over Ravi before he bent down and peered at him closely in the dim light.

"Are you all right?" the man asked in a voice Ravi finally recognized. "I'd offer you water, but—"

The guy didn't get to say anything else because Ravi punched him in the face.

"You asshole! This is all your fault!" he yelled as he surged to his feet and stumbled toward the door.

Under normal circumstances, he would have made it, even with his bag and the extra layers of clothes weighing him down. But the second Vision he'd had last night must have been a doozy because his legs still weren't working right. He'd just reached the door when thick arms wrapped around him from behind and lifted him off his feet. He struggled, knowing how dangerous physical contact was, but the bastard was as strong as an ox. His arms were like tree trunks, and his chest as broad as the side of a barn.

"Stop wiggling, you little shit, and calm down. I'm not going to hurt you. I'm trying to help. You'll get both of us caught if you go running out there blindly."

Ravi ground his teeth, but he eventually blew out a breath and forced his body to go limp, relieved another Vision didn't appear imminent at least.

After the man cautiously put him down, Ravi put some distance between them and growled, "Like you helped me last night, you Rift-blighted imbecile?"

My one chance, he sobbed internally.

In frustration, and with just a hint of caution, he tugged his hood back in place, hiding his face and putting another couple of feet between them. Best to not tempt fate. The one Vision he'd had involving this man was quite enough.

What in the Seven Hells do I do now?

He was so fucked.

Yesterday, he'd been so sure the gods had finally cut him a break, given him a way out that would protect the people he cared for most. He should have known better. The gods had cursed him with this life; why would they bother showing him kindness now?

He curled his hands into fists again as he saw red and took a step closer to the asshole who'd destroyed the only chance to escape he was likely to get. He couldn't vent his frustrations on the gods, but this guy seemed mortal enough.

Luckily, a good look at the man forced Ravi's brain to intercede on his body's behalf, stopping him from doing something really stupid. The guy wasn't much taller than him, but he was nearly twice as broad. Even in the weak early light coming through the cracked and dirty window, Ravi could tell this wasn't someone he should mess with. Wild, shaggy dark brown hair escaped the valiant efforts of the leather thong at the base of the man's skull. His throat, jaw, and cheeks were shadowed with thick stubble, making the bright pink slashes of two long, jagged scars along his neck and jaw stand out like lightning through storm clouds. His nose had obviously been broken a few times, and his heavy brows made him look threatening, despite the big calloused hands currently being held out in a conciliatory gesture.

"Hey, look. I was just trying to help," the guy huffed. "You don't want to go to one those night markets. Believe me. You'll end up somewhere even worse than whatever you got here."

His tone had just enough condescension to spike Ravi's temper again. Despite knowing he was physically outmatched, the temptation to throw another punch began to win the argument in his head. But then the guy's dark blue eyes caught the pale light, and they triggered the memory of that damned Vision. Suddenly, Ravi's cheeks burned from something more than anger. Flustered and unsettled, he hugged his bag close to his chest and spun away to pace the cramped, dirty space.

"Worse?" he fumed to cover his discomfort. "Are you kidding? You led me straight to a bloody brother. How could it be worse?"

"You saw that, huh?"

"Yeah, I saw that," he repeated sourly.

"To be fair, the brother was already looking for you," the guy said with a shrug. "He was a Finder. He felt your magic. I was just trying to get there first."

Ravi goggled at him as new terror flooded his body and his anger soared to keep pace.

"Oh, well that's just great," he practically screeched. "That makes it all better that you butted in where no one asked you and wrecked everything for both of us." Forgetting his earlier caution, he closed the distance between them and stabbed a finger into the air an inch from the man's crooked nose. "I told you to stay away from me. I *ran away from you*. Couldn't you take the hint? If you hadn't gotten near me, I never would have had that second Vision! I could've gotten away!"

"Lower your voice." The man's eyes narrowed as he calmly reached to push Ravi's finger aside, forcing Ravi to snatch it away before they touched. "*Second* vision? That's right. There were two. I forgot about that. The first was how I found you. So, what was it?"

"What?"

"The Vision. I heard the second one, the prophecy, but what was the first?"

Prophecy? How he found me?

"Wait." Ravi rubbed his temples, straining to think. "How did you know about the first? How *did* you find me?"

The big man shrugged. "I guess I'm what you'd call a Finder too."

At the second mention of that word, Ravi's heart thudded faster. He stared at the man, frozen.

"Hey, relax," the stranger said, gentling his tone. "Obviously, I'm not with the Brotherhood. I just happen to be gifted with a particular magic, just like you."

Just like me.

He flinched and glared to cover it. Too much was happening too fast. His brain was having a hard time keeping up.

"Tell me what was in the first Vision. It might be important," the man prodded, and Ravi lost his temper.

"Are you kidding me right now?" he hissed. "You know what? Why am I still here? Why am I even talking to you? I have to get out of here."

He made for the door again, but the stranger got there first and put one broad, scarred hand against it. "Where are you gonna go? They're looking for you now. They're looking for both of us. If you have another Vision, that Finder is going to lead them right to you."

Despair lapped at the edges of Ravi's anger, eroding it. "I had one shot," he gritted out, shooting daggers at the man with his eyes from the shadowed confines of his hood. "I had one chance to get out, and you ruined it. Now I'm even worse off than I was before."

"Then let me help you," the stranger said far too calmly.

"How?"

"Believe it or not, it's what I do," the man replied with a quirk of his lips that made Ravi want to throw another punch. "I wasn't in the area by chance. I've been to many of those markets. That's how I know you would have regretted going that route. I promise you."

Ravi took a couple of wary steps away from the man's very solid and imposing presence so he could think. He wasn't a fool. He knew the kind of men he'd have been dealing with if he'd stepped through that door last night. If this guy was either a buyer or a slaver himself, Ravi would have to be careful. Maybe this had all been some kind of trick or a trap to make him even more desperate to leave than he'd already been—desperate enough to sign his life away without a second thought.

He sucked in a breath and blew it out, trying to calm the warring voices in his head. He was getting paranoid. How could this guy have known Ravi's curse would flare up so spectacularly, right in front of a brother? No one knew his secret beyond the ragged little family he and Vic had cobbled together out of desperation. Unless he'd been using his magic to follow Ravi, but that seemed highly unlikely. Besides, any real slaver would have gladly abandoned him to the Brotherhood and fled for his life in that situation, but somehow Ravi was here and the Brotherhood wasn't.

"What happened last night, after I passed out?" he asked.

"You lit up like a bonfire, spoke a prophecy, and collapsed," the man replied with another shrug that seemed incredibly at odds with the blasphemy of his words.

Ravi groaned. "Then what?"

The guy shifted from foot to foot and grimaced. "I may have punched a fully-fledged member of the Brotherhood in the face and run away with you over my shoulders like a sack of potatoes."

Ravi could only blink with his mouth hanging open for a few seconds as that sank in. "Are you insane or just stupid?"

Surprisingly, the guy didn't seem to take offense. His dark blue eyes actually crinkled at the corners with amusement. "Maybe a little of both. Felt real good, though, the punching part at least. The other part, not so much. You're heavier than you look. And what's in that damned bag? I swear I have bruises all over my ass from it banging into me."

Ravi groaned and dragged a hand down his face even as he reflexively clutched his bag protectively to his chest.

This guy? *This* was the guy he might have to depend on to save his life?

If he'd had any faith left in the benevolence of the gods, he would have lost it then.

"How are you going to help me? And what's it going to cost?" Ravi asked as calmly and bravely as he could manage.

"I have contacts." The man folded his arms across his broad chest and glanced out the grimy window. "I need to get word to my partner, and she and I will decide the best way out of the city first. They're probably watching the docks already, and the gates, but we can't stay here, especially if you think you might have another Vision in the near future."

He turned back to Ravi as he said that last, a question in his eyes, and the small bubble of hope forming in Ravi's belly burst. He glared at the man before dropping his gaze to the floor. "I have no idea. I can't control it," he admitted bitterly.

The stranger grunted, but when Ravi reluctantly lifted his head again, the man didn't appear repulsed or fearful, only pensive.

"Then we need to move fast. I may have thrown the Finder off a little by giving him the wrong name." He smirked before his expression sobered again. "That will buy us a little time. But now that they know what to look for, the second you light up, they'll find us." He paused for a moment before he let out a long sigh. "If I leave you here to go get my partner, will you stay until I get back or will you do a runner?"

Ravi's heart skipped, and he shook his head vehemently. "You're not leaving me. It's your fault I'm in this mess. I'm not letting you off that easy. How do I know you won't just leave and not come back?"

Thick eyebrows lowered over angry midnight blue eyes as the man's expression hardened. "I carried your heavy ass for at least an hour last night. Do you seriously think I'd go through all that trouble just to walk away now?"

"I don't know you," Ravi shot back, moving to put himself between the stranger and the door. "How the hells should I know what you will or won't do? All I know is that you ruined the one shot I managed to get for myself, so now you're stuck with me until I'm safely out of Rassa."

Ravi was proud his voice didn't shake. He had no idea if this was a good idea or not, but he'd run out of options. He couldn't go home to their squat in Arcadia without putting Vic and the others in danger. He couldn't stay in the city at all anymore. His curse and the idiot across from him had made sure of that.

The guy's nostrils flared as he seemed to struggle with his own temper, but Ravi stubbornly held his ground. "I can't get us help until I find my partner," the man replied with obvious patience. "And if your gift could go off at any second, both of us getting to her is going to be dangerous. They'll be looking for two men matching our descriptions. It's better if I go alone. I give you my word, I'll come back for you."

Flutters of panic rooted him to the spot as he jutted out his chin. "No."

"Then how do *you* suggest we get to my partner without being spotted?" the man growled. "Or should we just hang around here until you have another Vision and the Brotherhood finds us?"

Without stepping away from the door, Ravi ignored his snide tone and turned to peer through the grimy window. No one moved in the narrow street outside, but he could hear the bustle of people not far off. The air was redolent of sewage and fish, which meant they were close to Arcadia, where all the shit from Rassat's elite literally ran downhill. He'd need to go outside to get his bearings, but they were at least near territory he knew well… and territory the Brotherhood only entered begrudgingly. Apparently, the Unnamed and the poor didn't need as much spiritual guidance and attention as the wealthier classes. But honestly, many of the people who lived in Arcadia preferred it that way.

"I can find someone in Arcadia to go get your friend and bring her back to us," Ravi replied slowly.

"That'll waste too much time. And how do we know we can trust this person?" he countered.

"It's my life too, you know," Ravi shot back. "I have people I trust. They can get word to your friend."

"Before we're spotted? Before you have another Vision?"

Ravi clenched his jaw and counted to ten. "I can't guarantee that, no. But there are plenty of places to hide in Arcadia, and plenty of people with no real love for the Brotherhood. Besides, I'm usually fine on the streets I know. The Visions mostly happen when I meet someone new or touch someone. As long as I stay awake and away from crowds of strangers, I should be okay."

The stranger in front of him looked skeptical, but Ravi stubbornly held his gaze. After facing off like that for a few more seconds, the man rolled his eyes.

"Fine. Let's just do *something* before we waste even more time," he huffed.

Ravi still had no guarantees the guy wouldn't run away at the first opportunity, but the big idiot was right—they were out of time. The streets would be filled with people all too soon.

"Follow me," Ravi said as he reached for the door latch.

He poked his head out and glanced both ways through the light morning mist before exiting their little shelter. Heading in the opposite direction of the bustling lines of laborers on their way to the docks, he clutched his bag close, scurried down to the far end of the street, and stopped. The stranger came up behind him, looming over him, and Ravi scowled.

"Can you try to look a little less…." Ravi swept a hand up and down as he fumbled for words.

"Less what?"

"Less, you know, big… thuggish."

"Thuggish?"

The guy actually looked offended for about a second before his lips twisted in that infuriating smirk.

"You're going to draw too much attention," Ravi huffed. "The leather breeches stand out enough on their own. Just hunker down a little. Don't look so damned puffed up. This is Arcadia. You need to look beaten down by life."

When the man blinked at him in surprise, Ravi winced. "You know what I mean."

"I take it you're not from around here either," the guy murmured blandly, and Ravi shook his head.

"I am now… or I *was*, anyway."

The realization of what he was about to leave behind hit him like a punch to the gut, and he clenched his jaw as his throat closed.

"Come on," he hissed.

They scuttled down every alley Ravi knew to avoid the main streets. At first, instinct led him toward home, or at least their most recent squat, but he changed course as soon as he realized it. The last thing he wanted to do was lead the Brotherhood straight to the others. He just needed to find a familiar face, that's all.

After about the fourth time they'd changed direction and hunkered down behind some trash at the edge of a square, his companion nudged him and cleared his throat. "Uh, I don't want to make you hit me again," he murmured, "but we appear to be going around in circles. And if your plan is to avoid running into people, this doesn't seem like the best place to be. Just throwing that out there."

Ravi scowled over his shoulder, but the big jerk wasn't wrong. He bit his lip, turned, and desperately searched the crowd again. Just when panic threatened, he spotted Sparrow scurrying through the thickening press of bodies, carrying a load that looked far too heavy for her tiny body, and his heart sang. He shot out of the alley and jogged after her before she could get too far away.

"Sparrow!" he called out as loudly as he dared.

She skidded to a halt, and a relieved smile spread across her face when she caught sight of him. "You didn't leave!" she cried as she hurried over. She dropped her burden and made as if to fling herself at him, but stopped just in time and gave him a rueful smile. "You're still here."

Ravi closed his eyes as pain tightened his chest before he nodded. "I'm here."

"Vic said you left. You didn't say goodbye," she accused, her full lower lip jutting out from grubby cheeks below a mop of tangled brown hair.

Ravi often forgot just how young most of the members of their cobbled-together little family were because of how fast they all had to grow up to survive. Sparrow looked so young right now, it hurt.

"I couldn't. I had to go while I had the chance and before I brought the Brotherhood down on all of us. I'm sorry."

Sparrow's eyes widened, and Ravi felt the weight of the stranger's presence at his back. "It's okay," he said to her. "He's going to help me." *I hope.* "Spar, I don't have much time. I need you or one of the others to get a message to this guy's friend." He turned to the stranger. "Where is she?"

"The Dog and Duck near merchant row. If she isn't there, then we have another meeting place behind the weaver's hall."

Sparrow grimaced. "Ezel is paying me a whole copper to take this bundle to the temple."

Seven Hells. That's in the opposite direction.

The stranger held out three coppers. "After, then. We need to find a place to hole up until she can get to us anyway."

Ravi sucked in a breath and nodded. They had to get off the street. Sparrow pocketed the money. Her eyes had widened at the coins but saddened as she turned back to Ravi.

"I'm sorry I couldn't say goodbye to everyone," he said. "I can't now either. But you'll all be safer without me. You know that."

Her lower lip trembled, but she didn't argue. "Who am I to deliver the message to?"

"My partner's name is Shura. Have you ever met a Cigani before?"

Sparrow shook her head, her eyes rounding again. "I heard they have skin darker than the oldest of sailors' and eyes as black as night… and they're mighty fighters, and if they declare a blood feud, they won't stop until every person bearing their enemy's mark is dead," she rattled off excitedly, bouncing on her dirty bare toes.

The stranger's lips quirked. "And they're ten feet tall and have claws and fangs," he added wryly. "They're not quite so scary as all that. They're just people, like the rest of us, trying to survive in a world that rarely welcomes them. Shura's skin is darker than yours and mine, and even his," he continued, nodding in Ravi's direction, "but more like toasted barleywine than an old sailor's hide. She does have dark eyes and thick black hair, though. If she's at the Dog and Duck, Faret, the innkeeper will know. Ask for him. If he says she isn't there, leave the message with him and then try to find her at the weaver's hall. She's kind of hard to miss, in Rassat at least."

"What's the message?"

"Tell her, Daks—that's me—Daks, uh, did as Daks always does. She'll know what that means. Tell her I need her to pack up and come to us as soon as she can."

He turned a questioning look to Ravi, and Ravi added, "We'll be in that place behind Tanner's Row. You remember it, right?"

Sparrow crinkled her little dirt-smudged nose, and Ravi smiled. "Yeah, I know. But it's probably the safest place right now. Go, deliver your bundle, and then run as quick as you can, okay? The red cloaks are on to us. We don't have much time."

Her eyes bugged again, this time with fear, and Ravi ached to pull her into a hug that would convey all of his emotions without words, but he settled for giving her a reassuring smile. "Go. I'll miss you, little bird."

It was a testament to the kind of life they lived that Sparrow only nodded in resignation, hefted her burden onto her shoulders again, and hurried off without another word or tear shed. Ravi's own instincts for self-preservation had him moving out of the street and into another shadowed alley without a backward glance.

"Come on," Ravi said wearily when Daks joined him. "I know a place we can hide."

Wisely, the big idiot didn't say another word as Ravi led him through more of Arcadia's narrow, trash-strewn alleys to the tanner's row—one of the few places in Rassat that actually smelled worse than Arcadia. At least the wind was up from the ocean and the air slightly cooler today, so the stench wasn't completely overwhelming.

Ravi pulled the edge of his patched and threadbare cloak over his nose and mouth as he ducked between loose boards in the back wall of one of the older buildings. He heard a quickly choked off gag from the big lump behind him as he also squeezed into the cramped, shadowy space. There was a reason he and Vic had kept this place as a last resort only. It would be warmer in the winter than outside, and no one would fight them for it, but that was the best that could be said about it.

"Gah. It's even worse in here than outside," Daks grumbled under his breath.

Ravi didn't bother to reply. The more air he used, the more he'd have to take in. He settled on the dirt floor as close to the outside opening as possible, and Daks crouched down across from him.

"Your girl will be able to tell Shura how to find this place?" Daks asked, giving the small space a skeptical once-over.

"Yes. She'll bring her here if need be."

"Who is Sparrow to you?"

"A friend."

"You trust her?"

"Yes."

Ravi could feel the weight of Daks's stare, but he ignored it. The man shifted and then shifted again. After a few beats, he stood up and prowled the space. Then he returned to his spot by the opening while Ravi tried to ignore him.

"How did *you* find it?" Daks asked finally.

"One of my friends worked here for a bit. We keep an eye out for likely squats for when the guard raids kick up again."

"Guard raids?"

"King's Guard comes through sometimes, clearing us out of abandoned houses and buildings, and we have to find someplace new to hide till they're done. The King, the Brotherhood, and the city council like to keep Rassat all neat and tidy."

He couldn't help the hint of bitterness that crept into his voice, and sure enough, Daks was studying him intently when he dared to look.

"What?" Ravi asked defensively.

Daks shrugged. "None of my business, I guess."

Ravi grunted and went back to staring out the opening to their hiding place, while Daks got to his feet and started prowling the small space behind him again. Could the man not sit still for even a second? Ravi gritted his teeth and glared at the rough wood in front of his face, trying to tune out the sounds of Daks's booted feet shuffling in the dirt and his breathing, both of which seemed to be getting louder by the second. With all the yelling and racket from the tanneries outside, the sounds shouldn't have been that annoying, but Ravi was tired and angry and already a little heartsick.

He was just about to snap at Daks to sit down when he heard footsteps approaching outside. He waved frantically at Daks as his heart thudded against his rib cage. Sparrow couldn't have delivered her message and made it back this soon, even if she'd run flat out from the temple.

"Ravi?" a familiar voice hissed.

"In here," he whispered, relieved.

When Vic's stringy blond hair popped through the opening, quickly followed by the rest of him, Ravi couldn't help the smile that spread across his face. Only a few short hours ago, he'd thought he'd never see his friend again. He wanted to drag Vic into his arms and squeeze the breath out of him, but he had to content himself with putting as much feeling into his grin as he could manage.

"What are you doing here?" Ravi asked.

"I should ask you that. What happened last night? I thought—"

Vic stopped and eyed Daks warily, and Ravi waved a hand. "It's okay. He knows. He was there."

"So, what happened?"

Ravi cast a sour look at Daks, his anger and embarrassment rising again. They were speaking in Rassan, but he had no way of knowing whether Daks understood. "I had a Vision. This guy showed up. Then a Rift-blighted brother, a *Finder*, came, and another Vision knocked me out. I don't even remember the second one, but he says I spouted some prophecy before I passed out."

Vic whistled and shook his head. "You really are cursed."

A bitter chuckle escaped him. "I keep telling you that, but none of you believe me. Why do you think I wouldn't let you come with me last night?"

"They're gonna be looking for you now, huh?"

Ravi closed his eyes and nodded. Vic sidled closer. Heat radiated from his thin body, but Ravi didn't dare lean toward it.

"What can I do?" Vic asked, giving him the splash of cold water he needed.

"Nothing."

"I'm serious, Ravi," Vic replied, leaning in earnestly.

"So am I. I don't want you or the others anywhere near this. The whole reason I left was to keep you safe. Sparrow's gone to get this guy's friend. I guess she's the one who told you where to find me?"

Vic nodded. "Yeah, she ran into Bett on her way, and Bett found me."

"Well, Daks here and his friend are going to get me out of the city. The best thing all of you can do is stay as far away from us as possible."

Vic's lips set in a stubborn line, and his pale eyebrows dipped over his long, slender nose. Ravi knew that look. He'd seen it by lamplight only a few hours ago as they'd argued over Ravi going to the night market alone. He'd won that one, and he'd win again.

"Be smart, Vic. Why the hells do you think I came all the way out to this gods-awful place? To stay as far away from the rest of you as I could. They're already searching for me. If I have another Vision, they'll be on us in no time."

Vic shifted uncomfortably, as he always did when the topic of magic came up, but he still jutted his dirt-smudged pointy chin out. "We take care of our own."

"That's what I'm doing," Ravi replied sadly.

They held each other's gazes in silence for a few heartbeats until the big lump in the room cleared his throat.

"Hate to break up whatever you two got going here or ruin your big self-sacrifice, but we might need all the help we can getting out of the city." Daks spoke in trade tongue, but obviously, he'd understood at least part of their conversation.

When both Ravi and Vic turned to stare at him, Daks shrugged. "I kind of want to make it out of Rassa alive too, you know. And so does Shura."

Vic grinned. "What can I do?" he asked, switching to trade tongue as well.

"Nothing," Ravi growled.

"Not sure," Daks replied at the same time. "Shura's usually better at this kind of sneaking around, planning things out ahead of time stuff. I'm more of a spur of the moment kind of guy."

Ravi stifled a snort and rolled his eyes, seriously reconsidering his decision to ally with this man. He sincerely hoped this Shura woman was everything Daks claimed, or they were all doomed.

Vic turned to face Daks directly and worried his lower lip. "If you can get out of the city, you can make it the rest of the way out of Rassa on your own?"

"Yeah. If need be. We've had to travel upriver to cross into Samebar before. We can do it again. My main worry is getting us out of the city itself without triggering another Vision that will bring the Finder or have them right behind us as we flee. The gate guards will be looking for us, and they'll be searching the docks too. I saw what looked like mercenaries with the brother last night, or at least they weren't in King's Guard uniforms. Heard anything about that? Has the Brotherhood started its own army?"

Ravi's stomach clenched as he and Vic exchanged a wide-eyed look. "I've never heard of it, if they have," Ravi said.

Daks glanced between them, looking pensive. "I'd really love to know what that was about," he murmured almost to himself before shaking his head. "But getting us out is more important. Do you know any ways out of the city other than the gates?"

Rassat sat across the river from Samebar's capital, Samet. Because of that, and because of its location at the mouth of the great Matna River, a stone wall had been erected around it to protect it from invading armies and pirate raids. No one got in or out without passing through one of the twelve gates magically constructed by the Brotherhood out of strong iron, and guard towers watched over the wall everywhere else. Ravi had heard of guards who could be bribed to look the other way—not that he or anyone he knew ever had enough coin for that kind of thing, but word trickled down even to them.

"You got coin?" Vic asked, as if reading Ravi's thoughts.

Daks grimaced, the move making the scars along his jaw flash white. "Not enough, if you're talking bribes. The guard might be on high alert for us. It would take a lot more than I'm carrying to make them risk it."

"What about the slavers?" Vic asked. "Surely they know a way to get in and out without being seen."

"No," Daks replied. "They rely on bribes at the docks if they have to, but mostly the guards don't care who's leaving the city as long as they stay gone. They won't risk getting caught with fugitives the Brotherhood is actively searching for. And again, it would cost a lot more than I have to even try."

"So, what then?" Ravi asked, his panic struggling to free itself from the stranglehold he had on it.

"The docks will be the most heavily patrolled," Daks replied. "They'll expect us to try there. It'll be safer to head out into the country. They can't patrol everywhere."

"What if you just wait until things die down?" Vic asked hopefully, and Ravi's heart broke a little more.

"It was a Finder, V," Ravi replied gently. "The longer we wait, the more likely I'll have another Vision that'll bring him right to me. They're getting worse. You know that."

Everything always came back to his gods-damned curse. He'd had to leave his parents and little sister years ago because of it, and now it was forcing him to leave his second family. His nostrils flared as his eyes prickled.

He caught Daks watching him with a cocked eyebrow, and he scowled at the man. It was Daks's fault Ravi had to rehash this painful conversation with Vic all over again. It was Daks's fault he wasn't on a boat somewhere already. He really wanted to punch the guy again, or at least punch something, but his hand still hurt from the last time.

"Look, we have an hour at least before Shura gets here, and we can make a plan," Daks said, breaking the heavy silence that had fallen. "Why don't we all try to rest a little. I'll keep watch, if you want to sleep."

"You're the one who was up all night. I apparently had plenty of sleep," Ravi replied bitterly.

"Only after you expended a great deal of magical energy tapping into whatever it is Seers tap," Daks shot back evenly.

His tone and the words he used drew Ravi up short. Daks talked of magic as if it were the weather or the price of wool at the market. Like it wasn't an evil thing to be hidden and shunned. Part of Ravi desperately wanted to ask what Daks knew about it, but a lifetime of hiding and avoiding the subject was hard to break, especially with a stranger… and in front of Vic.

"Really," Daks continued, "you should try to rest."

"I can't."

"Why?"

"Dreams," Ravi gritted out through clenched teeth, wishing the man would just leave it alone.

"He has Visions in his dreams sometimes," Vic explained so Ravi didn't have to.

"Are they Visions? Or are they Dreams? They aren't the same thing. The former is definitely an issue, the latter, not so much."

Ravi looked at Vic, who shrugged. "I don't know."

"It's unlikely a Dream will put out enough magic anyone outside this room will sense it. But if you don't want to risk it, you don't have to sleep. Just rest for a while. I'll keep watch."

With that imperious pronouncement, Daks turned his back on the two of them and settled by the opening, leaving Ravi wondering if he could trust that Daks really knew what he was talking about.

Just like me.

Ravi scowled at the man's back for a moment, but with little heat. He *was* tired. Sleep sounded wonderful, if only he could risk it. He glanced at Vic's worried face and sighed.

"You should go," Ravi murmured.

"No," Vic replied stubbornly. "I should have gone with you last night. Maybe none of this would have happened if I had."

Ravi shook his head. "They'd just be after you too. The whole point of my leaving was to keep you and the others safe, remember?"

Vic was small and lean, like most of the Unnamed, but he lifted himself to his full height, squared his shoulders, and jutted out his chin. "We keep each other safe. All of us, including you. I helped you find the night market, didn't I? I should have stayed with you."

"Having you there would have made it even harder to leave," Ravi admitted tiredly. He slumped on the dirt floor and leaned his back against the rough plank wall, clutching his bag in his lap. "It was hard enough sneaking out on everyone else."

He shot another sour look at Daks's broad back, resentful he and Vic weren't alone for this conversation, even though it was only a repeat of ones they'd already had. He wasn't being reasonable, but he didn't want to be reasonable. He wanted to be angry. He wanted to rage at the unfairness of it all, but he'd been doing that inside for so long he was bone tired of it.

Instead of letting it loose, he swallowed it, like always, and gave Vic a wan smile. "I can take care of myself. You have the little ones to think of. They need you, V. Staying here with me isn't safe. You know that as well as I do."

Despite the logic in his words, Ravi could admit to a surge relief and gratitude when Vic slid silently to the floor and scooted as close as he could to Ravi's side without touching him. They sat that way in silence for a while. Eventually, Vic sighed, drawing Ravi's attention back to him, and when Vic's head tilted down, Ravi followed his gaze to the stylized owl inked into his own wrist, barely visibly beyond the frayed edges of his tunic.

His heart squeezed a little more for his friend. Vic's life hadn't exactly been blessed by the gods either. He may not have been cursed with magic, but he was Unnamed. He had no family to claim him, so Ravi's family mark had always fascinated him. At one time, Ravi might've insisted that having a family mark hadn't done him any favors, but that wasn't exactly true. He'd had a loving childhood, before it all fell apart. He'd had a roof over his head, and he'd always known where his next meal was coming from. He'd had a life filled with laughter and books and love. That was a far sight more than many of the others in their ragtag little group could claim. He had no right to complain.

So much weight would fall on Vic's thin shoulders once Ravi was gone. Even in the bitterest of winters, when work was scarce, Ravi's ability to read and write had brought in enough coin or food in trade to keep the rest of them alive. He didn't know what they'd do without that extra bit he was able to provide. But they were strong. They had to be, growing up in Arcadia. He needed to believe they'd manage without him. And maybe someday he'd find a way to send help back to them, or send for them to join him.

Chapter Three

Daks tried very hard to ignore the pitiful duo curled up behind him as he stood watch at the opening. He had to wonder a little at their relationship, but it really wasn't his business. Getting emotional had landed him in this mess to start with.

Do the job. Get out. That's it.

He wouldn't bother with self-recriminations. What was the point? Shura would take care of that the first chance she got, and probably from now until the end of his life. The "I told you so's" would be legion. They would be written into the songs of her people and sung around campfires for centuries to come.

He couldn't wait.

He rolled his shoulders and stifled a groan. Nothing beat waiting for a tongue-lashing when you knew you deserved it.

Another waft of fetid air from the tannery behind them made him force down a cough.

Shura, where are you? Hurry, please.

After what seemed an interminable wait, footsteps alerted him that someone approached. His heart kicked up, as another, heavier set joined the first. Without turning his head, he waved a hand behind him to catch his companions' attention.

"Ravi?" someone hissed.

The voice belonged to the little girl, Sparrow, and Daks relaxed. He stood up and moved away from the opening as Shura squeezed inside behind Sparrow, dragging their packs. The little hovel was becoming crowded, but he'd never been so happy to see Shura's scowling face. Though after only a single hard stare from her, his smile of relief and greeting fell, and he wisely kept his mouth clamped shut while she shoved the packs into a corner.

She glanced around at Sparrow, Ravi, and Vic before returning her gaze to Daks. "Your message was vague, to say the least, but I'm going to have to assume we're meeting in this little part of Biton's Hellcave because something terrible has happened," she said in a deceptively even tone.

Might as well get it over with.

Daks cleared his throat. "I kind of stumbled on a gifted while I was just taking a midnight stroll to get some fresh air. And maybe that gifted was being tracked by a brother… and, uh, in the ensuing disagreement about which of us should be allowed to leave with the young man, I *might* have punched said brother in the face a couple of times."

Shura blinked at him for a few seconds before she closed her eyes and her entire body slumped in resignation. She dragged a hand down her face and took a long breath. When she opened her eyes, she shot another brief glance at their companions before pinning him again. "We will have words about this later," she promised as a muscle ticked next to her eye.

"I know," he replied contritely.

"I've been looking for you since I returned to the room to find you gone. I'd only just returned to the inn when your messenger arrived."

"I'm sorry."

She sniffed. "Later. First, we must get out of the city, obviously." She looked at the ragged trio again. "I assume we're not leaving without at least one of these; otherwise you would have come to me at the weaver's hall instead of forcing me to come to this horrid place."

He winced. "Yes. The gifted is coming with us." Daks took a deep breath before continuing, since he knew she was only going to get angrier with each word he said. "He's a Seer."

"So, no control over it whatsoever," Shura finished for him, her voice getting quieter by the second.

"Yeah." Daks swallowed. "And the brother was a Finder, so he'll be out looking for any magical signature." He waited a few beats, but when she only stared at him, Daks gathered his courage to throw the rest out there. "The brother had mercs out looking for us last night, so in addition to the King's Guard and the Brotherhood, we might have some paid swords to deal with."

"And there's no chance of leaving the gifted?"

Daks winced but shook his head stubbornly. He couldn't do it.

Her nostrils flared. "Is that all?"

"Uh, yeah. I think that about covers it."

"And, I take it, this Finder saw your face?"

"It was night, but the moon was full."

She glanced at the others again, and Daks was grateful for the reprieve. If they'd been alone, she'd have probably punched him in the groin by now and unleashed a string of Cigani curses on him and most of his lineage. As it was, she remained quite businesslike but for the tick by her eye and the muscle popping in her jaw.

"How long can we stay here without being discovered?" she asked, directing her question to Vic and Ravi.

"I picked it because no one ever comes here unless they have to," Ravi answered, eyeing Shura with justifiable trepidation. "None of the workers stick around a second after dark, if they can possibly avoid it. But if I have another Vision…."

Shura waved a dismissive hand. "I think we'll have to risk waiting at least until dark. Too many people out now, too easy to be spotted, especially if there are mercs out looking who aren't in any kind of uniform we can avoid." She paused a second to give Daks a glare. "If it was just the gifted, the Brotherhood might have tried to keep the search quiet, given all the troubles we've heard whispers of. But assault on one of their number isn't something they need to keep under wraps. They can use such a blasphemous offense to stir the public. Everyone could be looking for you two, for all we know. I'll check out the docks and see what I hear on the streets."

"We can help there," Vic chimed in eagerly.

"No," Ravi said, but Vic waved a hand at him.

"It's not putting us in danger to walk the streets and look and listen. Most people ignore us unless we get in their way."

"I don't want you to come back here," Ravi said, though his expression said the opposite. "If we're caught, I don't want you anywhere near us."

The two young men seemed to hold a silent conversation for a few beats before Vic sighed and looked away. "I can meet her somewhere else, then," Vic huffed, pointing to Shura.

Shura raised an eyebrow at Daks, and he shrugged in answer. He didn't exactly know what was between Vic and Ravi, but he wasn't above making use of whatever help they could get, and Vic seemed sincere.

"We can meet at the Dog and Duck," Shura said finally. "Faret will keep you safe until I can get to you." She turned back to Daks. "We still have that meeting with Maran we were supposed to attend."

Daks winced and stepped out of range, in case Shura decided not to wait to express her displeasure at the whole situation. "Oops," he said meekly.

She let out a disgusted sound. "I'll try to get to her for at least a quick meeting. She might have some advice or information on our current situation, if her daughter's claims are to be believed." She put a hand to her forehead and rubbed her temples. "Just stay here and try not to get into any more trouble until I can get back." She held her hand out. "Give me the coin and I'll do what I can."

After Daks handed over the purse, Shura turned to the others. "If you want to gather what information you can, that's up to you. I'll return to the Dog and Duck an hour before sunset bells. If you are not there, I'll go on without you."

She turned to leave without another word, and Daks wisely kept his mouth shut. He didn't like leaving all of this to her, but no one was looking for her. She should be able to move about the city with only the usual amount of attention thrown her way.

The other three in the room stood blinking at her sudden departure. Then Vic seemed to gather himself. He dragged a startled Ravi into the briefest of hugs before shoving him roughly away again. "Be safe, Ravi. Be happy."

He scurried out of their hiding place with Sparrow on his heels. Sparrow paused in the opening just long enough to throw a sorrowful look at Ravi before she too disappeared. The silence after their departure was so thick, Daks could almost feel it squeezing the fetid air out of the space. Clearing his throat uncomfortably, he moved to the packs Shura had brought and smiled in relief at the small bundle of food she'd crammed inside.

She still loves me.

He tossed Ravi a wizened apple before grabbing one for himself, trying hard to ignore the bereft look on what he could see of Ravi's hood-shadowed face. This wasn't his business. His business involved getting Ravi safely out of Rassa, into Samebar, and up to the Scholomagi. That's as far as he could or should go. He'd screwed up too much already not to remember that.

He'd finished his apple and had already begun rummaging for something else to eat by the time Ravi took his first bite. Satisfied the man had enough self-preservation to keep himself fed, Daks took up his position by the opening and tried to breathe in the slightly fresher air outside while he devoured a heel of dry, hard bread. He supposed he should be grateful the bread wasn't moldy with the way Shura had been looking at him, but would it have killed her to put some butter on it or a bit of cheese to make it go down easier? The waterskin only held water, not ale, and he sighed morosely.

After a few minutes, Ravi joined him on the other side of the opening, but he didn't seem interested in any more food or conversation, so they sat in tense silence as the rest of the world got on with its day.

The inaction made Daks antsy, but his body was tired after the night he'd had, so he didn't get up to prowl the room again. Who knew when his next chance to rest would come?

Instead of pacing to relieve his boredom, he took the time to really study his companion, cutting sideways glances at him so he wouldn't get caught staring. Despite the dirt and worry and the tattered hood blocking much of his view, Ravi was definitely more pleasant to look at than the grimy alley or dusty street beyond. He had an almost delicate angular profile, with a pointed chin, slender, straight nose, and lips that weren't full or thin but somewhere in between. The sharp slashes of his jaw and cheekbones saved him from being too pretty, but not by much. Still, it was his eyes that truly set him apart. Despite Ravi's obvious efforts to hide them, his eyes occasionally caught the light from outside, glowing gold, like amber. Daks had never seen eyes that color before, and he had a hard time not staring.

Now that he thought about it, last night he could've sworn he'd seen those eyes lit from within by some otherworldly light while Ravi had spoken that prophecy. But that had to have been a trick of the moonlight. Glowing eyes were a sign of Riftspawn, and Daks knew Ravi wasn't one of those. He would've sensed Spawn a mile away, and besides, Riftspawn eyes glowed red, and Ravi's had seemed almost silver.

Daks didn't usually go for the skinny, pretty ones—probably because the pretty ones never went for him either—but he could see the appeal, and he'd frankly always been more opportunistic than picky. The journey all the way up to Scholoveld would be a long one. Perhaps they could find a way to pass the time together, if Ravi ever got over that whole being-furious-with-him thing.

His stomach tightened as another thought occurred to him, and he turned his gaze back to the alley. Life probably hadn't been easy for Ravi on the streets. The pretty ones didn't last long outside the brothels. But gifted *and* pretty? Slavers like Tarek probably would have been frothing at the mouth to get their hands on him. Ravi had to have been either very smart or very lucky to make it this far and still be a little soft beneath his prickly exterior, or at least as soft as he'd been with Sparrow and that Vic guy. Maybe he hadn't been out there long on his own. Curiosity gnawed at him, but he shoved it down. Not his business. The boredom was torture, but better that than getting any more involved.

SHURA RETURNED just as the brilliant oranges, pinks, and reds of dusk faded to pale violet in the small patch of sky above the alley. The streets and tannery had slowly emptied of bodies and noise by then, and Daks was practically crawling out of his skin with the need to be doing something. Ravi had seemed infuriatingly content to sit quietly the whole time, lost in his own thoughts, so Daks didn't even have awkward conversation to distract him. The Seer would fit in great alongside the old farts at the Scholomagi, with their dusty old books and scribblings—a match made by the gods.

A shuffling in the alley caught his attention, and he sighed with relief. After he and Ravi stepped back to give her room, Shura squeezed through the opening and tossed two new packs on top of the others.

"As soon as the sun goes down and the rest of the streets clear, we need to move and move quickly," she began without preamble. "Maran has agreed to smuggle us out of the city—"

"She did?" Daks cut in, surprised.

Shura narrowed her eyes. "*In exchange* for an introduction to the High Council for one of her lieutenants," she continued pointedly. "This lieutenant will travel with us to Samebar."

Daks groaned. "That's all we need, more deadweight." He caught Ravi's outraged huff and shrugged. "No offense."

Shura's lips thinned as she took a step toward Daks, claiming all his attention again. "I'll remind you that this situation is none of my making, *Vaida*. If you think you could have negotiated better on our behalf, feel free to do so when we meet up with her people."

Finally sensing the danger he was in, Daks took a step back and threw up his hands. "No, no. I'm sure it was the best choice we had. Thank you, Shura, for taking care of everything."

"You're welcome," she sniffed.

Ravi stepped forward. "And Vic and Sparrow? Did you see them?"

Shura nodded. "They were at the Dog and Duck when I arrived. It is as we feared. The streets and docks are crawling with brothers and guards, plus there is talk of strangers bearing hidden weapons. Your descriptions are being spread, but it will be harder to catch up with us after dark. We need to leave tonight, though, before everyone in the city is looking for you."

Daks winced, and Shura merely blinked slowly at him for a long time in silent judgment.

When she stayed silent a bit too long, Daks cleared his throat and asked meekly, "Will you tell me the rest now, please?"

Her scowl eased slightly, and he relaxed. "The rebels are a real, organized group now, if still a bit small and underfunded. Maran says she is only one leader in their 'army.' She says unrest is spreading like wildfire, as we'd heard. There are rumors the brothers have lost their magics, that the gods are punishing them for their abuses of power by cutting the Thirty-Six off from their holy talismans, and the king does not seem to be working very hard to quell such talk. Other rumors of a barbarian invasion to the north, led by a mysterious wizard and a renegade brother, have everyone on edge, including the rebels. The people are frightened, and it won't take much for that fear to ignite into rebellion. She and her fellows are preparing for that moment."

"What do they want with the High Council?" Daks asked.

"Magic," Shura replied with a shrug. "They want to negotiate and bargain for potions and protections and the like, I assume. Rassans have been purposefully kept in ignorance about magic, and if the Thirty-Six have not lost their power, they're going to have to face them at some point, so they need to know how to fight with magic. Enemy of my enemy, and all that."

Daks snorted. "They won't get far with the power-hungry old bastards in Scholoveld. They won't share anything that isn't pried out of their cold dead hands." He shot a glance at Ravi and winced. "Except, you know, unless you're one of them," he amended.

"Not our problem," Shura cut in impatiently. "They bargained for guides and an introduction. That is all."

"True," he conceded, pride making his lips curl at the corners as he gazed at his partner.

"We meet them at the ninth gate an hour after dark. We'll hide you and this one in a wagon," she continued, crooking a thumb at Ravi. "When we're far enough away from the city, we split from the others. They could only afford to give us two horses, the one Maran's lieutenant will have and one for us, so we will have to share or switch off walking, but it should only take us a day to get to Urmat. We head for our contact there and hope he can get us a boat across the river. Once we're safely in Samebar, we'll figure out the rest."

With a grunt, Daks turned to Ravi and lifted his eyebrows. "Think you can hang on to your Visions for a day and a half?"

"I don't know."

"We take no chances at the gate," Shura said curtly.

She pulled a small stoppered glass vial out of the inner pocket of her cloak and held it up to the pale shaft of bluish light coming from the opening.

"What's that?" Ravi asked.

"Sleeping draught. When we get near the gate, you take it. You fall into a gentle, dreamless sleep, we stow you away in a trunk, and out you go, magic-sniffers none the wiser."

Even inside the depths of his hood, the whites of Ravi's eyes caught the light as he gaped at her and took a step back. "No way. What if something goes wrong? I'll be helpless. I won't be able to run. I won't be able to do anything."

"Young man," Shura began, softening her voice and her expression, "Finders will be at the gates. Not all, maybe, but we don't know how many or which. This is the only way to guarantee you won't lose control and give us away." She crooked a thumb at Daks. "This one carried you last night when you were out."

"It was his fault in the first place, and I didn't exactly have a choice in the matter!" Ravi argued.

"You got a better idea?" Daks asked.

Ravi turned his glare on him, his hood falling back a bit. "Yeah, I stay conscious."

"And we take our chances that all those new people you're around, the gate guards, possibly a Finder or other member of the Brotherhood won't trigger another Vision?"

Ravi closed his mouth with a loud click of his teeth coming together and stubbornly jutted out his chin. Daks raised his eyebrows to Shura, and she pursed her lips before turning to glance out the opening to the alley beyond. Barely a hint of light showed through the crack now.

"We are out of time for arguing," she muttered.

In one smooth motion, she pulled her dagger from its hidden sheath along her forearm. Before Ravi could do anything but yelp and take a step backward, she was at his side. She tapped him on the temple with the butt of her knife, and he dropped to the dirt at her feet.

Daks wasn't exactly shocked. He did grimace at her, though. "He won't be out long, and then what?"

She knelt next to Ravi's prone form, unstoppered the vial, and poured some into his mouth. He choked and spluttered, rousing enough to roll accusatory eyes in her direction before those eyes became unfocused and closed again.

"You carried him last night," Shura replied, stoppering the vial and putting it back in her cloak. "You carry him tonight."

"Are you kidding?" Daks whined. "Did I mention that I carried him for at least an hour last night? Do you know how heavy he is? A lot heavier than he looks, I'll tell you that."

She twisted her lips. "Poor, poor baby. You should be glad this is the only punishment you get for being so, so...." She let out a string of Cigani curses before visibly reining in her temper and smoothing out her features. "This is the plan. No one fights me on it unless it fails. You get him. I get the packs. Let us go."

After stooping to grab all four packs, she shoved them out the small opening and then followed, leaving him alone with an unconscious Ravi yet again. With a heavy sigh, he grabbed Ravi under the arms and dragged him through the opening, scraping his shoulders and upper arms against the rough wood and knocking a board loose in the process. Shura waited at the head of the alley, loaded down with their gear. This time, Daks was smart enough to drape Ravi's lumpy bag across his own chest before he hefted Ravi over his shoulders again.

He'd be lucky if he could move tomorrow.

"Lead the way," he wheezed as he joined her.

She took another sweep of their surroundings before heading north at a fast walk, and Daks stifled a whine and followed. Time passed agonizingly slowly. Daks had to use every ounce of his energy to keep his legs moving while searching every side street and shadow for possible trouble. If anyone ever asked him how long they'd traveled or what route they'd taken, he wouldn't be able to say, even at knifepoint. The entire journey was a blur of pain and dragging air into his lungs like a bellows. His throat hurt. His chest hurt. His thighs screamed alongside his shoulders and back.

So this is what the Seventh Hell feels like.

When they finally stopped in a dark alley, Daks unloaded his burden with a little less care than he probably should have and slumped to the ground next to him, gasping.

"I swear. That's it. I'm never. Going. To carry. Him. Again. No more. You hear me?" he panted.

Shura didn't bother to respond. She'd set their packs down too, and now she hovered at the head of the alley, focusing all her attention on the streets beyond. After a few minutes, the clop of hooves and the flicker of torchlight caught his attention. Shura's silhouette straightened in the wavering light, and she stepped out of the alley. Ravi moaned quietly next to him and shifted a little, but settled again. He was waking up, which could prove problematic, since the whole point of all this wasn't just to torture Daks, it was to get Ravi through the gate without any unfortunate magical incidents.

Gritting his teeth, Daks pulled himself to his feet and limped to the head of the alley. He spotted Shura easily amongst a small group around a cart. She looked his way, as if she'd felt him watching, and then she headed back to him with two of the strangers in tow, one of whom towered over the rest by a good foot at least.

"Daks, this is Haruk and Vahal. They'll be driving the cart," she said by way of introduction.

Daks nodded to both men, and then Vahal, the larger man, lumbered past them toward Ravi. Daks followed him and hovered close by while the giant stooped to pick Ravi up like he weighed nothing.

"He's waking up," Daks said, shifting anxiously as an odd twinge constricted his chest.

He shouldn't feel like he was somehow failing in his duty if he let someone else haul Ravi around for a bit. He was a practical man, after all. But his lips still twisted into a scowl as he sullenly followed them out of the alley.

At the wagon, Shura turned to him. "Haruk and Vahal will stow you two inside and leave by the ninth gate. We've decided I'm a little too, uh, *distinctive*, too memorable, so I'll join Maran's lieutenant and leave by the tenth gate. We'll meet up again in the woods outside Haruk's farm."

"We're separating?" Daks asked, eyeing the strangers uncomfortably. "Are you sure?"

She grimaced. "I'm not best pleased with the situation either, but they have a point. I draw too much attention just being who I am. We don't want to pique anyone's curiosity, and two small teams are less likely to be noticed."

And less likely the King's Guard or the Brotherhood will get all of the rebel's men in one incident if something goes wrong.

She moved past him to where Ravi lay propped against one of the large wheels to the cart, pulled the vial from her pocket again, and poured a bit more into his mouth. He coughed again but didn't rouse more than to crack his eyes for a second before closing them.

"Don't give him too much," Daks warned. "He may be heavy, but it's mostly bones. We don't want him out all night."

Shura threw him a sour look, like he should know better, and he cleared his throat uncomfortably.

"You know he's not going to let you anywhere near him again after he wakes up," he murmured as he threw her a crooked smile.

She shrugged. "I think he will have little choice. They could only spare a couple of mounts, and I'm the lighter of the two of us. He's more than welcome to walk the whole way to Urmat, if that is his wish."

Daks's smile widened. *This* was the Shura he knew and loved, not the sentimental stranger he'd encountered at the Dog and Duck. He still didn't like the idea of splitting up again, but he supposed the rebels had a point. The less attention they drew to themselves, the better off everyone would be. A couple of tired farmers going home from the city after a long day at the markets was as ordinary as the dirt beneath their feet, and just as forgettable. Shura, on the other hand, was another matter altogether.

They all pitched in unloading the cart so Daks and Ravi could squeeze into a crate behind the driver's seat at the front of the wagon. After a quick and largely unspoken goodbye with Shura, Daks settled Ravi into the box first and then climbed in beside him. There wasn't quite enough room for both of them to lie side by side, so he had to pull Ravi's inert body partway onto his chest to squeeze the rest of the way in. In other circumstances, he might've enjoyed the cuddling. He hadn't bedded anyone in weeks and wouldn't mind a little human contact. But the box was far too small and he hurt far too much to take any pleasure in it.

After putting the lid on the box, the others piled mostly empty crates, barrels, and sacks left over from a successful day at the markets in front of them. Thank the gods Daks wasn't claustrophobic or he would've been on the verge of panic by the time they were done. The bumpy ride to the gate was tortuous enough. He almost envied Ravi being allowed to sleep through it all, but the poor man would probably be covered in bruises by the time they were done. Daks did what he could to protect Ravi's head and shoulders, but he could barely move enough to brace himself within the confines of the box, so he wasn't sure how successful he was.

When the bouncing and rattling finally stopped, he held his breath and strained to listen as what sounded like gate guards questioned Haruk and Vahal. He tensed for a fight when the thud of boots moved toward the back of the wagon and someone began shifting the crates in front of him. As the noises grew closer, he silently cursed himself for not removing the dagger from its sheath at the small of his back, because he sure as hells couldn't reach it now.

Luckily, after a few tense moments, the rummaging stopped, and Daks blew out a long breath when the cart began moving again. They weren't safe yet, but they'd hopefully passed the worst obstacle.

Every single inch of his body ached by the time the wagon finally stopped again and Haruk called to him.

"We're far enough away now. You can at least come out of hiding and stretch," he said in accented trade tongue.

Crates and barrels suddenly moved and flickering torchlight flooded through the cracks of their hiding place. In other circumstances, Daks would have manfully refused the massive paw Vahal extended in his direction, but after the abuse he'd put his body through in the last day, he was embarrassed to admit he needed the help sliding out from under Ravi and climbing out of the box. His legs were asleep, and he had to roll his shoulders several times before he could work the crick out of his neck and lift up his head.

"Thank you," he murmured, and Vahal nodded.

"You'll need to stay in the back, but there's no need to cram into that tiny space. How is the other?" Vahal asked in a rumbling bass Daks could feel in his chest.

"Still asleep. I think he got the better end of that deal," Daks grumbled, and Vahal chuckled.

"Not far now," Vahal said gently before heading back to the front of the wagon.

Daks shoved some of the boxes aside to make room for himself and then crawled back in. He braced his back against a barrel a moment before Haruk snapped the reins and barked out an order, making the horse lurch forward. After the first new bump in the road, Daks tugged Ravi out of the box enough to cushion his head on one of Daks's thighs so the hard boards of the cart wouldn't do him any more damage than Shura already had. The last thing he needed was to have to carry the man yet one more time because he'd been brained unconscious again.

As the cart rumbled along the rutted road by the full moon, Daks draped an arm across Ravi's shoulders to hold him in place, settled himself as comfortably as he could, and tipped his head back to take in the stars littering the night sky. Away from the city and the smoky miasma of chimney fires, the view was breathtaking, and he was honestly too tired to try to make conversation with the men in front of him. He should be pumping them for as much information as he could, but Maran's lieutenant probably knew more than they did anyway, so he could afford to be a little lazy. He'd lost a full night's sleep to his own stupidity, after all.

He drew in a deep breath of clean sea air and blew it out again, allowing his mind to wander where it would as his gaze dropped to the rolling farmland they now traveled through. Shura was right. It was time for him to face facts and move on to some other job. His feelings were getting the better of him and he was making mistakes, possibly costly ones. If he quit, he could finally tell the High Council where to shove their bureaucracy, their greed, and their petty squabbles and venture out on his own… with Shura, of course. He might not be as young as he once was, but he and Shura were still young and capable enough they could find work anywhere. His gift would always be useful, even if it wasn't particularly flashy.

His glance drifted down to Ravi's cloaked head resting on his thigh. He couldn't save them all. And if he were truly honest with himself, he'd finally admit Josel was gone for good. He'd have found some way to contact Daks in the nearly ten years since his disappearance if he'd still been alive. He wouldn't have left Daks hurting if he'd had any choice in the matter.

Daks's hand tightened almost of its own accord on the shoulder beneath his palm. One more rescue and maybe his conscience would be satisfied and the old wounds inside him could heal. After that, maybe he and Shura could find a bit of land somewhere with the wages he'd saved over the years. They'd settle down, find a husband for him and a wife for her. They could be farmers like the rest of his family, and Shura could invite her clan to stay for as long as they wanted and return as often as they wanted.

He fidgeted, grimacing as he lifted one buttcheek and then the other to relieve the ache from the pounding it was getting. It was definitely not the kind of pounding he preferred. A small smile curved his lips as he glanced at Vahal's broad shoulders above him. If he wasn't doing this job anymore, he could find a mountain of a man like Vahal to climb on top of every night and hitch to the plow every day. Regular sex and not being on the verge of possible torture and death all the time had its perks, right? He glanced from Vahal's back down to Ravi's prone form again and pursed his lips. Or maybe he'd find himself a pretty little thing to curl around every night and hitch *himself* to the plow every morning instead. The options were limitless, really.

The fantasy lasted for only a few more minutes before he snorted and shook his head. Shura would be ready to kill him within a week, from boredom. She came from a nomadic people, so staying in one place ran contrary to everything she was. She'd do it for him, but he would be cruel to ask it of her. He wasn't exactly farmer material either... at least, not anymore. They needed a few more years of adventure under their belts before they could manage that level of settling down in any case... or the right partners to make the quiet life more interesting.

With a smile still on his face, he let his head fall back and closed his eyes. Shura would probably laugh herself silly if he ever shared half the shit that ran through his head.

He jerked awake when the wagon lurched steeply to one side, adding another bruise to Daks's already sore body.

"Almost there," Haruk called over his shoulder as he guided the cart off the road toward a small stand of trees. "This is where we'll wait."

As soon as Haruk pulled the horse to a stop, Daks eased out from under Ravi and crawled out of the back of the wagon, eager to stretch his stiffened muscles and shake off the lethargy that threatened to render him useless. Nothing disturbed the land around them beyond the sleepy chirping of crickets in the tall grass along the roadside, but he loosened the dagger in its sheath anyway and peered into the darkness beyond the torchlight.

"How long do you think it will take them?" Daks asked, twisting his neck from side to side and rolling his shoulders.

"Not long," Haruk answered as he climbed down from his box. "They should be able to move faster than this old cart, despite having to go the long way 'round."

"Thank you again for helping us," Daks said as both men moved to join him.

"'Tis a fair trade," Haruk murmured with a shrug as he pulled a pipe and a small cloth bag from his pocket and began to pack the bowl. "Things are happening here, happening fast. The whispers grow each day. Our prayers to the gods are being answered. If we are to take what the gods have given us, we must act and we must learn." He turned to glance over his shoulder into the back of his wagon before lighting a stick from the mounted torch and using it to light his pipe. "We'll need men and women like this one someday, I think. But there are many who'd disagree. Many who think magic is evil and should be snuffed out of all Kita forever. Lad will be safer in your land. Quanna, Moc, and Chytel willing, Rassa will be free afore too long, and without much bloodshed, and young ones like him will want to return to us."

Daks opened his mouth to give a polite, noncommittal response, but the sudden, rhythmic clomp of hooves on packed earth stopped him. He tensed as he held up a hand for silence and searched the darkness beyond the torchlight. The sounds weren't coming from Haruk's cart horse or the direction of the city, and they were growing louder. The men beside him immediately fell silent and also tensed. When a blur of white crested the next hill, Daks narrowed his gaze until the shape resolved itself into that of a riderless horse. He blinked for a moment in surprise before glancing at his two companions, but they were staring also, no sign of recognition or understanding on their faces. At last Haruk turned to him, and Daks raised his eyebrows.

"'Tis a bit odd," Vahal rumbled as he stepped away from the wagon toward the approaching creature.

The horse was very large and obviously well taken care of. It had no saddle, not even a bridle, but its long silvery mane and tail flowed freely, without a hint of a bramble or tangle. Shura's admonition that they would only have two mounts for the four of them rang in Daks's head, but he stayed where he was. He couldn't afford to risk upsetting his newfound allies, if they wanted the beautiful beast. He wouldn't be able to take it with him back to Samebar in any case.

The horse continued its sedate trot toward them, showing no reaction to Vahal's approach until they were within a few feet of each other and Vahal reached out to it. Then the horse snorted, arched away from his grasp, and bared its teeth at him. For each step Vahal took toward it, the horse took a step back, showing no signs of running away, but also not allowing Vahal to touch it.

"Easy there, boy," Vahal murmured in Rassan, continuing to try to get closer to it, but the horse would have none of that.

Appearing to lose patience with Vahal's attempts to capture it, the horse snorted again, lunged at him, and snapped at the air, forcing the big man to scurry backward. Apparently pleased with the result, the horse whickered and lifted its head proudly as Vahal cast a beseeching look toward Haruk. "A little help here?"

Haruk's lips quirked before he shoved his pipe between his teeth and strode purposefully over. He and Vahal approached the animal from opposite sides this time, while Daks watched in amusement. At least he had something interesting to pass the time until Shura got there. He folded his arms across his chest and rested against the side of the wagon as the two men tried time and again to coax the horse close enough to handle, but the animal continued to elude them, sending off periodic warnings of bodily harm with hoof and teeth, should they cross some internal line known only to it.

"I need to find a rope," Haruk finally puffed. "Maybe one of Daisy's leads will do the trick."

"Or maybe we should unhitch Daisy and bring her over. She's a mare. He's a stallion. We might be able to woo him to follow us home," Vahal suggested.

The two men had stepped back to give the horse some room as they discussed their options. The horse eyed them for a short time, but when they made no move toward it, the creature seemed to dismiss them completely and began walking again, right toward Daks.

Realizing the direction it was headed, Daks straightened and eyed the animal warily, keeping his hands unthreateningly by his sides. Amazingly, the horse didn't stop until it walked right up to him and rubbed its muzzle against his cheek.

"Uh, hi there," Daks said as his lips curved into an uncertain smile.

One huge pale blue eye captured his gaze and held. He wasn't exactly sure how long they might have stayed that way, but a sudden cry rang out behind him, and a pulse of that strange magic Daks had experienced the night before flooded his senses.

Seven Hells! Not now. Not so close to the city!

Forgetting the horse, Daks swung around in a panic. Ravi's back arched off the bed of the wagon only for a few seconds before he moaned and collapsed again. The horse squealed in distress and reared away as Daks vaulted over the side of the wagon, ignoring the animal completely.

"Ravi, are you okay?" Daks asked he knelt by Ravi's prone body. "Push it back if you can. Can you hear me?"

Magic tingled along his skin but dissipated quickly. "That's right. Push it back."

As the last vestiges faded to nothing, he blew out a relieved breath, but they weren't necessarily safe. That Finder or another could have been searching the area for any magical sign. And while a Sensitive's range was usually not that long, and scrying was forbidden magic in Rassa, after witnessing that brother use a summoning stone last night, Daks couldn't be sure of anything anymore.

"Is your friend okay?" Haruk asked, sounding spooked despite his earlier declarations of magical tolerance.

"He's seems okay now. I don't know what that was, maybe a nightmare," Daks replied, still frowning at the sleeping man in front of him.

"Okay. Good," Haruk breathed.

An outraged squeal rent the air.

Daks whipped around in time to see Vahal get knocked on his impressive ass by the enraged stallion. A leather strap swung from the creature's neck as it reared, but just when Daks thought it would trample the man, the thing settled back on the ground, flapped its lips at them, and sauntered toward the back of the wagon.

Bemused, Daks glanced between Haruk, Vahal on the ground, and the regal animal gazing benignly at him from a few feet away.

"Are you okay?" Daks called to Vahal without letting the horse out of his sight.

"I'm fine," Vahal answered irritably.

Daks cast a quick concerned glance at Ravi; then he scooted hesitantly toward the back of the wagon. He extended a cautious hand toward the horse's silver-and-pink muzzle, and it nuzzled his palm and gently lipped his skin.

"Oooooookay," Daks murmured.

"Feh," Vahal grumbled as he climbed to his feet and brushed himself off. "Do you two know each other?"

"No. I've never seen it before in my life."

"Well, it seems you have a new friend, then."

Daks cocked an eyebrow at the horse, but the creature just gave him what appeared to be a smug look. "I guess so."

Ignoring the strange horse for a second, he glanced back at Ravi and then anxiously scanned the horizon. They needed to get on the road before Ravi had another episode. A moving target was harder to find. He slid out of the wagon, past the horse, and walked toward the road, searching for any sign of Shura. If she took much longer, he might have to start their journey alone and make her catch up. But she and Maran's lieutenant had the horses, and Daks had a still-unconscious Ravi *and* all the packs stowed inside crates in the wagon, so that wasn't going to work. He worried his lower lip as he pondered his options until a nudge from behind nearly sent him sprawling in the dirt. He caught himself just in time and threw a glare over his shoulder at the white stallion. It shook its head and whickered in response.

Pursing his lips, Daks temporarily dismissed the problem of Shura and approached the animal. As before, it nuzzled his outstretched hand. Encouraged, Daks stepped close and ran his palm down the horse's neck to its shoulder, and it leaned into his touch. Something tingled at the edge of his consciousness, but when he tried to pin it down, it disappeared. Shrugging it off, he returned his attention to the horse. It really was a magnificent animal. Someone out there was obviously missing it, but they could definitely use another mount.

"What do you say, horse? If I sling some packs and an unconscious man over your back, are you gonna kick me and bolt?"

He'd need to rig up a bridle somehow, at least. He could ride bareback, but with only the horse's mane to hold on to, he didn't like his chances if it bolted. The stallion held his gaze with one calm pale blue eye until the sound of hoofbeats approaching made them both turn toward the road.

Even at a distance, with little more than moonlight, Daks would know Shura's silhouette anywhere, and his shoulders slumped in relief. He hadn't been overly worried for her safety, getting out of the city. No one was looking for her, and there shouldn't be any reason for her to be detained, but shit sometimes happened, and it was always better to have her where he could watch her back.

"Any problems?" he called when she was within easy earshot.

"No. Couple of gate guards got a little handsy, and I was tempted to remove said hands at the wrists, but calmer minds prevailed." She jerked her head toward her companion as she said that last, and Daks's attention shifted to the other rider.

Maran's lieutenant was a petite woman, possibly in her late twenties or early thirties. Her pale blonde hair had been coiled around her head in a modest thick braid that looked like it might reach her thighs when it was unbound. Even in the austere woolen tunic and leggings pious Rassans seemed to prefer, she was a pretty little thing, and Daks cocked an eyebrow at Shura as he fought a smile. "Calmer minds?"

Ignoring the comment, Shura lifted a hand in the other woman's direction. "Dakso Kavalyan, may I present Mistress Fara Sabin, Maran's right hand and our new traveling companion."

"Mistress Sabin." He gave her a brief nod as he heaved an internal sigh. "You can call me Daks."

She didn't look particularly useful in a fight—or anything else for that matter—but it was clear Shura was already fond of her, which could be a problem if they had to cut and run. He'd been proven wrong before, so he'd hold judgment for now, but the quality of her wool traveling garb and the delicate gloved hands holding the reins didn't make her seem like the kind of woman who was used to sleeping rough.

"A pleasure to meet you, Daks. And you may call me Fara."

One of Daks's eyebrows quirked in surprise. Rassans were normally quite fond of their titles and honorifics. Maybe she wasn't as prim as she appeared.

"Uh, Daks, what's that?" Shura asked as Daks felt the presence of a large body at his back.

He gave her a bland look and smiled. "A horse?"

Shura narrowed her eyes at him, and Daks smirked and held up his hands. "He just showed up. Maybe he'll be useful. Maybe not. But we don't have time for pleasantries right now. Ravi had another Vision… or something. The pulse of energy was brief, before it thankfully stopped, but that doesn't mean no one else felt it too. We need to get moving."

"Where is he?" Shura asked sharply, nudging her mount closer.

For some reason, when Shura's mare got close to the white stallion, it suddenly reared away, and Shura had to wrestle with it to get it under control again.

"Not so popular with the ladies, I guess," Daks quipped, even as he frowned in puzzlement at the stallion.

Shura dismounted, handed her reins off to Vahal with a nod of thanks, and approached the wagon with Daks on her heels. Ravi lay in the bed unmoving but for the gentle rise and fall of his chest.

"Still out?" she asked unnecessarily.

"Yeah. He only stirred briefly with the whatever that was."

"If he has Visions even when he's drugged, that could be problematic. I've never heard of such a thing before."

Daks shrugged. "Well, we weren't exactly planning to keep him knocked out all the way to Samebar, so that's pretty much moot, right?"

She glanced in his direction and cocked an eyebrow, and he narrowed his eyes at her. "I'm not carrying him all the way to Samebar, Shur. It's not happening. Besides, you could kill him, keeping him drugged up the whole time."

She only shrugged, grabbed a pack from the wagon, and carried it to her horse. When he continued to stare after her as she strapped the pack to her saddle, she huffed. "You were the one who said we needed to move, so *move*. If we need to get away from here fast, we'll have to ride double for a while. It'll be hard on the horses, but it'll put a greater distance between us and any followers to start, and we can walk them later."

"What about this guy?" Daks said, crooking a thumb at the white stallion that seemed to want to follow him like a puppy.

"You think you can trust it?"

"I have no idea."

"Then you ride it. We don't have a saddle or much extra rope. We can strap Ravi to my horse with the packs, and I'll ride double with Mistress Sabin while you take the other."

"Your great sacrifice is duly noted," Daks quipped under his breath as he fought a grin, and she shot him a glare.

"Perhaps I should remind you, yet again, of why we're in this situation," Shura replied icily, and Daks winced.

"That won't be necessary."

"You're sure?"

"Yup. I'm sure."

"Okay, then. Bring him here."

Though Vahal took a step forward, Daks beat the man to it and obediently dragged Ravi to the edge of the wagon bed as gently as he could. Shura's mare still seemed a little skittish because of the stallion, so Daks waved his arms at the big white brute until it snorted at him and took a few steps away. When Shura led her mare close enough, Daks took a deep breath, gritted his teeth against the coming pain, and hefted Ravi over the saddle with a grunt. Ravi stirred slightly at the treatment but didn't wake, and Daks frowned.

"How much of that stuff did you give him?"

"Enough," Shura replied curtly. "Don't fret. Maran's potion-maker promised no harm would come to him from taking it. He'll wake eventually, hopefully when we are a better distance from the city."

With help from Haruk and Vahal, Daks got Ravi and the remaining packs strapped to Shura's horse before warily approaching the stallion. If this didn't work, he'd be jogging behind the others for the next several hours or overburdening Shura's mount with his own weight on top of Ravi and the packs. Neither of those options particularly appealed.

"Well, horse, let's see how far your trust and admiration goes."

He'd rigged a quick rope halter, which the horse allowed him to tie on without so much as a twitch of complaint or unease.

"I bet someone is really missing you right now," he murmured in a soothing tone as he petted the stallion's neck.

Now for the big test.

He led the horse to the wagon and used the bed to lever himself onto its back. He tensed for the thing to rear or bolt, but nothing happened. He waited another few beats, but when the horse only turned its head to give him a placid, expectant look, Daks grinned. Maybe his luck was improving.

"Okay, let's go," he called.

Shura eyed him skeptically from behind Fara. "You sure?"

His grin widened. "Of course I am. No problem."

Shura shook her head and nudged their horse into a walk.

After giving Haruk and Vahal his thanks and saying his goodbyes, Daks collected the other mare's reins in his free hand and nudged the stallion after them. The two men both looked a bit jealous as he turned and waved, but they waved back until Daks's little party traveled around a bend in the road and they disappeared from view.

Chapter Four

FOR THE second day in a row, Ravi woke with every inch of his body aching and no idea where he was. The headache this time wasn't quite the same. It throbbed more than stabbed, but the fuzzy fog over his thoughts and the churning nausea made it almost as bad.

"Wha—?" he croaked, but his mouth and throat were so dry he couldn't get anything else out.

He licked cracked lips and blinked in what seemed to be early morning sunlight streaming through a canopy of trees as what sounded like a stream burbled happily somewhere nearby. If it weren't for the pain and the queasiness, the whole scene would have been rather idyllic, actually.

A cup brimming with clear water appeared in front of him, but he fumbled it, spilling half its icy contents onto his hands and over the ground. The water was so cold it made his teeth ache. Still, he sucked down as much as he could without a second thought, desperately thirsty for some reason.

When he blinked up at the kind soul who'd provided the life-giving draught, an all-too-familiar scarred, scruffy, disreputable face filled his vision, and Ravi's dreamy idyll vanished as a red haze descended. "You asshole! You drugged me? You *drugged* me?" he screeched, chucking the cup at Daks's head even as he winced at his own volume.

Daks's expression had been searching and concerned, but at Ravi's outburst, he ducked the missile and threw his hands out in front of him as he backed away. "Whoa there. That wasn't me." He crooked his thumb behind him at Shura and another woman standing near some horses. "Blame her. She's the one who did it."

Ravi gave Daks one last glare before shooting daggers at Shura, but when the Cigani woman lifted her eyebrows and took a step in his direction, Ravi yelped and scrambled to his feet.

"Keep her away from me!" he cried as he threw out a hand to brace himself on the tree they'd propped him against.

He didn't think he imagined the slight quirk to her lips, but her expression was bland and unreadable the next time he looked, so he couldn't be sure. Daks continued to make appeasing motions with his outstretched hands.

"Okay, let's all calm down a little. Shura's not going to do anything else to you. Are you, Shur?"

She was silent for far too long before she said, "Only when necessary."

"Oh, that's great. Just great. And who gets to decide what's necessary?" Ravi fumed past the throbbing in his skull.

Maybe this had been a terrible mistake. What had he been thinking, trusting these people?

He wished to the gods that he wasn't so unsteady on his feet and that he wasn't so ignorant of the world outside of the city. He had no idea how long he'd been out or where the hells they were or anything.

Cursed. I'm cursed. Why does no one ever believe me when I tell them that?

Daks took a cautious step forward, eyeing him warily. "Don't listen to her. I won't let anything happen to you. We're halfway to Urmat already. Another half-day's ride and we should be there. We'll find our friend, and he'll take us across the river to Samebar tomorrow morning. Easy as pie. No need for any more drugs or violence. Okay?"

Daks cast a meaningful look toward Shura, and Ravi relaxed marginally. He braced a second hand against the tree trunk and blew out a breath. He felt like he'd been run over by a wagon… and then dragged behind it.

"We're out of the city," he said unnecessarily.

"We are."

"Did anything happen?"

Daks paused a beat before shaking his head. "Nope."

Ravi narrowed his eyes. "Why don't I believe you?"

"Because you're very untrusting?"

Ravi scowled, and the big oaf just blinked at him innocently.

"You had another Vision last night, even while you were drugged," Shura cut in harshly. "But luckily it didn't last long enough to bring the entirety of the Brotherhood down on us, probably because you *were* drugged. This is why what I did was necessary."

Hells. Ravi closed his eyes, turned, and slumped against the base of the tree again in defeat. He didn't remember any Vision. He didn't remember *anything*.

Was he going mad, or was it just the drug?

Casting a glance at each of his three new traveling companions in turn, he struggled to calm his temper and think. If the big dumb brute was telling the truth, he only had another day before he'd be safely in Samebar. He didn't have to travel with these lunatics all the way to the school of mages. Maybe he could ditch them at the first town they came to on the other side of the river. Surely someone might want a Seer in their house or hold, even an untrained one. If all the stories were true, he wouldn't have to hide what he was in Samebar. Plus, he had other skills to offer. He could read and write, and he'd learned a bit of Sambaran before he'd been forced to leave his childhood home. He could put up with Shura and Daks for one more day, surely. He'd just have to watch his back.

"What now?" he asked in a slightly calmer tone.

"We're giving the horses and ourselves a little rest," Daks replied, seeming relieved. "I suggest you eat something, whether you're hungry or not."

After moving to one of the horses, Daks tossed him another wizened apple, and Ravi caught it and bit into it mechanically, not at all hungry. He suspected the lingering nausea was from the drug he'd been given, and he shot another ugly look at Shura, though the woman's attention was riveted on the petite blond standing beside her.

"Who's that?" he asked, jerking his chin in the woman's direction.

Daks glanced up from the pack he was fiddling with. "Mistress Fara Sabin. She's part of the bargain we struck to get us out of the city. She'll be traveling with us to Scholoveld."

The woman looked up at her name and nodded to Ravi, though her gaze seemed a bit uncomfortable. He gave her a nod in return, before biting another chunk off his mealy apple. His gaze wandered irritably over the rest of the sun-dappled clearing until it landed on the unsettlingly pale blue eyes of one of the horses. He shivered and looked away, pulling his patched, threadbare cloak tighter around his shoulders and drawing the hood forward. But when his efforts to rearrange his cloak met with no resistance, he realized something was missing.

"Where's my bag?" he asked, not even caring that his voice broke.

"In here," Daks replied, patting a bag strapped to the saddle.

"Give it to me."

Daks lifted an eyebrow at the demand but shrugged and undid the ties to the pack. The tightness in Ravi's chest eased a little after Daks handed him his bag. He clutched it to his chest like a lifeline.

Daks gazed curiously at him for a few moments before going back to whatever he was doing without comment, and while Ravi took a few breaths to calm down, he turned his attention to the white stallion with the blue eyes again.

"Why does that horse not have a saddle, and why does it keep staring at me? Is there something wrong with it?" he griped, needing something to complain about.

Daks cast a glance over his shoulder and shrugged. "No idea. I don't think there's anything wrong with him other than he only seems partial to me. He doesn't have a saddle because he wasn't part of the original bargain. He just showed up last night on the road, but I'm glad he did. We wouldn't have gotten as far as we did without him. I'll be sad to leave him behind when we cross the river tomorrow. He's a magnificent animal."

The horse arched its neck and whickered as if it knew it was being paid a compliment, and Ravi found his gaze caught by one bright blue eye. Something shivered and stirred inside him as he held that gaze—or the gaze held him—and he was too late to stop the Vision as it rolled over him.

"Shit!" Daks cried, and a horse neighed in distress, but the sounds were far away, muffled.

Ravi barely noted the pain of the back of his head bouncing off the tree trunk. His entire world had filled with a wall of grayness, smothering him. Splashes of light flickered through the gray like lightning in the clouds, and nausea swamped him as the world spun like he was rolling downhill. Almost as suddenly as it came on, the Vision vanished, leaving him gasping and reeling like a landed fish.

When he opened his eyes, Daks hovered over him. "Are you okay?" he asked calmly, gripping Ravi's upper arms in his big hands.

"I guess so," he croaked past the nausea.

Out of habit, he shook off the man's grip and dropped his gaze to his boots, huddling inside his cloak.

He wasn't okay, not really, and Daks was far too close.

Movement to his left made him scramble unsteadily to his feet, despite the lingering weakness and dizziness. He put the tree trunk between him and the rest of the group, even as he used it to keep himself upright. He couldn't let anyone else touch him and trigger another Vision. And no way would he let Shura anywhere near him right now. Who knew what she was thinking?

"What was in your Vision?" Daks asked in that same gruff, unruffled tone Ravi was coming to appreciate. For some strange reason, it soothed him more than any reassurances or tenderness would have.

He squirmed. He hated talking about his Visions, because most of the time they didn't make any sense until it was too late. This one had been so much worse. How could he explain a wall of grayness that left him feeling terrified? Normally, he at least saw something useful: a face, a place, some detail he could recognize later.

"It was nothing," he replied miserably.

"It can't have been nothing. I felt the magic," Daks continued, under his breath. "You definitely had a Vision. Tell me."

Ravi just shook his head, his anger and that feeling of helplessness and frustration rising again.

Daks growled and closed the distance between them. "Look. I get that you don't trust us. I get that you're angry with me and our methods. But I need *you* to get that if anyone was scrying, or if there's a Finder nearby, the Brotherhood and the Guard will know what direction we went in now, so if you have any information that might help us, we need to know it."

"And I'm telling you there was nothing!" Ravi shouted at him, all his frustration and fear spilling over. "Not a gods-damned thing! I saw a big swirling wall of gray. If there was anything on the other side of that, I couldn't see it. Something was blocking me."

They stood staring at each other for several beats, Ravi panting after his outburst and Daks seemingly trying to decide if he should believe him or not.

"We need to get going. *Now*." Shura's lips and eyes were hard when Ravi broke free and glanced in her direction. She'd already moved to one of the horses and was checking the straps on the saddle.

Daks let out a long sigh and dragged a hand through his already wild brown hair. "We don't know for sure if they even have scrying abilities… but she's right. It's best to be on the safe side. The sooner we get out of this Rift-blighted kingdom, the better I'll feel."

"We've had no reports of any such forbidden magics within the Brotherhood," the small blond woman, Mistress Sabin, said, frowning.

"I bet you haven't had reports of summoning stones either, but two nights ago a brother used one in front of me," Daks responded dryly.

Mistress Sabin's pale eyebrows lifted. "You saw this?"

"Yes."

"That is most worrying. Does Maran know?"

"I told her," Shura replied, still busily tugging on saddle straps.

Part of Ravi wanted to apologize for forcing them to rush, but he held his tongue and moved to join the others by the horses. Realizing there were only three horses for four people, he eyed each in turn and shifted from foot to foot.

"Where do I go?" he asked.

"Shura and Fara will switch to the stallion, if he'll let them. He doesn't seem to be tired at all from the long night. I'll take the saddle off the bay mare and put it on him. I'll ride the bay and you ride the roan. The situation isn't ideal, but they only have to make it a few more hours before they can have plenty of rest."

Ravi swallowed and eyed the horse Daks pointed to warily. With a grimace, he said, "I, uh, don't know much about horses."

Daks stared at him blankly for a few beats before understanding dawned. "You don't know how to ride?"

Ravi winced, and Daks shook his head. "Of course you don't. I wasn't thinking."

From a few feet away, Shura cleared her throat. She pulled a familiar glass vial from her cloak and waggled it in the air with a rather terrifying smile on her face, and Ravi stumbled back in dismay.

"Put it away, Shur," Daks murmured tiredly. "Stop teasing the poor man."

"Just saying," she replied with a shrug before tucking it back into her pocket.

Daks stopped messing with the saddle on the bay and walked over to where Ravi stood nervously eyeing Shura. "I told you no more drugs, and I keep my word. Besides, it didn't exactly work last time anyway." He stooped and offered his cupped hands. "Come on. I'll give you a leg up and get you settled."

Ravi held the man's midnight blue gaze for a moment, though he couldn't have said what he was looking for. With a final sigh of resignation, he set his worn boot in Daks's hands and allowed himself to be boosted into the saddle.

"Keep your feet in the stirrups. Hold on to the pommel," Daks ordered brusquely after he'd settled. "Try to move with the horse's rhythm, not against it. Keep your back straight and use your thighs to save your butt from too much pounding. We won't be going too fast to save the horses some, and I'll hold on to the reins and lead her. All you have to do is stay on the horse. Think you can do that?"

"Yeah," he replied a little breathlessly, grimacing at the stretch of his aching everything.

"Good, because we don't really have time for more of a lesson than that. If you think you're gonna fall, protect your head, tuck, and roll before you hit the ground."

With that bit of oh-so-helpful advice, Daks stepped away to help the others while Ravi shot a sour look at the man's broad back. His concern was heartwarming.

Daks had removed his cloak and jerkin despite the early spring chill in the air, leaving only a loose linen shirt tucked into brown leather breeches. Ravi eyed the leather-sheathed dagger at small of Daks's back uneasily for a moment before his gaze inevitably drifted downward. The way the supple leather trousers clung to Daks's ass may have been just a tiny bit distracting.

He closed his eyes and clenched his teeth. He would not notice how well the big idiot filled out those breeches or the way his back stretched the linen of his shirt. Nope. He would not. He was angry, *really* angry, and he had every right to be. Every time he thought Daks might be halfway decent, the big jerk would do or say something else to piss him off… or his crazy partner would. These were not good, kind people. He didn't know what they were exactly, but he knew what they weren't: trustworthy. Who knew what kind of contract he'd have to sign, what length of indenture they'd expect him to serve, to pay them back for their aid on the other side. He needed to remember he was just as much on his own now as he'd been when he left home the first time.

"You ready?" Daks called from the back of the other mare, and Ravi scowled but nodded.

Without another backward glance, Daks collected the reins of Ravi's horse and then urged his own into a walk. Of course, Shura hadn't waited for them, so they had to pick up the pace a little to catch her. Ravi simply gritted his teeth and tried to hold on as the two horses broke into a jarring canter. All the while, dark thoughts swirled in his head about what revenge he'd wreak on Shura… if the woman didn't scare him nearly witless.

THE RIDE to Urmat passed agonizingly slowly, particularly for the insides of Ravi's thighs, his ass, and his groin muscles. Any other time, he would have been fascinated and entranced by the gently rolling farmland and scattered copses of trees that provided tantalizing glimpses of the wide river beyond. He'd lived a long time within the walls of the city, and the town he'd grown up in was south of the capital, along the sea cliffs, so the landscape was quite different. He'd never been this far up the Matna before, and the rush of its waters would have been both calmingly familiar and awe-inspiringly new if he weren't fleeing for his life.

But he was. And fatigue clawed at him, despite his forced periods of unconsciousness. His head ached, his stomach roiled, and he desperately wanted to curl up somewhere quiet, just for a little while. Instead, he gritted his teeth, clutched his bag to his chest, and endured.

From what he could see of the others and their general lack of conversation, he wasn't the only miserable one in the party. The initial blame lay with the dumb brute in front of him, though, so no way would Ravi allow himself to feel guilty about it. He might've even taken some satisfaction from the misery of his "rescuers" if it didn't mean their tense silence left him with nothing to distract him from his own discomforts… and his heartache.

He missed Vic and the others already. Their lives had been harsh and even dangerous in Rassat, but they'd had each other. At least one of their little family could be counted on to sing a song or tell a story to lift everyone's spirits, no matter how hard things got or how empty their bellies were. Ravi was usually the storyteller. Every night the littler ones would beg him for a tale before bed. He hoped Vic remembered enough of the stories to take his place.

"Not far now," Daks called over his shoulder, stirring Ravi out of his threatening melancholy. "Urmat should be just over that next rise, if I remember right."

Ravi took a breath and straightened in his saddle. He gazed at the road ahead, but he couldn't see anything beyond the hill Daks mentioned and trees to either side of them. As he squinted against the sunlight, hoping for his first look of Urmat, a sudden odd tingling sensation shivered along his arms, and the hairs on the back of his neck stood up.

"Uh, Daks?" Ravi called shakily as his stomach twisted in fear. *Not now. Not again.*

He couldn't be having a fourth Vision in less than two days. He refused to believe it was possible.

Daks turned to look at him over his shoulder and was nearly pitched from his horse when the stallion carrying the two women suddenly stopped in the middle of the road right in front of him, forcing his mare to startle and dance. Daks scowled at his mount as he dropped Ravi's reins and struggled to get her under control.

"Shura, what the hells? Why did you stop?" Daks growled.

"I didn't," she growled back as she tugged on her reins and nudged the stallion with her knees. "This damned horse of yours won't budge."

Ravi's tired mount seemed perfectly content to rest when its lead was no longer being tugged on. She calmly ambled to the side of the road, dropped her head to a tuft of bright green spring grass, and started grazing, ignoring everything else. Still feeling shaky and afraid of passing out if he did have another Vision, Ravi swung a leg over his saddle and slid awkwardly to the ground. He realized his mistake as soon as his worn boots touched the road, but too late to stop his numb legs from crumpling and dropping his ass in the dirt, knocking the wind out of him. His erstwhile mount swung around to eye him for a few seconds before returning to her grazing.

Silently cursing his legs, the horse, Daks, and anything else he could think of, Ravi struggled to his knees. The tingling still shivered along his skin as he fought tears of frustration. Not bothering to try to get to his feet again, he closed his eyes and prepared to fight the threatened Vision as best he could, remembering Daks shouting "push it back" at him before. He didn't exactly know what that meant, but he'd try.

Except the strange shivery feeling wasn't followed by the rush of a Vision. In fact, it faded all on its own, leaving him only a little cold and disoriented.

He blinked. Had it really been a Vision or something else?

His old granny on his mother's side used to say she caught the "chills" sometimes before bad things happened. As a small child, Ravi had dismissed her ramblings as superstitious nonsense, because that was what the rest of the family did. They told him she was harmless, just a little addled, but he was rarely allowed to spend much time with her. Was this what she'd felt? He'd sometimes wondered if she was like him, only the family had protected her instead of—

"Why are you on the ground?" Shura's harsh voice cut through his reverie, and he felt himself flush.

He glanced around and caught all three of his traveling companions staring at him with varying degrees of exasperation, disquiet, and curiosity. He narrowed his eyes and huffed out a breath as he struggled to his feet.

"I felt something before the horses stopped," he admitted reluctantly, tugging his hood back in place and slapping road dust from the folds of his cloak.

"What did you feel?" Daks asked sharply.

Ravi winced. No way was he going to mention his granny's chills. He turned away from Daks's intense stare and shrugged. "I don't know. Just, something feels wrong."

He winced at how stupid that sounded and gave another helpless shrug. If he ever hoped to win a cushioned seat at some lord's high table as pet prognosticator like the ones he'd read about in old tales, he was going to have to practice a more theatrical flourish with regards to any "feelings" he might have, but right now he just felt ridiculous.

No one spoke for several seconds, so Ravi cut a quick, reluctant glance back to Daks. Instead of appearing irritated or dismissive, the man was watching him even more intently than before.

After another few beats of silence, Daks said, "Let's get off the road."

Shura quirked an eyebrow at him, but shrugged and nodded to Mistress Sabin to dismount.

"Are you all right? Do you need help?" Daks asked him neutrally as he also climbed down from his horse.

"I'm fine. I just need to get a little feeling back into my legs."

Daks pursed his lips but said nothing. He spun on his heel and headed for the stallion. "You take the mares. I'll take this stubborn brute," he called to Shura as he moved to collect the stallion's reins. At Daks's urging, the horse decided to cooperate and moved into the woods without hesitation while Shura glared at the animal's swaying rump.

"Now what?" Shura snapped once they were off the road. "We were almost there."

Daks pursed his lips as he scanned the area around them. "I don't know what's wrong with Horse, but we can walk from here if we need to. You know as well as I do that ignoring a Seer's bad feeling is not a wise move. It could be nothing. It could be something. A little caution won't hurt. We're all tired, and even *I* would love to be in a boat crossing the river right now, but we have a few hours before sundown. We can do a little scouting first."

Shura sighed. "I'll do it." She turned to Mistress Sabin. "Will you take these for me, Mistress?" she asked somewhat formally, offering the reins she held.

"Of course. And it's Fara, remember?" the small blond said with a shy smile.

Ravi watched in astonishment as Shura's normally harsh expression softened and her lips curved. "Thank you, Fara," she practically cooed.

Shura disappeared into the woods before Ravi could do anything but gape at her. But when he turned to Daks, he found the man grinning after her like some lovesick fool. Unaccountably irritated, Ravi rolled his eyes, stomped over to nearest tree, and flopped down at its base. It was just as well he planned to leave these people as soon as he could manage it. They didn't make any sense to him at all. Maybe being absolutely insane and confusing was a Sambaran thing he'd have to get used to. He should probably be paying more attention in case they were all like this, especially if he wanted to live there.

He dropped his head in his hands and closed his eyes. He needed a real night's sleep or he'd be of about as much use as that sack of potatoes Daks compared him to only a little more than a day ago.

Had it only been that long?

Before he could let that realization sink in, Shura came hurrying out of the shadows, and he lifted his head.

"There's a company of King's Guard camped outside the town's borders on this side of the bridge," she said without preamble.

"Seven Hells," Daks swore.

"They shouldn't be there," Mistress Sabin protested. "Our reports said they left the city three days ago for the north. They should have been well past Urmat and over the Kun river by now."

"The information I received from my contact was the same," Shura agreed.

Daks cocked an eyebrow at Shura and grinned again, and Ravi lost his patience. "Well, whoever you talked to was wrong. They're obviously still here. Who cares why. What does that mean for us?"

"It means we're going to have to alter our plan a little. That's all," Daks replied evenly.

Before Ravi could growl anything unflattering back at him, Daks turned to Shura. "We'll have to skip the bridge and take the long way around to Emok's place. We should have enough tree cover not to be spotted, and I think I remember a shallow crossing not far from town. I doubt they'll have any scouts out this close to the capital, beyond the usual watch on the Matna. I wish I knew what delayed them, but I'd rather just get the hells out of here than risk trying to find out."

Catching Ravi completely by surprise, Daks walked over to where he sat and offered his hand. He almost reached for it, but stopped himself, shook his head, and climbed to his feet on his own. He never touched people for a reason, and he needed to remember that until he was safely out of Rassa.

Daks withdrew, and his face hardened a little, but he said, "Thanks for the warning. Don't ignore those feelings. If you sense anything strange like that again, let us know. I'd rather be overly cautious than walk into a hornet's nest."

A warm feeling spread through Ravi's belly despite his best efforts to will it away. No one had ever thanked him for anything that came from his curse before. Part of him now stupidly wished he'd taken that hand, despite the risks.

"Sure," he replied uncomfortably, not looking at him. "I'll do my best."

Daks was silent for a few beats before he turned and walked back to the horses. "Let's get started. We'll lead the horses through the woods and around the town. We'll have to hope to the gods that the Rael isn't too swollen with spring runoff, and that Emok is home and can take us across in his boat right away. If we're lucky, he might be able to throw a little information about the company of soldiers and maybe a little ale into the bargain."

Chapter Five

They weren't lucky, and Ravi shot a glare at Daks's oblivious back as they approached a cabin that looked like it hadn't been lived in for months. They were all still damp from the waist down from the icy river crossing. Ravi's worn boots threatened to fall apart after the dousing they'd received, and he felt like he'd never be warm again.

Cursed. I'm cursed. And Daks, the big idiot, should have known better. The gods can never pass up a chance to shit all over you if you invoke luck.

"Well, that's disappointing," Daks said far too calmly as they came to a stop a short distance from the seemingly abandoned home. If Ravi could have murdered with a look, Daks would have collapsed on the spot.

Shura made a sound of disgust in the back of her throat, and for once, Ravi agreed with her. Mistress Sabin crossed the last few feet and peered through what was left of the grime-covered windows.

"Looks like no one has been here in a while," she said unnecessarily.

Without another word, Daks dropped the stallion's reins and strode off down a worn path that, by the sounds, must lead to the Matna. When he came back only a few minutes later, his expression was grim and he was shaking his head.

"No boats, not even a skiff we could borrow and make two trips." He let out a frustrated growl and dragged a hand through his shaggy hair, dislodging more of it from the leather tie. "I'll have to go into town and scout out another option. Maybe Emok had to move for some reason."

"We'll both go," Shura said.

"No. Someone has to stay here with these two," Daks countered.

"I can take care of myself," Mistress Sabin replied quietly but firmly. "We'll be fine until you return."

Ravi didn't intend to make any such brave declarations. He would *not* be fine, and he could *not* take care of himself.

That wasn't completely true. In the city, his home, he knew how to get around, where to run and hide, and how to be smarter than the average bully, guard, or brute. He'd taken care of himself and his newfound family for years. But here he was utterly out of his depth, in a forest, with an entire company of armed men not far off. He came from a long line of scholars and scribes, not soldiers, fisherman, or woodsmen.

His face must have reflected some of his dismay, because after he caught her looking at him, Mistress Sabin turned to the others and said, "Why don't Shura and I go? That would make more sense anyway. If anyone is looking, they're looking for you, not us. Two women traveling alone will not be that out of the ordinary this close to the city, and I may see a familiar face who can help us. I haven't traveled to Urmat more than once or twice in my life, but I might recognize someone from our meetings."

Daks frowned and shook his head. "You won't know our contact."

"I don't know his name, but I may know his face. Besides, Shura knows him, right?"

Daks and Shura exchanged a long look before Daks finally sighed and nodded, his expression grim. "In and out," he said brusquely. "If anything feels wrong, leave, and we'll think of another plan. We can always sneak down to the docks at night and steal a boat if we have to."

Mistress Sabin's thin blond brows drew down disapprovingly, and her lips set in a hard line. "These people rely on their boats to live. I won't be a thief and leave a family to starve."

"Then pray for better luck than we've had thus far," Daks shot back with a shrug, and Ravi winced.

Mistress Sabin continued to scowl at him, but Shura stepped between them and lifted an arm. "Come, Fara. We should hurry."

Mistress Sabin's face softened as she turned her attention to Shura again, and she moved in the direction she indicated, only throwing a single disapproving glance back at Daks as they retraced their steps up the path.

Fidgeting in the heavy silence that followed, and overly uncomfortable with the large blue eyes of the white stallion trained on him, Ravi cleared his throat and moved closer to Daks. "What now?"

Daks grimaced. "We wait."

Ravi hugged his bag closer to his chest and scanned their surroundings. Beyond the clearing with the abandoned house and the dirt track they'd used, all he could see were trees and more trees. The rush of the river nearby called to him in the vain hope that Daks had somehow missed a boat somewhere along the bank. It was a slim hope, but Daks was obviously not infallible, and anything was better than standing around doing nothing.

While Daks fussed with the horses, ignoring him, Ravi turned and followed the small track he'd taken earlier to the river's edge. The bank was steep and rocky where it wasn't choked with reeds or tree roots, but the water moved past at what seemed a fairly sluggish pace. Though Ravi hated to admit it, Daks hadn't missed a boat among the reeds. He found nothing beyond a few frogs and birds as far as the eye could see.

He turned and glared at the towering trees behind him as if they were somehow at fault, before returning his frustrated gaze to the river. The opposite bank didn't seem *that* far off. Maybe he could risk swimming it. He wouldn't be able to carry a pack or cloak. In fact, he might have to leave his bag and extra clothes behind, which would hurt, but surely someone would take pity on him on the other side before he froze to death.

"If you're thinking of swimming or bathing, I wouldn't."

He jolted at Daks's voice and nearly pitched forward down the slope into the water. Daks caught his shoulder to steady him, but

Ravi quickly shrugged it off and scowled as he stepped away from the edge.

How did someone so big move so silently?

"The bottom is muddy," Daks continued, his expression unreadable as he stared at the rushing water. "It sucks at your boots if you try to walk on it, and that's where it isn't filled with rocks that could trap an ankle. The currents are a lot stronger than they look, especially where it gets deeper toward the middle. Plus, it's cold as hells this time of year, and farther than it seems."

He shot a glance at Ravi, and despite Ravi's less than welcoming expression, his lips curved at one corner as he casually propped a shoulder against a nearby tree, folded his arms, and crossed his ankles.

"You know, yesterday, in that hiding place you found us that smelled like it came straight out of the Seventh Hell, you sat like a rock for hours," he continued. "Today you're fretting like a mare getting ready to birth her first foal. What gives?"

"Are you kidding me?"

"What?"

Ravi swung to face him fully and glared in disbelief. "Uh, there's a whole company of soldiers camped on the other side of town that could discover us any minute. We don't know why. We have no way across the river. You were dumb enough to mention luck *twice* now where the gods could hear you. And we're in the middle of the woods, where who knows what wild animals or even Spawn could attack us at any second. I think I have good reason to be a little anxious."

Daks quirked an eyebrow, and his infuriating crooked smile grew. "Yesterday you were in the same city as Blagos Keep, surrounded by brothers and King's Guard, with a Finder hot on your trail."

"But it was *Arcadia*, a place I know, with people I could ask for help. I'm useless out here. I don't know anything about surviving in the wilds."

Daks snorted. "This is hardly the wilds."

Ravi's fists balled at his sides. "Don't mock me."

Daks's smile fell away, and he blew out an irritated breath. He pushed himself off the tree and turned back toward the trail to the cabin. "I need to check on the horses, and then I'm going to sit and rest while I still can. I suggest you do the same. It's been a stressful couple of days for all of us."

"And whose fault is that?" Ravi yelled at his retreating back.

Daks's shoulders stiffened, but he didn't slow his pace. "Stay out of the water," he growled.

Ravi continued to glare after him for several long moments before he gave the opposite bank of the river one last longing look, huffed out a tired breath, and trudged back up the trail to the cabin. Daks was brushing down the white stallion he'd oh-so-cleverly named Horse, apparently, cooing praise at the animal, who seemed to be soaking it up and preening. For some reason this irritated Ravi even more, and he flopped onto the ground as far away from the two of them as he dared.

They occupied opposite sides of the clearing in uncomfortable silence for the next couple of hours, until Ravi felt as if he might crawl out of his skin with anxiety. He needed sleep, but he didn't dare until they were on their way across the river. The air was damp and cool, but he found himself sweating as each hour the ladies were gone ticked past, and Daks's own usually calm veneer sloughed away, bit by bit.

What's taking them so long? Has something happened?

He didn't bother voicing the questions aloud. Daks was probably thinking the same thing, given the way he was acting. Besides, Daks didn't have any more information than he did.

The woods around him didn't become any more comforting as the sun dropped lower and lower. The shadows grew, and his surroundings took on an even creepier, more ominous feel. The quiet noises of the forest were all wrong, softer than the bustle of the city, but that much more noticeable for the lack of anything beyond the soft susurration of the Matna.

By the time the sun actually sank below the horizon, casting the sky in eerie indigo light, he found himself jumping at every crack of a dead branch falling to the ground, chitter of a squirrel, or hoot of an owl. His hopes of getting across the river that night had sunk with the sun, until Daks finally crushed them altogether.

"We should start collecting firewood," he said, making Ravi jump. "We'll need to wait to cross until morning at this rate, and we might as well have a hot meal tonight."

"Are you sure?" Ravi asked. "I mean, they could come any second, and we could be on our way."

"Even if they show up before full dark, we still need to get to whatever boat they've found. The moon might still be nearly full, but I don't relish a night crossing, and I'd imagine whoever they enlisted to help us won't either. It will be simple enough to douse the fire should we get luc—uh, should they get here in the next hour, but we might as well be warm while we wait. I wouldn't mind something hot to eat or drink either."

He stepped up to the door to the cabin and tried the lock. It held against his first couple of shoves, and Ravi was about to offer to pick it if he could find a bit of wire or something similar in one of the packs when Daks threw his shoulder against it and the door gave way.

Ravi rolled his eyes.

That's right. Why use thought and precision when you have brute force?

"It's a bit dusty, and the mice seem to have had a grand time inside, but at least we'll be under a roof if it decides to rain." He went to retrieve the packs, and Ravi's shoulders slumped in growing disappointment and defeat as he moved to help.

He only took two steps before the world spun and all the hairs on his body stood on end.

No!

He fought the Vision, imagining himself pushing at it, like Daks had said, but he failed miserably. It swept over him like a tide, and all he could do was go under.

Shura and Mistress Sabin hurried down a shadowed alley, away from raucous laughter and a borderline blasphemous tavern song Ravi had heard many times in Rassat. The women weren't running, but they moved quickly, and their expressions were worried. Shadows followed them, calling after them, but Ravi couldn't understand the words. The women stepped around a corner and ran straight into a crowd of men in King's Guard colors. They turned, but more men stood behind them, drunkenly hanging on one another. These men also had splashes of guard blue mixed among their clothing.

"What's your hurry? We just want to talk," one of the men called, and several of the others laughed.

"Let us pass," Mistress Sabin said firmly, lifting her dainty chin and glaring at them.

Shura seemed to be fingering something inside her sleeve, but Mistress Sabin laid a hand on her arm.

"Awww, don't be like that," another guard said. "Here we are, risking our lives every day protecting the kingdom. The least you can do is share a few kind words with us while we're trapped here with nothing to do."

"If you want to talk to someone, I suggest going to the town temple. I'm sure the brothers there will have plenty to entertain you with. Shall we call them?" Mistress Sabin shot back, but her eyes darted nervously around.

As if by some unspoken accord, she and Shura took a cautious step back, toward the smaller crowd of men behind them.

"Damn brothers are why we're stuck here in the first place," another of the men slurred out, and the crowd suddenly stilled and cast nervous glances around them.

"Careful, Roald, don't let the red robes hear ya talkin' like that," someone cautioned, and the men sniggered.

"We have business elsewhere. Let us pass," Mistress Sabin called, her voice turning a bit shrill with nerves.

One of the guards took a step forward. His uniform looked finer than the others. "And what business is that?"

"We're visiting family."

The man eyed them suspiciously. "She's not visiting any family here," he said, nodding toward Shura.

"Not that it's any of your business, but we do trade with her family," Mistress Sabin said, lifting her chin. *"It was my understanding the King's Guard is supposed to protect Rassans. Is this how you go about your work? Should I ask your superiors?"*

The crowd around them grumbled, and the man who'd stepped forward shifted uncomfortably. "Very well, Mistress. You may go… but the Cigani can't. We need to know what she's doing in our land."

The man's words were almost as slurred as the others', and Ravi's stomach dropped.

"Ravi! Push it back! It doesn't have to control you," Daks's urgent voice finally cut through the others filling his mind, and Ravi shook his head, trying to dislodge the magic somehow. He struggled out of Daks's grip and nearly fell over when he actually succeeded. At least he hadn't passed out this time.

"It's Shura and Mistress Sabin," he panted, fighting to stay upright as the clearing came into focus around him. "They're in trouble, or… they will be. I… think."

"Where?"

"I don't know. A tavern with music playing. An alley nearby."

"What trouble?" Daks was already moving toward the horses.

"King's Guard, a lot of them."

Daks swore under his breath as he mounted Horse bareback. "Stay here."

"Wait!" Ravi ran after him. "You don't know where you're going. There were over a dozen of them. What are you going to do?"

"Bash some heads!" Daks shouted over his shoulder, and Ravi would have called his tone almost gleeful if not for the worry tightening the man's face.

Left with the packs, the mares, a churning mass of anxiety and fear gnawing at his stomach, and the beginnings of a Vision headache, Ravi let out a frustrated growl.

What the hells was he supposed to do now? *Damn the man!*

Daks galloping into town on a white stallion was sure to raise some eyebrows and call way more attention than anyone wanted, the idiot. Luckily, full dark had almost fallen, so maybe the *entire* company of soldiers wouldn't be out looking for them before dawn. Ravi hugged himself and eyed the creepy forest surrounding him. When one of the two mares snorted, he nearly jumped out of his skin and clutched a hand to his breast.

He could hide out in the cabin and maybe try to start that fire Daks had talked about. The mares should be fine outside by themselves, right?

He worried his lower lip and glanced back and forth between the path Daks had taken and the cabin as another thought occurred to him. He didn't really need them anymore. In the chaos Daks's "heroic ride" was sure to create, he could sneak into town along the riverbank and find a small boat for himself and paddle his way across. Mistress Sabin might be too noble to steal, but Ravi hadn't had that luxury in a long time. Surely one little boat wouldn't mean the difference between life and death for a family. He could pick one of the nicer ones, a boat that looked like the owner had coin to spare. He'd leave it tied to the opposite bank, clearly visible from the other side so it could be retrieved in the morning. No harm. No foul.

His stomach clenched as he continued to stare in the direction Daks had gone. His chest tightened with a foreboding he didn't understand, and shivers danced along his skin.

"Shit."

He groaned, took two determined steps toward the cabin, and stopped. He spun on his heel and took two steps toward the path to the river. He stopped again and scowled over his shoulder. The feeling nagging him got worse whenever he turned away from town.

Was it his conscience or magic?

With a pained sigh, he closed his eyes and hung his head in defeat. Daks had said to listen to his feelings. And why was he following the word of that big idiot?

Because he was an even bigger one.

Or because Daks was the only person ever, including himself, to actually see something of value in the curse he'd been saddled with.

For once in his life, his curse had actually been of some use, so how could he ignore it now?

Daks had saved him from the Brotherhood, no matter the circumstances. Ravi owed him, even if he'd never admit it to the man for fear of losing what little desperate leverage he had.

Even as he led the placid mare he'd ridden earlier to a rock to help him climb into the saddle, his hands shook and he continually questioned his sanity.

I'm not a fighter. What possible help could I be? And why should I try to help these lunatics anyway? I'd probably be doing them a favor going off on my own, wouldn't I?

But the feeling driving him wouldn't relent.

Grasping the reins tightly in his sweaty palms, he nudged the animal with his thighs the way he'd seen the others do. The mare ambled a bit but seemed loath to leave her companion or the clumps of tender spring grass surrounding the cabin. He nudged her a little harder, this time with his heels. She lurched into a trot that made him yelp, and it was all he could do to stay in the saddle.

This is a terrible idea. This is an incredibly terrible idea.

He should have tried to run to town instead. At least he would have gotten there in one piece.

By the time he saw the rooftops silhouetted black against the indigo sky, his ass and thighs were screaming. Pulling hard on the reins, he was nearly pitched over her head as the mare came to an abrupt halt. His dismount was something less than graceful, and the horse threw an accusing eye over her shoulder at him as he winced and patted her side clumsily.

"Sorry. Sorry. But just think, I could die tonight and you'll never have to see me again, so there's that," Ravi quipped somewhat hysterically.

Without allowing himself any more time to consider what the hells he thought he was doing, he looped her reins over a nearby fence and trotted into town, his bag thumping against his flank with each step. If she managed to pull herself loose and wander off, he supposed he deserved it.

Having never been to Urmat, Ravi didn't know exactly where to go. The town was big, probably owing to its proximity to Rassat and having sprung up around the junction of two rivers. A large stone bridge connected the two halves, but Ravi was pretty sure his Vision had been on the near side of it.

As the houses and shops grew closer together and more people appeared in the streets, he stopped in an alley to catch his breath and think. Most taverns tended to be as close to the town's hub of activity as possible—without being *too* near the temple, which dominated the center of every town and village in Rassa. If he could find Urmat's temple—the very thought of which made him queasy—he could work outward from there. Surely the music would lead him the rest of the way, as long as he got close enough to hear it.

He closed his eyes and spun in a circle until the internal tug that had gotten him this far drew him in one direction. Light spilled from windows and the occasional lantern carried by passersby, but Ravi tried to stick to the shadows and avoid people as much as possible. He finally stumbled to a halt when that strange foreboding riding him simply vanished, leaving him bereft instead of relieved. He searched the darkened streets helplessly. Just as he was beginning to get desperate, faint strains of music reached his ears, and he took off running, recognizing the tune from his Vision. *This is it. It's happening now.*

The street he blundered into was at once familiar and foreign as he tried to meld the memory of his Vision to the reality. A large door to a well-lit building opened, and that familiar music spilled out into the night, along with a crowd of young men in splashes of guard blue. Ravi's heart squeezed as he panted for breath.

Now what?

Instinct more than anything had him ducking into the shadows as the men passed. He couldn't see enough of their faces to know if he had the right group of soldiers, but how many gangs of drunken guards could there be in a town like this?

He probably didn't want to know the answer.

The men ambled down the street singing, laughing, and being generally obnoxious to everyone they passed, until something caught their attention and the whole group stumbled to a halt.

Ravi's stomach dropped as he turned in the direction they were staring. He spotted Shura and Mistress Sabin at once and frantically searched the shadows around him.

Where was Daks?

DAKS SWORE under his breath as he hunkered down behind a stack of wooden crates. Shura and Fara had just disappeared down an alley, followed by a group of soldiers. While Daks watched, eight of the men split off in another direction, but Ravi had said a dozen, so the others must be swinging around to block them in from the other side.

Dammit!

If he'd just waited and gotten a little more information from Ravi, he might not have wasted so much time blundering around in the dark and stopped the incident before it started. He hadn't even asked what side of the river to check. He'd heard "Shura" and "danger" and lost his senses. But honestly, who knew there could be so many taverns in a pious Rassan town? He'd been slacking on his last trip through here, because he apparently hadn't gotten drunk in even half of them.

He blew out a breath and pushed the recriminations aside so he could think. Shura could take care of herself, but not against twelve armed men while trying to protect someone else. Plus, they needed to get out of this with as little bloodshed as possible, and the only weapons she had were her daggers. If any of the guards were killed, the whole company would drop whatever they were doing and come after them, but Shura would choose a quick, lethal strike before allowing herself or Fara to be hurt.

Leaving his own dagger sheathed at his back, he ripped a cudgel-sized board off one of the broken crates at his feet and hurried after the four men behind the women. If he could neutralize them, they could all slip away before the others caught up. He wished he had a way to get Shura's attention without alerting the guards in front of him, but he didn't. And the men were clustered too closely together for Daks to pick them off quietly one by one.

Brawl it is, then.

Shura would get the hint soon enough.

As he ran to catch up, he hefted his makeshift club, testing its balance before swinging it in a controlled arc toward the skull of the nearest guard. The man dropped like a rock. Obviously, his friends spun around at this point, but Daks dropped another one with a shot to the temple before any of them could do more than cry out in alarm.

The two remaining men reached for their belts, but someone higher up must have wisely forbidden them from drunken carousing in the city while armed, because none of them sported swords.

Thank the gods for that at least.

The men did have belt knives, but they'd barely unsheathed them before Daks clocked a third man and the fourth dropped to the ground, revealing Shura behind him.

"We need to go, now," Daks said, spinning back the way he'd come.

Shura didn't question him; she simply grabbed Fara's hand and followed.

Shouts rang out behind them, and Daks gritted his teeth. He hadn't been fast enough, and the other guards had spotted them. He angled away from the more densely populated area of town, hoping to lose their pursuers in the shadows, but a feminine cry from behind forced him to swing around.

Fara had been yanked off her feet and away from Shura. The guard who'd caught up to them still held the back of her cloak as Fara struggled to free the clasp at her throat.

Daks did a quick count. Six men converged on them. The other two must have stayed behind to check on their fellows, but it probably wouldn't be long before they followed.

Shura feinted with her dagger at her nearest attacker and used his distraction to get through his guard and crack the heel of her palm under his chin. His head snapped back, and he toppled to the ground. Fara struggled free of her cloak, and without a moment's pause rolled to the side, grabbed the boot of the nearest man, and yanked him off his feet. The small woman leapt up and struck out at another man with her fists and booted feet barely a second later, her movements a blur.

She hadn't been lying. She could take care of herself.

Though relieved to see it, Daks wasn't going to let the women have all the fun. He waded into the fray with his club, jabbing at stomachs, cracking arms and wrists, and smashing noses. He didn't have enough room to really swing his club without endangering the women, but he could still do a fair bit of damage.

The soldiers obviously hadn't been expecting all three of them to fight. It took them a few precious moments to understand the danger, but they were recovering quickly, and Daks feared his strikes might have to get deadlier soon. Especially since the noise was drawing unwanted attention.

Heads poked out of windows and doors, and exclamations of dismay grew louder as lanterns came alight inside darkened houses. One shout for the guard became two and then six and so on, echoing down the streets. They'd have company soon.

Three of the soldiers had fallen to the ground, leaving the other three still fighting, but Daks spotted the remaining two plus a couple of their recovered fellows running toward them. They were out of time.

He was just about to shout a warning to the women when the sound of hoofbeats and an angry neigh rent the air. Horse charged into the approaching group of men, scattering them. Daks's jaw dropped. He threw a glance at Shura, only to find her just as stunned even as she continued to struggle with the man in front of her. Unfortunately, one of the men on the ground chose that moment to rise behind her with his belt knife poised to strike. Daks cried out and lunged toward him, his heart in his throat, knowing he'd be too late. But a second before the guard would have sunk his dagger into Shura's unprotected side, Ravi emerged from the shadows wielding a brick. He slammed it into the back of the guard's head and the man crumpled to the ground.

Daks didn't have time to spare for more than a relieved smile as he redirected his momentum to barrel into two of the men directly in front of them. Uncaring for any damage he might incur, he tackled them to the street while Shura dispatched the last. The other four were still trying to escape the hooves and teeth of the enraged stallion. Daks had no idea how the beast had untied himself from where he'd left him, how he'd found them, or what had pissed him off, but he was glad Horse seemed to be on their side.

"Come on!" he shouted to all four of his companions. "We'll split up and meet back where we left our packs! Go!"

Shura snagged Fara's cloak off the ground took her hand again and ran, but Ravi stood frozen in place, staring down at the bloodied guard at his feet and looking a little glassy-eyed. Daks grabbed his wrist and dragged him away. Hopefully, going in opposite directions would slow any pursuit, but he still ducked down as many twisting dark alleys as he could, with Ravi stumbling along behind him.

At the head of one alley, Daks skidded to a halt, panting. On instinct, he spun on his heel, grabbed Ravi's shoulders, and shoved him into a recessed doorway. Ravi's mouth opened, but Daks clapped a hand over it and pressed himself close. With his other hand, he drew the hood of his cloak up, hoping the dark material would hide both of them in the shadows.

"Stay still," he whispered breathlessly, his lips pressed against Ravi's ear as their chests brushed together with each heaving breath.

Booted footsteps echoed off nearby buildings, and flickering torchlight followed soon after as several men ran along the street nearby.

Ravi's gasping breaths warmed Daks's palm. He drew back enough to search Ravi's wide eyes, to make sure he was calm enough to stay quiet, then pulled his hand away so the man could get some air. They huddled, pressed closely together in the alley, until the searchers moved on. But even when the threat had passed, Daks wasn't in any hurry to step away. His lips curled as he was reminded of other times he'd been breathless and wrapped around a man in an alley.

Good times.

Ravi shifted slightly, brushing against him, and Daks's cock twitched despite a slight unpleasant twinge and wetness seeping from his side. A fight like this always left him horny. Shura had explained it quite pragmatically to him once. It wasn't the blood and the mayhem. It was facing death and needing to reaffirm life to keep himself in balance with the universe… or something like that. He hadn't completely understood her Cigani wisewoman speech, but he'd gotten the impression that she was speaking from experience, which meant he wasn't the only one. That was enough.

"You shouldn't be this close. It might trigger a Vision," Ravi whispered in a somewhat strangled tone, and Daks reluctantly stepped back.

"Are they gone?" Ravi asked.

"I think so. Are you all right now? You seemed a little out of it back there."

Ravi huffed and moved farther away from him. "I'm fine."

"Okay then, let's go."

He didn't grab Ravi's wrist this time; he just took off at a fast walk in the opposite direction the searchers had gone, hoping he could swing back, once they'd gotten out of the town proper. He spared one glance to make sure Ravi was following before he broke into a jog.

By the time they reached the trees past the edge of town, they were both puffing like bellows, but at least he was pretty sure no one was following them.

"The horse," Ravi wheezed.

"I know. He was. Amazing," Daks panted absently, scanning the darkness around them and trying to get his bearings.

"No. The mare," Ravi continued. "I left her. At the. Edge of town."

Daks groaned and let his head drop back for a second as he struggled for breath. Too late to cry about it now. They'd lost two horses tonight, since he'd left that gorgeous, wonderful, life-saving white stallion behind as well.

"Don't worry. We probably shouldn't take the road anyway," he replied as his heart settled a little. "We have the one for our packs. She'll have to be enough. We can lead her through the woods on foot."

"To where?" Ravi asked, his tone dismayed.

"Away from here. North, probably."

"Probably?"

Daks ground his teeth. "We'll talk when we catch up with Shura."

"Why? Because she's the only one with a brain?" When Daks made no reply, Ravi growled. "So, that's it? That's all you've got? Just run into the woods? I swear, you must pray to Ruko, god of mischief and bad luck, every day of your life, because he certainly loves you."

"I don't pray to any gods, particularly not Rassan ones. And I have some ideas of what to do next, but I'd rather talk it out when we're all together, okay? Does that work for you?" he snapped back.

Ravi sniffed but didn't say anything else, and Daks set off into the woods without another word. Luckily, the trees hadn't filled in with summer growth yet, so he could still catch a glimpse of the moon and stars often enough to keep his bearings.

"I hope you at least know where you're going," Ravi grumbled behind him.

Daks held his tongue and his temper for two reasons and two reasons only. One, he was tired and had to save his breath. And two, Ravi had saved Shura's life tonight, possibly twice. For that, Ravi would have his eternal gratitude… or at least enough gratitude to let the sniping roll off his back.

Their trek to the cabin was blissfully uneventful—not that you'd know it by the grumbling and swearing going on behind him every time Ravi stumbled over a bit of uneven ground or an exposed root in the dark. But as the cursing went on, Daks found himself fighting a smile more and more, his humor returning. The skinny Seer had a mouth on him when riled, Daks had to give him that. He could also admit to finding that a little bit sexy… but again, that might just be the aftereffects of the fight still coursing through his veins.

He made sure to hide his smile any time he glanced back to make sure Ravi was keeping up, though. No need to add any more fuel to that fire. Ravi might need that energy to make it through the rest of the night.

When Daks finally stepped out of the trees and into the clearing with the cabin, he skidded to a halt, making Ravi stumble into him from behind.

"What are you doing?" Ravi griped.

Daks didn't reply. He was too busy blinking in disbelief.

All three of their horses waited placidly for them beside the cabin. The mares had been grazing but lifted their heads at his and Ravi's approach. Horse stood apart from the others, keeping watch. The beast eyed him with unsettlingly calm eyes that almost seemed to glow in the moonlight, and Daks was helpless to do anything but stare back. Then Horse lifted his head, breaking contact to glance beyond him, and Daks shook himself and turned to find Shura and Fara coming up the track.

The women were both breathless, their faces anxious, but neither looked injured.

"Are you all right?" Daks asked, glancing between the two of them.

"Barely a scratch on us," Shura replied, narrowing her eyes at him. "But I should probably be asking you that, since you're the one bleeding."

"What?" Ravi exclaimed.

He stepped in front of Daks, pushed the hood of his cloak back, and studied every inch of him until his gaze locked on something, and even in the moonlight Daks thought he paled.

Daks glanced down at the spot on his side that had complained for most of his flight from town.

"Flesh wound," he said with a shrug as it began to sting now that he'd acknowledged it. "One of 'em got a lucky hit. I don't think it's bleeding anymore, and we have bigger things to worry about."

Shura pressed her lips together unhappily but didn't bother to argue. They'd been through this before, and she trusted him to know when a wound was serious enough to need tending. Ravi, on the other hand....

"Don't be ridiculous," Ravi snapped. "If you faint from loss of blood or the wound putrefies, who's going to make sure I get safely to Samebar? You owe me. You promised."

"It's fine," Daks argued tiredly. "It's nothing that can't wait until we're a safer distance away and holed up for a rest."

Ravi turned to Shura. "And you're okay with this? He's your partner. Shouldn't we at least bind the wound, just to be sure?"

Shura pursed her lips and regarded Ravi with steady, unblinking eyes until Ravi looked away and threw up his hands. "Fine. Whatever. I don't know why I bother. You're all crazy."

In the dark, Daks was the only one who caught Shura's lip twitch as she fought a smile. She stepped past both of them, moved to one of the mares, and began fiddling with the straps.

"Where will we go now?" Fara asked, breaking the uncomfortable silence that fell after Ravi stopped ranting.

Before Daks could answer, the sound of ripping cloth came from behind him, and he turned and cocked an eyebrow at Shura.

"Lift your jerkin and shirt, *Vaida*."

"Shur, we really need to get moving," he argued.

"It will take only a few moments. The *Vechi* is right—we have that much time while we talk."

Daks cleared his throat to cover the snort that almost escaped him. *Vechi* in Cigani was a type of small, irritating bird that was noisy and a general nuisance, but harmless.

Without further argument, he lifted his bloodied and rent tunic and shirt out of the way. The slash wasn't deep. He'd known that by the feel alone. It had crusted with dried blood already and only seeped a little from one end. He could have managed without binding it, but it probably would have reopened a bit when he climbed into the saddle.

As Shura pressed a pad of cloth to it and began wrapping a binding around his middle, he grimaced and said, "I believe the best plan is to keep going north. We've unfortunately stirred a hornet's nest back there, and once they piece together what happened, we'll be risking a lot if we hang around and try to go back for a boat." He lifted his gaze to Fara. "I assume you had little luck finding a contact, and that's why you were gone so long?"

"Yes." She threw a glance down at Shura before continuing. "Your man, Emok, died over the winter of a fever, they said. We gently prodded inn- and tavern-keepers for information while I searched the common rooms and squares for familiar faces, but had no luck. With the influx of soldiers, the town is uneasy and suspicious of strangers. The soldiers are awaiting a contingent of brothers to join them on their journey north. The good news is, none of the Thirty-Six are expected. Lending some credence to the rumors we've been hearing. But that's about all the good news."

"Everyone was on edge," Shura added as she worked. "The soldiers aren't happy to be saddled with the brothers or with being forced to wait. The townspeople aren't happy with bored soldiers roaming their streets, drinking and causing fights. That might work to our advantage some, since the elders of the town won't automatically assume the soldiers are innocent of instigating our little scuffle. Infighting may slow any organizing."

Daks hissed as Shura pulled the binding tight and tied it off. "We should still put as much distance between us as we can," he said, lowering his clothing back in place. "Ravi had a Vision. That's how we knew to come to you. But that might also have attracted more attention."

At Shura's sharp look, Ravi winced, but he jutted out his chin and asked, "But if they're all headed north, should we really do the same? Especially if there's some unknown trouble up there?"

"We could try to swing south again, but that's closer to the Finder searching for you and more of the Thirty-Six. Plus, we might run into more soldiers being sent north, not counting the problems with finding a boat big enough to cross the river as it widens closer to the sea," Daks answered soberly. "I think our best bet is to go north along the Matna until we find a village where we can buy passage across. We don't have much coin, but we have some fine horseflesh to trade." He walked over to where Horse stood and patted the animal's neck and shoulder. "Though I'll be very sad to walk away from this remarkable fellow, to be sure."

"He certainly seems to like you," Shura said. "How on earth did you find him again?"

"I didn't. He came back here all on his own."

"Huh."

Daks left out the part where the beast had apparently led the other mare back as well. They didn't have time for him to try to wrap his own head around everything that had happened, let alone discuss it with the others.

"Come on. Let's mount up," Daks ordered as he moved to transfer one of the saddles to Horse. "Ravi, you're with me. Fara and Shura will ride the two mares and take the packs."

His side complained as he hefted the heavy saddle onto Horse's back, but he ignored it. The scar would be ugly if he continued to rip it open over and over, but it certainly wouldn't be his first.

"I don't... I don't think that's a good idea. What if it triggers a Vision?" Ravi said, approaching him uncertainly.

"It's a risk we'll have to take. I'll have you in front of me, so you won't fall off either way. Besides, I've touched you often enough in the last couple of hours and nothing has happened."

Ravi made an odd noise in the back of his throat but wouldn't meet Daks's gaze when he glanced at him.

"Give me your boot," Daks ordered.

Ravi hesitated only a moment before stepping into his cupped palms and allowing Daks to boost him up. Then Daks climbed up behind him. Shura strapped the packs to the other saddled horse before helping Fara mount and then taking the mare without one for herself. The situation wasn't ideal, but that had been the case since he'd stepped off the boat in Rassat, and he had a bad feeling that wouldn't be changing anytime soon.

Chapter Six

Daks kept them just inside the trees for better cover, rather than riding on the road. The going was slower, but everyone looked to be on their last legs anyway, and he wasn't faring much better. Galloping down the packed dirt road to put as much distance between them and the town as they could was what his gut was telling him to do. But the risk to their necks and the horses' legs in the dark wasn't worth it.

At first Ravi had held himself stiffly in front of Daks, keeping a few inches between them, but as their ride wore on, exhaustion seemed to win and he slowly slumped back against Daks's chest. When he was sure Ravi had nodded off, Daks wrapped an arm around his slim waist, just to keep him on the horse, of course. With Ravi's warm back snuggled into his chest and his slow, even breathing lulling him, the brisk early spring air on Daks's face and the fear of being followed were the only things keeping him awake. But when he found himself nodding off despite his best efforts, he called over his shoulder to Shura. "We need to find somewhere to rest before I fall off a horse for the first time since I learned to ride."

Ravi stirred in his arms, and Daks tightened his hold despite the stab of pain in his side.

"We're all tired," Shura agreed, casting a worried glance back at Fara.

She tugged on the reins until her mare ambled to a halt, and then she swung out of the saddle. "I'll take a look around."

The other mare and Horse stopped as well, and Daks did his best to stay alert while he waited for Shura to return.

"What's happening?" Ravi croaked, sitting up. "Where are we?"

The Seer

"I'd say we're halfway to the Kun river," Daks replied. "Shura's finding us a place to rest for a few hours."

Fara urged her horse alongside theirs and said, "I've heard of a few places up closer to the crossing that are at least partially sheltered."

Daks gave her a tired smile but shook his head. "I'd rather stay away from places *anyone* has heard of, but thank you," he replied. "We just need a decent clearing shielded from the road where the horses can eat, drink, and rest, and we can do the same."

"Do you think we've gone far enough?" Ravi asked, furrowing his brow.

Daks experienced an unexpectedly intense pull to smooth his fingers over that brow and gripped the reins tighter.

"I think we've gone as far as we should tonight," he answered gruffly as he swung his leg over Horse's rump and dropped to the ground. "Plus, now that I've had a chance to think a bit, I'm beginning to wonder if they'll come after us at all."

He groaned as he stretched tired muscles, but when he caught Ravi's skeptical look, he explained, "There's nothing to connect us to the search in Rassat. The soldiers just got into a drunken brawl in an alley with some travelers. Shura's a bit distinctive, I'll grant you. But the men might also be loath to admit two women and a man took them all out—with your help of course," he added, giving Ravi a tired smile. "That should work in our favor. If the company is waiting for a contingent of brothers to join them, they can't venture far. Add in how dark the alley was, and that they were probably doing something they weren't supposed to, and we might be in the clear for a while, as long as no one really got too badly hurt."

"It's possible," Fara agreed.

Shura chose that moment to emerge almost silently from the shadows, spooking one of the mares into snorting and making the rest of them jump. "I've found a glade not far from the river. There should be a bit of grazing for the horses, and it's shielded from the road by a slope. Come."

She moved to take the reins of Fara's mare as the woman dismounted.

When Ravi didn't move, Daks stepped in close and murmured, "We'll need to walk the horses from here, since we're going deeper into the woods and the grade gets a bit steep closer to the river."

Ravi jerked and blinked sleepily at him.

"Oh. Right." He swung his leg over and dropped awkwardly to the ground.

When he wobbled a little, Daks automatically shot out a hand to steady him, unaccountably pleased when Ravi didn't flinch from his touch. Ravi was fairly adorable when he was too sleepy to scowl and hurl abuse. Although he was kind of cute when he was fuming too.

Daks huffed out a breath and shook his head as he shifted Horse's reins to his right hand and moved to follow Shura's retreating shadow. He obviously needed rest too.

They followed a deer track deeper into the stretch of woods between the river and the road. Daks wasn't looking forward to the journey back uphill, but he'd be better rested then at any rate.

When the rushing of water was loud enough that they must have been within mere yards of the river, the land flattened out, and the thick tree trunks opened into a small glade ringed by half-buried moss-covered boulders that seemed to sparkle in the moonlight. His skin tingled, and the hairs on his arms lifted as he stepped into that circle of stones and the Singers' tales his mother used to spin for him before bed came to mind.

Tired though he was, he opened his senses and searched with his gift. The hum inside the ring was definitely different from outside it, but the same could be said of any holy temple, old battlefield, or mage's workroom. It could mean anything. He knew what trap spells and curses felt like, and this wasn't it. There was no threat here, nothing active, only some faint energy clinging to the place like the river mist filling the air. None of the rest of their party seemed uneasy. Horse hesitated slightly before entering the ring, but that was it. Daks was getting spooked by nothing, and he gritted his teeth, irritated with himself.

To help settle both of them, he took the saddle off Horse and rubbed him down with a few handfuls of dead grass as Shura and Fara saw to their mounts and Ravi slumped in a heap on the ground away from everyone else. They'd need to do a more thorough inspection of the horses in daylight, but his arms and his side protested every movement by the time he'd done a cursory job of it. He gave the stallion's rump a quick pat and walked away, not bothering to tie him up. If Horse hadn't left him by now, he probably wasn't going to.

"Help me with these branches," Daks said, waving to catch Ravi's attention.

They started dragging dead branches out of the woods and driftwood from the bank of the river and the women eventually joined in, making the job go that much faster. They could've gone without a fire, but the spring air wasn't quite warm enough yet, and they'd had a hard and sometimes wet journey so far. A little warmth and light to chase away the shadows and the misty damp was well worth the extra effort.

When Ravi turned to head back into the woods to get more wood, seemingly in a trance, Daks put a hand on his shoulder to stop him.

"We've got enough for now. Curl up somewhere and try to get some sleep."

As a sign of how tired he must have been, Ravi merely turned on his heel, shuffled to one of the saddles they'd set on the ground, and slumped against it, wrapping his patched, threadbare cloak around himself. Daks frowned at the ragged bit of cloth as a cool breeze ghosted over his skin. He'd need to get something heavier for Ravi if they had to go too much farther north, or the man might freeze at night.

With a disgruntled sigh, he moved to his pack and pulled out his spare jerkin. After taking off his own cloak, he pulled the second jerkin on over his bloodstained clothes, then draped his cloak over Ravi's unconscious form. He patently ignored Shura's raised eyebrow as she hurried to the spot they'd cleared for the fire and set to work with flint and steel. Dead grasses from the glade and pine needles made starting it easy, despite the mist coming off the river, and the pine branches they'd collected soon popped and blazed cheerily enough to dry out the rest of the wood.

Shura groaned as she sat on the ground and held her hands out to the flames, making Daks smile.

"Both of you try to get some rest too. I'll take first watch," he offered.

"You sure? What about your wound?" Shura asked, frowning at his side.

He waved a dismissive hand, making the wound in question twinge. "It can wait. I was the one sitting on my ass while you two searched the town for aid. I had plenty of rest then. And I sure as hells don't want you stitching me up half asleep by firelight. I'll wake you in a few hours to take over, and we'll worry about the wound then."

She didn't look completely happy about it, but she nodded wearily.

As he expected, both her and Fara dropped off nearly as fast as Ravi had, leaving him alone with only his thoughts and the fire to keep himself awake. He was almost glad he'd given up his cloak, because if he'd been any warmer, he might never have stayed conscious.

His gaze strayed to Ravi's sleeping form often as the minutes ticked past, remembering the weight of Ravi's body in front of him in the saddle and the heat of his breath as they stood crushed together in that alley. The first thing Daks planned to do when they were safely in Samebar was to find himself a willing bedpartner. And this time he wouldn't be anywhere near as picky as he'd been in the Dog and Duck. Male, reasonably clean, breathing, and willing would be his only criteria.

He threw an envious look toward Shura and Fara's huddled forms. The ladies had steadily shifted closer together in their sleep, until mere inches separated them. They were practically spooning each other. He glanced at Ravi again, and his lips curved wryly. What would happen if he just happened to curl up at Ravi's back when Shura took the next watch?

Probably another punch to the face, he thought, his grin widening.

Still, Ravi's occasional physical responses to him made him wonder.

With a sigh, Daks shook himself and forced his gaze back to their surroundings. He should really be trying to formulate a plan instead of daydreaming about getting laid.

IN WHAT seemed to have become the new norm since he'd met Daks, Ravi woke aching in nearly every part of his body and with no clear idea of where he was. At least this time he remembered going to sleep. Wood smoke and the crackle of a fire registered first, then a chill in the air that had him scowling and snuggling deeper into his cloak. Bracing himself for the pain, he tried to stretch his legs out, wincing when the chafed skin and strained muscles of his inner thighs made themselves known.

That was new.

He couldn't wait to find out what this day would bring—a broken leg perhaps? Loss of a finger or toe?

After only a few halfhearted tries to get his body unlocked from the fetal position he'd slept in, he gave up and lifted his head instead. Opening sleep-crusted eyes in the predawn gloom, he noticed Shura first, where she crouched next to what was left of a fire. She gave him a brief, neutral nod of acknowledgment before lifting her gaze beyond the circle of firelight again. Mistress Sabin huddled beneath her cloak not far from Shura, and Daks lay to their right, presumably out cold as well.

Ravi frowned at the big lump and attempted to dredge up a glare, until he realized the man wasn't wearing his cloak. Only then did the comforting extra weight on top of him register. Glancing down at himself, he recognized the dark, thick wool draped over him, and his stomach fluttered. He buried his nose in the fabric, but only for a moment, and only because it was chilled… not for any other reason.

A memory of heat rolling off a hard body as Ravi was pressed into a doorway surfaced, which in turn recalled the first Vision he'd had the night he'd met Daks. He scowled, sat up, and removed the cloak. He was not a pawn of fate, and this big lump and his crazy partner were not to be trusted—even if the man had looked pretty heroic riding off to Shura's rescue, and he'd been quite gentle and solicitous when Ravi's Vision had come on.

Nope. Not going there.

Stubbornly lifting his chin, he shoved the aches and pains aside and climbed to his feet. He felt Shura's gaze follow him as he walked around the fire and dropped the warm, heavy cloak over Daks's prone form. He hadn't asked for it. He didn't owe Daks anything for his kindness.

Last night he could have gotten himself killed. But while he hoped to dredge up a little energizing anger over that, he wasn't particularly successful. First, because he was still tired. Second, because the ambush hadn't been the women's fault. And third, and most importantly, because he had no one to blame but himself for getting involved. He could have kept quiet about his Vision. He could've lied and left the women to their fates. Even when Daks left, he could've stayed inside the cabin and let things play out as they would. But he hadn't done any of those things. Instead, he'd run after Daks like he thought he should be the hero in one of his grandfather's old books, riding in on a white horse to save the day.

Idiot.

He clutched his bag to his chest as the sick thud of brick meeting skull echoed in his memory, swallowing as his gorge rose. He would have been perfectly happy to have lived his entire life without knowing what that sounded like… or what it felt like. That man might be dead now because of him. The tales never talked about that part. He was done being the hero. Never again.

After relieving himself in the woods, he moved back to the saddle he'd slept against, sat down on the cold, hard ground, and cleared his throat to get Shura's attention.

"I can take over, if you'd like to get more rest," he offered quietly enough he hoped he didn't wake the other two.

She studied him for a few beats, making him shift nervously inside his cloak.

"I would take you up on that," Shura finally murmured. "But sunrise is not far off, and we should be on our way as soon as we're able. If you can rest more, I recommend you do so while you can."

He started to ask a question, but she'd already turned her gaze away, dismissing him, so he let it go.

Too cold and unsettled to fall asleep again, he untied the water skin from the saddle behind him and took a long pull as he scanned their surroundings for something to distract him. Dying firelight flickered off spring leaves, new and dead grasses, weathered tree trunks, and worn, half-buried boulders, but not much else. The scene was actually quite peaceful if he discounted what might be lurking in the semidarkness beyond. The horses seemed unperturbed, though, so that was probably a good sign nothing waited to jump out at them.

A flicker or light drew his attention back to the stones, and he squinted more closely at them. He'd been too tired to pay much attention last night, but looking at them now, they formed an obvious circle that couldn't have been natural.

A small tremor of giddy excitement passed through him. Could this be a Singers' ring? An *actual* Singers' ring?

He clutched the bulky shape of the book hidden in his bag and smiled, remembering the countless hours he'd spent in his grandfather's home, tucked away with forbidden volumes of history and lore—books the Brotherhood had banned but his family had held on to in secret. His smile fell. At least when it came to protecting knowledge, his family had been brave enough to do the right thing.

Shaking off the old bitterness in favor of something far more pleasant, he set the water skin aside, stood, and approached the nearest stone. If the Singers actually existed, one of them might have touched this stone with his own hands, done wonderful feats of magic with it. Veins of translucent milky white running through the gray rock periodically captured and reflected the flicker of firelight. Intrigued, he leaned closer and reached out to run a finger along one such vein, but before he could touch it, he was suddenly knocked aside. Letting out a startled yelp, he lost his balance and landed hard on his butt.

Four long white knobby legs ending in gleaming black hooves filled his vision. He glared up at the stallion until Horse dipped its head and leveled that unsettling blue gaze at him. Quickly breaking eye contact as a strange, unpleasant shiver ran along his skin, Ravi rolled away from the animal and shot to his feet.

"What's wrong?" Shura called sharply.

Ravi huffed and threw a glare in the stallion's general direction without meeting its eyes. "I have no idea. This dumb horse just came up and knocked me over."

"Wha—?" Daks croaked, sitting up. His hair was even more of a mess than usual, framing his scruffy, stubbled face in a dark, bushy halo that had been matted down on one side.

Ravi frowned even harder to smother a threatening giggle, dusted off his ass, and moved back to the fire with the others, away from the damned horse. He'd apparently also woken Mistress Sabin, because the woman stirred out of her cloak cocoon and blinked owlishly at him across the dying flames.

"Sorry," Ravi muttered to no one in particular. "You should keep that thing tied up," he continued, scowling at Daks. "It's a menace."

Instead of rising to the bait and giving Ravi an excuse to vent his frustration and embarrassment, Daks merely yawned and said, "He's a perfect gentleman with me."

"Now that we're all awake, we might as well discuss our next moves," Shura cut in blandly, stopping any snarky reply Ravi might have made.

He huffed out a breath. She was right. The sooner they got going, the sooner he'd be free of these infuriating people and their equally annoying animals.

He plopped back on the ground and folded his arms across his chest as Daks shook out his cloak and put it on without a word. He didn't meet Daks's gaze when the man came over to him and grabbed the waterskin Ravi had drunk from earlier. Daks loomed over him as he upended it into his mouth, and Ravi tried very hard not to look at the part of Daks's anatomy that was currently at eye level, encased in supple, form-fitting leather.

"Our next best chance at getting across will be Reyan," Daks said. "We're only half a day's ride away. The town isn't as large as Urmat, but we should be able to find someone with a boat for hire who won't ask too many questions. If we hurry, we could get there and across the Matna long before any word of us could possibly come up from Urmat *or* Rassat. We'll just be simple travelers needing a quick ferry across, nothing for the villagers to concern the guard with."

Daks continued to hover as he spoke. The wool of his cloak brushed Ravi's shoulders, making it hard for him to add much to the conversation. He felt the heat rolling off the man, and he scowled and hugged his own ragged cloak tighter around himself, pulling the hood up to hide his face even as he rolled his eyes.

At least the idiot hadn't said "What could possibly go wrong?" But his blind optimism, given everything that had happened so far, didn't inspire a great deal of confidence.

Shura didn't seem to share his attitude either, judging by the pursing of her lips, but she didn't contradict him.

"Do either of you know anyone in Reyan?" Mistress Sabin asked.

"I doubt it. It's been quite a while since we've had to travel this far from Rassat," Daks answered, sharing a look with Shura. "Other, uh, associates of ours normally deal in the more rural territories, but we don't know who their contacts are."

Mistress Sabin worried her lip. "I *might* know someone. Maran has family in the North, near Reyan. They could possibly be willing to help, but I make no guarantees."

"That's better than nothing if we run into trouble," Daks replied. "Do you think they'll have a boat?"

"I don't know. They're not fisherman. They're farmers, from what I recall."

"It might be worth it to look them up anyway," Daks said, sharing another silent conversation with Shura with just a look.

The slight stab of jealousy Ravi experienced surprised him. Why should he be jealous? Their easy companionship? Their loyalty to each other? He'd had that with Vic and some of the others, and he'd have it again someday, once he got settled in Samebar.

Daks suddenly crouched down next to him and began to rifle through the packs they'd piled behind the saddles, pulling small cloth-wrapped parcels out. Ravi gave the man a disgruntled look and scooted farther away.

"There's still enough food for today, but not much more than that," Daks said as he stood, dusted his breeches off, and started moving about their campsite, finally putting enough space between them that Ravi could relax.

"I'll take the horses down to the water and fill our skins, while the rest of you divvy up the food," Daks continued.

Shura and Mistress Sabin moved as one to the parcels and unwrapped a couple of heels of bread, dried fruit and meat, and a small wheel of cheese.

Ravi got to his feet and hovered nearby, feeling useless. "Should I, uh, get some wood for the fire?" he asked as Daks disappeared into the trees with the horses in tow.

Shaking her head, Shura said, "We have enough coals to toast the bread and soften the cheese. We'll be leaving soon, so there's no need. Come. Eat. Everyone will need their strength."

Mistress Sabin eyed him warily as he closed the last few feet between them, but Ravi was used to that look from anyone who knew his secret. Even Vic had worn a similar expression sometimes, when he thought Ravi wasn't looking. He guessed he should be grateful Mistress Sabin didn't make the Holy Trinity symbol of Quanna, Moc, and Chytel with her hands and sing a warding hymn every time he came near.

He claimed his share of breakfast from Shura, ducked his head, and hurried to the other side of the dying fire to eat, separate from the women. Shura hadn't stinted on his portion, and he stopped halfway through his breakfast and opened the flap of his bag to save the rest for later.

"Eat it all, Ravi," Daks's deep voice rumbled behind him, making him start.

"You said it was the last," he argued, tipping his head back but not quite meeting the man's eyes.

"We'll reach Reyan this afternoon," Daks replied gruffly. "Even if something happens and we have to keep traveling, we aren't going to be able to go much farther without resupply. The horses need more than a few spring shoots and grasses. Hells, even if all goes well, we'll have to get more food from the town to tide us over on the other side... one way or another."

He turned toward the women as he said that last, and Mistress Sabin shifted and frowned at him. Ravi glanced between the two of them until Mistress Sabin flinched away from his gaze. He silently swore and averted his eyes before tugging his hood forward and tucking into what was left of his food—doing it because he was still hungry, not because Daks had ordered him to.

When they had finished eating, Daks and Shura saddled one of the mares and Horse, while Ravi threw dirt on the fire. After some discussion, in which Ravi's opinion was largely ignored, Daks and Shura decided to keep the riding arrangements the same as the night before. Begrudgingly, Ravi had to admit the stallion miraculously seemed to still be faring much better than the mares, despite having to carry two grown men on his back much of the night. Ravi could also reluctantly admit he was the biggest liability in their party, so complaining too loudly about anything wasn't a great idea, no matter how much he wanted to.

He stubbornly refused Daks's offer of help and climbed into the saddle himself, despite the protests of his aching body. He held himself stiffly in the saddle for the entire ride, trying to avoid any accidental contact with the brick of a man behind him, but it wasn't easy. He swore the damned stallion was in on some dastardly plan to make his ride as uncomfortable as possible, jostling him back against Daks's chest any time he started to relax.

Daks had attempted to start light conversation with him a few times, like the ladies were doing behind them, but Ravi had stubbornly refused to be drawn out, and Daks had quickly given up. Of course, Ravi paid for that bit of spite by having nothing to distract him from his discomfort. But at least the sun had warmed him enough he was no longer cold and miserable, just miserable.

As the journey dragged on, the lure of Daks's hard chest and thick arms hovered at his back, tempting him. Maybe he could let go for just a little while. Daks didn't seem averse to touching him, quite the contrary really. It had been so long since he'd been touched or been able to touch anyone without fear. What would be the harm, really? He could just lean back a little bit, to ease his sore muscles.

Daks suddenly pulled on the reins and ground out a curse, jolting Ravi out of his argument with himself, heart pounding. When Ravi twisted around to glare at him, Daks's jaw was set in a hard line.

"What is it?" Shura asked as she drew alongside them.

"Pain priest," Daks growled and cursed again.

"You're sure?" Mistress Sabin asked, eyeing him askance before scanning their surroundings.

"He's a very talented Sensitive," Shura said. "If he says he feels one, then there is one."

"Maybe more than one," Daks replied absently.

"A Sensitive?" Mistress Sabin asked, her expression wavering between seeming distaste and curiosity.

"You'd call him a Finder, if he were a member of the Brotherhood," Shura explained, her expression hardening ever so slightly. She turned her attention back to Daks. "More than one Pain priest in a little town like Reyan?"

"This is a problem," Daks muttered.

You think? Ravi's stomach twisted, and he seemed to be having trouble getting enough air into his lungs.

"Keep calm." Daks's voice rumbled in his ear as a large, warm palm settled at the join of his neck and shoulder and gave it a little squeeze. "Breathe and keep control."

Ravi closed his eyes and tried, not bothering to shake the hand off him, though he didn't want to admit how comforting he found it.

"They're in the town," Daks continued, his voice calmer and more assured. "I'm close enough now that I can feel them, so we're going to have to avoid it until we have a plan."

Ravi let that voice wash over him, ignoring the one in his head reminding him how much Daks's confidence and certainty had been worth in the past.

"I'm the least, uh, noticeable of all of you. The brothers should have no reason to question me. I can go into town to ask about a boat or find Maran's family," Mistress Sabin offered, her gaze locked on Shura rather than either of the two men.

"We can both go, as we did before," Shura said with a reassuring smile.

Mistress Sabin shook her head even as she grimaced in apparent apology. "I think it best if I go alone this time. Word may be on its way already from Urmat, and you are… *distinctive*, Shura. My coloring may be a bit fairer than most Rassans that live this far south and east, and a woman traveling alone a little odd, but not so noteworthy as all that. I should be able to make my inquiries and leave without causing much fuss."

Shura and Daks exchanged a long look this time. Eventually Daks nodded, but he didn't seem happy about it.

"This trip has been more harrowing than you'd originally bargained for," Shura said to Mistress Sabin. "We are very grateful for your help."

Mistress Sabin smiled and her cheeks pinked. "I'll admit I hadn't anticipated this much excitement. It makes me doubly sorry Maran and the others couldn't risk finding us a boat out of Rassat's harbor instead."

"None of us could have foreseen all the difficulties we've faced," Shura replied, making Ravi wince. "Thank you for sticking it out, when you could have safely returned to your people."

Mistress Sabin blushed darker. "I wouldn't be much help to my people if I gave up at the first sign of adversity."

Ravi was the only one close enough to hear the low groan Daks let out before he pointedly cleared his throat. "Still, we're grateful to you, Fara. But we should get moving if we want to stay ahead of those who may be chasing us."

"Oh. Right." The mistress's face flushed even darker as she seemed to suddenly remember he and Ravi were there. She urged her horse forward and wrinkled her brow at Daks. "Where should I meet you?"

If Ravi hadn't been staring at Daks over his shoulder, waiting for his answer, he might have missed the quick glance Daks shot his way as he said, "I think we should keep our distance from the town, but I don't like staying so near the road, and there will be too many people by the river. If I remember right, there's a festival space to the west of town across a shallow stretch of the Kun, where they hold their high holy days. We'll swing wide of town and meet you in the woods behind it."

"All right. That should be easy enough to find. I'll meet you as soon as I can." With one last small smile for Shura, the mistress nudged her mare toward town.

When she was far enough away not to hear them, Daks turned to Shura and asked, "Are you sure we should trust her?"

Instead of immediately jumping to her defense, as Ravi half expected given some of the flirting he'd witnessed over the last couple of days, Shura shrugged and pursed her lips, gazing in the direction the mistress had gone. "I don't know. But our options are somewhat limited at present. If we can get across to Samebar cleanly and quietly, I'd much prefer it to trying to steal a boat and supplies under the noses of pain priests. Ordinary men might not be able to do much, even if we're spotted crossing in the dark of night, but a stone-wielder could use their magic to sink us or force our boat back to Rassa with little effort, particularly if they're warned of our presence in time to prepare."

She shot a glance at Ravi, but was much less subtle about it than Daks had been, and Ravi flinched and turned away.

Yeah, he knew he was the problem. He always knew it. The thought of being the reason some poor villager was taken as an offering and tortured to recharge a pain priest's stone made him almost as queasy as the fear of being captured by the Brotherhood.

Daks swung off the saddle behind him, then reached up and offered him a hand. "Come on. We'll need to cut through the woods, and Fara may be a little while. We might as well give the horses—and our asses—a break and walk the rest of the way."

This time, Ravi took it and allowed Daks to help him down. Shura dismounted as well, and Daks led them across the road and into the woods on the other side.

None of them bothered to talk much during their trek. Picking their way through the underbrush required a bit of attention, and Ravi needed to save his breath. He was used to working long hours, running errands, stacking crates, and any other odd jobs he could get in Rassat, but this was a whole different level of exertion, and the constant anxiety and fear didn't help.

When Daks finally stopped, the woods around them didn't appear any different from what they'd been struggling through, and he gave the man a questioning look.

"The green is over there." Daks pointed to a slightly brighter area off to his right.

Feeling completely out of his depth, Ravi simply nodded and slumped onto a fallen log. The other two settled farther up the log while the horses were left to graze nearby.

After only a short rest, the silence began to feel oppressive. The only sounds around him were the occasional trill of birdsong and rustle of branches in the breeze.

"Do you still feel them?" he asked Daks, cocking his chin toward the town.

"Yes. Members of the Thirty-Six are hard to miss. The relics they wear are quite... *loud*, for lack of a better word, very distinctive, especially when *charged*."

He'd said that last with a grimace, and Ravi worried his lip as he studied the man. Daks might be an impulsive brute, but he knew a hell of a lot more about magic than Ravi did. The scholar in him longed to pummel the man with questions, draw out everything he knew, and write it down in a journal, but he bit the words back. He'd have plenty of time to learn from actual wizards when he reached Samebar.

"Will Mistress Sabin be able to find us here?" Ravi asked instead.

Both of his traveling companions were staring at him now, and he squirmed.

"She should have no trouble," Daks replied kindly. "The festival green isn't hard to find. Anyone in town should be able to point her in the right direction. I've kept back a bit because the big guy over there stands out like a sore thumb." Daks nodded in the direction of the white stallion, who gazed placidly back at them. "But I should be able to see her when she makes it to the tree line."

"What if she doesn't come back?"

Shura's jaw hardened, and Ravi winced.

"If she doesn't come, we'll wait until dark, and I'll make a foray into town to explore our options," Daks replied evenly. Shura opened her mouth, but Daks shook his head at her and placed a hand on her arm. "I'm less—what was the word she used—*distinctive* than you are… or at least I can be when I want to. If anyone could have possibly sent word up from Urmat, they'll be looking for you. I'm just a unsavory dark-haired type they may have caught a glimpse of in a dark alley. They were following you, and the farther we get from Rassat, the more attention you will draw."

She sniffed but didn't argue with him.

"You'd steal a boat, with members of the Thirty-Six around?" Ravi asked nervously.

Daks grimaced. "Not if we don't have to. As Shura said, we risk magical attack even if we manage to get a boat big enough for all of us to go at once. I'd rather find someone amenable to a trade, someone with no great love for the Brotherhood, or with no great love for law and order in general… though I'm not sure Fara was the right person to send on such a mission."

"She will get us information, and we can go from there," Shura huffed, as if they'd had this conversation already, and Daks grunted noncommittally.

Chapter Seven

Daks cracked his neck and rolled his shoulders as he resisted the urge to get up and pace the clearing. They were all anxious. He didn't need to make it worse by prowling like a caged animal, but he sure as hells wanted to. Sitting on his ass while he left his fate to a stranger went contrary to everything he was.

He glanced pensively over at Ravi, huddled beneath his ratty cloak, the hood pulled all the way up despite the warmth of the spring sunlight filtering through the trees. Had he done the right thing? Each time things went from bad to worse, he asked himself that question, and he was still afraid to answer it.

Seers were always the most unpredictable of the magic users. Even after hundreds of years, the scholars hadn't perfected training them or predicting when their power would manifest. At least half of the Seers he'd ever met were borderline insane... *but* they had their own tower at the Scholomagi and were well taken care of, particularly now when any tiny bit of information they could glean from their gifts was necessary. Ravi would be better off there than here at least, right?

Despite his best intentions, Daks stood and started pacing. He didn't like it when he had too much time to think. He started questioning everything and tying himself in knots. He'd been cut adrift by the High Council. He had no clear directive anymore, no one else calling the shots. Was he making good decisions?

"How long has she been gone?" he asked impatiently.

Shura raised an eyebrow at him. "Not more than two hours."

"Mmf," he grunted and went back to pacing.

"Sit down and rest, *Vaida*, or you will reopen your wound, since you haven't yet let me stitch it closed."

"It's fine," he grumbled, even as he settled himself on the fallen tree again.

That wasn't exactly a lie. It hurt... *a lot*. But it had only bled a little since he'd jarred it getting on the horse that morning and then again when they'd stopped. He'd probably be in more pain if he let Shura wield the needle on him than if he just left it to heal on its own, anyway.

Feeling the weight of someone's stare, he glanced up to find Ravi studying him with concern. Even shadowed by his hood and obscured by the stringy strands of tangled auburn hair he hid behind, those gorgeous amber eyes caught the afternoon sunlight like jewels before the man quickly averted his gaze.

Liquid gold like brook-cooled ale after a hot summer day working in the fields back home.

Ugh. Dear gods, it's come to this.

He was waxing poetic over a crabby little man's eyes. Next, he'd be carrying a harp and skipping through the wildflowers.

"Shur, give me something to do," he whined.

"Hush," she hissed, and he was on the verge of growling at her when he realized she wasn't looking at him and her body had tensed.

He followed her gaze, searching the trees until he finally spotted movement across the clearing. After a few tense moments, he recognized a familiar blond head and gray cloak and confirmed that she was alone.

Shura stood by his side practically vibrating like a coiled spring until he said, "Go on. We'll wait here."

Despite his recent concerns, she didn't go running blindly toward Fara like some lovesick virgin. She swung in a wide arc from their location, moving silently but quickly through the undergrowth. Daks sometimes wondered if her people didn't have some sort of innate magic, the way they could move with such deadly grace and stealth through even the roughest terrain, but he'd never sensed it if they did.

From their hiding place, mostly shielded from the clearing, he watched Shura approach Fara cautiously. Eventually, she must have decided all was safe, because she stepped out of the shadows and into the sunlight, startling the other woman and her horse. Daks grinned. She loved doing that to people.

The women exchanged a few words before Shura led the way back to their hiding place in a far more direct line than she'd taken out.

"Any success?" Daks called when they were within easy earshot.

"Yes and no," Fara answered, blowing out a breath as she allowed Shura to take the reins of her mare and lead it to the others. "Reyan is not a large town," she continued, closing the last few yards between them. "Not like Urmat. And having two members of the Thirty-Six in their midst has made everyone edgy. But I'm afraid we don't only have them worry about. The people I talked to said the brothers have been given their own small contingent of soldiers, and they're questioning anyone coming down from the North as well as patrolling the two riverbanks near town. I don't think we'll be able to get anywhere near a boat without being spotted and questioned."

"And if we make a dash for it, the pain priests will likely be sent for," Daks finished for her, frowning.

"So exactly what part of that is success?" Ravi squawked.

Shura narrowed her eyes at him, and Daks took a step forward, blocking their view of each other.

Despite Ravi's tone, Fara's grim expression lightened a little as she answered, "I've found Maran's family. They are well-known and liked in the community... a great deal more than the soldiers and brothers at the moment. Their farm isn't far up the Kun. We can keep to the forest until we find a safe place to cross. We might get a little wet again, but we should be given a safe place to rest and dry off on the other side."

Daks pursed his lips. "You think they'll be sympathetic?"

"Any time Maran has spoken of her family, it has been with pride," she answered somewhat defensively. "I heard nothing in town that would make me think otherwise."

"I'm sure they're good people," Shura gently interjected. "And they may dislike what is going on as much as the rest of us. I think what he's asking is, do you believe they'll be willing to take the risk of helping us? Because it is a risk. They have to live here once we're gone."

"They know what happened to Maran's boy. They'll help," she replied confidently.

After meeting Shura's questioning gaze, he gave her a small shrug, letting her know he'd accept her decision. Anything was better than sitting around doing nothing, and honestly, they didn't have a lot of options. They could send Fara back to town for supplies and simply go around in hopes of finding better luck farther north. But that was about the only other option left to them if the waterways were being closely watched. He sure as hells didn't want to risk a night crossing with pain priests nearby. Just the thought made him shudder and his stomach clench.

"Lead the way, Fara," Shura said with a soft smile.

Daks shot a quick glance to Ravi. The man was worrying his lower lip, and a deep *V* had formed between his pretty eyes, but he didn't say anything. He merely fell into line behind them as they moved to gather the horses and followed Fara upriver.

Crossing the Kun was not particularly pleasant. At least the river was still shallow and slow-moving, despite the icy snowmelt, so he only got wet up to his waist leading Horse over the rocky bottom. His chest tightened and his hands clutched convulsively on the reins the higher the water climbed, but luckily Shura was the only one who seemed to notice—because she was the only one craning her neck to check on him every five seconds. They were all shivering by the time they reached the far side, but the lure of solid ground and the possibility of a good, hot meal and a roof to sleep under tonight egged him on.

The family's house and barns weren't difficult to spot, once they reached the edge of the trees. The large stone-and-wood structures perched on a hill far enough from the river to be safe from floods, but close enough for easy access to the water for their crops. Despite Fara's obvious faith in Maran's family, she didn't argue when Daks recommended she approach them on her own while they kept hidden. They were far enough from Reyan that there shouldn't be any guard presence, but given their luck so far, he wasn't taking any chances.

The woman was all smiles when she finally returned, easing the last of the tightness in Daks's muscles that he hadn't been able to work out through pacing the riverbank.

"They'll help," she said brightly, her cheeks flushed. "They recommend we wait until after dark and the extra laborers they've brought on for planting season have gone home. They'll put us up in the house to avoid being seen by anyone outside the family. We'll have plenty of hot food, beds, and warm water to wash in."

Her enthusiasm was contagious. He found himself smiling along with Shura. He cut a glance to Ravi, who seemed oddly silent, but the man had his hood pulled forward and his head bent, so Daks couldn't see any part of his face.

"I guess we wait, then," Daks said into the silence, his smile fading a little.

As far as they were from town, they still heard when the temple bell rang at sunset for evening prayers. Even in this overly-pious kingdom, farmers and other workers weren't expected to travel to the temple at dawn and dusk, but they did have to stop whatever they were doing and sing one of the hundreds of interminable hymns the Brotherhood had concocted.

Daks hadn't noticed much in the way of prayer from Fara before, probably because they'd been a bit preoccupied with running, but he saw her draw a little away from the rest of them now. He shot a glance at Ravi, but the man remained still and silent where he'd propped himself against a tree to wait.

Finally, Fara rejoined them, her face alight and smiling again. "We should be able to go now. The workers will probably have headed home before the bells to sing with their families."

Daks didn't need to be told twice. He hopped to his feet and went to gather Horse's reins while Shura and Fara collected the other two. The women had almost crossed the dirt road outside the tree line when Daks realized Ravi wasn't with them. He swung around to find Ravi still sitting at the foot of the tree.

"Ravi, what are you waiting for? Let's go," he called.

"I can't," came the muffled reply.

"What's wrong?" Shura said, coming back to him.

"I don't know."

He handed the reins to Shura and walked back to stand over Ravi's huddled form. "Are you hurt?"

"No."

"Then what?" he asked, losing patience.

"You know what," Ravi said with equal harshness, seeming to fold in on himself even more. "People? A *house* full of people I've never met? What do think is going to happen when I get near them? In case you've forgotten, there's two pain priests only a few miles away. If something happens, do *you* want to take the chance they won't find out?"

Daks grimaced and dragged a hand down his face. Ravi was right. He'd been so focused on a hot, hearty meal—with maybe some blessed ale to wash it down—a soft bed to sleep in, and the chance to clean up that he'd forgotten all about Ravi's little Vision problem.

"Daks?" Shura called from where he'd left her.

"It's fine," he replied. "We're just going to have to alter the plan a little."

He dropped to one knee, grimacing at the pull on his wound. When Ravi finally met his gaze in the fading light, Daks murmured, "We won't go in the house. We'll keep clear."

Ravi shook his head. "There's no reason you all can't. I can wait outside, in the barn maybe. You need to get that taken care of," he said, nodding to Daks's ribs. "I'll be fine on my own."

Daks's lips curved. "What happened to not letting me out of your sight until you're safely out of Rassa?"

Ravi rolled his eyes, but his lips twitched. "I doubt you could sneak away on me. I'll stick with the horses to make sure, though."

"Come on," Daks said, only wincing slightly as he rose to his feet again. "We'll figure it out once we get closer. I'll scope out one of the buildings farthest from the house and leave you there while we talk to the family. We're all cold and damp. I think we can risk getting a little closer than this."

He returned to Shura and took Horse's reins.

"Let's get going. I'll explain on the way."

This time, Ravi followed them as they trudged upward around a newly planted field toward the farm. When they neared the outbuildings, Daks kept his senses opened for any tingle of magic from Ravi—or from anyone else for that matter—but luckily nothing surfaced. Perhaps the gods were finally going to give them a break, though he didn't dare say it out loud.

He'd explained the situation to the two women as they walked, while Ravi remained mute behind them. Shura had quickly agreed keeping Ravi away from others was the safer course, and Fara had only given Ravi an uneasy glance before nodding her acceptance as well. The woman was going to have to get over her obvious distaste for all things magical before she reached Scholoveld, or at least learn to school her expressions better. Her face showed way too much of what she was feeling, and the High Council would eat her alive.

Not my business, he reminded himself again.

RAVI COLLAPSED on the first bale of hay he found in the small barn Daks led him into, wrapping his cloak tightly around himself and hunkering down. He was so tired, he'd probably sleep for a week when they finally reached Samebar… *if* they ever reached it.

He'd assumed living in near-constant fear of his Visions for the last ten years and scratching out a meager existence on the streets of Rassat would have hardened him enough to make this journey, but he'd been so very wrong. He missed his found family. He missed the familiar places and people that made up his second home, such as it was. He even missed the smell of the city, which he never would have thought possible.

The others were talking quietly amongst themselves, but he didn't bother to listen. They were the ones who'd deal with the family. He was so far out of his depth his input wouldn't be of much use anyway. And right now he was the most problematic; best to just keep his head down.

"We're going in to talk to the family, before they come in search of us."

Daks's voice coming from right above him shook him out of his thoughts enough to nod in acknowledgment before curling up and closing his eyes again. He probably shouldn't risk sleep, but he could rest quietly until hopefully someone brought him something to eat. He had a long, lonely night ahead of him.

"Ravi?"

He jolted awake, his heart racing. A large shadow loomed over him, backlit by flickering lamplight. He blinked, and Daks's scarred face came into focus. His normally shaggy hair was wet and combed flat against his head, making him look a little less disreputable than usual. Although that impression was probably sweetened by the bowl of steaming stew the man held out to him.

Ravi took the bowl and greedily shoveled a heaping spoonful into this mouth, mumbling a quick "Thank you" around chunks of potato, meat, and carrots in a thick, delicious gravy. He should take his time and savor the meal. He hadn't eaten anything this good in a long time. But he couldn't seem to stop cramming more in.

"You keep eating that fast, you're going to get a stomachache," Daks warned as he settled on the bale next to his.

He held out a chunk of bread, dripping in butter, possibly as incentive to heed his words, and Ravi stopped inhaling the stew long enough to accept it with another murmured thanks. Daks was probably right. He might regret eating this much later, but it sure felt like a tiny slice of Quanna's gardens in the Beyond right now.

"There's plenty more where that came from. Vasin, Maran's uncle, has been quite generous. His harvest last year was apparently outstanding, so we needn't feel bad taking what's on offer," Daks said as he eased back against a post and stretched out his legs.

"He's all right with us here?" Ravi managed between slower bites.

Daks nodded. "Mostly because of Fara. It's her mission he sympathizes with. But that's good enough for me. Once you've eaten, I have a bucket of warm water and some soap and flannels for you to wash. They've agreed to clean and mend your clothes at the house, so they've sent along some spares for you to change into."

He nodded toward a small pile of cloth and a covered wooden bucket on the ground. Ravi eyed it uncertainly as he finished mopping up the last of the stew with his bread, feeling shame heat his cheeks. The clothes weren't rich or ostentatious, just serviceable linen and wool—probably someone's hand-me-downs—but their quality far outstripped his own thin, ragged, patched, and stained garments. Maran's family would likely prefer to burn whatever he gave them, if he agreed. Honestly, his clothes might disintegrate with a strong washing at this point anyway.

"I'll wash and see to my clothes," he said. "If they can provide needle and thread, I can tend to my own things."

Daks sighed and sat up. "They're not going to steal your clothes, Ravi. They're mending my torn tunic now. I can tell you, they do good work, and they seem happy to 'contribute to the cause' in whatever way they can. You should let them."

"Do they know what I am?" Ravi asked, deflecting.

"They do. I personally wouldn't have shared that bit of information unless I had to. But Fara is apparently of high moral fiber so...." He shrugged.

He'd said that last as if the words left a bad taste in his mouth, and Ravi had to fight a small smile. He didn't always appreciate the man's pragmatism and definitely not his partner's—but it was useful where Mistress Sabin's blind idealism was not.

When Ravi remained silent, Daks huffed and stood up. Ravi didn't miss the hitch in the man's breath or the way he favored his side, and he winced in sympathy.

"Look," Daks continued, "I'm going to leave you the bucket and the rest. Use it however you like while I go get the bedding they offered. I'll be back in a little while, and you can hand over the clothes or not… up to you."

Once he'd gone, Ravi finished the last of his meal and then gladly availed himself of the warm water and soap. Such things were a luxury in Arcadia. Ordinarily, they washed in sea water or cold well water if they were willing to risk it, and not at all in winter. The air was still cold enough he was shivering by the time he pulled on the clean borrowed clothes, and he moved closer to the lamp Daks had left, if only for the little bit of warmth it shed. His cloak had several new tears in it and the hem was caked in dirt, further tempting him to hand it off to someone else and hope they could work a miracle on it, especially now that his full stomach was making him sleepy.

The sound of footsteps jerked his attention away from the sorry cloth in his lap in time to see Daks suddenly come to a halt at the edge of the lamplight. The man held an inordinately large stack of brown wool bundles in his thick arms, but it was his expression that caught and held Ravi's gaze. Daks stood as if frozen, gaping at Ravi like he'd never seen him before. Ravi supposed this might have been the first time the man had seen him fully without his cloak, but that was hardly worthy of the wide-eyed stare he was receiving. The only really noteworthy feature he had were his eyes, and Daks had seen them plenty of times by now.

"What?" Ravi asked, shifting self-consciously.

Daks blinked and cleared his throat. "Uh, I guess I didn't realize your hair had so much red in it. You, uh, look different."

Ravi really wanted to ask if "different" meant good, but he bit his tongue. He didn't care what this man thought about how he looked. He didn't care what anyone thought as long as they left him alone.

"Those blankets for me?" he asked instead, since his wet hair seemed to be sucking what little warmth he had out through the top of his head without his cloak.

"Yeah," Daks replied, crossing the space between them and moving to one of the small stalls made of rough-cut boards beyond. "They said we could put down as much straw as we want to sleep on."

As Ravi watched him pull a knife from somewhere inside his clothes and cut the ties binding a bale together, his words sank in and Ravi frowned. "We?"

Daks just kept working. He lifted another bale into the stall and cut it open, before raking the hay into two sizable, oval mounds.

"I don't need a babysitter," Ravi said finally, but Daks merely grunted.

"I should be safe enough on my own," he tried again.

"Mmhmm."

Ravi had to stifle a yawn even as he narrowed his eyes. He shouldn't have eaten so much.

Daks shook out one of the cloth bundles and laid the blanket over one pile of straw before doing the same for the other, while Ravi continued to fidget. Daks would be warmer, more comfortable, and probably happier inside with the others.

"Put this on," Daks said, shoving another bundle at him. "Have you decided about your clothes?"

Fighting another yawn, Ravi shrugged and looked away, embarrassed. "I guess it's okay if they want to see what they can do with them," he muttered reluctantly.

With another vaguely affirmative grunt, Daks collected the pile of clothing Ravi had taken off, rolled it up, and tucked it under an arm before turning to leave. "I'll be back with something hot to drink and some more food," he called over his shoulder as the darkness beyond the lamplight swallowed him.

Ravi stared after him for several moments, worrying his lower lip before he finally looked down at the bundle of cloth he held. The heavy greenish-brown wool turned out to be a cloak. Like the other borrowed clothes, it wasn't new, but it was comfortingly thick and free of holes, stains, or patches. He slung it over his shoulders, pulled up the hood, and nestled into it with a happy sigh. For tonight at least, he'd be warm. And the deep hood made him feel safe from prying eyes, even if a part of him had actually enjoyed the way Daks had been looking at him.

By the time Daks returned with two steaming clay mugs, Ravi had already buried himself beneath the heavy blankets on one pile of straw, and he was fighting to keep his eyes open. He propped himself on an elbow and accepted the mug he was offered with a muffled "Thank you," before sipping at the herbal mixture heavily sweetened with honey. He let out another happy sigh at the warmth seeping into his hands as he watched Daks settle into the other makeshift bed over the rim of his mug. The tea was helping to revive him a little, but the need for sleep still weighed heavily on his eyelids. The longer the silence between them stretched, the more Ravi squirmed inside his cocoon.

"Do you think it's safe for me to sleep here, this close to town?" he finally asked, not sure if he really wanted to hear the answer.

"I think you need sleep. We all do."

Ravi studied Daks's face from the concealment of his hood as his full belly, soft bed, and honeyed tea made him a little dreamy-eyed. The man wasn't exactly unattractive. The warm, flickering light from the oil lamp smoothed some of the harsher edges of his face and softened his roguish appearance. Now that someone had finally taken a brush to his unruly mane, Ravi wondered how soft it would feel under his fingers.

He clenched the mug tighter in his hands. Clearing his throat, he asked, "What if I Dream? Will they know? Will I lead them to us?"

"Have you had a Dream since we left the city?"

"Other than what you two told me about, I don't think so."

Daks waved a hand. "I don't think that was a Dream either. I think that was the beginnings of another Vision—though I can't explain how it happened while you were drugged or why it cut off so abruptly. That was a new one for me, I'll admit. But I didn't sense anything while you were asleep by the Matna, so I think it's safe to risk it now. You can't go on without sleep."

"And you can sense things they can't?"

It irritated him a great deal that he knew so little about magic. His entire family line, going back generations, prided themselves on the acquisition and dissemination of knowledge, and yet he was completely ignorant of something so huge.

"I can," Daks replied simply, annoyingly.

"But that brother in Rassat could sense what you did."

"He was a Sensitive, like me, not a pain priest. I don't think his gift is as strong as mine either. It took him longer to find you, and he probably lived in the same city as you for years."

Ravi could almost see Daks's chest expanding with each word, and he smothered a smile against the lip of his mug.

"The members of the Thirty-Six are different," Daks continued without prompting. "I've never heard of a pain priest being a Finder as well. They are two different gifts. The priests would most likely be able to sense you if you were actively using your gift within close proximity of them. And possibly out this far, *if* you have another prophecy surge like the night we met—though they'd probably have no idea what it was. But anything other than that, they shouldn't be able to sense from this distance. If anything that big happens, I'll definitely feel it, and we'll have time to get away before they find us out here. Vasin can say he scared some vagrants out of his barn. Now stop worrying and go to sleep. Get what rest you can, while you can, or we'll have to strap you to the saddle with the rest of the baggage when we head out again."

Daks smirked as he said it and shot him a wry sideways glance. Ravi scowled, even if the man couldn't see it. "I can keep up with the rest of you."

"Good. Now get some sleep."

Daks rolled away from him and snuffed the oil lamp. Ravi's tea had cooled enough for him to drain the mug without burning his tongue. He upended it, savoring the last few honeyed drops before setting it aside and burrowing deeper beneath his blankets. Their breathing, the wind, and soft night noises beyond the barn were the only sounds to break the silence until Ravi summoned the courage to ask what he'd been too afraid to in the bright light of day.

"They'll know how to help me at the Scholomagi, right?" he whispered into the darkness, half hoping Daks was already asleep.

"Yes," Daks replied nearly as quietly. After a few moments, Ravi heard the rustle of straw as Daks shifted onto his back and sighed. "They'll help. I can't guarantee they'll be able to give you complete control. Sight is a tricky gift to have, because it's almost as receptive in nature as being a Sensitive, only I think you're channeling instead of absorbing. I can't really explain it better than that. I'm no teacher or scholar."

Ravi took a few moments to digest that. It wasn't as if he'd been expecting a miracle to happen once he reached Samebar, but he wished Daks had sounded more definite.

"You'll have a place at the Scholomagi, though," Daks continued, as if sensing his unease. "The Seers have their own tower and are quite well taken care of. You won't have to be afraid of having Visions anymore. They won't hurt you in Samebar for being gifted, for being different. No one will take you away or force you to do anything you don't want. You don't even have to stay in Scholoveld, if you don't want to. Your gift isn't the kind that could prove dangerous without training, so there are no laws to make you."

"But there are for others?" There were so many things he didn't know.

"For some, but only if the gift is deemed dangerous. Then you're required to go for training to protect the innocent and ungifted from harm."

"Okay," Ravi murmured as a hundred more questions bloomed in his mind.

"It will be different," Daks said around a yawn. "There are laws that govern the gifted, and some of them don't always seem fair. But you have my word you will be far safer than you are here. Shura and I have helped dozens of gifted to better lives in Samebar. You'll see."

"Why?"

The question escaped him before he could grab it back, and he winced. The last thing he wanted was to have Daks questioning why he was risking so much for a perfect stranger.

Idiot.

"Why what?" Daks asked.

"Nothing. Forget it."

"Go to sleep. You can ask me whatever you want in the morning."

RAVI STRUGGLED to free himself from the last vestiges of his Dream as he lay panting in his woolen cocoon. Opening his eyes, he clung to the weak indigo of predawn outside the barn like a lifeline, dragging himself free of the sea of muddy gray-brown still trying to drag him into darkness. The Dream had been the same as his Vision on the road, a terrifying gray wall, but different. This time a stranger had been with him in the miasma, calling out something in Sambaran, as lost and afraid as he was.

He shook his head and sat up, dislodging the blankets from his shoulders, welcoming the shock of cold air on his skin to bring him fully awake. Even as the last clinging cobwebs of the Dream fell away, his heart began to pound for a different reason—fear of discovery.

Had that been a Vision? Could a brother be on his way to the farm even now?

His gaze locked on Daks's sleeping form as he tried to control his breathing. The man appeared to still be asleep, oblivious to anything wrong. Should he take that as a sign his Dream hadn't been that "loud" and he was panicking for nothing, or that Daks was just a sound sleeper?

As he stared at the man, his pulse and breathing slowed. He couldn't fathom why, but Daks's mere presence had a calming effect on him. It made no sense. The man was infuriating and as impulsive as a toddler in a sweets shop. But Ravi could feel the tension leaching from his shoulders and chest as the seconds ticked past and Daks's chest rose and fell in a slow, even rhythm. He looked warm and solid, close enough Ravi could touch him if he just reached out.

What kind of lover would Daks be? How would those big, hard hands feel on Ravi's skin? Would all that infuriating bravado and overconfidence translate to something dominant and hot between the bed linens?

Ravi's body tingled as memories of that other Vision flooded his mind, pictures of himself naked on his back, looking up at an equally naked Daks hovering over him, his cocky smile gentled somehow, his dark blue eyes filled with tenderness.

Ravi threw his blankets off the rest of the way and climbed to his feet before stomping out of the barn to relieve himself. The thought of lying with that man was utterly ridiculous, a pathetic fantasy because he was lonely and scared. Vision or no Vision, he'd prove to the gods he was the master of his own fate. Besides, he'd have plenty of better options to choose from once he reached Samebar. He'd been propositioned enough on the streets of Arcadia to know he was at least moderately attractive to both men and women. He didn't have to settle for a rogue and a lunatic, even if the memory of being pressed against that hard body made his stomach flutter and his skin flush with warmth. There would be plenty of other hard bodies in Samebar to choose from—hard bodies that weren't attached to that irritating mouth.

Disrobing enough to relieve himself in the chill morning air helped cool any lingering heat. And by the time he returned to the barn, Daks was awake and sitting up, blinking groggily at him. His bushy hair had dried into an oddly misshapen halo about his head.

"What now?" Ravi asked crisply so he didn't have to acknowledge that a sleepy Daks might just be a tiny bit endearing.

Daks grimaced and sighed as he pushed his blankets off and climbed to his feet. "Breakfast, I hope," he answered, his voice still rough with sleep.

"And after? Did you even discuss a plan yet?"

"Yes, we '*discussed a plan*,'" he bit back, giving Ravi a grumpy glare. "Can I take a piss first before I lay it out for you, or do I need to hold it?"

He was moving toward the door to the barn as he spoke, so Ravi assumed he wasn't expecting an answer.

A short time later, Daks poked his head through the door again and called, "I'm going to the house to see what's on for breakfast and if they have any blessed caffe'. I'll bring back what I find. Stay hidden, in case the farmworkers start showing up."

He didn't linger long enough for Ravi to give a reply, which was just as well. The promise of something hot to eat and drink was enough of a distraction, and Daks was obviously not a morning person.

Ravi moved to their makeshift beds and began shaking out and folding up the blankets. He collected their empty mugs and the oil lamp and set them near the opening of the barn before moving back to a straw bale in a shadowed corner to wait, wrapping his borrowed cloak tightly around him and pulling up the hood.

When Daks returned with a steaming mug and a bowl of some kind of porridge smothered in butter and dried fruits, any grumpiness on Ravi's part was completely forgotten. He tried to go a little slower with this meal than the one last night, hoping to forgo the slight stomachache he'd experienced after gorging himself, but it was a challenge. Two hearty, delicious meals in a row, without having to worry if he was taking too much away from the little ones or feeling guilty for not sharing, was a luxury he hadn't had in years.

A small lump of porridge dripped from his spoon onto the cloak and he winced, setting the bowl aside to wipe at the mess.

"Are my clothes ready?" he asked, hoping he hadn't left a grease stain on the good wool.

"They're packed," Daks answered around a mouthful of porridge. "The family are filling our bags with supplies as we speak. They rose early so we could be on our way before the workers show up after morning bell."

"Packed?" Ravi asked, momentarily forgetting the rest of his porridge.

"Yes. We've decided it's too risky to attempt a crossing here. Not only could we run afoul of the brothers midcrossing, but questions will be asked of everyone in the village even if we aren't caught. It'll be safer for everyone if we go farther north."

"You said that last time," Ravi pointed out dryly as his chest tightened with worry.

Daks sighed and rested his bowl in his lap. "I know. According to Vasin, extra soldiers have been sent to villages all the way up the river, and any strangers are highly scrutinized. Our best bet is to swing away from the King's Road and travel narrower byways through the marshes, avoiding towns and only returning to the Matna when we're close to Traget. If all the rumors are true, which Vasin seems to think they are, and the Thirty-Six are afraid to go any closer to this supposed wizard and his band of barbarians and possible rogue brother up north, we shouldn't have to worry about your Visions anymore. Plus, Traget is the largest town with the largest market beyond Rassat, so strangers coming and going shouldn't catch anyone's notice."

"Traget?" Ravi asked, his voice cracking as the porridge curdled in his belly. "But that's nearly to the Northern Mountains. We might as well cross the border on foot."

"Not quite," Daks replied, his stupid lips quirking in that smug way Ravi hated. "It's only three days' steady ride. Vasin has agreed to give us enough supplies for the journey, and he can spare us a mule to help carry the packs, or one of us, if it comes to it. He's got a cousin in Traget who'll get the beast and the horses back to him next time they run the merchant barges down the river, and we can get new horses once we reach Samebar."

He seemed so pleased with this, Ravi could only stare at him for a few beats before he found his voice. "Three more days? In the boglands?" he all but whined.

"They're not so bad as all that," Daks replied, waving a dismissive hand. "The marshes are a little challenging, but not if we stick to the marked paths. Vasin is drawing up a map, and he says there aren't many people traveling that way these days, since it's planting season. Those who are moving away from the troubles in the North would take the King's Road to the larger towns along the Matna, so we shouldn't have to worry about running into anyone. And if you have another Vision, there will be no one for miles to sense it. Win win."

Why Ravi had allowed himself to think Daks was even moderately attractive for more than two seconds, he couldn't quite fathom right now. But given that Ravi had only ever read about the boglands and the North of Rassa, he couldn't exactly argue the man's logic either, not effectively anyway. The distance had seemed a lot greater than three days' travel on the maps in his grandfather's study, and the swamps so much more ominous in some of the stories than Daks made them sound. But he *had* always wanted to see them, though definitely not under these circumstances.

"Can't we try a few other villages upriver from here? Surely there has to be *one* where we can hire a boat to get across. There can't be a pain priest in every town."

Daks shook his head. "With the fuss we created in Urmat, and the villages being similarly flush with guard companies, the risk is too high. Shura and I aren't familiar enough with this area to know who to approach, and Mistress Sabin isn't either."

"Surely this Vasin knows someone," Ravi tried again, his hopes sinking.

"That he can get in contact with quickly? Who'd be willing to take the risk? No. This is the best, safest solution."

Ravi sucked in a breath and swallowed any further protests. It was obvious they'd made up their minds without him. He didn't relish another three days in the saddle, though. He wouldn't be able to walk by the end of them.

"Finish your breakfast. We'll be leaving soon," Daks said curtly before digging into his own bowl again.

Ravi lifted his bowl and obediently shoveled the nearly cold porridge mechanically into his mouth, though it didn't taste as delicious as it had only a few minutes ago.

"My clothes?" he asked when he'd swallowed the last of it.

"I told you. They're packed. What you have on now will do better for the colder climate anyway."

"These aren't mine, though."

"They are now."

Before Ravi could argue, Daks stood, collected the bowl from him, and then headed for the door.

"We'll be back with the horses in a few minutes," he called brusquely over his shoulder.

Ravi glared at his retreating back until his gaze seemed to drop lower of its own accord. *Why did the man have to be so, so—bossy? Solid? Thick?*

"Irritating," he settled on with firmness, as the man's firm, round ass disappeared from view.

Chapter Eight

THE FIRST day into their journey through the boglands, Daks began to regret his earlier optimism pretty much immediately. It rained. All. Day. Long.

No one spoke. They all rode in heavy, wet silence, hunched over their saddles, trying to keep as much of the cold rain from finding its way inside their cloaks as they could. Even the horses' heads were bowed as they trudged along berms that only marginally kept them out of the swampy muck to either side and sometimes narrowed to little more than overgrown deer tracks.

As sullen silence seemed to be Ravi's normal state of being, when he wasn't arguing or complaining, Daks couldn't tell if he was as miserable as the rest of the party. He sat stiffly in the saddle and hadn't leaned back against Daks's chest even once—which was a little disappointing. Daks could have used some physical comfort while being surrounded by so much damned water.

Never again, he promised himself. He was never coming back to this sodden, Rift-blighted kingdom again if he could help it.

That night they made camp where the "road" finally widened enough to fit them all and a few straggly trees provided some cover. The rain made any attempt at a fire futile, so they simply tucked into a meal of dried meat, cheese, and bread and curled under what cover the trees could afford.

Ravi hadn't said more than two words all day, and after taking his ration of food, he settled under a tree as far away from the rest of them as the small clearing allowed. Daks frowned at him but didn't say anything. They were all wet, tired, and cold. Making it an early night meant they could start fresh in the morning, and hopefully Shura's sky god, Tomok, would have finally emptied his bladder by then. When Shura and Fara curled up together under a second tree, Daks shot one more disgruntled look in Ravi's direction before finding his own slightly drier place to bed down with a bottle of ale... *alone*.

As she'd done the day before, Shura took point when they headed out in the morning. She had the best sense of direction and tracking abilities of all of them. He was relying on her to keep them from wandering off the barely visible track and getting hopelessly mired in the foul-smelling muck.

Daks and Ravi brought up the rear on Horse while Mistress Sabin tugged the pack mule behind her mare in between. The rain had finally stopped sometime in the night. And even though water dripped from every reed, leaf, or vine, and heavy mists blanketed the ground all around them, at least Daks didn't have to feel the constant maddening beat of droplets on his head and shoulders, and the wool of his cloak might actually have a chance to dry.

He tried to distract himself from their agonizing, plodding progress by studying their surroundings, but even when the mists lifted somewhat in the afternoon, there wasn't much to see. The boglands were aptly named, even if the title wasn't particularly imaginative. Clusters of trees like the ones they'd slept under dotted the landscape where the ground rose above the waterline, but beyond that remained only a sea of tall grasses, broken by pools of reed-filled, brackish water.

How could anyone choose to live out here? But Vasin had warned them to stick to the border tracks because the bog-dwellers weren't particularly welcoming to strangers.

By midmorning, the clouds had passed enough for the sun to filter weakly through the fog, but that only added to the otherworldly feel of the place, and he scowled and tightened his hands on the reins to keep from shuddering.

"Nice place," he quipped, anything to break the oppressive silence. "Can't imagine why more people don't settle here."

Ravi startled in front of him, as if Daks had woken him, and Daks experienced a little niggle of guilt, but only a niggle. He was so *bored*. Beyond keeping an eye out behind them and using his gift to scan for pain priests, Spawn, or large gatherings of people, he had nothing to do but stare at the back of Ravi's hood, the women's cloaks, and the rumps of the horses and donkey ahead of him. It didn't help matters that the place was as eerily oppressive to his other sense as it was to look at. He didn't try to stretch his gift too far, partly because he wasn't sure he wanted to know what lived out there.

"No one really knows how many people actually live in the boglands," Ravi said quietly, and Daks sighed with relief. He was spooking himself.

"Oh?" he prodded.

"In Rassat, it's said that temple postings out here are more of a punishment than an honor, reserved for troublemakers in the Brotherhood," Ravi thankfully continued. "The people don't like outsiders, and I don't think I've ever met anyone who came from here in Rassat."

"That's what Vasin said at the farm. They come out to trade sometimes, but that's it.... Which hopefully means they'll leave us alone, as long as we do the same for them."

"Do you, uh, *sense* anything out there?" Ravi asked hesitantly.

"If you mean pain priests, then no, I don't sense any nearby. I'm keeping my senses open, just in case. If there are any within a few miles of us, I'll know it. As I said before, though, I won't be able to feel if another Sensitive is nearby."

Ravi remained silent for a few beats before he asked, "What about other things?"

Daks cocked an eyebrow at him, but Ravi still faced forward, and his hood was up, as usual. "Other things?"

Despite Daks's heroic efforts at keeping a considerate distance between them, Ravi's ass brushed the front of his trousers as the man shifted in the saddle. Between that and their eerie surroundings, Daks was grateful Vasin and his family hadn't been stingy with the ale when he'd resupplied them. He'd need it tonight.

The Seer

He swallowed an aggrieved sigh, did a little shifting of his own, and struggled to pay attention as Ravi cleared his throat and replied, "Yes, *things*. You know, like magical things or *Spawn*?"

Ravi nearly whispered that last word, and Daks had to fight a smile. But then the more he thought about the question, the quicker his smile fell away. How hard it must be for the people of Rassa to have so little control of the world around them, to be so dependent on such a small group of brothers to protect them.

In Samebar, nearly every town and village had at least a few wardstones or a Sensitive or *something* to warn them if Riftspawn were in the area. A select few even kept enchanted weapons to be handed out in the event of an attack, though those were expensive and had to be recharged periodically if the spellwork wasn't of a high enough caliber. Hells, even in Ghorazon, they had their enigmatic village witches to rely on, and there was no limit to how many witches or mages there could be beyond nature itself.

Rassans had only their faith and themselves until a member of the Thirty-Six could be called to the area they're needed. Who knew what damage a monster from the Rift could wreak before the Brotherhood arrived? Without magic, they were helpless to do anything beyond destroy the body, if they could, releasing a Wraith to possess some other poor creature or even one of their own, starting the cycle all over again. And even when the Brotherhood arrived, the village or town had to pay a heavy price for their aid. He'd never been able to understand how the Brotherhood maintained its power, its monopoly on magic, when there were so many other options in the world—easier, more efficient ways of protecting the people.

"I'd know right away if there was a Spawn within a mile of us. You don't have to worry about that. They practically scream to be noticed."

"And Wraiths? Or… maybe ancient magical objects, like before the coming of Blessed Harot? Would you be able to feel that?"

Ravi's tone had taken on an odd, excited note that made the hairs on the back of Daks's neck stand up. Unwilling to admit just how much the eeriness of their surroundings was getting to him, Daks opened his senses for one more sweep, just to be sure, but all was the same as it had been.

"I haven't had much experience with Wraiths," Daks admitted reluctantly. "In Samebar, when a mage kills a Spawn, its Wraith is captured in a crystal and taken back to Scholoveld for destruction, if it isn't destroyed in the killing. But from everything I've been taught, Wraiths can't wait long before they find a new host. I doubt there would be any just hovering about in the bogs like ghosts."

As soon as he said the word, he wanted to take it back. Ravi finally swung around to look at him, his amber eyes wide as his hood fell back enough to expose a touch of that damnable auburn hair.

"Can you sense ghosts?"

Daks grimaced and wanted to smack himself on the forehead. He dragged his gaze away from Ravi and eyed their dreary surroundings once more, reminding himself he wasn't a superstitious man.

"If they exist, I've never sensed them. Why all the spooky questions all of a sudden?" he asked, deflecting.

Ravi immediately stiffened, and Daks was filled with equal parts regret and anticipation as he waited for Ravi to snap something cutting back at him. But before he could, a familiar tingle shivered along Daks's skin and he lurched forward, wrapping an arm across Ravi's chest as the man let out a strangled moan and arched his back. Magic flowed over and through Daks as Horse snorted and jerked beneath.

"Push it back, Ravi. Don't let it take over," Daks urged as he tightened his grip on the reins and his hold on Ravi.

Ravi's muscles strained against him only for a few moments before he went limp. Lucky for both of them, most of Ravi's weight was supported by the saddle, and Horse wasn't particularly skittish. Daks managed to settle him and keep them both from falling.

"Daks?" Shura called.

He glanced up to find her twisted in her saddle, looking back at him with concern.

"We're all right."

"Another Vision?"

A glance at Fara showed her biting her lip and staring wide-eyed, and Daks grimaced.

"It wasn't a big one, and there aren't any members of the Thirty-Six around, so we should be okay," he replied grimly. "This is why we took the long way around."

Shura remained quiet for a few beats before she asked, "Do we need to stop?"

"No. I've got him. Keep going."

She pursed her lips but nodded and nudged her horse back into a walk as Daks settled Ravi's unconscious form a little more comfortably against his chest. In another day and half, they would be at Traget, so if Ravi was going to have a Vision, now was the best time to do it, when they were halfway between large settlements. Daks just hoped it was the last until he could get him across the river.

"Drink this," Daks said, handing over the waterskin when Ravi finally stirred.

Ravi sat up straighter in the saddle and sadly pulled out of Daks's embrace. He didn't meet Daks's gaze as he took the skin and downed a large gulp from it before handing it back.

"Thanks," he murmured.

He sat hunched in silence in front of Daks for a while as the horses plodded across the marshy ground, and Daks decided not to push. If the Vision was important, Ravi would have said so.

"How long was I out?" Ravi asked morosely.

"Not long. A few minutes at most."

He heaved a long sigh, and Daks cringed for him. He knew a little of what it was like to have this thing inside you that you didn't want, that made you different, forcing life choices on you you'd otherwise not have made. His situation hadn't been exactly the same. He didn't have to fear for his life when his gift manifested, but it turned his world upside down anyway, and with not much in the way of compensation.

If he thought Ravi would welcome it, he'd wrap an arm around him again to show him he wasn't alone. But he doubted the gesture would be appreciated. Ravi would probably be glad to see the back of him as soon as they reached Scholoveld, if not sooner... and sentimentality was a trap at any rate.

"It was the same Vision... or *lack* of Vision, I had before," Ravi huffed out finally, though Daks hadn't asked.

"The gray wall?"

"Yes. I don't know what's happened, but I never thought this curse could actually get worse. Still, having the damned Visions but not being able to *see* anything is definitely worse, so much worse."

"Things can always get worse."

Ravi swung around and met his gaze with a scowl. "Not helping."

Daks's lips quirked as he shrugged. "They'll get you sorted at the Scholomagi. They'll help you figure it out."

"You're sure about that?"

"Of course."

Ravi's lips twisted skeptically as he narrowed his eyes, and Daks had to fight a smile. The truth was, he had no idea what was wrong with Ravi's Visions, and he also had no idea if the crackpots in the Seer's tower could help him. But what was the use in wallowing in fear and indecision if they were going to the Scholomagi anyway? Besides, poking at Ravi was too entertaining to resist, and he needed something to distract both of them from their woes.

"You'll see when we get there," Daks continued with the airy bravado he knew would irritate Ravi the most, and Ravi harrumphed and faced forward again, allowing Daks to indulge in the smile he'd been fighting without getting punched or ordered to get off the horse and walk. The only downside was, he seemed to have killed what little conversation Ravi was willing to share, leaving him with nothing to do but stare out into the gloom again.

After they stopped for lunch, everyone seemed to perk up a little, which helped keep Daks from going completely insane. Shura and Fara did most of the talking, since Ravi seemed mired in his own thoughts, but Daks was content to listen. Shura seemed positively chatty, which was a little unsettling. He'd give her no end of grief about it when their little adventure was over, but definitely not now. She might stop.

The Seer

The sun finally burned through most of the mist by late afternoon, warming the air a bit, and their ride might have been almost pleasant if not for the pervasive smell of rotting vegetation and squelch of mud beneath the horses' hooves. At least they were making better time, despite Shura having to dismount periodically to scout ahead when the trail became too obscured, or sometimes even submerged, the deeper they went into the bogs.

Though he felt ridiculous, each time they stopped, he found himself reaching out with his gift, still a little spooked. Every once in a while, he thought he caught the hint of something—something old and buried deep, something sleeping, like the vibrations of the ring of stones they'd camped in near Reyan—but he couldn't be sure. He needed to stop or he'd have one hell of a headache by nightfall. Nothing was close enough or active enough to threaten their progress. That's all that mattered. Trying to pry ages-old secrets out of a swamp was a waste of his time and energy. He couldn't sense ghosts because there *was no such thing as ghosts*, and they'd be headed out of this accursed swamp tomorrow.

Never again.

By the time they found a dry space to camp that night, the itch between Daks's shoulder blades, like someone was watching him or had an arrow trained on him, was driving him crazy. He dismounted before Horse had even come to a stop and didn't hang around to make sure Ravi got down safely.

"I'm going for firewood if I can find anything dry in this Rift-blighted place," he called over his shoulder, because no way was he sitting around in the dark tonight.

He was sweating well before he'd finished collecting a sizable pile of wood, and Shura cocked an eyebrow at him each time he returned with another armload, but she didn't comment. Thankfully they'd climbed enough of a rise that a copse of pines had been able to survive the wet. They'd have plenty of bright, cheerful flames from a crackling, popping fire that would drown out any eerie swamp noises.

Possibly sensing his surly mood, the others puttered with the horses and the gear, while giving him a wide berth. That was fine. He needed the reminder that this was a job, a job that would come to an end as soon as they reached the Scholomagi… and then he'd have to figure out what came next. From the way Shura had been fluttering her eyelashes at Fara, maybe he'd have to remind her of that soon too. A few nights sharing blankets was one thing, but they would both be walking away eventually.

Once he got the fire lit, Shura fed the horses their ration of grain for the day while Fara prepared stew, and then everyone settled around the fire to eat in companionable silence. Daks tried to relax. He sipped at a bottle of ale as he stretched his boots toward the flames, but that spot between his shoulder blades continued to itch. Ravi staring pensively out into the shadows beyond the campfire, as if searching for something, didn't help. For the life of him, Daks couldn't see anything but darkness peppered with starlight when he followed the man's gaze.

Finally, he couldn't take it anymore and he growled, "Are you having one of your *feelings*?"

Ravi frowned at him. "No. Why?"

Now everyone was looking at him oddly, and Daks felt like an ass for bringing it up. "No reason," he mumbled. "Just checking."

"Is everything all right?" Shura asked, eyeing him.

"It's fine." He took another swig from his bottle.

"Then, do you think we might risk a little music tonight?" Fara asked wistfully. "Last night was so dreary, I wouldn't mind some cheering up."

"I don't see why not," Daks replied a little too quickly. "Anyone close enough to hear would be able to see or smell our fire anyway."

Shura cocked an eyebrow at him, and Daks cleared his throat. "I mean, if you want to, that is."

"Oh good," Fara replied as she stood and went to the packs.

When she returned to the fire, she unrolled a small wooden flute from a square of wool and put it to her lips. After a few practice notes, the soft, breathy strains of an unfamiliar tune rose into the night, as if carried by the swirls of smoke and sparks from the fire, and Daks let out a long sigh and slumped back against the pack he'd propped behind him. Fara played well. It was probably some Harotian hymn, but the music was soft, sweet, and just a little achingly poignant, so he could hardly complain.

Fara started another tune without being prompted, and Daks passed his bottle to Shura and then to Ravi. Shura began singing a husky countermelody to the music, punctuated by the little cries and vocal modulations traditional to her people, and Daks felt a warmth spread in his belly as he gazed at her. She rarely sang outside a gathering of her clan. He hadn't been aware of how much he'd missed it until that moment.

Eventually, Fara set her flute down and accepted the bottle, but the ensuing silence after everyone sung her praises and thanked her was oppressive. With nothing better to do, Daks turned his gaze to Ravi, only to find the man staring off into the darkness again.

"Ravi, are you *sure* you're not having one of your bad feelings?"

Ravi started and blinked at him as if he'd been somewhere far away. "Yes, I'm sure."

"Then do you mind telling us why you keep staring out into the darkness like you can see something we can't? You're freaking me out."

Ravi clutched that damned precious bag of his against his chest and grimaced. "It's nothing. It's stupid. Sorry. I'll stop."

Now Daks felt like a jerk for saying anything, and he sighed.

"Please, don't apologize," Fara cut in, before Daks could come up with the right thing to say. "I'm sure it's not stupid at all. If you have something you'd like to share, I think we'd all like to hear it."

Some of that warmth he'd lost earlier returned to Daks's chest as he threw an encouraging smile at her. She'd been a little standoffish with Ravi since they'd started this journey, and he was glad to see her making an effort, particularly when Ravi's embarrassed grimace softened into something uncertain but hopeful.

"I've always wanted to see the boglands," Ravi said hesitantly.

"Why?"

The question came out a bit more derisively than he'd intended. He started to take it back, but when Ravi's expression turned from hesitant and embarrassed to irritated, Daks decided to hold his tongue. He liked it when Ravi got fired up. It made life more interesting. For good measure, he threw Ravi his cockiest grin and drank deeply from the bottle that had somehow made it back to him, while cocking an eyebrow at him challengingly.

To his delight, Ravi rolled his eyes and turned to Fara, haughtily dismissing him. "My family are all scholars, scribes, and teachers. I was raised surrounded by books and stories. Some of them, uh...." He bit his lip and cringed slightly. "Some of them proscribed by the Brotherhood."

His hands tightened on his bag again, almost reflexively, confirming Daks's suspicions about what it contained. That must be one important book.

"Anyway," Ravi continued, "there's a story about the boglands that I was always very fond of. I used to read it over and over as a child, and I wanted to see the place, to feel what they felt. It isn't quite as romantic as I'd imagined." His face flushed darker in the firelight.

"What story?" Shura asked, surprising Daks.

He really shouldn't have been surprised. Cigani were famous all over Kita for their love of stories and storytelling. She must have surprised Ravi too, because his eyes widened before he glanced at Fara and grimaced. "Perhaps I shouldn't."

"No, please," Fara urged. "That would be lovely. Too many stories have been lost since the coming of the Brotherhood, I think. Times are changing. They shouldn't be lost altogether."

Ravi licked his lips.

"If you're sure," he said hesitantly.

"Please."

He nodded and took a pull from his waterskin before sitting straighter against the tree trunk and drawing in a long breath.

"In the reign of King Hatal the Mighty, before the coming of Blessed Harot, Rassa was a much more savage place than it is today," he began, his voice taking on a melodic quality Daks hadn't heard before. "Lesser nobles still fought constant battles over territory. Pirates, barbarians from the mountains, and other tribal peoples made annual raids on the border settlements. And Riftspawn and rogue magic users roamed freely throughout the land, leaving only destruction and despair in their wakes. Lawless and godless, the people suffered greatly."

When Ravi paused for breath, Daks threw him a smirk and cocked an eyebrow, making Ravi grimace apologetically and clear his throat. "The book was obviously a copy of a much older manuscript, probably done after Harot's ascension, but obviously before the Brotherhood started destroying such things," he qualified, his cheeks pinking in the firelight as he shot a nervous glance toward Shura.

"Keep going," Daks said.

With another nervous glance at Shura, Ravi cleared his throat again. "Well, okay, uh, King Hatal had three sons. Rolf, the eldest and heir, was much like his father: undefeated in battle, determined, and merciless. His second son, Ero, was the more poetic, fanciful type, with some small talent for magic. Women and men alike swooned over Ero's handsome face, his intricate illusions, and his skills with the lute, rather than in battle. But despite their vast differences in personalities and skills, King Hatal was said to have loved his two elder sons equally, even more than the magic sword that had made him invincible in battle and given him the crown. Volumes are filled with praises for both princes, even before Rolf ascended to the throne and Ero wedded Princess Darutha, heir to Samebar, ensuring peace between the two kingdoms for decades… but this story isn't about them. This is the story of Ael, Harat's youngest and mostly forgotten son—the scarred prince of Rassa."

Ravi cut the briefest of glances in his direction, so brief Daks might have missed it if he hadn't been watching the man so raptly. Ravi's amber eyes glowed in the firelight—not that otherworldly glow they'd had when he'd spoken his prophecy, but something warmer, happier, as if this was the real Ravi he hadn't shown them before.

As he spun his tale into the night, Daks couldn't tear his gaze away. If he were honest with himself, he was more entranced by the storyteller than the story itself, but he got the gist of it.

Scarred across much of the left side of his face by the fire that had killed his mother, Ael had withdrawn into the world of books and away from the rest of his overachieving family—perhaps a little like a certain Seer they all happened to know, though Daks was just guessing on that. At nineteen, Ael had fallen in love with a young, eager scholar of a lesser noble family and kept it hidden from his father for fear of the man's disapproval. The lovers intended to run away together to avoid any political marriage the king might try to force Ael into, but they were discovered and betrayed.

Ael's young scholar, Balin, was forced to leave Rassat in disgrace and return to his family's hold in the boglands. But only a week after his dramatic departure, word reached the king's court that the hold had been beset by a giant Riftspawn. Forbidden to leave but desperate with fear for his love, Ael had stolen King Hatal's magic sword and fled to his lover's aid. The sword was said to make its bearer invincible in battle, and he needed all the help he could get. Daks definitely would have done the same; no sense taking any chances if you didn't have to.

Ravi's melodic voice washed over Daks as he continued to weave the tale of the prince's difficulties and trials on that journey, but Daks kind of got distracted with watching Ravi's mouth and his eyes for a little while… until Ravi reached the good part, where Ael slew the horrid monster, saving his scholar love from certain death. Even Fara, as obviously ill at ease with any discussion of magic as any Rassan, sighed in relief and clapped when the magic sword felled the beast with a single strike.

"Excellent fireside tale," Daks called. He let out a burp and sat forward, smiling. "Almost makes this place seem—"

"Hush. The *Svatna* is not done with his tale," Shura interrupted sternly. Surprisingly, she'd used the Cigani formal title for a storyteller, which meant she honored his skill.

Ravi couldn't have known that, but he seemed flattered by her intervention on his behalf just the same, as he smiled shyly at her and nodded before resuming his narrative.

"The tale is far from over. You see, in his desperation to save his beloved, Ael had forgotten something. He'd forgotten the Riftspawn's Wraith. As soon as he plunged the sword into the monstrous creature's heart, the Wraith fled from its dying body and into the nearest host it could find. Wounded and weakened by his ordeal before Ael could reach him, his lover, Balin, was no match for it. It possessed him fully, shoving the man Ael knew and loved aside. A creature of hate and savagery and darkness stared back at Ael through his lover's eyes, and the prince cried out in despair and wept as he dropped the sword and wrestled with Balin to keep him from disappearing into the swamps.

"After his family assisted in capturing him, poor Balin lay bedridden and fevered for days, bound and under guard. But Ael never left his side. What was left of Balin's beleaguered family rallied around them with little hope, for no one had ever heard of a Wraith leaving a living body before.

"The family said their goodbyes and made their preparations, trying to come to terms with the inevitable, but Ael refused to see reason. He called to his lover night and day, begging him to fight, to come back, until his voice gave out. Still, he fought any attempt to remove him from that bedside.

"In the middle of the night on the fourth day, Ael woke to Balin's sweet voice calling to him as he used to. Desperate with fragile hope, Ael met his lover's gaze to find the soft brown eyes of the man he loved no longer glowing red and filled with feral rage.

"'Balin?' he croaked hesitantly.

"'I am here,' his love whispered back. 'Set me free. Let us leave this terrible place together.'

"Delusional with grief and lack of sleep, Ael allowed himself to be persuaded to untie his love and help him outside. So scrambled were his wits, he did not notice Balin had brought the wretched sword with them. In the moonlight, wrapped in heavy mist, Balin kissed his love tenderly and without urgency, until Ael's legs shook and threatened to buckle. A flash of metal was Ael's only warning before the sword found its bloody sheath."

Fara gasped in horror, momentarily taking Daks out of the story, but Ravi continued as if he hadn't heard.

"Ael cried out in agony as Balin's body dropped to the ground, Balin's hand still on the hilt of the sword buried in his own chest.

"In shock, Ael looked on as the air around his love shimmered into life. The Wraith rose from his Balin's body like mist and hovered in the air. Fear held Ael paralyzed, trapped before the red, glowing eyes of the writhing insubstantial creature, but the Wraith did not move any closer. It did not attempt to take him over as it had done Balin. When a sudden cry rang out behind him, it shook Ael out of his trance, and he turned to find Balin's family pouring out of the farmhouse they'd fled to after the destruction of their hold. When Ael turned back to the Wraith, it had vanished.

"With another anguished cry, he dropped to his knees by his lover's side and collected him in his arms as tears streamed down his face.

"'Why?' he cried. 'We could have beat it together. We could have found a way.'

"'This was the way,' Balin whispered back.

"All hope lost, Ael rocked his lover in the moonlight as Balin's family huddled in a circle around them."

"He's dead?" Fara squawked indignantly when Ravi paused for a drink of water.

Daks agreed, even if he wouldn't admit it out loud. But Ravi held up a hand and shook his head as Shura glared at Daks and Fara until everyone settled again.

"The wound forced the Wraith out, but it did not kill him as Balin had obviously expected when he'd kissed his love goodbye.

Though the magic of the sword had never failed before, somehow, this time, it did. Balin still breathed.

"Swallowing his grief and pain, Ael carried his lover back inside, and the family called for the healer. The woman did what she could, but even with her talismans and herbal remedies, she feared she could not save him.

"The family wept and wailed anew until the poor healer sighed and admitted reluctantly, 'I may know someone who can help. But beware, she will demand a high price.'

"'Anything!' Ael and the family cried out together.

"The healer did not seem surprised, but she did not smile as she left them and ventured off into the mists alone.

"They waited a night and a day while Balin clung to life and Ael clung to him. At last, when night had fallen again on the second day, a knock came at the door. A wizened old woman, draped in rags, her hair a massive nest of tangles threaded through with vines and leaves, stood haloed in the moonlight when they opened the door. The family froze in fear at the sight of her, but Ael saw nothing beyond a chance for his love and rushed forward to bring the woman inside.

"She smelled like the bogs themselves, and Ael thought she might have something living inside that nest of hair, but he took her arm as if she were the most beautiful of court maidens and led her to Balin's sickbed.

"'Please, can you help him?' he cried.

"The woman ran a wrinkled, clawlike hand in a sweeping motion over Balin's prone form, murmuring to herself in a tongue Ael did not recognize.

"'I can, but it will take a great deal from the land. Why should I sacrifice so much for one man?' she asked in a voice like the rustling of dead leaves.

"Nonplussed, the family grew angry. What could she mean? Of course a man's life was worth so much more than any other creature or stretch of earth.

"'I love him more than my own life,' Ael cried. 'Whatever you ask in return, I will give.'

"The old woman studied Ael for a long time, making Ael's insides quake, but he didn't turn away. She had one dark eye, black as midnight, and one pale and milky like the full moon. Ael thought he saw stars glittering in the darker one, but it might have only been a trick of the light.

"Eventually she released him from her gaze and stared out the window for a time. Then she smiled, revealing an even row of teeth somewhat sharper than Ael expected. They gleamed greenish yellow at him and a shiver ran down his spine.

"'It waits out there for you,' she said cryptically.

"'What?'

"She shook her head. 'Tell the others to leave us, and I will name you my price.'

"Despite the objections of the others, Ael was a prince, and when he bade them leave, they had no choice but to obey.

"No one knows all that Ael agreed to in that room, for he never spoke of it again, even to Balin. The only thing that is known of that night is that Ael had one of Balin's cousins take him to the deepest heart of the boglands. Once there, the cousin watched in dismay as Ael tossed the magic sword into the murky waters, and it sank below the surface, never to be seen again.

"As if by some miracle, the next morning, Balin's wound had nearly healed, and he was able to sit up in bed and speak with his family and his lover.

"The old hag stayed at the farm for three more nights. Each day Ael would collapse in his lover's arms and sleep like the dead. Each night, despite any pleas from Balin or the family, Ael would follow the witch out into the dark and return, sweaty, pale, and exhausted.

"No matter how hard anyone entreated, Ael could not be brought to speak of it. But on the third morning, the swamp witch packed her bag of trinkets and charms and disappeared into the mists, leaving the two young lovers to rest and heal, wrapped in each other's arms. Safe and happy together at last.

"They say the sword is still out there, that no one in all the intervening centuries has been able to find it, no matter how hard they searched. They say whatever magic the witch worked with Ael hides it, or that she may have even called forth a god to protect it, a god that still haunts the deep places, waiting to snack on the unwary or anyone brazen enough to trespass in search of the sword. No one knows for sure, and the boglanders refuse to tell."

A heavy silence followed that last ominous pronouncement, and goose bumps flared along Daks's arms... until Horse whinnied behind them, making everyone jump.

"Nonsense," Daks blustered gruffly, shaking off the chill that had run along his spine. "Believe me, if there was a magic sword that powerful out there, someone would have hired a Sensitive to find it, or the Brotherhood would have used one of their Finders and confiscated it centuries ago."

Ravi's lip curled evilly as he shrugged. "I can only relate what the book said. Perhaps there is a god or something out there protecting it, waiting for the time when it's needed."

His amber eyes got a little dreamy, and Daks felt an answering tug in his chest... and lower. He scowled and turned his attention to the mist-shrouded darkness around them, opening his senses wide, searching for what felt like the thousandth time since entering this horrid place. Nothing but miles and miles of tangled, wet, rotting land met his senses. The hum of the place was eerie but harmless.

"If there were a god out there, or some other centuries-old bog monster Riftspawn, I'd be able to sense it," he huffed.

Horse snorted, making him jump again, and Daks threw a glare over his shoulder. Sometimes he swore the damned horse was laughing at him.

"So what happened to them after? Ael and Balin?" Fara asked.

"The histories are hazy on anything beyond their time in the boglands," Ravi replied with a somewhat self-conscious shrug, his dreamy expression fading. "The only thing they seem to agree on is that the prince and his love left Rassa together. Ael had stolen and lost his father's famous magic sword for the sake of a single man, so obviously, the king sent men in search of him and wasn't too pleased when they came back empty-handed. But Ael disappears from the histories after that, and only the other two princes, Rolf and Ero, are mentioned." Ravi's expression brightened as he turned to gaze out into the darkness again, and his voice turned wistful. "I like to think they found happiness and the peaceful, quiet life they always wanted, anonymously in a faraway library somewhere, maybe the scholar's guild library in Zehir or…." He shot a quick glance at Daks. "Or maybe the great library at the Scholomagi."

"Well, if they were at the Scholomagi, there'd be a record of it somewhere in that dusty old heap," Daks said with a chuckle. "They love their records."

He'd had no idea Ravi was such a romantic under all that crabbiness. It was sweet. His enthusiasm was contagious, and Daks briefly toyed with the idea of hanging around Scholoveld for a while after they delivered Ravi, to see if they could solve the mystery. But he quickly came to his senses again when a cold breeze blew smoke from the fire into his face. He shifted uncomfortably under Ravi's bright, hopeful gaze and added, "But we need to get there first, so enough stories for one night. Let's get some sleep so we can get to Traget all the faster tomorrow."

He felt a twinge of guilt when Ravi's open expression shuttered, but it was for the best. They'd all be parting ways soon enough, getting all romantic and dewy-eyed over a story—or a storyteller—would only lead to more pain later.

Shura took the first watch, and Daks curled up in his bedroll. One more full day of riding and they'd be out of this eerie place for good and in Traget buying their passage to freedom.

Chapter Nine

In the morning, Shura roused Ravi from another uneasy dream of that terrifying gray wall with a steaming mug of tea and some melted cheese on toasted three-day-old bread. He mumbled a hoarse thank-you as he sat up and took the offered meal, struggling to shake off the last cobwebs of sleep.

The ubiquitous fog crowded around them, much like his dream, shrouding everything beyond their little circle in dirty white and concealing the rest of the boglands from view. Ravi couldn't decide if this was a good thing or a bad thing as he bit into his toast and chewed.

Like he'd admitted to the others last night, after perhaps too much ale, the bogs had been a lot more romantic in his childhood imaginings. But the reality possessed a certain haunting charm of its own, a sense of mystery, of waiting and longing that could definitely fuel countless stories. Who knew? After this adventure, he might have a story or two of his own to tell… if they ever made it out of Rassa.

"The fog is worse today," Shura said, drawing him out of his thoughts before his mood could sour any more.

"We should be out of it soon enough," Daks replied with his characteristic unwarranted optimism, though his tone seemed more clipped and businesslike than his usual smug drawl. "We head back toward the Matna and the King's Road today."

He stood by the horses, checking straps and fiddling with their packs, his back ramrod straight, his attention fully focused on the task. Instead of the leather breeches Ravi had come to appreciate, he'd donned wool trousers and a linen tunic cut in the Rassan style.

He'd also tamed his bushy mane of hair into a braid down the back of his head that ended in a severe knot wrapped tightly in a leather cord. Even his whiskers had grown out enough to mask the scars on his jaw and neck, making him look almost respectable in the morning light.

The clothes should have been comfortingly familiar to Ravi, but they didn't hug the man's ass and thick thighs nearly as well. And for some reason Ravi couldn't quite fathom, his fingers itched to free Daks's hair from that uncomfortably tight-looking braid.

He shook his head and turned his attention back to what was left of his breakfast. Too many days of close contact with the man after more than a decade without touch had his mind going places it had no business. Whether or not he found the man attractive at all was pointless and irrelevant. Besides, Daks hadn't so much as looked in his general direction this morning. He'd obviously imagined the interest he'd seen in the man's eyes last night during his story.

Tales were tales and real life was real life. He was doomed if he hadn't learned that by now.

"Let's get going. We're wasting daylight, such as it is," Daks ordered without bothering to look up from whatever he was doing.

With a sigh, Ravi stood, walked to a pool of brackish water, and rinsed his mug before washing the grease from breakfast off his hands. After relieving himself behind one of the few moss-covered, drooping trees, he moved to stand behind Daks to silently await his turn to mount.

Without acknowledging him, Daks called out, "Shura, I want to give Horse a bit of a rest today, so I'll ride your mare for a while."

Ravi frowned at Daks's back before swinging a nervous glance in Shura's direction, hoping that didn't mean what he thought it meant.

The woman's black brows furrowed. "Is he showing signs of strain?"

Daks shrugged, still without deigning to acknowledge Ravi's existence. "I don't think so, but he's borne double the weight of the others for most of our journey. I think it best not to push him, just in case."

Much to Ravi's dismay, Shura simply shrugged and came toward them as Daks stepped away from the stallion. Ravi was tempted to voice an objection. He might be able to use his curse as an excuse not to come in close contact with yet another person. But they were in the woods, still a day's ride from Traget, so even if he had a Vision, it probably wouldn't be a big deal. Plus, it would mean admitting he was as scared of Shura as he was, *and* that he preferred having Daks pressed against his back. Neither seemed appealing, so he kept his mouth shut and prayed the woman wouldn't dump him off the horse at the first opportunity... or knock him out again at the first sign of a Vision.

The morning passed so slowly it was agony. Ravi kept himself as stiff in the saddle as he could without every muscle in his body cramping, making sure no part of him touched any part of her, if he could help it. Since she was still the best tracker, they took the lead on Horse, but the unnaturally heavy fog made traveling quickly impossible. They had to stop frequently for Shura to get down and check the track.

By what he thought might be noon, judging only by the slight change to the brightness of the fog around them, he'd fallen into a miserable stupor. No one had spoken a word in at least an hour, and even when they did speak, the fog seemed to muffle the sounds. He would have liked to throw a few glares back at Daks as he silently swore at the man for making a miserable trip even worse, but he doubted Daks would have been able to see him do it, and he sure as hells didn't want to risk locking gazes with Shura in the attempt. He only roused when the stallion suddenly stopped, making Ravi yelp and clutch the saddle.

Shura tugged on the reins and clucked at the beast, but it didn't move. After a few more tries, she let out what sounded like a curse in what was most likely Cigani and dismounted.

"What is it?" Mistress Sabin called behind them.

"Shura?" Daks called from farther back.

"Wait," Shura replied, holding up a hand as she took a few steps away, studying the trail and the heavy mist before tipping her head back and squinting upward.

"This is wrong," she growled. "I must have missed a split in the trail in all this blighted fog. We should have been heading north and east by now, according to the map farmer Vasin drew for us. We've been heading farther into the boglands for too long." She swore another couple of times in her own language while Daks let out a curse of his own. "It's a good thing this horse is so damned stubborn, or it might have taken me another hour to realize it," she muttered, coming back to them.

"We're lost?" Ravi asked and winced as his voice cracked.

Shura narrowed her eyes at him. "Not lost. We just missed the track back there. We'll have to turn around and try to find it, if this blighted fog will let us."

She was obviously not in a good mood, so he clamped his mouth shut on any further commentary while she pulled the map from one of the packs. Daks dismounted too and started toward them.

Deciding to take the opportunity presented to him, Ravi dropped awkwardly to the ground to get some blood back in his legs and unlock his spine. Once he was on his feet, his bladder complained, and he moved away from the others as Daks and Shura bowed their heads over the map. Finding somewhere private wasn't much of a challenge in the heavy curtain of fog, so he didn't have to venture far off the trail. He could still hear the others discussing their predicament, but as soon as he was "alone," their voices sounded strangely far off, and an ominous feeling tingled along his spine, sort of like….

Hells!

His chest tightened as he nervously searched his surroundings. This wasn't a Vision, though, but one of those feelings Daks had told him to look out for.

"Guys," he called, rushing back to them.

As he drew closer, the mist cleared enough for him to see Shura coming toward him, with Daks a close second. He was just about to explain when he tripped over something hidden in the long grass.

As he struggled to right himself, a rope snapped taut near his head, forcing him to duck to the side. He let out an embarrassingly high-pitched yelp as he broke into a stumbling run toward the others.

Daks cried out a warning, and Ravi spun around in time to see the large tree limb barreling toward him, but not in time to do anything more than close his eyes and cringe. The wood caught him in the chest and sent him flying. Before he could even register the pain of the blow, he hit the water. Momentarily stunned, all he could do was sink below the murky surface until instinct took over and he flailed his arms and legs. The bog wasn't deep, but mud and reeds beneath the surface clutched at him, tangling worse the more he struggled. He started to panic, clawing at whatever clung to his legs as foul-smelling water tried to force its way into his nose and mouth. But then a large body crashed into the water nearby and a strong arm wrapped around his middle.

"Ravi, stop! Stop struggling! I got you," Daks yelled, and finally the man's oddly strained voice registered through his terror and he went limp with relief.

Daks pulled him to the solid ground and collapsed next to him as Ravi fell to his hands and knees and started coughing out the foulness he'd inhaled. His chest hurt a lot where the limb had hit him, and it took every ounce of his concentration to try to pull air into his lungs after each cough.

"Ravi, are you all right? Where are you hurt?"

Daks's voice shook so much Ravi hardly recognized it. He wanted to say something comforting back, but he couldn't get enough air. Trembling fingers fumbled at his throat, and soon the unbearable weight of the sodden wool cloak fell from his shoulders. Ravi sucked in a relieved breath, thinking he might at last have enough air for a thank-you or a reassurance, but it stuttered in his chest as Daks's big, frantic hands began roaming his body.

"Tell me where you're hurt," Daks rasped.

Ravi had almost reached the point where every breath was no longer agony, but he hesitated, oddly enjoying the attention. Then guilt made him pull away and wave Daks off with one limp hand.

"Give me… a minute," he wheezed. "Breath… knocked out of me."

He settled onto his ass, his boots still trailing in the mud, and put a hand to his diaphragm while he propped himself up with the other.

"Shura, are you okay?" Daks called harshly, and Ravi turned to find her nodding as she held her left arm close to her body

"It just clipped my shoulder," Shura bit out, before turning to glare at Ravi. "What were you thinking? Of all the idiotic, useless—" She let out a string of words in her own language Ravi didn't understand, but he was pretty sure they weren't flattering, until Daks cut her off.

"That's enough, Shur. It wasn't his fault, and I'm all right."

They shared another one of their long looks, before Shura nodded once, begrudgingly, and turned to Mistress Sabin, who hovered at her elbow.

Ravi clenched his jaw in both guilt and anger and attempted to struggle to his feet. Daks appeared at his side before Ravi got even halfway up, though he didn't seem completely steady either. They were both soaked to the skin, shivering, and covered in muck that smelled as bad as it looked.

"I'm okay," Ravi protested, which was mostly true.

He'd have a huge bruise on his chest and it hurt to breathe, but he could stand without aid. Daks's dark blue eyes seemed a little wild when Ravi met his gaze, but after a few seconds of study, Daks nodded, blew out a shaky breath, and withdrew his hands. Without another word, Daks turned and headed toward the women.

"Is it bad?" Daks asked Shura.

Her dark eyes were oddly intent as she studied Daks's face. "No. It'll hurt for a while, but I can still use it."

To demonstrate, she flexed and rotated it while Mistress Sabin pressed her lips together in obvious disapproval.

"What happened?" Mistress Sabin asked.

"Trap," Shura answered grimly.

She was still watching Daks closely, but she spared a small glare for Ravi before turning back to stare at her partner... but Daks's eyes had that vacant look they took on when he used his gift.

After a few seconds, he shook his head. "If there's anyone out there, I can't sense them. There's no magic."

He moved to the branch that had struck them and crouched down, examining the ropes. "This has been here a while. I don't think it was meant to do any real harm, only deter unwanted visitors. It's just our bad lu—" He cleared his throat. "We just ventured too far from the safe path."

"But that's dangerous, leaving something like that out here," Mistress Sabin protested. "Anyone could chance upon it. That could have killed a child."

"I imagine anyone out here who's supposed to be would know how to avoid it. I think the moral of the story is, don't stray too far from the road."

Ravi winced, but how could he have possibly known? As if the bugs, the muck, the wet, and the cold weren't enough, he had to worry about traps too? He'd only wanted to pee.

"Ravi, can you travel?' Daks asked brusquely, jerking Ravi's attention back to him.

"Yes."

Even if he couldn't, he certainly wouldn't have admitted it.

Cursed. I'm cursed.

"Good. Let's get the horses turned around and see if we can find that trail we missed."

Without a backward glance, Daks moved to where the horses and the mule had retreated and began sorting them out. Luckily for all of them, Horse seemed to have corralled the other three and kept them from bolting in the excitement.

Daks didn't seem at all bothered by the fact that he was soaked from the neck down anymore, but Ravi shivered again as he grabbed his sodden borrowed cloak off the ground and made his slow, somewhat pained way to join the others. At least the fog seemed to be lifting. That was something.

"We should take a look at your wound too," Shura called out as she approached them.

"It's fine."

"*Vaida*, you may have torn the stitches we put in at the farm," she argued.

Daks shook his head. "It'll wait." He turned to Ravi, his face set in a frown. "You can change into dry clothes now if you need to, but I'm going to wait until we're closer to Traget and I can find a clean stream or pool in the river to wash in."

Ravi's lovely borrowed clothes were clammy, covered in mud, and smelled of bog, but he shook his head and said, "I'll wait."

With a brusque nod, Daks turned to Shura. "Take the mare up front. We'll follow."

While Ravi blinked at him in surprise, Daks collected the heavy sodden cloak from him and walked to the mule. When he returned, he carried Ravi's old cloak, freshly cleaned and mended.

"Climb up," Daks ordered, handing him the cloak and nodding to the stallion.

His face was still set in a heavy frown, and Ravi wanted to snap something biting to defend himself. He hadn't done anything wrong. Daks had no right to be mad at him. But since he hadn't exactly been looking forward to sharing another ride with Shura, especially while she was angry with him, his chest hurt, and he smelled like he did, he kept his mouth shut. He'd say something later… *much* later, like when they were safely in Samebar kind of later. Then he'd tell both of them to go to the Seven Hells.

Much to everyone's relief, Shura found the track they should have taken easily, now that the fog had cleared some. The entrance was completely overgrown, and Ravi probably would have missed it even on the second pass, but he didn't try to offer those words of comfort to her. Her scowl was nearly as forbidding as Daks's.

The rest of their ride that day was still miserable, despite the air clearing and the sun brightening the farther they headed away from the bogs. Damp, muddy, and shivering, Ravi had to work for each breath around the throbbing band of pain across his chest. Having

Daks's big body pressed to his back, solid and warm, helped, but he wouldn't mention that either. Best to keep quiet and hope everyone forgot he was there.

The sun had sunk low in the sky by the time they crossed the shallows of the Bael river a few hours south of Traget. When Daks dismounted on the far bank and said he was going to head upstream to wash and change, Ravi followed him. He wasn't looking forward to the frigid water, but the promise of clean, dry clothes gave him courage.

He kept his hood up and trudged along silently, lost in his own thoughts, until Daks stopped abruptly and began stripping. Ravi stood rooted to the spot as Daks removed each piece of muddy clothing and tossed it into a small pool of water nestled among the reeds and rocks, seemingly unconcerned or unembarrassed about having an audience. Biting his lip, Ravi turned away, wondering if he should find his own bathing place, but the sounds of splashing drew his gaze back to Daks like a lodestone.

The man was undeniably well put together. Barrel-chested and broad shouldered, with thick arms and thighs—everything about him was thick. Ravi swallowed against a suddenly dry throat. When Daks caught him staring, the frown he'd sported for hours morphed into that infuriating grin, and he winked and quirked an eyebrow, making Ravi flush and turn his head away again. The man was impossible.

"Should we, uh, do something about that?" Ravi asked, waving a hand behind him in the general direction of Daks's midsection. Daks snorted and Ravi's cheeks flamed hotter.

"Your bandage. Your stitches," he qualified.

"You could come check it out for me if you'd like," Daks replied with a smile in his voice.

Ravi tried to glare at him, but Daks just shrugged and lowered himself into the pool with a hiss and shiver. He began washing himself and his clothes while Ravi hovered uncertainly on the bank.

When minutes passed and Ravi still hadn't joined him, Daks let out a heavy sigh and said, "If you're feeling prudish, find another pool upstream and set to. The sun isn't going to get any higher, and we have a few more miles to go before we reach any settlements around Traget. We'll miss the last ferry tonight, but I'd like to find Vasin's cousin, drop off the horses, and find somewhere to settle before true dark sets in."

"Fine," Ravi huffed, lifting his chin stubbornly, "but at least turn around and give me some privacy."

Daks's mocking smile faded as he shot an odd glance over his shoulder at the river before rolling his eyes and turning his back to Ravi. The man had churned up the silt a bit in the pool where he was, so Ravi should try to find a cleaner spot upriver. But with his luck, he'd have a Vision and drown, or something else equally horrible would happen.

At least that's what he told himself as he began to disrobe.

He brought his soiled clothes with him into the water to try to wash the worst of the muck off, as Daks had done. The water was cold enough to make him gasp, but he gritted his teeth and plunged in anyway.

Without soap, his clothes wouldn't be anywhere near as clean as when he'd received them, but they'd be slightly more presentable. When he turned back after pounding a particularly difficult stain on the rocks, he found Daks watching him as he the man bobbed lazily in the water nearby.

"It's not as cold, once you get used to it," Daks murmured.

His eyes had gone a little heavy-lidded, and his voice had deepened and softened somehow. Feeling uncomfortable and a little short of breath, Ravi shook his head and turned his back again.

"You're crazy. It's still freezing."

Small waves lapped at his hips as he felt Daks approach, but Ravi didn't turn around.

"I could help warm you up if you like."

Daks's voice was downright husky, and a shiver ran down Ravi's spine that had nothing to do with the icy water. If he weren't already covered in goose bumps, he would have been now, and his sudden difficulty breathing had nothing to do with the line of bruises across his chest.

He stood frozen, clutching his wet clothes, the air heavy and silent but for their breathing and the rush of the river beyond their quiet, secluded little pool.

Why not?

This hadn't exactly been what he'd dreamed of for his first real sexual encounter as an adult, but when had reality ever lived up to his dreams? Daks was big and warm. He was also handsome in his own peculiar way, despite being a little rough around the edges. Ravi had wondered more than once what his skin felt like, how his mouth tasted, and what those big hands would feel like on his body, touching sensually rather than clinically.

It had been so long since he'd been able to really touch anyone. His hands suddenly ached to map the planes of Daks's body, to feel the ridges of muscle and bone and trace the scars with his fingertips, but he gripped the clothes tighter in his fists and swallowed against the need vibrating through his body.

Why not? Because I can't risk it. That's why not.

Not yet anyway.

He didn't have the strength to actually step away from all that offered heat and comfort, but he had enough to clear his throat and say, "I thought you said we needed to get going."

"I suppose a couple of minutes here or there wouldn't hurt," Daks replied, the shrug obvious in his tone.

That note of indifference broke the spell. This was not what Ravi wanted. A couple of minutes of stolen pleasure with a virtual stranger wasn't worth the risk. He wanted more… at least a bed, for Harot's sake. Besides, Daks had either ignored him or growled at him all day—except for the part where he jumped in the bog and rescued him from drowning.

Why did the man have to be so confusing?

With an enormous exertion of willpower, Ravi stepped to the side and climbed up the bank, uncaring that Daks was watching.

"No, you were right before," he said, his voice becoming more determined as he spoke. "We should push on. I'm hungry and I'm cold."

He didn't bother to look back as he dried himself as best he could on his cloak and dressed in his old clothes. Despite being freshly cleaned and mended better than he'd ever managed on his own, the feel of their worn, patched layers against his skin was comfortingly familiar. And when he donned his slightly damp, ratty old cloak and his ratty old boots and tugged the hood up to hide his face, he breathed out a sigh of relief. This was who he was… for now, anyway.

No more touching. No more letting his guard down.

Maybe when they'd crossed the Matna into Samebar and were safely nestled into an inn, he might reconsider Daks's offer. That is, if the man wanted to repeat it when there might be more tempting options available. But that was a chance he'd have to take.

Without waiting for Daks, he bundled up his wet, soiled clothes and headed back to where they'd left the others. Daks didn't say anything when he returned a few minutes later, dressed in his old leather breeches and tunic. His expression was unreadable as he encouraged everyone to mount up. He didn't look as cross as he had earlier. He didn't even look disappointed, which niggled Ravi's pride a little. Obviously, Ravi's rejection didn't hurt that much, which should have made him feel better, affirming that he'd made the right choice. But it still stung, and he kept his back ramrod stiff and rode in stony silence for the rest of their journey.

The ground and air dried out significantly the farther they traveled away from the boglands, and Ravi sighed in relief when the horses finally turned onto the broad, wonderfully dry King's Road, despite the increased danger they were in.

As they drew nearer to Traget, the houses along the road grew closer together and more and more people appeared, going about their daily business. Ravi hunched deeper inside his cloak and stared at the back of the stallion's head, praying silently to any god who would listen to take pity on him for once and keep his Visions at bay. He'd been concentrating so hard on not looking at anyone that he jumped when Horse finally stopped and Daks dismounted.

Blinking blearily in the fading light, he spotted a small cabin with a light in the window and a smoking chimney a short distance away.

"If Vasin's directions are correct, this should be the place," Daks said as Shura and Mistress Sabin also dismounted. "We've obviously missed the last ferry, so let's see if this cousin of Vasin's will allow us to set up camp on his land tonight, and we'll head for the ferry at first light."

"I'd also like to talk to him," Mistress Sabin said.

Daks pursed his lips and shot a glance toward Shura before he nodded.

"How are you? Any bad feelings?"

It took Ravi a couple of seconds to realize Daks was actually talking to him for the first time since they'd left the river. When he did, his chest warmed a little at the man's concern, until he realized Daks was asking about his curse, not his well-being.

"Nothing yet. But I probably should avoid new people as much as possible," he admitted just a little petulantly.

"Okay, you stay here with Horse, and we'll take Vasin's cousin the other three animals and be back as soon as we can."

"You're keeping it?" Shura asked, lifting a skeptical brow.

Daks shrugged, and his lips curved ruefully. "He wasn't part of the original bargain, and honestly, I'm not sure he'd stay wherever we put him anyway. He likes me. What can I say?"

Shura snorted. "No accounting for taste."

Ravi smirked in the shadows of his hood.

Daks gave her a playful scowl. "He can carry our packs, and we'll need horses for the journey to Scholoveld anyway. He'll be one less thing we'll have to bargain for on the other side."

"You'll have to pay for his spot on the ferry."

"We have enough," Daks replied without meeting her gaze.

Shura studied him for a few moments before rolling her eyes. "Let's go. I'm tired and hungry."

Ravi climbed down from the stallion's back as the women led the mares away. Everything ached, but that wasn't anything new. He started to search for a good tree to settle against when he felt someone watching him. Daks had hung back from the women and was studying him with a concerned frown.

When Ravi lifted his eyebrows in question, Daks said, "We'll be back soon. If you sense any trouble, anything at all, get on the horse and ride away. We'll find you."

With that pronouncement, he spun and strode off to join the others, leaving Ravi feeling irritated and confused all over again. He was having a hard time keeping up with Daks's mood swings. One minute the man was cranky and aloof, the next concerned and solicitous, and then the next angling for a quick tumble in the reeds.

Thankfully, Daks was true to his word and returned swiftly, before sitting on the damp cold ground in the dark with only a horse for company lost its charm. Ravi's heart skipped a beat when he first heard the crunch of boots approaching, but Daks called out to him before he could truly panic.

His relieved smile drooped in confusion when he realized Daks was alone in the circle of light provided by the lantern he carried.

"Where are the others?"

"Fara wanted to pump the man for as much information as possible, rebel business I guess, and Shura stayed to listen in."

"Oh."

Daks paused expectantly, but when Ravi didn't come up with anything more intelligent than that, he shrugged. "With the number of soldiers and brothers in town, he recommended we err on the side of caution and move no closer tonight. He didn't seem hostile, but he wasn't as encouraging or helpful as his cousin. We'll likely not get much more out of him than permission to stay on his land, maybe some food, and this." Daks held up a small flask. "Fara still wanted to try to get him to open up, but I wasn't in the mood to tiptoe and needle for hours."

He moved to the tree next to Ravi's and sat on the ground at its base. After uncorking the bottle, he took a swig before offering it to Ravi. "No fire tonight. Too risky with soldiers on patrol. Don't want to draw attention unless we really have to." Ravi accepted the bottle and nearly choked on the strong spirit it contained. "Luckily," Daks continued as he coughed, "the night shouldn't be too cold, although the clouds are looking a little ominous. Pray to whoever you like that the rain holds off until we're across the river tomorrow."

When Daks lifted his hand, Ravi returned the flask to it willingly, wiping his watering eyes.

"Settle in. Get comfortable," Daks continued after taking another swig. "Shura said they'd try to wheedle something hot out of the guy, but if they can't, we'll dig out what's left of the food in our packs when they get back."

That seemed to be the extent of Daks's conversation for the evening, because he leaned his head back and closed his eyes. Ravi worried his lower lip as he studied the man for a few beats in the lantern light. It appeared he would be getting distant and aloof Daks again, and he wasn't sure if he should be relieved or disappointed.

Either Shura and Mistress Sabin were better at extracting information than Daks thought or they gave up early, because it wasn't long before they joined them. They'd even been able to acquire some hot meat pies and a small pot of stew, and Ravi practically inhaled his portions with so much gratitude it made his eyes a little misty. He'd never complain about the food they'd cooked on the journey, but a hot meal with fresh meat, herbs, and vegetables compared to dried, was a thing of true beauty he hadn't been allowed often enough over the last ten years to take for granted.

Daks remained mostly silent during the meal, and though he offered the flask around, no one took him up on it. After a while Ravi began to think maybe one of them should have, if only to limit the amount left for Daks, and apparently, he wasn't the only one. He caught Shura eyeing her partner worriedly several times during the meal and after, which didn't exactly inspire confidence. She didn't say anything, though, and Ravi began to get angry.

Screwing up his courage, he decided to try to catch Shura alone. If anyone could get Daks to behave, it was her. Ravi certainly didn't want to try after everything that had happened between them earlier. Besides, he might lose his temper completely and say something he shouldn't, and he still needed these people for a few more hours at least.

When Shura rose and left their little circle of lantern light, probably to relieve herself, Ravi waited a few minutes and then followed. He hung back at the edge of the shadows to allow her some privacy, but when she returned, he held up a hand to stop her.

"I think you should do something about him," Ravi said, his voice cracking slightly under her forbidding stare.

She didn't bother to ask who he meant. "He's fine."

Ravi narrowed his eyes and lifted his chin, his temper overtaking caution. "He's not fine. He's been drinking from that flask since he came back. We've only got one more day before we're in Samebar. He can't wait one more day?"

Her lips pressed together as she folded her arms across her chest. "I assume you come to me because you believe I know him better than you, so accept it when I tell you he will be fine."

Seeing that she'd dug in her heels, Ravi blew out a breath and decided to take a different tack. "But is he okay? I mean, he did save me this morning. If there's something I can do…."

He left the words hanging, and her expression softened a little as she studied him before turning to glance at her partner and then at Mistress Sabin. When she turned back to him, her dark eyes held a deep sadness he'd never expected to see, and it threw him off balance.

She studied him for a few beats more before she seemed to make a decision. "The journey tomorrow will be challenging for him." She said the words as if each one hurt her to admit. "We will not speak of this again, but if you must know the why of it, I will tell you. He has no love for water. Many years ago, before I met him, he nearly drowned, and the resulting illness cost him dearly. After this morning's little dip, and with tomorrow looming, he is not entirely himself."

Ravi blinked at her in surprise and screwed up his face. "Uh. He has a fear of water and he comes to Rassa, the wettest of all the three kingdoms? Are you serious? Good gods, the only place worse for him would be the Southern Isles."

Her frown returned full force as her eyes narrowed. "Don't make me regret telling you. He may not be the most pleasant of companions until we are all safely on the other side of the Matna tomorrow, but don't let that get in the way of doing as you are told, *when* you are told. Do not argue. Do not question. He has risked much to get you to safety. Remember that. He has crossed the Matna many times, and he will do so again. He will do as he must."

With that, she spun on her heel and headed back to Mistress Sabin's side, leaving Ravi to trail pensively behind her. Daks had fallen asleep by the time he got back, still clutching the flask to his chest, and Ravi studied his face in the lamplight. At least some of his strangeness made more sense now.

He saved me.

Despite his own fears, and despite all the trouble Ravi had caused, Daks had saved him.

Why?

From the way Daks had talked, Samebar had plenty of Seers. One more, and an unreliable one at that, couldn't be worth all this effort. Ravi had purposefully played up the guilt card, and Daks had given his word, but Ravi lived in the real world. He knew how much a man's word was worth. If it weren't for him, Shura and Daks could have just hopped on a boat back to Samebar and been somewhere safe by now.

"Why?" he whispered aloud this time.

"What?" Shura asked.

Embarrassed, Ravi mumbled, "Nothing."

"Go to sleep. We have an early start tomorrow."

"Good night," he said as he curled his cloak around himself and turned his back.

"Good night," Mistress Sabin said, and someone snuffed out the lamp.

All fell silent around them but for the periodic call of an owl, the chirping of insects, and Daks's light snores. The air was heavy, cool, and damp, reminding Ravi of Daks's concerns about rain. He curled into an even tighter ball and sent up a prayer to merciful Quanna that the weather would hold until they found shelter on the other side.

Tomorrow, his new life began. He clung to that knowledge as too many other worries, thoughts, and feelings vied for attention in his head.

Chapter Ten

Daks had their gear repacked and secured to Horse well before sunrise. Not that he'd be able to tell the exact moment the sun crested the horizon beyond the heavy clouds that had rolled in, but he'd worked mostly in complete darkness despite his roaring headache and queasy stomach. Whatever was in that flask Vasin's cousin gave him, it sure packed a punch.

Once he'd dressed in the less conspicuous, though slightly worse for wear, Rassan style clothing again, he roused everyone else. They all groggily agreed not to bother with breakfast. They could find something in the market square if they had time before the first ferry left. And if not, they'd eat at Eben's comfortable and well-stocked inn on the other side. They were so close, Daks could almost taste Eben's famous ale and meat pies already, and he licked his lips despite the angry gurgle in his belly.

Tipping his head back, he glared up at the clouds. He absolutely refused to allow whatever bad luck, sick twist of fate, or that Rassan god of mischief Ravi accused him of praying to even one more chance to get in the way.

"Everyone ready?" he called brusquely.

After receiving sleepy, disgruntled nods in return, he took Horse's reins and started a brisk walk toward Traget. Luckily, Vasin's cousin didn't live too far outside of the town proper, and they reached the outskirts just as the temple bells began to ring for morning hymn. Like everyone around them, Daks reluctantly paused and piously bowed his head when the bells rang out, taking the opportunity to search their surroundings with his gift while everyone was busy praying.

The hum of a large town, with so many bodies crowded together, made it nearly impossible to discover any subtler magics from this distance, but at least he didn't feel any members of the Thirty-Six. The rumors were accurate thus far.

Opening his eyes, he scanned the people around them and the market up ahead. He didn't like the amount of guard blue he saw, but he wasn't surprised. They'd been warned. He imagined, once the morning hymns were sung, there would be a great many bloodred robes joining the throng too, which made him itch with the need to get moving.

Since he was stuck until the bells stopped, he closed his eyes and sent his gift out again, just in case. And this time, a strange tingle caught his attention from the direction of the market. It was too subtle for active magic, but it didn't feel like a charm or an enchanted object either. Frowning uneasily, he strained to find it again, but like a scent on the wind, it was gone before he could identify or locate it.

When the bells stopped and the people around them began moving again, Daks blew out a breath, clenched his jaw, and charged ahead. Whatever he'd sensed didn't matter, as long as it didn't get between him and that ferry. He was done being curious for the rest of his Rift-blighted life—or at least until he started getting fat and bored back home. At the moment, he was very much looking forward to a little comfortable boredom.

Traget's marketplace was larger and more diverse than any other in Rassa, outside of the king's city. Merchants and farmers were already at their stalls, hawking their wares to passersby as soon as the bells stopped and customers in garb from all over Kita had begun to fill the streets—perfect for a few strangers heading toward the ferry to blend in and remain largely unnoticed.

So why was he gripping the reins so tight his fingers lost feeling?

Because it would be just their shit luck for something to go wrong. And even if nothing went wrong, he still had the lovely river crossing to look forward to.

I hate water. I hate boats. I hate ferries. I hate everything about this cursed kingdom.

As they made their snaillike progress through the bustling market, he kept his head low and reminded himself not to scowl so much or he'd spook the locals. The ferry didn't leave Pazar to return to Traget until after the morning bells. Vasin's cousin had assured them the schedule hadn't changed. And even when it arrived, passengers and carts had to disembark before anyone could board. They still had plenty of time.

Keep calm. Everything will be fine. You're almost there and you've done the ferry before. It's good and sturdy.

But even as he tried to convince himself nothing was wrong, a sensation of being watched prickled along his spine. He searched the people around him as best he could without drawing any more attention their way and found nothing but smiling merchants hoping to catch his eye, bored soldiers, and the odd surprised look when a passerby spotted Shura. Ravi shuffled behind him, his head bowed and hood up. He'd switched back to the better quality borrowed cloak and boots that morning, so he looked like any other servant trudging through his daily labors and was largely ignored, with Shura drawing most of the mildly curious looks.

Daks could have blamed the sensation of being watched on her, but he didn't spot anyone actually staring. One of the reasons they'd decided on Traget was because visiting Cigani merchants weren't unheard of in the market. She shouldn't have been that much of an anomaly, yet the itch between his shoulders persisted.

Finally, when he couldn't take it anymore, he gave up all pretense of being sneaky and boldly searched their surroundings. He didn't spot the man until his second pass around the market. Leaning against the side of an inn, several merchant stalls behind them, stood a tall, red-bearded older man in plain homespun clothing, holding a tankard in one hand while his other rested on the hip of the rather pretty dark-haired youth pressed to his side. After studying the man for a few seconds, Daks realized the jerk was staring at one member of their group in particular, but it wasn't Shura.

Scowling, Daks dropped back to stand closer to Ravi, blocking the red-beard's view. The man met Daks's gaze with bright, amused green eyes, and the bloody bastard actually winked. Ravi let out a startled noise when Daks dragged him against his side, but Daks didn't take his eyes off the red-beard. He glared hard at the man, but that only made the bastard's grin widen.

In a parting gesture he hoped red-beard understood, Daks also bared his teeth, but in a much less pleasant manner. With Ravi still clamped to his side, he began pushing more forcefully through the crowd.

Pimp, procurer, slaver, or just horny old goat, whatever red-beard was, he'd need to find some other lamb to pounce on.

By the time they reached the ferry landing, Daks was sweating hard, and Ravi had pulled away from him, giving him a confused scowl. That was fine with Daks. Ravi could stay angry until they were all safely in Samebar. Shura lifted her eyebrows at him, but he gave her the look that said they'd talk about it later.

"How many?" the thin little man taking the coins at the landing asked in trade tongue, not bothering to look up from his tally slate.

"Four and a horse," Daks replied, palming the sad little pile of coins left in their purse.

The man glanced up at him then, assessing before cocking his head to study Daks's companions. "Four coppers a head, and a silver for the horse," he said in a monotone.

Daks gave a purely internal wince. He hoped Eben would be fine with taking credit for their stay at his inn, because Daks *really* didn't want to give up that horse. A beast like that was worth at least twenty times that much. He'd take the cost out of his own salary when he reached Scholoveld.

"Done," Daks said begrudgingly as he counted out the coins for the three of them and the horse.

Then Fara stepped forward to hand over her portion.

"We can only take two of you now, and not the horse," the man added, after taking their coin, and Daks tensed.

He glanced in confusion at the few people who'd been ahead of them in line and at the number of people still disembarking the sizable ferry.

"Why?"

The man tipped his chin toward a large, heavily-laden wagon in a fenced yard behind him. "That goes on first thing. Merchant paid extra last night."

As he spoke, a man in plain but quality wool clothing led a large horse toward the wagon and began hitching it up.

"If you want to go together, you'll have to wait for the next one."

The man holding the slate returned Daks's glare with a bored stare of his own, and Daks was sorely tempted to wipe that bland expression off his face, but he held his temper. Too many guards around.

"What's wrong?" Shura asked in Cigani at his elbow.

"He says only two of us can cross now, and not with the horse," he replied in the same language.

Shura threw a glare at the man too, which seemed to have a slightly better effect, but he still lifted his chin stubbornly and waved for the people in line behind them to come forward, calling, "First ferry is full. Taking payment for the next."

The couple behind them, a young man and woman in plain homespun carrying bundles of pastries, eyed them warily as they took a few nervous steps forward, and Daks took pity on them and stepped to the side.

"You go. Take the Seer with you. Fara and I will follow with the horse," Shura said as soon as they were out of the way.

Daks shook his head. He didn't like the thought of separating now, even for only a couple of hours. They were so close to the safety of their home kingdom, but a very large body of water separated the two. He wouldn't be able to come charging back to help if anything happened.

"You need to get *him* out of here," she said, tossing a look at Ravi. "You know this. So then it is either you or I who must go with him, and I—" She hesitated and cast a furtive, almost shy glance toward Fara. "I would prefer to stay and go on the second ferry."

Daks was tempted to tease her, but one narrow-eyed glare from her stopped him. "I don't like it," he said uselessly.

"Neither do I. But this is the best we have. He is the reason we rush. There may be no pain priests here, but there are plenty of soldiers. And if they're fortifying against a wizard, I would assume they would have at least one Sensitive here as well. The Seer must go first."

Daks lifted a troubled gaze to the town behind them, remembering the strange feeling he'd had and the man watching them in the market. She was right. They had to get Ravi out first, before anything else could happen.

"Ravi," he called, "you're with me."

Ravi startled as if he'd been miles away, but he moved to Daks's side without saying anything. Shura moved to Fara's side and explained the situation. Then they all waited in heavy silence as the last of the debarking passengers trundled up the landing toward the market.

The ferry consisted of thick tree trunks lashed together, with a layer of planks nailed to the top and a railing to keep anyone from accidentally pitching into the water. A huge rope, as thick as Daks's arm, spanned the narrowest spot on the Matna and was connected to a large wheel on either side. Massive horses turned the wheels on each bank to pull the raft across while the current tried to push it downriver. Everything about the setup seemed sturdy and well-maintained, but Daks's stomach still churned just thinking about trusting his life to it. He had no intention of letting anyone else see his distress, but Shura knew and eyed him with concern, which only made him more irritable.

Swallowing against the sudden tightness in his throat, he turned his back on the water so he wouldn't have to think about it more than absolutely necessary, now that it was almost time. Ravi stepped closer to him, close enough Daks could feel the heat from his body and the brush of his cloak against the back of his hand. Daks glanced down at him curiously, but Ravi's head was bent as usual, hiding his face within the shadows of his hood.

"Are you all right? Is your chest hurting you?" Daks asked.

"I'm okay... just ready to be across the river and away from all these people," he answered tightly.

Daks nodded.

"Soon," he replied, trying to sound reassuring despite the fear riding him.

Daks shifted from foot to foot as he waited for the last of the passengers to get out of the way. Focusing on his breathing, he sucked in a long, slow breath and blew it out again, studiously ignoring the sound of rushing water at his back and the thick, dark clouds overhead. When Horse suddenly snorted and raised its head, Daks nearly jumped out of his skin. He scowled at it, but the stallion was looking over its shoulder, back toward the town.

Daks searched the milling throng for anything amiss. A few brothers in russet robes had joined the crowds heading toward the market, but none of them seemed to be paying them any attention. But as Horse continued to stare fixedly at something, the hairs on the back of Daks's neck rose. He sent his gift out one more time when his other senses failed him, and that odd whisper of magic brushed his consciousness again. His heart kicked up, and he searched every shadow and every face until his eyes stung. When he spotted the red-beard and his companion again, he tensed. The man had moved from his perch by the inn and was watching them from the edge of the market now.

"Shura," he murmured under his breath, "red beard, northern end of the square. Can you see him?"

Both women turned in the direction he indicated as he felt Ravi shift and tense by his side.

"I see him," Shura replied.

"He's watching us. I saw them earlier too. I didn't think it meant anything, but there they are again. He's clearly watching us, right?"

"He is. He's not a guard or a priest," Shura said.

"No, I don't think so."

"Do you sense anything?"

"Maybe... I'm not sure." Daks dragged a hand through his hair, his fingers catching in the braid, and gritted his teeth. "I don't like it."

"Forget it," Shura said firmly. "Go. Get on the ferry. They can watch all they like. It changes nothing. He can't be a mage, not in Rassa—unless he has a death wish—so whoever he is, he can't interfere with your crossing."

"But you'll still be—"

"For an hour, maybe two. I'll keep an eye on him, but we will be fine here. We can handle ourselves."

Daks closed his mouth, swallowed his anxiety, and nodded. To keep arguing with her would only insult her and piss her off, neither of which he wanted to risk.

"Loading next ferry. Next ferry loading!" the little man with the slate barked out, and Daks grimaced.

He searched the space where red-beard and his companion had been once more, but the two men were gone.

"Just be careful, okay?" Daks said, holding her gaze.

She smiled. "Always. See you on the other side, *Vaida*."

"You better."

He turned away from her and forced himself to walk to the ferry while Ravi shuffled along silently behind him. The cart and horse were loaded onto the ferry first before the other passengers were allowed to squeeze on around it. Daks gave the cart and driver an ugly scowl as he moved to the far side of the deck, making the man start and eye him nervously.

Once he'd found them an empty spot, he gripped the rail tightly and kept his gaze riveted on the far shore, away from the swirling murky water below him and the thickening clouds above. He really hoped the rain would hold off until Shura managed to make it across, not that a little rain should make the crossing more dangerous, but he thought he just might've glimpsed a flash of lightning in the far-off mountains. If that storm moved south, it could delay the next ferry considerably.

A horn blared behind him, and the ferry jerked as the rope pulled taut a few moments later. He swallowed thickly and breathed in the fishy, damp air through his nostrils before blowing it out again through his mouth. He took several breaths like this until he could release his white-knuckled grip on the railing.

Ravi pressed closer to his side, and when Daks glanced down at him in surprise, Ravi's bright amber gaze held his, shadowed with concern.

"Will you be all right?" he asked quietly.

Daks frowned. He hadn't thought he was that obvious. "I'm fine."

It came out a little gruffer than he'd intended, but Ravi didn't look away.

Ravi was silent for a few beats before he licked his lips and said, "Shura told me what happened to you, years ago. I just... I wanted to say thank you for what you did in the boglands and for all this, now. I haven't said it yet, and I should have. If there's anything I can do to help, I will."

Despite the pitch and sway of the chunk of wood barely separating them from watery death, Daks felt his lips curve. "Don't get soft on me now. You're going to make me think you might just like me a little."

Ravi's open, concerned expression closed off, and Daks was immediately sorry. He shouldn't poke. He knew he shouldn't, but he just couldn't seem to help himself sometimes.

Ravi took a step back, putting distance between them, and Daks felt the loss like a punch to the chest. Without thinking, he released his death grip on the railing, snagged Ravi's hand, and squeezed it.

"I'm sorry. I'm an ass. If Shura told you, then you know why, but that's no excuse. I appreciate the gratitude, but it's not necessary. I'm partly to blame for the mess in the first place, remember? Plus, that bit by the river yesterday wasn't fair with everything else going on. I shouldn't have teased you." He was rambling. He knew he should stop but couldn't seem to stem the nervous flow of words. "We'll be safe on the other side in no time, and we'll both get a good, hot meal and a long rest… and maybe start over? How's that sound? Good? Eben has some of the best ale in Samebar, and believe me, I've sampled ales from north to south. It's—"

Ravi's cold hand suddenly squeezed his, shutting Daks up. Ravi wasn't looking at him anymore, he was staring down at the water. Daks couldn't read his face, but all the color had drained from his cheeks.

"What is it?" Daks asked when Ravi didn't move or speak again. The rest of the people on the ferry were chatting and laughing, but the silence coming from his companion was deafening.

"Ravi?" he prodded again.

Ravi took in a long, shuddering breath and slowly lifted his gaze to meet Daks's. The look in his amber eyes made Daks's guts clench.

"I… I was wrong," Ravi whispered hoarsely. "I thought that my Visions were blocked somehow. For a while, I even tried to convince myself those Visions could have been about what happened to us in the boglands, but I knew it wasn't true. It didn't *feel* true."

"Okay. You're starting to scare me here," Daks replied breathlessly. "Are you having one of your feelings? I don't sense a Vision."

"Not exactly. It just clicked. The water… it's the same color as in my Visions, the *exact* same color. It's coming. I can feel it."

"What's coming?"

"The wall. The gray wall."

Daks's skin grew cold as he turned to look upriver again, past the treetops, to the mountains, and then up to the sky. The clouds had darkened, and the lightning was more pronounced now, as was the pitch and yaw of the ferry. He wasn't imagining it.

"You're sure?" Daks asked, hoping Ravi would say he wasn't.

Ravi scowled at him and tried to pull away, but Daks tightened his grip on the hand he held. "I'm sorry. I'm just trying to understand."

"*I* don't understand most of the time," Ravi hissed, casting a nervous glance toward the other passengers. "I just *know* things sometimes. Like pieces of a puzzle, they make no sense until they click together. I don't know how I know, but it's happening and soon."

His lips trembled, and he sounded just as frustrated and frightened as Daks felt, so Daks sucked in a breath and tried to calm himself. They could figure this out.

A tingling started where Daks held Ravi's hand, and Daks groaned inwardly. He shot a glance to Ravi's face, but he already knew what he'd see. Ravi's eyes had paled from their usual golden hue to almost silver in the weak light filtering through the clouds. He gasped and clutched at Daks's hand.

Daks quickly searched the faces of their fellow travelers, but thankfully none of them seemed to have noticed anything wrong.

"It's okay," Daks whispered as he pulled Ravi against his chest, supporting him and wrapping his cloak around them both. "I've got you, and we're almost halfway across. No one will come after us now."

"That's not what worries me," Ravi gasped as he leaned into Daks for support and shuddered. "It's going to happen, Daks. Here and now."

"The same as before or different?"

"The same."

The fat rope that carried them across the river creaked as the boat strained against it from the water rushing toward them, and Daks gulped and eyed the clouds in the distance again as he held Ravi close. Rotating to shield him from the others, he let the magic of the Vision wash over him. When he finally spotted the sheets of what had to be rain falling from those far-off clouds as blue and orange slashes of lightning arced through them, he groaned, closed his eyes, and clutched Ravi almost convulsively.

Fuck me.

Before fear could paralyze him, Daks gripped Ravi's shoulders and pushed him an arm's length away. "Okay, Ravi, snap out of it," he ordered harshly, giving the man a shake even as his own knees quaked. "Are you weak? Are you going to let this thing control you? No? Then push it away."

Ravi swayed with the pitching of the raft and blinked at him, a bit dazed at first before his eyes finally cleared and then narrowed in hurt and anger.

Daks smiled grimly. That was exactly what he needed. He needed Ravi angry and focused, not dazed and afraid, because he was only a few seconds short of pissing himself.

"I think I know what your Vision means now, and it's not good," Daks said breathlessly.

"What?" Ravi spat, still obviously hurt and fuming.

"Flash flood. Warm wet spring, plus a sudden storm with heavy rain upriver means a wall of water coming our way. That has to be it."

He paused to give Ravi a chance to contradict him, but when he only swallowed visibly and nodded, Daks's stomach sank. He'd kind of been hoping Ravi would argue, but he took his disappointment manfully on the chin.

When he was sure Ravi could stand on his own, Daks took his hands away and gripped the rail of the ferry instead so Ravi couldn't see them shake. After a couple of deep breaths, he started shucking his clothes.

"Take off your bag, your cloak, your jerkin, and your boots, *now*," he ordered. "You don't want anything weighing you down."

"We're going to swim?"

Ravi's voice cracked on the last word, but he pulled the strap of his bag over his head, then undid the clasp of his cloak and let it fall.

"If your Vision is right, I don't think we're going to have much choice. We're not even halfway across yet."

Daks stopped talking and closed his eyes as a wave of nausea swept over him. His worst nightmare was about to come true, and there was nothing he could do about it but try and survive. He was not a superstitious or religious man, but he was really beginning to think there was something to this curse thing Ravi had moaned about to his friend back in Rassat. Or maybe some of the tales Shura's people told of their vengeful gods were true. Maybe there was some water god out there Daks had cheated all those years ago, and they were going to keep trying to drown him until they succeeded.

Pull yourself together.

He was seriously losing it.

"Oy, what you two doin'?" the ferryman called from his perch behind them.

When Daks turned to look, he found every person on the ferry watching them in curiosity or dismay.

"You need to get yourselves ready," his conscience made him yell back. "There's a flood coming. Unhitch the horse, and do what you can to remove any excess clothing or weight that might pull you under."

He was proud to say his voice only shook a little bit as the people stared at him with various expressions of disbelief.

"You're barmy," the ferryman called, even as he shot a fearful glance upriver.

"I'm telling you it's coming. I've seen it," Ravi piped in, lifting his head and meeting the gazes of the entire group of strangers, one by one.

Daks was actually quite proud of him. He didn't flinch once as each person who met his gaze jerked their eyes away and took a step back. Still, Daks grew irritated with their reactions pretty quickly and growled, "What have you got to lose other than a few minutes on the other side putting your things back on and hitching up the horse again?" When they all just continued to stare at him in silence, Daks threw up his hands. "Fine. We warned you. If you choose not to listen, it's on your heads."

A sudden gust of wind smacked into Daks and the deck heaved beneath them, making him lunge for the railing again, Ravi right beside him. Dismissing the other fools, he looked to Ravi. "We'll go to the very front. When you see it coming, dive as far away from this thing as possible so you don't get hit by any debris or taken down with it."

"You really believe me?"

Daks frowned. "Of course I believe you. I've seen what you can do, Ravi. Your gift is strong."

"Not strong enough."

Emotions chased each other across Ravi's lovely face, as easy to read as those books he was so fond of—fear, pain, guilt. Daks forgot his own very real terror long enough to cup Ravi's cheek in one palm and meet his startled gaze.

"You've had no training, no chance to explore and learn about what you can do. Even the Seers in the tower at the Scholomagi can't always decipher what they're given, and never right away. Don't blame yourself for that. The future is ever-changing. I refuse to believe we have no choice in it, and that it's already planned out for us. You've given us enough warning to stand a chance. Be proud of that."

Ravi swallowed and nodded before his gaze strayed to his bag, lying discarded on the deck, and Daks's throat tightened in pity.

"I'm sorry you have to leave it behind. I can tell whatever's in there is important to you."

After a moment, Ravi sighed and shook his head. "It's just an old book. I know it by heart by now. It's a reminder of the life I used to have. I think this is a sign it's time to let it go. It's not worth my life."

"Still, I'm sorry."

Ravi's expression opened a little as he returned his gaze to Daks's face. "You're not as bad as you want people to think," he said. "I'm sorry I called you so many unflattering names."

Daks couldn't help a smile. "Did you?"

"Well—" Ravi's lips curved ruefully. "—I guess most of them were just in my head."

He might have laughed if another gust of wind hadn't hit him. The storm was getting closer. The people on the boat had apparently also noticed this because they had begun peppering the ferryman with worried questions.

Good. He'd done what he could for them. They'd listen or they wouldn't. Not his problem.

He grabbed Ravi's elbow and led him toward the very front of the ferry, leaving most of their belongings behind. While the others were distracted, he took the opportunity to surreptitiously undo the buckles on the carthorse's harness straps, yoke, and collar, ignoring any indignant protests from the merchant. It was no guarantee the poor thing wouldn't drown, but at least it had a fighting chance if the ferry went under. The humans could decide their own fates.

A calming numbness finally took over his fear as he took the last steps to the head of the ferry and gazed longingly at the distant riverbank. His hands had stopped trembling and his mind had cleared. This might change at any moment, but he was glad for the reprieve. He'd be no use to anyone shaking and vomiting in a corner.

The other passengers continued to squawk and squabble behind them, periodically yelling something in their general direction, but Daks let it roll over him. Ravi's breathing was fast and erratic, and Daks couldn't exactly blame him, despite the damage it was doing to his own obviously short-lived calm. When Ravi suddenly tensed beside him, Daks closed his eyes and swallowed. After a breath, he reluctantly turned to face upriver and opened them again.

At first he saw nothing beyond what he'd seen before—clouds, distant rain, lightning, and choppy water—but then he spotted it, a wave of frothing white spreading far past the river's normal banks and rolling toward them. Someone shouted behind him, and a woman screamed.

All at once, several people started cursing, and the ferryman began blaring on his horn, hopefully warning those on shore. Daks spared a moment to worry about Shura, hoping they'd retreated to the market to get some food as she'd said and would be far enough away they wouldn't be hurt. Then he turned to Ravi.

"I think I forgot to ask if you could swim," Daks admitted with a forced, breathless chuckle.

Ravi rolled his eyes, but his face was pale and worried. "I lived near the sea my whole life. Bathing in the sea was free. I can swim. You're the one who nearly—"

Daks put a finger to his lips, cutting him off. He didn't want to hear the D-word right now.

"I can swim. That thing Shura told you about was because I fell through some ice and got trapped." He eyed the approaching wall of water with his heart in his throat. "We need to go. We need to get as far away from the ferry as possible. Don't look back. Don't worry about me. Jump in and swim as hard as you can… like your life depends on it."

Ravi swallowed visibly and nodded.

They both climbed over the railing and balanced on the narrow strip of wood on the other side as the ferry rocked more violently. They exchanged a single weighted glance before Ravi dove into the water and Daks jumped in after him.

Daks broke the surface sputtering and scrambled to find Ravi. The rapidly increasing current had already put several yards between them when Daks finally spotted him, but at least Ravi didn't seem to be struggling beyond his fight to swim against the flow. Without wasting another second, Daks ducked his head and swam with all his might. He couldn't help Ravi any more than he could help himself, and if they'd tried to stick together, they probably would have gotten in each other's way. He didn't even bother looking upstream. He couldn't do anything about what was coming.

When the leading edge of the flood hit him, it sent him tumbling helplessly beneath the surface. He had no idea which way was up or if he'd ever stop spinning. The initial impact eventually let go, and he scrambled toward the light, bursting through the surface and gasping for air only long enough to hear a loud crack from the direction of the ferry behind him before another wave took him under again.

The next few minutes felt like an eternity of fighting to keep his head above water. He couldn't even gather enough strength to truly swim, even if he'd known what direction to swim in. His heart pounded as the icy water dragged at him. He was tiring too quickly, and his hopes of surviving this were draining away with his strength.

At last the waters stopped tossing him around like a doll long enough for him to spot the shore not too far away. He had no idea which shore it was, but it didn't matter. He swam for it, pushing past pain and exhaustion. He had a moment to think he might just make it, and to wonder if Ravi had fared any better, before something huge and hard slammed into him from behind. Stars burst behind his eyelids before all went dark.

Chapter Eleven

Ravi had never been so exhausted in his life by the time the river spit him out into a muddy tangle of reeds, roots, and dead branches along the shore. He coughed water out of his lungs for what felt like ages until he collapsed, gasping, in a heap in the mud. He woke with a groan when stinging rain started pelting his face.

Could the gods not give him even a second of reprieve? What had he ever done to them?

With another groan, he rolled onto his hands and knees. He had to stay that way, with the heavy rain stinging his back instead, for a while before dizziness and fatigue passed enough for him to attempt to stand. In nothing but his sodden underclothes, he staggered through pools of slowly receding floodwaters to a tree trunk and leaned against it. The tree's canopy of leaves gave him some shelter from the pouring rain as he wiped at his eyes and squinted at his surroundings. The curtain of water falling from the sky made discerning anything impossible, so he slumped against the base of the tree in defeat.

He had no idea where he was or what had happened to Daks. A wave of fear and abject desolation threatened to swamp him. Everything hurt. The bruises across his chest made breathing that much harder, and he was shaking with cold as the rain blotted out the rest of the world. He needed to find Daks. That was the only thought running through his head over and over again, the only thing keeping him from surrendering to the darkness that threatened at the edges of his vision, but he couldn't seem to manage much more than that. He couldn't make himself stand up again.

He huddled in misery against that tree until a new sound intruded on the constant but slowing patter of rain and rush of the river, a snort and the dull thud of hooves on wet ground. Fear and uncertainty spurred him unsteadily to his feet as he peered through rain and growing mist. The hoofbeats drew nearer. Drawing on what little strength and courage he had left, he stepped around the tree and searched the woods until he spotted a decidedly equine-shaped blurry blotch of white.

Whether friend or foe, Ravi couldn't huddle out there alone forever. He had to take a chance whoever was riding that horse would be willing to help. He stumbled toward the shape as it continued to approach him. When he could finally see the animal clearly, he blinked several times and shook his head, thinking surely his mind was playing tricks on him.

"Horse?" he called, still not quite believing it.

The stallion snorted and trotted the rest of the way to him. Ravi nearly wept when he put a palm to the animal's snout and Horse nuzzled him.

"How?" he croaked.

He glanced back at the river through the trees in confusion. What he could glimpse of it showed it flowing in the direction he remembered. He was on the opposite bank from where they'd started that morning. He was in Samebar. So how the hells did the animal get there? He had to be Horse, though—their packs were soaked and dripping water, but still tied to his saddle.

"Oh, Horse," he cried, burying his face in the stallion's damp neck and letting a few tears fall. "I don't know how you got here, but I can't tell you how glad I am to see you."

Before he could truly give in to his feelings and bawl all over the beast, Horse side-stepped him and started walking.

"Hey!"

Ravi tried to grab the halter, but Horse dodged his grasp and kept moving. Ravi went down several times in his attempts to follow the animal on exhausted and shaking limbs. Each time Horse would pause, as if waiting for him to get up, before he would start walking again.

"Please," Ravi rasped, almost sobbing with fatigue. "I have to stop."

Horse let out a whicker, flaring his nostrils before angling toward the river, and Ravi whined in the back of his throat and stumbled after him. They'd almost reached the bank before he spotted what Horse was headed for through the thinning rain. A dark shape with bushy hair was hung up in the branches of a downed tree, bobbing in the shallows. Ravi let out a hoarse cry and stumbled into the water.

"Daks! Daks, can you hear me?"

Daks only continued to bob in the water, and Ravi's throat closed. Struggling through the muddy shallows, he finally managed to reach the man. Daks's eyes were closed, and a bloody lump marred the side of his head.

"Daks? Wake up. Come on, wake up."

His hands shook as he patted the man's cheeks gently, but Daks's eyelids didn't so much as twitch. The sound of a large body splashing into the water next to him made Ravi jolt. Horse closed the last few feet, breaking dead branches along the way until he dipped his head and gripped the collar of Daks's shirt between his teeth and started backing up, dragging Daks toward the shore.

"Careful," Ravi said somewhat unnecessarily, as all he could do was watch for a few beats before dragging his own battered body after them.

When Horse stopped, Ravi dropped to his knees in the mud next to Daks's prone form and rested a palm on his chest. The first signs of movement beneath his palm almost had Ravi in tears again, but he swallowed them back.

"Thank the gods," he whispered.

Horse snorted again, startling Ravi into glancing at him, but the beast just eyed him calmly.

"Thank you too," Ravi said with a weary smile. "Now what do we do?" He searched their surroundings but saw nothing beyond trees, mud, and more rain. "I need to find help. We need to get him dry and warm somewhere and find a priest or herb woman or something, whatever they have for a healer in this kingdom. Come on, Daks, you gotta wake up. I don't know anything about this place. I can't do this on my own."

Daks's face was so pale and his skin so cold Ravi's stomach hurt every time he looked at the man. Just as Ravi was trying to decide if he had the strength to drag Daks deeper into the woods, out of the worst of the rain, Horse moved in close and laid down next to them. When Ravi just gawped at him, Horse swung one disapproving pale blue eye in his direction and stared.

"Uh. Okaaaaayyyy."

Ravi struggled to his feet and eyed the animal in confusion until Horse let out another whicker and nudged Daks's body with his muzzle.

"I guess if you stay like that, I could try to get him draped over you." He worried his lip as he eyed Horse skeptically. "Then I can try to climb on, maybe?"

Plan made, Ravi began the agonizing process of trying to pull Daks's heavy, inert body over packs. At one point, he was tempted to leave the packs behind to make the process easier, but he had no idea if he'd need their contents. He was sweating and panting by the time he got Daks in place and had to take a break to catch his breath.

"And he said *I* was heavy," he gasped.

Before Ravi could muster the energy to secure Daks somehow or climb on himself, Horse apparently decided he'd had enough and got to his feet, with Daks slung precariously over his back. Ravi yelped and lunged to keep Daks from sliding off, even as he scowled at the animal and cursed under his breath.

Before the wave of dizziness his sudden movement caused subsided, Horse had already started walking away, back the way they'd come.

"Hey!"

Ravi staggered after him but could barely keep up. He had no idea how far they walked. He was so absorbed in his misery and just putting one foot in front of the other that he literally ran into Horse's rump, knocking himself back on his ass in the mud, when the animal suddenly stopped.

Thinking all kinds of nasty thoughts, Ravi lifted his head to scowl and glare but stopped when he spotted the dark shape of a building through the rain. After scrambling awkwardly to his feet, he staggered toward it, his hopes rising until he got a good look at the place and he groaned. Three of the four walls of the small log structure were still intact, but the fourth and part of the roof had been caved in by the large tree that had fallen on it. It was obviously abandoned, but it would provide shelter out of the rain, and Ravi didn't think he could walk any farther.

"Hello?" he called out as he approached, but received nothing but the splat of rain in response. He tried again in Sambaran, for good measure, but still nothing.

At least the tree hadn't hit the door, so he wouldn't have to clamber over the trunk and through branches. He never would have been able to get Daks inside, if that were the case. He wasn't sure if he'd even have the strength to drag Daks through the doorway, as it was.

When he pushed on it, the slightly rotted, moss-covered door creaked loudly on rusted hinges. Gray light streamed through the door and filtered through the branches spanning the hole in the roof. Strangely enough, part of the tree was still alive, despite having toppled over, and small green leaves sprouted along the branches and caught the rain. Ravi wiped away the water still dripping into his eyes and scanned the mostly empty space bleakly before taking a deep breath and jutting out his chin. He'd lived in worse over the past decade.

He stomped a bruised and battered bare foot against the floor to announce his presence to any current inhabitants. Only small rustlings and scurryings answered him, which was good. He wouldn't have to try to wrest the place from anything bigger. A quick survey showed him the fireplace and chimney were still intact, and he allowed himself a weak smile. There were a few bits of old, broken furniture strewn around, and some of the branches on the underside of the fallen tree looked dead enough to burn.

He limped back to the doorway and found Horse calmly waiting outside with Daks still slung over his back, unmoving.

"Right," he said, mostly to encourage himself to keep going. "Let's see about getting the big jerk inside. Are you going to cooperate again?"

As if Horse understood him, the animal dropped down before Ravi even reached its side. Ravi stared wonderingly into Horse's eyes for a few seconds, before turning away again with a shiver. He dragged Daks from its back, wincing when his strength failed and they both hit the ground harder than he'd intended.

Horse whickered at him, and Ravi huffed. "I know. I know. I'm trying, but you obviously felt how heavy he is. And if you hadn't noticed, I just survived a flood."

With a series of grunts and curses, Ravi managed to drag Daks into the abandoned cabin and out of the rain, but only as far as he needed so the big lug's body wasn't blocking the door. Ravi shouldn't have been surprised, but Horse tried to come through the door right after them, only to be stopped by the bulk of the packs tied to his saddle. Horse turned to look at them, as if they offended him, and Ravi let out a raspy chuckle. The stallion then swung a baleful eye in his direction, and Ravi laughed harder, only to start coughing soon after.

"Looks like you aren't as mystical and amazing as you like to let on," he wheezed after the coughing subsided.

Horse lifted his head haughtily and turned away from him.

Ravi studied the animal in the rain for a few beats before shrugging. He really couldn't afford for Horse to wander off, and the cabin had plenty of room. With effort, he stood, limped over to it, and began undoing the straps holding the sodden packs to the saddle. After all four had plopped to the ground outside the door, Horse primly stepped over them and entered the cabin to take up residence against the far wall.

"Anything else I can do for you, Your Highness?"

Horse swung his head over his shoulder toward the dripping saddle on his back and Ravi groaned. With numb fingers, he fumbled at the straps. The saddle hit the ground with a loud thud, but that was the best he could manage.

He shuffled out into the rain one last time and dragged the packs inside. He had no idea if anything in them would still be useful, but he remembered Daks had stowed the last of their food in one of them, and he'd be hungry eventually.

After closing the door, he sank down by Daks's side and searched the man's face. The cut on the side of his head had mostly stopped bleeding, but he still showed no signs of waking.

"Don't you dare die on me," Ravi whispered to him, fighting another spate of tears. "You promised me you'd get me to Scholoveld. I'm not there yet, you big jerk."

Unable to move even one more inch, Ravi spooned against Daks's back, draped an arm over the man's waist, and fell into a damp, cold, miserable sleep.

DAKS WOKE to the crackle and pop of a fire and the smell of wood smoke. The second he tried to open his eyes, he regretted it, as pain stabbed through his skull. He let out a moan and winced, but that was a mistake because his side reminded him of the knife wound he'd gotten only… how many days ago was that now?

"Daks?"

At the quavering note in Ravi's voice, Daks forced his eyes open despite the pain. Ravi knelt next to him, silhouetted by firelight coming from a hearth Daks didn't recognize.

"Where are we?" he croaked through cracked, dry lips, and Ravi immediately offered him a waterskin.

Daks drank greedily, surprised at how thirsty he was.

"I don't know. Somewhere in Samebar," Ravi answered with a shrug. "Horse led me here…. I'm so glad you're awake, I can't even tell you."

Ravi's voice broke on those last words, and Daks pushed the water skin away to look at him. Ravi's gorgeous auburn hair lay in lank tangles about his face. Daks's spare jerkin hung overly large on his lean frame. What he could see of Ravi's trousers was dirty, wrinkled, and torn at the knees. Dull, dark-ringed amber eyes gazed back at him over sallow, sunken cheeks.

Gods, he looked awful.

Daks tried to sit up, but his body was surprisingly slow to respond. He reluctantly gave up after a few unsuccessful tries and sank back beneath the pile of heavy wool covering him with a grunt.

"What happened?"

"You don't remember?"

He strained, trying to think past the throbbing in his head. "We were on the ferry to Pazar. Then the flood hit."

As if triggered by the memory of it, Daks started coughing, and he had to close his eyes and ride the wave of pain for a few moments before he could open them again. His chest ached dully, he was as weak as a kitten, and his vision blurred in and out. Beyond that, he absolutely refused to acknowledge the stirring panic in his belly when old and new memories of struggling in the water threatened to surface.

He wasn't in the water anymore.

Ravi studied him with glassy, haunted eyes, his brows drawn down in worry, so Daks pulled himself together and cleared his throat. "Are you all right? Are you hurt?"

"I'm okay," he said, though not particularly convincingly.

Daks's own concern only increased as Ravi's gaze turned a bit vague and he shivered.

"Ravi, how long have I been out?"

"Two days," he replied hollowly.

Two days?

In dismay, he searched Ravi's face again. "Have you slept?"

He nodded. "That first night, sort of. I couldn't stay awake. But not since. The wolves. I had to keep watch."

"Wolves?"

"They came for the—" He grimaced and swallowed as he focused those haunted eyes on Daks again. "For the bodies...

along the riverbank, from the flood." He paused again and hugged himself. "I couldn't bury them. I didn't have a shovel or anything, and I had to get back to you. They come after dark. I can hear them out there."

The more he rambled, the more worried Daks became. He looked like he might fall over any second.

"I found food, though." Ravi jerked his chin toward the wall, and Daks followed the movement to a small wooden cask next to the hearth. "It's just grain, but it's better than nothing. It didn't get too wet inside, so it should be good for a few more days. You want some?"

He started to stand, but Daks caught the edge of his jerkin and tugged, not hard, because he didn't have the strength, but Ravi sank back down anyway.

"Ravi, look at me." He waited until Ravi met his gaze. "You need to sleep."

"Can't. Wolves. Need to keep watch."

Daks shook his head. "I'm awake now. I can keep watch."

Ravi frowned at him. "You're hurt."

"And you're dead on your feet."

Ignoring the pain, Daks pushed himself up enough to brace on one elbow and lift the pile of clothes covering him aside, which seemed to take an appalling amount of effort. Cool air rushed in despite the fire in the hearth and goose bumps broke out across his naked skin, but he was more concerned with how much his arm shook trying to hold that little weight.

"I'm not that hurt, Ravi. Come on. Get in. Lie down. You're exhausted."

Ravi jutted his chin stubbornly and shook his head.

"Look at me," Daks said, more forcefully this time, drawing Ravi's bleary gaze back to him. "I've got this. I know I failed you on the river and after. You had to do everything, and I'm sorry for that. But I'm awake now, and apparently, we have Horse too, somehow. We can keep watch while you sleep. I'll wake you if anything happens."

As if his body had only been waiting for the right excuse, Ravi crumpled onto the nest of grasses next to him. Gritting his teeth against his body's complaints, Daks scooted closer, rearranging the pile of cloaks and spare clothing over both of them.

Ravi stiffened slightly and looked up at him when Daks brushed his side, and Daks smiled gently down at him. "Don't worry. I won't touch you more than necessary. But you're freezing. We need to get you warm."

Ravi held Daks's gaze for a few beats before his face softened into a tired smile and his body relaxed. "It's okay to touch me now. I want you to. It's been so long. Please. I need—"

His voice caught, and something stirred in Daks's chest, a worryingly familiar sensation he hadn't experienced in over a decade. He scooted closer to Ravi, curled against his side, and cupped a hand to his cheek. Ravi's eyes fell closed as he nuzzled into that hand, and that thing in Daks's chest flared brighter.

"I thought you were dead when I found you by the river," Ravi whispered brokenly, his eyes still closed. "And then you wouldn't wake up. I kept hoping, calling to you, but you wouldn't wake up."

A tear slid from beneath his eyelashes and down his cheek, and Daks's throat closed. "I'm sorry, but I'm awake now," he murmured back. "You did that. You saved me. Now it's my turn. Let go, Ravi. I'll be here when you wake up. Trust me."

"Not your fault."

"Go to sleep."

As Daks tenderly smoothed the hair away from Ravi's forehead, he watched the man's struggle to stay awake and it made him smile, Ravi being as stubborn and contrary as ever.

Daks stayed with him for a long time after he finally lost the battle and his breathing evened out, just watching him and enjoying the warmth and solidity of his presence. If Shura could see him now, she'd give him no end of grief for the disgustingly sentimental smile he couldn't seem to wipe from his face.

Gods, he missed her already.

Let her be safe, he prayed to who or whatever might be listening. He threw a nervous glance over at Horse, but he didn't have the strength or desire to try to unpack what the stallion's presence meant just then.

Inevitably, he grew restless after an hour or so, despite his exhaustion. If he stayed in that warm cocoon, he'd definitely break his word and fall asleep. Besides, according to Ravi, he'd lain around uselessly for two days. That was long enough.

He eased away from Ravi's side and struggled to his hands and knees. Climbing to his feet took far longer than it should have, but he managed it, and he only had to wait a few seconds for the dizziness to subside.

After finding his leather breeches and his other tunic in the nest of clothing and grasses Ravi had built for him, Daks shuffled to a roughly repaired chair—the only stick of furniture in the whole cabin—to try to get dressed. Horse whickered from his corner of the room, and Daks's lips twisted in a wry smile despite the throbbing in his head.

"I don't know how you did it. And your preternatural abilities are starting to make me question some of my most firmly held beliefs—particularly since I've sensed no magic on you whatsoever—but I'm glad you're here."

He still flatly refused to explore the implications of Horse's presence any further than that. Sure, he'd left the animal on the other side with Shura, and now he was alone on this side, but that didn't have to mean anything. Ravi would have told him if he'd seen Shura along that riverbank. Daks wouldn't panic, at least not until they made it to Pazar and learned more.

Fading orange light filtered through the tree branches near the roof of the cabin when Daks heard the first howls echoing outside, and his blood chilled. But Ravi had done a great job of finding shelter for them. The cabin walls and door were still sound, and he'd piled branches as a barrier around where the tree had broken through. Ravi had done a fantastic job at taking care of them all around, and Daks cast yet another proud, sappy look at Ravi's sleeping face.

Gods, he wished Shura was there to give him shit for it before he went completely soft.

"Come on, you," he murmured to Horse as he stood up. "We need more water and wood before the sun goes down, and I'm not sure I'm up to both collecting it *and* carrying it."

He'd regained a little of his strength from downing two more skins full of water and the last of the cold grain porridge Ravi had made, but he definitely wasn't at full strength yet. Hopefully the wolves would be content with what they could scavenge along the riverbank for one more night and they could all agree to leave each other alone. At least Horse still looked in fine fighting form. The damned beast didn't have a scratch on him.

When full dark had fallen, Daks had a second pot of porridge bubbling in the cookpot, plus a decent reserve of downed branches to feed the fire. He'd already eaten the first full pot on his own with a small portion of dried meat from the packs that seemed to have survived Horse's swim. The grain had been a lucky find, though he was pretty sure whoever lost it wouldn't agree. He felt a slight twinge of regret for all the people on the ferry, but there wasn't much he could have done for them. Hells, he couldn't even save himself.

Ravi finally stirred and sat up, rubbing his eyes.

"Hey, I've got dinner going... such as it is," Daks said.

Ravi bit his lower lip before smiling shyly back, and Daks's heart squeezed disgustingly again.

"How's your head?" Ravi asked, climbing slowly to his feet.

"Better. A little food and some more water took care of most of the pain. I'll make it."

Ravi looked much better too. He was charmingly rumpled, but the dark circles under his eyes and grayish cast to his olive skin had faded.

After accepting the wooden bowl of gruel Daks offered him with a nod of thanks, he sat cross-legged on the dirty plank floor of the cabin, refusing the chair Daks offered to vacate. That stung Daks's pride a little, but if he were honest, his pride would have taken a bigger hit later when he couldn't get up off the floor without help. His little supply gathering mission earlier had wiped him out.

They ate in silence for a while, and Daks thought the gnawing pit in his stomach might have finally been satisfied by the time he finished his second meal. With a sigh of relief, he stretched his legs toward the fire and patted his full belly. The makeshift bed looked awfully good right now. He just needed to force himself out of the chair to go to it.

"How long did I sleep?" Ravi asked somewhat hesitantly, drawing Daks's gaze back to him.

"Probably not enough. The sun only went down an hour or so ago."

After another couple of beats, Ravi cleared his throat and dropped his gaze to the empty bowl in his lap.

"Uh, about earlier," he murmured without looking up. "You were right. I was pretty out of it. I'm sorry for the whole tears and begging you to hold me thing. It had been a rough couple of days."

"You don't need to apologize for anything."

Ravi grimaced. "After the other day by the river, and you saving me in bogs... hells, this whole trip, I haven't been exactly myself. And then last night... I'm never that weak and needy, I swear. I can't afford to be."

Ignoring the protests of his body, Daks pushed out of the chair and crouched next to Ravi. When Ravi finally glanced up at him, Daks cupped one flaming cheek in his palm and said, "There's nothing weak about you. And you saved *my* life too, remember?"

"I didn't do much."

Daks frowned. "After nearly drowning, you somehow got me out of the water and all the way up here. You could have left me there. Hells, you could have left me *here* and taken the horse to find help, but you didn't. You stayed and took care of me, kept yourself awake for two days watching over all of us. That's not weak. I owe you my life."

Ravi's blush only deepened, heating his palm, and Daks grimaced. This conversation had gotten far too serious and perilously sentimental. Time for a different tack.

Forcing his lips into his best grin and dropping his voice low, Daks added in Rassan, "And as far as begging me to touch you, you don't *ever* have to beg for that, beautiful. I'll give you as much or as little as you want, anytime, anywhere."

He half expected Ravi to huff and glare at him, or possibly even shove him away, so he was stunned when Ravi lifted heated eyes to meet his gaze. His tongue poked out to wet pink lips before he whispered, "You think I'm beautiful?"

"I *know* you're beautiful," he replied honestly.

Ravi's answering smile was the sweetest Daks had ever seen, before it turned wry and sexy. "And if my response to your offer is: a lot, right now, and right here?"

The sudden huskiness in his voice went straight to Daks's cock. Forgetting all about any pain or exhaustion, he sank to his knees between Ravi's spread legs, cupped Ravi's jaw, and captured those soft pink lips for the first time. Ravi tasted of the porridge they'd just eaten and an underlying salty sweetness that had Daks groaning and pushing deeper. Ravi's kiss seemed a little unsure at first, reminding Daks that he probably needed to slow down. But the soft sigh Ravi made as he opened up and his tongue came out to play made it difficult to think beyond the need to have more.

As Daks slid a hand behind Ravi's back to draw him closer, Ravi wrapped his arms around Daks and pulled himself up, as if seeking as much contact as possible.

"Maybe we should go somewhere a little more comfortable," Daks murmured breathlessly against Ravi's lips between kisses. "Can't quite get to all of you like this."

"Good idea."

Ravi let go and rolled away. After he got to his feet, he began shucking his clothes, any hesitation gone, so Daks happily did the same. His movements weren't quite as graceful, but he didn't care anymore. Lust had a wonderful way of making things like pain, exhaustion, and embarrassment seem stupid and unimportant.

Before Daks could look his fill, Ravi slid that hot, lithe, long-limbed body beneath the pile of cloaks and clothes. *Next time*, he promised himself.

As soon as he scooted into their nest, Ravi wrapped those long legs and arms around him. The way Ravi clung to him made it feel like he had eight limbs instead of the usual four, and Daks grinned.

"I'm not going anywhere," he whispered into Ravi's ear before kissing the shell and working his tongue downward.

Ravi arched and moaned before tightening his hold. "You almost died," he whispered back.

Daks stopped his kisses long enough to give Ravi a good hard squeeze in return, before running his palm in soothing patterns over Ravi's back, flank, and ass. "You did too. But we're okay now."

"Are we?" Ravi gasped as he pumped his hips, rubbing his already hard cock against Daks's belly.

Daks grabbed a firm, round asscheek in each palm, encouraging him to move, as his own cock slid along Ravi's crease. "We will be."

He kissed Ravi again, long and deep as they explored the planes of each other's bodies. When they were both sweating and panting, with cocks hard as stone and leaking, Daks ordered, "Lie back."

Ravi's expression turned just a little uncertain, and Daks smiled wryly.

"Trust me."

Ravi hesitated only a second longer before releasing his hold and settling back onto their makeshift mattress, staring up at Daks with so much trust and need, Daks's heart squeezed. He smoothed a palm over Ravi's chest until the bruising across his sternum caught the firelight.

"Are you sure you're okay?" Daks asked, running a gentle finger over the mottled skin.

Ravi quirked an eyebrow and reached for the puckered, reddened skin along Daks's ribs. "Are you?"

A wry smile spread across Daks's lips. They certainly made a pair.

Without answering, he gently lowered himself to cover Ravi's body and kissed him slow and deep. Their cocks pressed together between their bellies, and Daks slid his hands down to Ravi's thighs, tugging, encouraging Ravi to lift them to cradle him again. They both moaned when he pumped his hips. Ravi's long fingers slid up his back to tangle in the bushy mess of his hair, tugging and dragging his nails along Daks's scalp as they rutted together and kissed messily.

Ravi gasped and moaned against his lips as Daks groaned and his need built. Finally, he couldn't take it anymore and he arched up, spat in his hand, and reached for their cocks. Grasping them both in his calloused palm, he pumped Ravi's long, pretty cock alongside his own. Watching them slide through his fist was so damned hot, he didn't want to take his eyes away from it. But when Ravi gasped and his hips jerked, Daks's gaze shot to Ravi's face.

His cheeks had flushed a deep red. Sweat beaded along his hairline and glistened on his throat. Even as he panted, moaned, and arched beneath Daks, gripping his shoulders convulsively and squeezing Daks's hips with his thighs, he never took those gorgeous eyes off Daks's face.

When Daks thought he might not be able to hold his own orgasm off any longer, Ravi finally closed his eyes, threw his head back, and cried out. Hot seed spurted from his cock onto his belly and Daks's fist, adding to the slickness in his palm. Daks continued pumping until Ravi collapsed back into their nest and let go of Daks's shoulders. Daks released his spent cock and pumped his own fast and rough. He was so hot, it didn't take long before he let out a long, low moan and his seed mixed with Ravi's all over his belly and chest.

He watched in deep satisfaction and pleasure as their releases puddled and joined on Ravi's lovely warm olive skin. When he finally glanced up, he caught Ravi watching too, and Daks grinned smugly at him before collapsing against Ravi's side. As the rush from his orgasm faded, all of his injuries reminded him of just what he'd put his body through recently, and he had to stifle another moan of the not-so-good kind. He took small consolation in the fact that Ravi wasn't exactly springing back demanding a second round either.

Choosing the wiser and much less fun option, Daks snagged the shirt he'd removed earlier and handed it to Ravi to clean up as he said, "We should get some sleep. We have at least a few miles to travel tomorrow and only the one horse."

Ravi rolled to face him and frowned uncertainly. "Okay. If that's what you want."

Daks gave him a gentle smile as he cupped Ravi's cheek. "I didn't say it was what I *wanted*. I said it was what I thought we should do. There's a difference."

Ravi's lips quirked into a shy smile before his expression turned unreadable as he searched Daks's face.

"What?" Daks asked.

Ravi flushed. "I…. You… you didn't, uh…."

"Didn't what?"

Ravi groaned and rolled so his back was to Daks. "Never mind."

Daks might have been exhausted, but he'd have to be dead to let that one slide. Grinning, he pushed himself up and scooted until he'd spooned Ravi's back. Ravi tensed at first. But when he relaxed and pushed back against him, Daks hooked an arm around his waist and rested his chin on his shoulder.

"Didn't what?" he poked again.

After blowing out an aggrieved sigh, Ravi said, "Obviously, I don't know a lot about this sort of thing. Not being able to touch anyone for ten years severely limited my, uh, interactions. But I'm not naïve or stupid either. I know what the men who approached me in alleys and on the streets at night wanted. I knew what some of the others who stayed with us did for coin when work was scarce or, *hells*, what they did with each other for fun when they could find a quiet corner. I guess I was expecting you to want to—"

He flung a hand in the air and waved it around instead of finishing that sentence, and Daks's grin widened. He was tempted to make Ravi actually say the words, but decided to take pity on both of them. He was too tired.

He nuzzled playfully behind Ravi's ear. "There were a lot of things we didn't do tonight. And I'm very much looking forward to doing all of them that you'll let me… once both of us have seen a healer, had a chance to get a little more rest, and we're safely tucked up in a real bed." As he spoke, he reached for Ravi's hand and threaded their fingers together. "Eben's inn in Pazar has wonderful soft beds, fine food and drink, warm fires, and a bath house out back with barrels of steaming hot herb-scented water big enough for two. When we get there, you and I are going to eat and drink our fill, soak every last ache away, and not leave one of those beds for a whole day at the very least," he promised.

Ravi shivered in his arms and pushed his ass back, making Daks's cock twitch, but he told it to be patient. He wasn't in any kind of shape to follow through on any of its promises right now.

"You make it sound like Quanna's gardens of plenty," Ravi replied, a smile obvious in his voice.

He pressed his cheek to the top of Ravi's head. "Not quite. But once I've had a little rest and healing and we're in that bed, I'll get you to those gardens, don't you worry."

Ravi snorted, and Daks could almost feel the man roll his eyes.

"Sleep, Ravi. Save your strength for the journey tomorrow."

"Are you taking the first watch?" Ravi asked around a yawn.

"No. We'll both sleep. You did a great job with this place. The door might be old and a bit beat up, but it's still solid, and so are the walls and the barricade you made. Plus, we've got Horse over there, a proven fighter. We can let our guard down for the night. The wolves should be well-sated with what they've scavenged from the river bank. They shouldn't bother with us."

"Ew," Ravi murmured, and Daks winced.

That was a sure way to kill the mood.

"Sleep," he ordered, curling protectively around Ravi's body. "Trust me."

Chapter Twelve

The trip up to Pazar might have been arduous and long, but Ravi didn't remember much of it once they reached the inn Daks had waxed so poetic about. He'd spent far too much time dreamily reliving the night before, eyeing his strong hands, and leaning back into the warmth and solidity of that broad chest. The weight of that big body on top of him, surrounding him, holding him with those thick arms, kissing him with those lips that could be so soft and then so hard and needy....

He groaned silently and surreptitiously pressed a palm to the front of his trousers as they handed Horse off to a groom and turned toward the inn. Riding in a saddle with a hard cock for hours had not been a comfortable experience, but with Daks so close, he couldn't seem to help it. It was like a switch had been flipped inside him, and all he could hear was his dick and his skin begging for more. Daks hadn't helped matters either, teasing him relentlessly. Ravi'd been tempted to walk the rest of the way, just to get a little relief, but after their journey and another dunking in a river in Horse's packs, his old boots might not finish the journey.

Even now, as Daks greeted the mountain masquerading as an innkeeper in Sambaran and Ravi struggled to keep up with the foreign words, his eyes kept straying to Daks's mouth, his hands, and his ass. When Daks caught him, his lips twisted into that smug, infuriating grin, but for some reason Ravi's cock had decided it didn't hate that grin in the slightest.

Daks finally seemed to remember Ravi wasn't Sambaran and switched to trade speak with an apologetic smile, and Eben, the innkeeper, followed suit, just in time for the conversation to turn inevitably to the flood.

"It was terrible," the huge, tawny-bearded man said. "The inn is high enough up, we didn't know it was happening until we heard the shouts and screams from down by the water."

"Did you lose any people?" Daks asked solemnly. "Did anyone else from the ferry survive?"

"Weren't sure who all was on the ferry, mind, but the ferryman was one of ours, and he hasn't been found. Old Taun runs the horses and the crank on this end. He was injured. Broken leg. One of the horses had to be put down. He said a few waiting for the ferry were swept up in it. I think Mawd lost her nephew, cracked his head on a rock, found him a half mile downriver." Eben grimaced. "A few houses flooded, but we'll be fixin' 'em up soon enough. Ferry rope snapped. That'll take a bit more time, but we're still here, and boats are running across until then."

"Have you seen a Cigani woman in town?" Daks asked.

"You mean that woman you traveled with before, right? I remember her. But no, haven't seen her, sorry."

Daks's face fell. "If she'd been able to get a message across, it would have been delivered here. She knew where we were headed."

Ravi shifted uncomfortably, wanting to touch him, to give what comfort he could, but he wasn't sure what the rules were between them yet, so he held himself still.

"Sorry," the innkeeper murmured again. "If a message comes, I'll let you know. And I'll keep an eye out and spread the word you're looking."

"Thank you," Daks replied, his voice sounding weary and tight. "We need to find your healer. Can you tell us where?"

Eben nodded. "Hers was one of the houses caught in the flood, so we set her up in Aver's common house, down near the market, since he has the room. Lots of cuts and bumps around these days; you may have a wait."

"You think you can find me a spare pair of shoes or boots until I can get to a shop?"

"I'll see what I can do."

"Thanks. We'll visit the healer after we've had our meal, and then come back for the bathhouse, if that's all right with you."

"Of course. We'll be ready for you. The spring waters will do you good too, mark my words." Eben gave them each a nod before heading toward what Ravi assumed was the kitchen, but he stopped halfway and came back. Leaning in close, he whispered, "Now, I don't traffic in gossip as a general rule, but you being from the Council and all… the few boats that've come across since the flood have carried tales of a wizard on the other side, if you didn't know already."

"A pain priest?" Daks asked sharply, making Ravi's stomach jolt.

"Nooooo. No robes. No stone 'round his neck. They're saying he just lifted his hands and pushed the waters back from the town." Eben shrugged as if embarrassed. "Now, I know what the waters did on this side, and I never heard of a wizard strong enough to do that on his own, with no time to prep or potion… except maybe in the old tales. So I don't know if it's true. But since I can tell you're worried about your friend, I thought I should mention it. If this man did as the people are saying, and most of the town was saved from the worst of it, chances are, she's okay."

Ravi shot Daks a startled glance, but Daks looked just as confused as him.

"You think that might be the same wizard—" Ravi began excitedly, hoping to offer Daks some comfort through words if not through touch, but Daks put a hand on his arm and gave him an almost imperceptible head shake.

"Thanks, Eben," Daks said. "I hope you're right."

The innkeeper glanced between them for a moment before shrugging. "Like I said, I don't know for sure if it's true. But you shouldn't give up hope just yet."

"I won't," Daks replied.

When the enormous man lumbered out of earshot, Ravi asked quietly in Rassan, "You don't trust him?"

"What?" Daks had obviously been lost in his own thoughts because he frowned in confusion.

"You stopped me from talking about the other rumors we'd heard."

"Oh, right. No. It isn't that I don't trust him. He's probably heard the rumors already anyway. But if he hasn't heard everything we have, I prefer to keep that to ourselves until I can report to the High Council." He paused for a second and grimaced. "Sorry. I'm sort of conditioned to not share any more information than I absolutely need to. I shouldn't have interrupted you. I'm sorry."

Daks's gaze grew distant again, and Ravi decided not to press. Shura wasn't the easiest person to like, but Ravi found himself worried for her and Mistress Sabin too, and not only for Daks's sake. It was amazing what sharing an adventure and almost dying could do to your feelings about someone. Perhaps he would have a tale worthy of writing down someday after all. The thought reminded him of what he'd been forced to leave behind on the ferry and his chest tightened with loss before he shoved the feeling aside. Dwelling on it wouldn't make him feel any better. He'd meant what he said. He was starting over for the second time. It was time to leave his first life behind.

They dug into the heaping bowls of hot, meaty stew and warm buttered bread, while Ravi allowed his mind to wander to more pleasant things as he glanced at his companion frequently. Daks only remained mired in his own thoughts for a short while before he caught Ravi's gaze and his lips curved slyly.

"Told you this place would be worth the journey," Daks murmured.

"You did."

Daks's eyes hooded as he licked his lips. "After the healer, I'll keep the rest of my promises too."

Something fluttered in Ravi's overstuffed belly, and his cock twitched.

Not now, he scolded his wayward dick. They still had to walk through the town.

Their inn rested alongside a few other shops and taverns at the top of a hill overlooking the town square and the river beyond. Ravi had been too distracted to note much else about Pazar when they'd arrived, especially since they'd come from the forest road rather than the shore. Daks had taken them inland from the cabin until they'd reached that road, possibly to make their journey easier, but also so neither of them would have to see any more of the devastation the flood had wrought or deal with too many scavengers.

To his outsider's eye, Pazar looked much like Traget. The houses, shops, and inns were constructed of similar rough-cut beams, rock, and plaster. People filled the streets, hawking their wares or filling their baskets. But there was one striking difference between the two towns—the *color*. Yellow, red, orange, and purple flowering plants, banners, and even some painted murals adorned many of the buildings. Instead of the dull grays and browns of Rassan dress, even the lowliest Sambaran seemed to have a splash of color somewhere on them, be it a ribbon holding back loose waves of flowing hair or a brightly dyed leather belt or scarf.

It might have been his imagination, but the people seemed brighter and happier too. Rassans weren't overly demonstrative people. In fact, they were quite proud of their reserve. He knew that, but the contrast was still striking as he surreptitiously studied the people they passed. It made him wonder if Rassans had ever been that free, if maybe the Brotherhood had taken their joy along with everything else and they just didn't realize it.

He shook his head at his own philosophical meanderings. He'd lived in Arcadia for a long time. Life was hard there, but he'd still seen children laughing and people smiling as they sang their hymns and went about their work. Surely there were plenty of places in Rassa where people were as happy as these. Just because someone didn't wear that joy out where everyone could see it didn't mean it wasn't there, right?

The press of bodies around them made Ravi wish he'd dug his old cloak out of their packs before they left, even if all their clothes were badly in need of washing. He wasn't used to being around this many people without his hood to hide behind, and he found himself edging closer to Daks with every minute that passed. After the second time Ravi bumped into him, Daks threw him a sideways glance.

Daks didn't say anything, but Ravi almost tripped over his own feet when Daks grabbed his hand and threaded their fingers together. Swallowing his shock, Ravi stared at him questioningly, but Daks kept his gaze locked on where they were going. After shooting a slightly embarrassed glance at the crowd around them, Ravi allowed the comfort of Daks's grip to make its warm way up his arm and into his chest. He had so many new things he'd have to get used to, but this one he'd do gladly if Daks let him.

A new life. A new start.

He lifted his chin, met a few curious stares from passersby, and reciprocated their nods of acknowledgment and greeting like he was anyone else who belonged there. He even smiled a few times, though the stretch of his lips felt awkward.

The healer was a no-nonsense lean older woman with sharp, assessing brown eyes and a steel-gray braid that trailed down her back. By the cluster of injured people sitting in neat rows in the tavern's common room, she had her work cut out for her, but she didn't bat an eye when Daks and Ravi came in. After questioning them to make sure neither was in any immediate danger, another woman in a white apron wrote their names on a slate and directed them to a bench.

Ravi had dozed off at least twice in the time it took for the healer to get to them again. He supposed it was lucky for them they hadn't arrived on the first day or two after the flood or their wait would have been even longer. The whole time, Daks clasped Ravi's hand in his lap and held him close to his side with an arm around his waist, and Ravi drank in the contact like sunlight after years of rain.

The woman in the white apron came to them first. She cleaned the wound on Daks's head and removed the stitches along his ribs before the healer came to join them. Ravi hadn't been nervous up until that point, but when the healer pulled a glowing green stone out of her pocket and leaned in close to Daks, he flinched. Daks's hand tightened on his, and he gave Ravi a reassuring smile.

"It's okay."

Blowing out a breath, Ravi sat still and watched closely as the woman passed the stone over the wounds. A lifetime of prejudice wouldn't be overcome in a few hours, but he supposed he'd have to get used to it sometime. He was going to a school for mages, after all. Before Ravi's astonished eyes, the raised and reddened skin on Daks's side faded to pink. Next, the healer moved the stone to his head, closed her eyes, and whispered. Ravi could actually see the hairs on Daks's arms lift as she worked and the lump began to shrink and the gash form a scar.

"That's the best I can do for now, I'm afraid," the healer said wearily. "I've sent a request to the High Council and the king for another healer and more healing stones, but towns and villages all along the river are calling for aid, so I don't know what we'll get or when."

"It's fine. I wouldn't ask for more than that. Thank you," Daks said, lifting and flexing his left arm before running cautious fingers along his scalp.

"Your turn," the healer said, turning to Ravi.

He reared back. "Oh no. I'm okay."

"I'll judge that," the older woman said firmly.

"No, really. As you said, you need to save your strength and your—" He waved a hand at the stone, unsure what to call it other than blasphemy.

"Sit still," she ordered, and when Daks squeezed his hand, Ravi stilled.

"Your tunic," she said, pointing.

Reluctantly, Ravi lifted his tunic and shirt to expose the bruising on his chest, but the woman didn't place the stone there. Instead she rested a cool palm over the area and closed her eyes. Given that she was the only one other than Daks to touch him in a long time, Ravi flinched, half expecting a Vision to overtake him, but nothing happened beyond a slight tingle along his skin beneath her hand.

"It doesn't hurt. I promise," Daks murmured, and when Ravi glanced at him, the man was smiling wryly.

Ravi blew out another breath and tried to force all the muscles in his body to relax. He could only imagine what his expression must have looked like to prompt Daks to say that, probably not very attractive at all. That was something else he'd have to get used to without his hood.

He jumped a little when a slight warmth spread beneath his skin where the healer touched, though the sensation was far from unpleasant.

"There you are," she said, withdrawing her hand. "You'll need to be careful for a while. I didn't take care of all of the bruising, but I mended the small crack in one of your ribs, which should keep you out of immediate danger."

"Thanks."

The woman looked even wearier now, and Ravi was almost sorry he'd come. He'd been in some pain, especially after their journey today, but he could have healed on his own in time, and there were more people in line behind them.

"Thank you, Healer," Daks said formally. "I'll also send word to the High Council on your behalf when I report in, and they'll reimburse you for our healing as well."

The healer's lips quirked in a mirror of Daks's usual wry grin. "I won't hold my breath, Agent. But lucky for both of us, you have a hard head, so perhaps you'll have better luck than I."

By the time Daks had dragged them to a cobbler, a clothes merchant, and to yet one more shop to send his message—which he did by simply holding a rock the man behind the counter gave him and closing his eyes—and they returned to the inn, Ravi was completely overwhelmed with the strangeness of it all. He wanted to find his cloak and curl up somewhere dark and quiet. He tried to argue when Daks procured flannels, robes, sandals, and soap for the bath house he'd been going on and on about. But all Daks had to do was crowd him into a quiet corner and kiss him breathless, and Ravi followed along like a puppy from then on. Ravi wasn't completely sure he liked being so easy to manipulate, and he glared down at his cock with disapproval of the choices it was making for him, but he still went.

The bath house turned out to be a separate structure behind the inn, and as they stepped inside, mineral and herb-scented steam enveloped them. In the center of the room, hot coals smoked beneath a grate piled with large rounded river stones littered with leaves and flowers. At first Ravi couldn't understand the purpose until a woman ladled water over the stones and more steam filled the air. Five large half barrels, big enough for two people to sit in, ringed the room, but only one other was occupied.

"It's suppertime," Daks said quietly, as if reading his thoughts. "We should have a little more privacy, but not as much as I'd like."

The deep, husky rumble of his voice vibrated through Ravi's belly and his cock pulsed hopefully, making Ravi scowl down at it again and shift uncomfortably. A "little" privacy definitely wasn't enough for him, no matter what his cock thought. No way was he going to get naked in front of strangers with Daks anywhere near him. He'd die of embarrassment.

He started backing up, but Daks caught his hand and squeezed. Ravi met his gaze and melted under the sweetness and reassurance he saw there. Dammit, he'd had no idea how charming Daks could be when he chose. Either that or Ravi was just too besotted to think clearly anymore. He preferred to blame Daks.

"Gentlemen, welcome," a small woman dressed in a cream-colored linen blouse, tan skirt, and light blue apron said, approaching them. "Are you sharing a bath today?"

"We are," Daks replied. He cast a quick glance at Ravi before he added, "We'd like a privacy screen as well, please."

The woman smiled knowingly at them, making Ravi's face heat even more. "Of course, sirs. This way, please."

As she led them to one of the barrels at the back of the room, Ravi murmured under his breath, "We're not doing any funny business in this place, screen or no screen."

Daks beamed that infuriating grin at him. "Of course not. But I figured you'd appreciate the bit of privacy for your modesty's sake, if nothing else. I'm only thinking of you."

Ravi narrowed his eyes at the man, almost certain Daks was laughing at him or lying... or both.

The instant Ravi sank into the steaming, scented water, he forgot all about any worries over modesty or irritation with Daks. Not caring who heard, he let out a long, low moan as every tight muscle in his body seemed to melt into a puddle all at once. He hadn't had a hot bath since that last winter with his family more than a decade ago. He'd forgotten how good it could feel.

"You keep making noises like that and I'm going to have a hard time respecting your finer sensibilities," Daks said huskily as he climbed into the tub with him.

Ravi tried to think of something clever or cutting to say in return, but his mind had apparently melted as well.

Daks let him float on his own for a while before tugging Ravi into his lap and murmuring smugly in his ear, "Told you you'd love it."

Ravi let his head fall back against Daks's shoulder as he allowed the man to support him in the water. Daks was right, though Ravi wouldn't give him the satisfaction of admitting it out loud. Ravi relaxed in a pleasant dreamlike state until Daks began to gently wash him with a soaped flannel that smelled of lavender and spices. He tried to voice an objection. He really did. He was perfectly capable of washing himself. And they might have a reed screen between them and any other patrons or staff, but someone could still hear. But Daks's ministrations felt so good, Ravi couldn't seem to get his voice to work or his mouth to utter anything but quiet, breathy moans. He squirmed in Daks's lap as the man soaped between his legs, his big hand sliding over Ravi's hardening cock teasingly before dipping lower to massage his balls and then farther back.

Ravi let out a little whimper when a soapy finger ghosted over his hole, and Daks's hand returned along the path it had taken.

When he regained enough control to speak, Ravi hissed, "We need to go to our room now."

"You sure?" Daks asked, that stupid smile in his voice. "We haven't used the full hour yet."

With a monumental feat of strength, Ravi pushed himself off of Daks's lap and spun in the water to face him. He narrowed his gaze at the man and gritted out, "Yes. Now."

He'd waited ten Rift-blighted years for a night of unbridled sexual hedonism. He wasn't waiting any longer.

Despite the teasing in Daks's tone, Ravi had felt the man's hard cock pressed to the small of his back, and Daks's pupils were blown so only a narrow ring of blue circled the black. The man wasn't as in control as he liked to pretend, and that somehow made Ravi even hotter. He needed to get to that big soft bed Daks had promised before his legs wouldn't carry him anymore.

How they got up to the room, Ravi couldn't say. He vaguely remembered Daks murmuring something to the ladies who worked there as they clumsily dressed in the robes, collected the rest of their clothes, and stumbled toward the inn proper, but that was all.

As soon as the door closed behind them, Ravi launched himself at Daks, kissing him and tugging the robe from Daks's shoulders. Daks chuckled into their sloppy kiss as he yanked at his own belt, freeing the knot, before doing the same to Ravi's. Naked, smelling of herbs and the first pungent musk of need, they fell on the bed together in a writhing heap. It was only when Ravi's chest twinged, reminding him that he wasn't completely healed, that he remembered Daks's injuries too.

"Are you. Okay? I'm not. Hurting you. Am I?" he gasped between kisses.

Daks rolled on top of him, covering him with that big body in a way Ravi knew he'd never get enough of. After bracing himself up on his elbows, Daks gazed down at him with an achingly tender smile as he brushed Ravi's unruly damp, curling hair out of his face.

"I'm fine. Are you okay?"

"Yes."

"Good."

Daks burrowed his arms under Ravi's shoulders, slid one palm down to grip Ravi's ass while the other moved to cradle his neck, pulling him into another long, teasing kiss. Ravi hooked his heels around Daks's thighs and writhed against him, seeking friction for his achingly hard cock even as he clutched at Daks's back.

When Daks finally broke their kiss, Ravi whined and tried to pull him back again, but when he began moving down Ravi's body, kissing, licking, and caressing as he went, the whine turned into incoherent sounds of encouragement. He arched into each touch, shaking with need and anticipation, moaning and gasping. Every nerve was on fire and starved for attention.

When Daks's hot mouth closed over the head of his cock the first time, Ravi nearly shot off the bed. Daks chuckled around his length, sending vibrations of pleasure that had Ravi flopping back onto the plush mattress. With one palm flat against Ravi's chest, pressing down even as he caressed him, Daks began working his way up and down Ravi's shaft, licking, sucking, and gently nibbling, until he took Ravi's entire length inside.

With a cry, Ravi exploded into Daks's mouth mortifyingly quickly. He'd tried to hold on, but the teasing in the tub, followed by all of Daks's ministrations since then, overwhelmed him. This wasn't the first time someone had used their mouth on him, but what Daks could do with that mouth of his far outstripped any of the youthful fumblings with the boys in his childhood village. He now understood why so many people made such a big deal about it.

Still, as he came down from his orgasm and Daks settled on top of him again, brushing the backs of his fingers along Ravi's cheek and peppering him with gentle kisses, Ravi couldn't help a wince of embarrassment.

"Sorry," he murmured with a grimace.

Daks's eyebrows drew together. "For what?"

Ravi squirmed. "You know, not, uh, lasting longer than that."

Daks grinned. "Beautiful, we have all night. That was just the first round."

Shyly, Ravi wrapped his arms around Daks's shoulders and held his gaze. "I didn't take care of you."

"I can be patient."

"Since when?" Ravi snorted.

Daks merely cocked an eyebrow and grinned. Ravi studied his face before running the tips of his fingers along the pink scars on his jaw. "You're different than I imagined you'd be," he said absently.

Daks's grin widened. "You fantasized about me?"

Of course Daks would only hear that part. Scowling, Ravi huffed and tried halfheartedly to push him off, but the man's solid bulk didn't budge. "I was going to say, I just didn't expect you to be so… so tender, I guess." Then he cringed at how stupid and lovesick that sounded.

He pushed at Daks's chest, harder this time, wanting to hide his embarrassment, but Daks cupped his jaw and kissed him until Ravi melted again.

When he finally drew back, Daks said, "As Shura will gladly tell you often—and in any language you choose—I can be a bastard. I know it. But not when it counts. Not with people I care about."

Ravi bit his lower lip as his stupid heart fluttered, but he was absolutely not going to ask for any more reassurances than that. Instead, he whispered, "Daks, I want you to fuck me."

Daks's gaze darkened as he stared into Ravi's eyes. His tongue snaked out and wet his lips before he asked, "Are you sure?"

"Yes."

Despite his nervousness, his cock started filling again at the thought of being so wrapped up and filled that he could feel Daks everywhere at once. He'd done without for so long, he ached to be overwhelmed with sensation and had no interest in being patient.

Daks cleared his throat. "Just to be clear, you've never done this before, have you?" Before Ravi could even think of frowning, Daks added, "I need to know so I don't hurt you or expect you to know something you don't."

Ravi flushed but shook his head. "I haven't."

"You don't have to, you know. If you'd rather wait, or try something else, I'm quite flexible—"

"I want to. I want to feel you in me, on me, around me, everywhere."

To Ravi's immense relief, Daks groaned and smiled that sexy smile of his as he pumped his hips, letting Ravi feel how those words had affected him. Which was good, because Ravi wasn't sure he could have managed more convincing than that without dying of embarrassment. His proper Rassan reserve had suffered enough for one day.

After a brief peck on the lips, Daks climbed off him, leaving Ravi feeling surprisingly—and appallingly—bereft. Gods, he hoped that was only a temporary reaction to the sex and all the attention he'd received, because he didn't like feeling this needy and vulnerable.

Luckily, Daks returned to the bed quickly, before Ravi had to explore that thought any further. Daks carried a small corked pot in his big hands, his cock proudly leading the way. The man really was thick all over, and Ravi's stomach fluttered.

When Daks uncorked the pot, Ravi caught a nutty, sweet aroma he couldn't quite place, but he stopped even trying when Daks dipped two thick fingers in and drew them out. They glistened in the light from the single window, and Ravi's breath stuttered as his nerves jangled, despite the throb that pulsed through his cock. Back in Arcadia, he'd heard horror stories from some of the others... but he'd heard good stories too, and he trusted Daks. He didn't quite understand *why*, but he did.

He relaxed back against the pillows and spread his legs in invitation. Daks drew in a sharp breath as he lowered himself to kneel between Ravi's thighs and gazed down at him with heated eyes. He bent and kissed Ravi sweetly as he lifted one of Ravi's thighs over his hip and gripped and kneaded his ass. Ravi wrapped his arms around Daks's barrel chest, pulling him closer as the heat built between them again. But when Daks teased a single blunt finger against his opening, Ravi unconsciously tensed and had to force himself to relax.

"We don't have to do this, you know," Daks murmured as he placed tender kisses along Ravi's jaw and down his neck. "There are plenty of things we haven't done yet. You could fuck me instead, for instance."

The finger massaging his hole stilled, but just the feel of it there made Ravi's belly ache, now that he'd had a bit to get used to the sensation. He was so wrapped up in the feel of it, it took a few seconds to process Daks's words.

When he did, his eyes popped open. "You'd let me?"

Daks's lips curved in that grin that had somehow become more sexy and adorable than infuriating. "Like I said before, I'm quite flexible," he murmured playfully, despite the heat in his eyes.

Storing that information for later, Ravi shook his head. "Not this time, but good to know." Working up some courage to give the man a grin of his own, Ravi said, "I want you to show me how it's done first." He paused a beat before adding challengingly, "If you think you can."

Daks quirked an eyebrow, and his grin widened. "Oh, I can."

"Then stop talking and get fucking," Ravi ordered with more boldness than he felt.

Thank the gods, Daks didn't accept Ravi's bravado at face value. Instead, he seemed to take hours teasing, caressing, and working him open until Ravi was a trembling, needy, breathless mess. His cock was so hard he could pound fence posts with it, and when Daks grabbed the backs of Ravi's thighs, bent him nearly in half, and pushed his tongue into Ravi's hole, Ravi almost lost control and came right then.

"Daks," he gasped in a strangled whisper, "please."

He felt Daks grin against his skin, his stubble rubbing against sensitive flesh, before he lowered Ravi's legs to either side of his hips and draped himself over Ravi's chest. "Please what?"

Despite the blissful tingles flooding his body, Ravi narrowed his eyes at the man, and Daks chuckled. "As you command," he said. Then his grin faded slightly and he added, "It might be easier on you your first time if you roll over."

Ravi shook his head. "I want to see you."

Daks seemed surprised for a second before his expression softened as he nodded. He slid his big, rough palms down beneath Ravi's thighs again and helped him angle his hips upward. Ravi sucked in a breath at the first pressure of Daks's cock against the entrance to his body, but Daks had more than prepared him, and with gentle coaxing, Daks was able to push slowly inside. The stretch was strange and a bit uncomfortable at first, but the sensation of fullness was still incredible.

After a few panted breaths and giving his body time to adjust, Ravi needed more. He locked gazes with Daks and said, "It's okay. Move."

The first long slide in and out of his body had Ravi arching off the mattress, overwhelmed with sensation. He moaned and tightened his grip on Daks's upper arms. Locking his heels together over Daks's ass, he flexed his hips, urging Daks to go deeper. As he pressed slowly inside again, Daks bent and captured Ravi's lips, kissing him long and slow. They rocked together for a long time, Ravi adjusting to Daks's rhythm as the strangeness and discomfort morphed into pleasure like nothing he'd ever experienced.

Daks tightened the arm under Ravi's shoulders, lifting him and molding their bodies as closely as possible while he fucked him, and Ravi simply rode the wave of sensation. Trapped between their bodies, his cock wept as Daks pushed into him over and over, hitting that spot inside him that made him gasp and dig his fingers into Daks's ass and back, begging for more.

"Daks," he panted, "I need...."

"What do you need?"

He drew back, which wasn't what Ravi wanted at all. He craved the contact. But when Daks began stroking Ravi's cock as he fucked him, Ravi's world exploded in sparks of pleasure.

"Okay. That," he moaned helplessly.

Daks barked out a breathless chuckle before increasing his pace, thrusting into him harder with each pump of his fist on Ravi's cock. The pleasure built beyond Ravi's ability to hold it back, and he arched off the bed with a cry as his orgasm swept over him, coming in spurts over his belly and Daks's fist. Daks eased his grip on Ravi's cock while the last of the aftershocks rolled over him, but didn't let go completely as he pounded into him. When Daks threw his head back and grunted, stilling inside Ravi and flooding his channel, it forced a few last dribbles from Ravi's cock.

Still inside him, Daks leaned in for another tender, wet kiss before pulling out of Ravi's body and slumping to the mattress next to him. They both lay still, filling the room with the sound of their rapid breathing until that evened out as well. Without a word or opening his eyes, Daks snagged his robe off the floor and used it to clean Ravi off before tossing it aside and flopping onto his back again. Ravi's body ached and his skin tingled in the absence of Daks's touch, but that needy creature inside him finally seemed to have been appeased—for now, anyway. For the first time in days, he didn't mind having a few minutes to himself to absorb everything that had happened.

His lips curved in what had to be an embarrassingly dopey smile as he turned to study Daks's sprawled form. He had the oddest impulse to thank him but managed to bite his tongue. Daks's contented smile was already smug enough. He'd be insufferable if Ravi spouted half the lovesick things running through his mind right now.

Daks's eyes were closed, his hair spread out in a bushy halo around his head, and sweat beaded in several tantalizing places along his skin. All too soon, Ravi found himself licking his lips as renewed desire awakened in him. He was trying to decide if his body could possibly fulfill even half the promises his mind was making when a knock at the door made him jump.

More than a decade of fear and caution made his heart race as Daks grunted and rolled off the bed.

"Probably supper," Daks mumbled on his way to the door.

Naked and still rumpled from sex, Daks just opened the door and bade the serving girl on the other side to enter, while Ravi yelped and scrambled to get under the bedlinens. The girl's eyes widened and her cheeks pinked, but she scurried inside, set her tray down on the table, and scurried back out again.

"What?" Daks asked when Ravi glared at him.

Ravi spluttered at the man's thick-headedness until he caught Daks grinning at him. The bastard knew exactly what he did. Ravi growled and threw a pillow, which Daks deftly caught out of the air.

Ravi was searching around the bed for something else to hurl at the man when Daks argued, "She's seen worse, I'm sure."

Ravi simply glared back, and Daks tried to look contrite. It wasn't convincing at all.

"Sorry," Daks murmured, marginally more convincingly as he sidled to the bed carrying a slice of soft bread positively dripping in butter.

Instead of just offering it to Ravi, Daks climbed onto the mattress and kept coming until he loomed over Ravi, his smile turning wicked.

"Forgive me?" he asked, fluttering his eyelashes.

Ravi might have laughed at the absurdity of a scoundrel like Daks trying to act coy, but he was distracted by both his stomach and his cock clamoring for his attention at the same time. Both ended up winning.

He couldn't call what happened next a meal exactly. There was too much kissing and fondling and licking going on. But at the end of it all, his stomach was full again, and his balls were empty, and he was so exhausted he probably couldn't have climbed out of that bed if someone had set it on fire.

They made love once more, sometime in the night. Ravi's ass was too tender to try that part again, no matter how tempted he was, but Daks was either incredibly imaginative or had tons of experience to draw from, because Ravi's suddenly insatiable libido was not in any way left wanting.

For once in his life, the gods had been generous, handing him so much more than he would have ever thought to ask for. Which, of course, meant something horrible had to be waiting for him right around the corner, but he'd worry about that tomorrow.

Chapter Thirteen

Daks had overdone it as usual. But he wasn't sorry.

The sun streaming through the small window in the room Eben had given them made Ravi's messy auburn hair blaze red and painted warm yellow streaks across his body, but luckily hadn't woken him yet. Daks could have a few more minutes of laziness to look his fill without getting caught.

He'd tried to rouse himself earlier in the morning and at least go down and order breakfast, but his body had quickly countermanded that idea. Was he really getting too old to fuck all night? What a horrible thought. He'd blame it on being knocked unconscious for two days after nearly drowning instead.

He shivered. Even thinking the D-word made his stomach quail.

He forced his gaze back to Ravi and let it wander over the hills and valleys of his lanky body, which was a much more pleasant usage of his time. He couldn't afford to deal with any of the rest right now. For one thing, Eben's ale was far too expensive for him to buy enough to drown his sorrows in, especially since he wasn't 100 percent sure the High Council would actually cover his expenses this time. And for another, he still hadn't heard anything of Shura.

Ravi was awake and watching him when Daks's gaze climbed back up to his face.

"Morning," Daks murmured, grinning even wider when Ravi's cheeks darkened.

He had a feeling that would never get old.

"Morning," Ravi replied quietly.

But as Ravi continued to study him soberly, Daks's grin faded. "Something wrong?"

"Just thinking."

Daks winced internally. Quirking an eyebrow and forcing his grin back in place, he rolled off the mattress and moved to collect his clothes, despite the loud complaints of his body.

"Thinking goes better on a full stomach. I'll pop down to the kitchen to see what I can get for us."

"Daks," Ravi said, his tone far too serious.

Daks froze, bent over with his trousers half on, and reluctantly met Ravi's gaze. "Yeah?"

"I had a Dream last night, after… you know." Ravi's cheeks grew a little darker.

Daks ducked his head and pulled his trousers the rest of the way on, though he didn't bother to knot the ties at the front.

"A Dream about what?"

"I know what you're going to do."

Daks snorted and dropped onto one of the two plain wooden chairs by the table so he could tug on his boots. "Even *I* barely know from one minute to the next what I'm going to do."

When only heavy silence met his words, Daks sighed, set his shiny new boots back down, and met Ravi's gaze. Impatience, irritation, worry, and something else all chased across Ravi's face. The man really was going to have to learn to hide his feelings better or the crusty old bastards at the Scholomagi would eat him alive.

"I *Dreamed*," Ravi repeated. "But even if I hadn't, I'm not an idiot. You're going back for her. You can't *not* go back for her, because you love her."

Daks slumped against the back of the chair and dragged a hand down through his tangled hair. Ravi couldn't have waited just a little while longer for him to have some caffe' before bringing this up? He hadn't even acknowledged the plan to himself yet. He kept hoping any second she would walk through that door. Damned Rassans and their prohibitions on magic. If they'd been able to carry message or tracking stones, he'd know she was safe. He wouldn't have to cling desperately to hope.

"Because she's family," Daks replied tiredly.

"I know."

Ravi's tone was gentle with acceptance and even approval, and Daks met his gaze again as that familiar sensation fluttered in his chest.

"When will you leave?" Ravi asked neutrally.

"Tomorrow, I think." No sense in trying to avoid it now. "I'll make the arrangements today and give her just a little longer to get across or send a message, but it's been three days since the flood. I should have heard something."

"Yes."

"Your Dream didn't happen to say whether or not I was successful, did it?"

Ravi winced and shook his head. "Only that you were going. Which was as useless as always, since I could have figured that out on my own."

Ravi's jaw tightened as he scowled. He drew his knees up to his chest and wrapped his arms around them, forcing Daks to join him on the bed and pull him into a hug.

"It's okay," he murmured into Ravi's hair as he pressed a cheek to the top of his head. "Can't expect you to win all my battles for me."

Ravi barked out a bitter laugh. "Yeah, right. I should have known the one time I actually want a Vision, my curse refuses to cooperate. When it could get me killed, I was having one practically every day, sometimes more than one. And now that it could actually be useful, of course they've stopped."

"When we get you to the Scholomagi, they'll be able to help you figure it out. Until then, no one, not even you, should blame you for not being able to control it. Give yourself a break."

His leg was starting to cramp, so Daks eased back into the pillows and tucked Ravi more comfortably against his side. They lay in silence for a while until Ravi sighed and lifted himself over Daks, straddling his body and boldly meeting Daks's gaze.

"I need to know something before you go," Ravi said somberly. "I need to know why."

"Why what?"

"Why did you help me?"

Daks frowned. "We already talked about that. It's my job, remember?"

"And that's it? It's just your job? You traveled the length of Rassa, risking the Brotherhood and the King's Guard. You dove in to save me from the swamp when you're terrified of drowning. And you nearly drowned again trying to get me to safety, all because it's your job?"

Daks squirmed, uncomfortable with where this conversation was going but unsure how to stop it, especially with Ravi essentially pinning him to the mattress.

"I gave you my word," he replied, hoping that would be the end of the conversation.

"And that's it? That's your answer?" He paused, and when Daks couldn't come up with anything to say, he sighed and nodded. "Okay. That's what I needed to know."

Ravi climbed off him and scooted to the edge of the bed. Unable to bear the sadness and disappointment he'd seen in Ravi's eyes, Daks wrapped an arm around his middle and dragged him back. He didn't think about what he was doing. He simply rolled Ravi onto his back and covered him with his body. Though he was obviously upset, Ravi didn't struggle or lash out at him, like Daks half expected him to.

"What do you want me to say?" Daks asked, his chest constricting.

"Nothing," Ravi said without meeting Daks's gaze. "I wanted the truth. Now I have it."

Fuck.

Daks was screwing this up. Why did things always have to be so complicated? Especially before he'd had a chance to get some caffe' in his system so at least half his brain would have been working.

"Why did you stay with me, Ravi? Why did you save *me*?" Daks asked.

Ravi met his gaze then, his amber eyes filled with cold anger. "No. You don't get to ask me that. If all this," he continued, waving his hand between them, "was just a bit of fun after a few hard days of work, then so be it. I would have had to be a complete idiot to think otherwise. Go make your plans, and I'll make mine."

That last pronouncement had a finality to it Daks didn't like at all, and he tightened his grip on Ravi's arms.

"Just give me a second here, okay?" Daks whined.

"Why?"

Daks growled and narrowed his eyes at Ravi. "I've got a lot on my mind, if you hadn't noticed. You're pushing me, and I haven't even had breakfast yet."

Ravi blinked at him for a second before he snorted out a laugh. Then he closed those oh-so-pretty eyes of his and sighed. "You're right. You are who you are."

"What's that supposed to mean?"

"I'm *agreeing* with you," Ravi huffed.

"Well, stop."

Ravi cocked an eyebrow at him and just stared until Daks couldn't take it anymore. With a groan, he pressed his forehead to Ravi's and closed his eyes.

"I care about you," Daks whispered into the close space between them. "Is that what you want to hear?"

"*Of course* I want to hear that. Anyone would," Ravi whispered back.

"Okay, well I do. I never would have agreed to be your first if it was just about blowing off some steam. I'm not an asshole when it really counts. I told you that."

"Okay."

Daks blew out a breath and rolled onto his back to stare at the ceiling because he couldn't stare into those damned gorgeous eyes anymore.

"This isn't easy for me, talking about feelings. There are reasons I don't do *this* anymore," he admitted reluctantly, waving a helpless hand between them.

"I'm not asking you to write me a poem, Daks," Ravi huffed back at him. "Just be honest with me. I need to know I'm not making a complete fool out of myself. That's all. I'm not exactly an expert at this kind of thing either."

"You're not… making a fool of yourself, I mean. But there's things you don't know. Even Shura doesn't know all of it, whatever she might have told you about my past."

"She didn't say much. All she said was that you nearly drowned and that it had cost you a great deal more."

"Well, she's guessed, but she doesn't know. I met her after, when I was a little reckless and didn't give a damn anymore if I got hurt."

"What happened?" Ravi prodded after Daks stopped there.

Daks's lips curved despite the twisting in his gut. Ravi wasn't the kind of man to let him off easy, particularly when there might be a story involved. But Daks was no storyteller, and his hesitation had already made a way bigger deal of this than it was.

"Look, it's not some great mystery. I just don't like to talk about it. I fell in love a long time ago… when I was first sent to the Scholomagi for training. Jos was older than me. He had some small talent with magic, but not enough to ever earn him a spot on the High Council or anything." Daks risked a quick sideways glance and found Ravi watching him intently. "He was originally from Rassa. He'd escaped all on his own, so that's why he'd pushed for the program to rescue others like him from the Brotherhood. He's the reason I got involved in it. I would have followed him to the Seventh Hell if I had to."

The old pain had dulled considerably over the years, along with memories of their too brief time together. Sometimes it seemed like another life entirely, but if that was true, what did he have left to keep him going? This was why he didn't look too closely inside. He might not like what he saw.

Clearing his throat, he continued, "When I fell through the ice on a mission in Samebar, I was sick for a long time. Jos stayed with me while I recovered, until he received word from his family that a cousin had shown signs of a gift. I couldn't go with him, and he couldn't wait until I was better. My family had to drug me to keep me from trying… and then I never saw him again."

"He died?"

"No. Well, yeah, I guess he had to have, but I never found out one way or the other."

Ravi placed a gentle hand on his arm and squeezed. "I'm sorry."

Daks laid his hand over Ravi's and gave him the best smirk he could manage. "I've spent the last ten years of my life looking for a man I knew, deep down, I wouldn't find, obsessed with keeping his mission alive while our support and funds from the Scholomagi dwindled and finally disappeared. No one cares about what I do anymore, but here I am, still trying to do it. Heh. You might say I'm just a tiny bit slow to get the hint."

"I care," Ravi said, pressing closer. "I wouldn't be here if you hadn't—"

"Screwed everything up?"

"Given a damn," Ravi corrected with a glare. "I meant what I said on the ferry. I'm sorry for putting all the blame on you, for not being more grateful for everything you tried to do for me. I can admit that now… and more, if I thought you wanted to hear it."

Ravi bit his lower lip then, and his stern gaze softened into vulnerability. That feeling inside Daks, the one he'd experienced only once before and had been fighting to keep buried even deeper than his fears, struggled to break free. But now wasn't the time.

He rolled them until he was on top of Ravi again. Ravi opened so sweetly for him when Daks pressed their lips together, and Daks tried to say all he could without words.

When he pulled back to allow them to catch their breaths, he whispered, "I do want to hear it, whatever you want to say to me, just not yet, not until Shura is safely home and I can put all that behind me for a while, okay?"

"Yeah?" Ravi asked uncertainly, his pupils blown wide, his lips swollen and pink.

"Yeah."

Ravi swallowed and nodded. "Okay."

They never got around to eating breakfast. By the time Daks clambered out of bed on somewhat shaky legs and pulled his trousers back on, the inn kitchens had already started preparing for supper. The best he could wheedle out of them was a tray of cold meats, cheese, dried fruits, and bread.

As they ate, Ravi seemed pensive, but not nearly as sad as earlier. Daks sure as hells hoped he'd done the right thing. Shura would laugh her ass off at him when he told her… or maybe she wouldn't, given how she'd been acting with Fara.

After lunch, Ravi insisted on accompanying him down to the river to see about hiring a boat to the other side. It took a little while to find someone willing to take a promise of reimbursement from the High Council in lieu of ready coin. Daks had to save what coin he had for the trip back, in case they couldn't rely on Fara's coin for any reason he refused to contemplate.

Eventually they found a merchant who already had a trip planned to sell his wares at the market in Traget and was willing to take Daks along—if he helped row and unload on the other side. Daks reluctantly agreed.

Beggars can't be choosers, after all.

"I'll help too," Ravi offered, and Daks jolted.

"Uh, no, you won't."

"Yes, I will."

"Excuse us a moment." Daks gave the merchant a tight smile before taking Ravi's arm and walking them out of earshot.

"You're not going," Daks said flatly.

Ravi lifted his chin, his amber eyes flashing as he yanked his arm free from Daks's grasp. "I am."

"Have you lost your mind? We just spent the better part of two weeks in misery, running from the guard and the Brotherhood, to get you here, and you want to go back? In case you haven't forgotten, you nearly drowned a few days ago crossing this very river."

"I haven't forgotten you nearly drowned too," Ravi shot back.

"All the more reason for only one of us to risk it."

"I know why you have to go, but you shouldn't have to do it alone," Ravi practically growled.

His gold eyes had drawn to narrow slits, his jaw clenched, and his pretty lips pressed in a stubborn line, and Daks was entirely unprepared for the little baby bird flutter behind his ribs. This was probably not the correct response, but he couldn't seem to help it. His lips curved in a sappy little smile, and he rushed in to steal a kiss.

Caught off guard, Ravi sucked in a breath, and Daks chased it with his tongue. Despite his anger and frustration, Ravi didn't shove him away. He melted into the kiss, trembling just a little, and Daks's heart twisted some more. Even if the thought of crossing the river alone again terrified him. Even if he knew having Ravi next to him would help immensely, he'd never let it happen. Ravi was just as scared as he was and fighting hard not to show it.

Though it pained him, Daks ended their kiss and took a step back. Ignoring his first impulse to deflect from the emotions swirling inside him by poking the bear a little more, he blew out a breath and decided to be a grown-up… just this once.

"I can't tell you how much it means to me that you're willing to risk so much, but you're not thinking clearly," he murmured as kindly as he could. "You may not have had a Vision in days, but the risk is still there. We talked about this before, remember? With a rogue wizard or a rogue brother only a day's ride away at this supposed barbarian encampment—or even in town if the new rumors are to be believed—the Brotherhood is guaranteed to have a Finder here, and we've no quick way back across. You saw the number of brothers and soldiers in the market."

Ravi's eyebrows drew together, and he worried his lip. He wanted to argue, Daks could see it in his face, but he had to know Daks was right.

"I'm going to be okay," Daks continued, closing the distance between them to cup Ravi's cheek. "I'm not any happier about crossing over again than you are, but I'll be quicker and less noticeable on my own."

"You're barely healed," Ravi protested weakly.

"I'm healed enough. It's just a boat ride. I'll ride over, find out what happened to Shura, and ride back. No one's looking for me in

Traget, and I'll feel that much better knowing you're tucked up safe and comfortable here. Do it for me, okay?"

Daks fluttered his eyelashes for dramatic effect, and Ravi's lips twisted sourly. He glared at Daks for a few beats before he huffed out a breath and folded his arms across his chest.

"You better come back, and quickly. You still have to get me to that magic school you've been bragging about," he huffed.

"I will," Daks replied with a grin. "There and back again… that's it. And—"

Ravi clapped a hand over Daks's mouth. "Don't you dare say a single word about how easy it will be or 'with any you-know-what,' or I swear to the gods I'll deck you."

Since he had been about to say something along those lines, he wisely kept his mouth shut when Ravi removed his hand.

"Come on," Ravi ordered as he spun on his heel and headed back to the boatman. "Let's get this over with and go back to the inn. I'm tired and hungry."

Chapter Fourteen

Ravi didn't accompany Daks down to the river the next morning. They said their goodbyes without words while they were still in bed, Daks insisting Ravi naked and freshly fucked was the picture he wanted to take with him over the day or two they'd be separated.

Ravi hadn't argued; he wasn't sure why now. It probably had something to do with Daks's admittedly impressive skills in the bedroom. Daks might be an impetuous walking disaster anytime other than when he was fighting or fucking, but damned if he didn't make up for it.

Daks had kept him up half the night—literally and figuratively—possibly to distract himself as much as Ravi. It had worked... mostly. But now that Ravi was alone, the anxiety he'd managed to ignore for hours came back full force. He tried to tell himself he was being stupid and overly dramatic. His emotions were all over the place because of the idiot now trying to get himself killed... *again*. If he'd ever needed a reminder that real life was nothing like the stories he loved, the gods were making it perfectly clear to him now. He and Daks had made it out of Rassa. They'd survived a flood together. He should have his happily-ever-after by now, shouldn't he?

Unable to stand the close confines of their room any longer, Ravi got dressed and headed down into the slowly awakening inn. Without being asked, Eben brought him a light breakfast, which Ravi managed to eat half of before his stomach threatened mutiny. He pushed the remainder around his plate while he eavesdropped on the steadily increasing conversations around him as the common room filled. He heard smatterings of Sambaran, trade tongue, and even a little Rassan, the latter making his heart constrict with a longing he hadn't expected.

Alone in a foreign kingdom, without Daks's seemingly endless energy to distract him, all that he'd sacrificed started hitting home.

He wasn't given much choice in the matter. If he hadn't left his old life, the Brotherhood would have taken it from him eventually. But still, he could mourn just a little, in private, all that he'd left behind. He missed Vic and the others terribly.

"Daks won't be too happy if I let you waste away to nothing while he's gone," Eben said gruffly as he held out a hand for Ravi's plate.

"Sorry. I'm not particularly hungry today, I guess."

"You're not ill, are you?"

"No."

Ravi tried to think of something else to say but came up empty. He shifted uncomfortably under Eben's scrutiny.

"He'll be back, you know," Eben finally said. "Like weeds in the cobbles, that one always springs back, no matter how many times you think he's gone for good."

Ravi's lips curved fondly at that. "Have you known him long?"

"Ten years or so, I guess. He comes through at least a couple of times a year on his way to Samet or back up to Scholoveld. We're not close, mind, but he's the type of man that leaves an impression."

Ravi's smile widened. "He is."

"He told me to take care of you while he's gone, so if you need anything, food, drink, more clothes, another hour in the bath house, you just let me know."

"I don't have any coin for such things," Ravi admitted.

Eben grinned, baring slightly crooked teeth behind his beard. "Don't worry about that. We'll be billing the Scholomagi. They may be tight-fisted, covetous old bastards, but they always pay their debts. I have a letter of approval from Agent Daks that'll cover everything you might need, here and on the road to Scholoveld—" He cut off with a grimace and shrugged apologetically. "Only if you need it, that is."

Ravi frowned as Eben's words sunk in. "If I need…? Wait, you mean if I need to go the rest of the way alone?"

Eben cringed. "I just meant you're taken care of, no matter what."

If the man had hoped to ease Ravi's anxieties, he'd done a crap job of it, but Ravi forced a smile and nodded. "Thanks."

"Just, uh, let me or one of the others know. Whatever you need," he finished awkwardly as he backed away.

Ravi returned to their room and started rummaging through their belongings to see if Daks had left any other notes or provisions behind, but he found nothing, and he rolled his eyes at himself. What had he been expecting? A romantic farewell letter urging Ravi to go on without him should he never return? Declarations of undying love? A single rose?

Sometimes he thought those stories he loved as a child had ruined him for real life.

He slumped onto the bed and put his face in his hands. What was the matter with him? Daks had been gone less than two hours and he felt like he was losing his mind. The man's scent hadn't even had time to fade from the bedlinens.

He buried his face in those linens and breathed, trying to calm down. He was so wrapped up in inner turmoil, he missed the first tingling along his nerves. By the time he pulled his head out of his ass enough to realize what was happening, he was too late to even try to stop the Vision from barreling through him. Luckily, he was already on the bed, so he didn't have far to fall when his world spun out of control.

Daks stood alone in a forest. The setting sun cast long shadows around him, but Ravi could just make out Daks's face. It bore the exact same expression it had when they were together on the ferry and the flood was raging toward them—controlled terror. He held a dagger in one hand and a short sword in the other as he faced off against something hidden in the darkness. Ravi's perspective suddenly shifted, as if he were now looking through Daks's eyes, and what he saw made his heart stop. Peering out at him from between two trees was a pair of glowing red eyes, eyes anyone would recognize even if they'd never seen them in real life—Riftspawn!

The Seer

Ravi rolled off the bed and onto the floor, gasping and fighting the last clinging tendrils of his Vision. As soon as he could get his limbs to obey him, he got to his knees and used the bed to push to his feet. He staggered out of the room and down the stairs. When he spotted Eben, he rushed the man.

"Eben! Please tell me there's some way I can get a message to Daks."

The big man looked at him, confused. "A message? Sorry, I don't think so. He didn't know where he'd end up, or at least he didn't tell me."

Ravi groaned. "Please. This is Samebar. Don't you have some sort of magic you can use? There has to be something. Daks showed me the message stones."

Eben shook his head. "They only work if you've got the matching stone with you. Daks wouldn't have taken anything like that into Rassa. It's too dangerous, if you're caught."

"Then I need to get across."

"He said you should stay here."

Ravi barely came up to the man's collarbones and probably weighed half of what Eben did, but he was sorely tempted to punch him. "I'm going. Either you help me or I figure out a way to do it on my own."

Eben gaped at him, doing a fair impression of a landed fish, and Ravi threw up his hands in frustration and stomped off. Following the path down to the river he'd taken with Daks yesterday, he managed to locate the same boatman. After the fourth rejection he received, he was getting desperate.

"No coin, no passage," the asshole said, repeating the same line he'd heard far too many times already.

"You took the note from my friend," Ravi insisted.

"Aye, a note for passage from an agent of the High Council. You're not an agent of the High Council."

"If I don't get over there, he might not make it back to make sure you get paid," Ravi gritted out through clenched teeth.

"Don't need him to. I got the note."

Ravi wanted to scream, but he forced his anger and panic down, desperately trying to come up with a solution.

"What if I had something to barter?" he asked hopefully as a thought occurred to him.

The grizzled older man eyed him skeptically. "What?"

"A horse. A magnificent stallion, strong, healthy, smart, with the endurance of ten horses. He's sitting in a stable up at the inn as we speak." As the man's eyes lit up with guarded interest, Ravi leaned forward. "If I or my friend don't make it back to see you're paid in full from the Council, the horse is yours. I'm sure it's worth at least twenty times one little passage across the river, right?"

The man sucked his teeth for a moment before he gave Ravi a begrudging nod. "Bring me the horse and you have a deal."

"What? No."

He shrugged. "No horse, no deal."

Ravi's teeth were going to crack if he didn't stop clenching his jaw so tight. "Fine," he huffed and stomped his way back up to the inn.

The stables attached to the inn were in chaos when Ravi first got there. Several stall doors hung open, and horses, goats, and donkeys wandered freely while a short, round-bellied man shouted orders at two young boys and a small pile of wet straw lay smoldering in the center aisle. Ravi searched the smoky space and blew out a relieved breath when he found Horse standing calmly in his stall, surveying the chaos around him with what seemed to Ravi to be regal amusement instead of fear or anxiety.

"What you want?" one of the boys asked him sourly while tugging on the lead to a rather recalcitrant mule.

The boy received a cuff on the ear from the round man, who hurried over. "Sorry, young sir. We've had a little mishap this morning, but it'll be under control soon. What can I do for you?"

Ravi wasn't exactly dressed for the part of a "young sir," but he supposed the stable master had seen him come in with Daks, which hopefully meant he wouldn't have any trouble.

"I'm here for our horse," he said as confidently as he could muster. When the man hesitated a fraction of a second, Ravi added, "We'll take him out of your way for a little while so you have one less thing to worry about. I'll get him myself, no need to trouble you."

He started walking before the man could form a reply. And as he'd hoped, the man had too much on his hands to put up much resistance. Ravi blew out a relieved breath as he led Horse out of the inn yard and down toward the river without further incident. He tried not to meet Horse's unsettling eyes as he handed over the reins. If the boatman ran off with Horse, Daks would probably kill him. But he might not live long enough to kill him if Ravi didn't get across the river.

The trip back across the Matna was interminable. Luckily for him, he was too worried about Daks and the Riftspawn to spare any thought for the terrible memories the churning waters below him might have conjured up.

Scholoveld is in the mountains, not an ocean or large river in sight of the place, he promised himself. Before a few days ago that thought wouldn't have made him feel better, but he could do without any large bodies of water for a while.

As they neared the opposite shore, he caught his first glimpse of red robes in the market above the landing and his breath quickened. Tightening his grip on the side of the small boat, he retreated farther into the shadows of his hood, closed his eyes, and willed himself to remain calm. The reality of trying to find Daks in all that bustling humanity started to sink in past the fear that had impelled him there, but what choice did he have? No one would do it for him, and if he didn't go, he had a terrible feeling he'd never see Daks again, and it would be all his fault for not trying.

Perhaps noticing his distress and finally taking pity on him as they neared the landing, the boatman said, "Your friend headed toward the market when I dropped him off. When he asked me the best places to go for information and gossip, I told him Hamul's place, the Ram's Horn, if that helps any. It's one street over from the market so a little less crowded at midday."

"Thank you."

The man grunted, leapt into the knee-deep water to pull it ashore, and waited for Ravi to scramble awkwardly out.

"We'll be back to see you're paid in coin and collect our horse," Ravi declared with far more confidence than he felt.

The boatman only shrugged and pushed off again, climbing nimbly back into the vessel as it floated away on the current, leaving Ravi alone.

This is such a bad idea.

Swallowing his fear, he headed up the landing toward the market, skirting the edges of the crowd and keeping his head down as much as possible. One or two men in red cloaks and splashes of guard blue caught his eye, but not as many as when they'd come through before, which seemed odd. But perhaps they were out in nearby villages cleaning up and rebuilding with those who hadn't the benefit of a mysterious wizard's aid, like the rumors said. The market did look remarkably untouched, compared to the other side of the river.

He huddled inside his cloak, quickly turning away anytime a brother or guard got close, sweating and shaking with nerves as he searched desperately for any sign of Daks. After only a few minutes, he gave up on the crowded market altogether. He'd just have to trust his instincts that Daks wouldn't have stayed there for long.

Like the boatman had said, one street over, things were much calmer and less crowded. He blew out a relieved breath once he'd reached a quiet spot and wiped the moisture from his forehead.

Please, please, please, just let me find Daks. Don't give me any more Visions until we're back in Samebar, please. I won't even complain about the next one if you just wait.

He spotted the Ram's Horn's painted signboard and hurried over, but he hesitated outside the open doorway, unsure how to proceed. The place looked cramped and dark inside, the last place Ravi should be going if he wanted to avoid close contact with people. But he wouldn't get any information lurking outside.

Hoping to remain inconspicuous, he sidled over to the large, slightly grimy window next to the door and peered inside. Unless Daks was hiding in the back, he wasn't in there. He glanced at the sky and winced. The sun was moving across it far too quickly. He needed to find Daks before sunset.

"Can I help you, sir? Would you like some of Hamul's fine ale? Best in Traget."

Ravi jolted and turned to find a young woman with a tray of flagons balanced on her hip, smiling at him expectantly. He licked his dry lips but winced apologetically. "Sorry, no. I'm, uh, looking for a friend of mine who might have come through this morning. Could you tell me if you saw him?"

Even as he spoke, he tensed for the tingle that meant a Vision was imminent, but felt nothing. Blowing out a relieved breath, he tried to give the woman a disarming smile.

"You'll have to be more specific than that. I see lots of friends 'round here," she said with a wink. "Maybe a little ale will loosen your tongue."

Ravi's regret wasn't feigned as he shook his head. "Sorry. I haven't any coin."

Her sunny smile lost some of its brightness, and she turned to go back inside but stopped when Ravi caught her sleeve.

"Please, miss, I'm sorry. I'd buy some if I could. I just need to know if my friend was here. He's about my height but much broader of chest and shoulders. He has dark hair he keeps tied back and has a couple of scars along his jaw. He would have been asking about a friend of his, a woman."

She pursed her lips and cocked an eyebrow at him until Ravi let go of her sleeve. When he gave her another mumbled apology, her smile returned, although it seemed a little more wicked now.

"I remember your friend. Thick man he was. Only stayed for a single pint, though, more's the pity," she said with a wink.

Ravi's heart lurched. "Do you know where he went?"

Her eyes widened as she leaned toward Ravi. "Oh yes. He came in looking for the Cigani woman."

"Yes, that's them!"

"You know her?"

Her tray of wares remained forgotten on her hip as she stepped closer to him.

"I do. They're… they're my friends."

"Gods," she breathed, before she seemed to remember herself, made the sign of the Three, and searched their surroundings nervously.

Ravi did the same, but luckily no Brotherhood scarlet or guard blue caught his eye.

"Your friend helped a lot of people here. My nan might have been killed if not for her," she whispered.

"She did?"

The woman nodded. "When the flood came, we all heard the horn and the shouts and screams and came running. Everyone was in a panic, but they never would have been able to get out of the way if it hadn't been for the *wizard*." She lowered her voice even more. "The brothers and the guard couldn't have done anything, not without one of the Thirty-Six. But the wizard, he just lifted his hands and the floodwaters hit some sort of wall no one could see, saving everyone in the market."

"How did Shur—I mean, the Cigani woman fit in?"

Her face clouded. "The guard tried to go after the wizard while he was working his magic to save us. They aimed their bows at him an' all. The young man who was with the wizard saw them, pulled a dagger, and started running, but it was the Cigani woman who got there first." Her eyes rounded again and her cheeks pinked. "She was *amazing*, her and her little blond friend. They cut through the whole lot of king's men like chaff. Never seen anything like it."

"What happened next?" Ravi prodded impatiently, when the woman's eyes got a little dreamy and far off.

"The wizard knocked out the remaining guard before they could harm his companion, who'd jumped into the fray, but the Cigani woman got hurt somehow. They took her with them when they left, as more men were being called." She scowled then and spat on the ground. "Wizard could've helped us so much more if they'd let him."

Ravi blinked at her in surprise. "You'd trust a wizard?"

She shrugged. "I've lived in Traget my whole life. I've seen all sorts come across that river and heard all kinds of stories about what magic does for people in Samebar. Times are changing, and not a day too soon, if you ask me." She only paused a beat before she made the sign of the Three again and added, "Gods willing, that is."

"Alanna!" someone shouted from inside the pub.

The woman winced. "Gotta go."

"Wait!" Ravi called, rushing forward, "Does Daks, the man I'm looking for, does he know all this?"

"Oh yes. It's all they can talk about in the pub these days while the soldiers lick their wounds."

"Where did they take her, the Cigani woman?"

"To the barbarian settlement, I suppose," she replied with a shrug. "North and west, up the Bael toward the mountains is what people say."

Ravi groaned as she disappeared inside. How the hells was he supposed to find Daks in the wilderness, especially when the man had a few hours' head start?

Without any logical hope, he allowed the memory of his Vision to pull him toward the northwestern edge of town. But as he stared at the encroaching wilderness beyond the farms, his heart sank. He had no supplies, no money, no one to ask for help, and no clue what he was doing. He also had no way of getting back across the river.

He could only partly blame his curse this time. If it had come only a few hours earlier, he could have sent Daks off with a warning, or insisted on going with him. But he'd also let his feelings drive him to do something utterly stupid… yet again. Daks was a bad influence that way, to be sure.

He took a breath and closed his eyes. He was here now. He couldn't flounder around helplessly. He hadn't survived for a decade on his own in the streets of Rassat for nothing. He could do this. Daks needed him.

Inside, he strained in search of that feeling: the one that had led him through the darkened streets of Urmat, the one that had brought him here. At last he felt it, a flutter deep inside, and the more he focused on it, the stronger it got, tugging him in only one direction, like a compass needle. He had confirmation he was headed in the right direction. Now he just had to figure out how to get there in time.

The northwestern road rose steadily upward away from the ferry landing, so he had a good view of Traget and the guard encampment just outside it… *and* the small temporary corral they'd built for their mounts.

Heart in his throat, he started jogging toward it, keeping low, inside the tree line. Did he really think he could steal a horse in broad daylight from the King's Guard?

The camp seemed mostly empty right now. Perhaps they were somewhere licking their wounds, like the barmaid had said. Besides, he'd already taken one page out of Daks's book. Why not two? If he slipped in from the back and took out part of the makeshift fencing, he could steal away in the confusion of escaping horses, right?

His hands shook, and he couldn't quite get a full breath, but he kept going, straining for any tingle of danger his gift might give him. He was only about twenty yards from his target when a bolt of alarm shot through him. Without hesitation, he heeded the warning and dove into a cluster of thorny bushes, hopefully out of sight.

A few seconds later, two men—one in a guard-blue tabard and one in crimson robes—stepped from between some tents and headed straight in his direction.

"I'm telling you, I felt something out here," the brother said irritably.

"I'm not contradicting you, Brother," the guard replied with obvious patience. "But you've said that several times over the last few days and we haven't found anything. We're all exhausted. No one would blame you for taking a rest."

"You obviously don't know my brothers. The wizard was in this town for who knows how long, and I didn't sense him. The villagers we interviewed told us he'd eaten their food and drunk their ale, *sitting at a table in the middle of the market square.* And yet I never sensed him. It is my duty to protect Rassa from creatures like him. I was sent here for this specific purpose—to give warning and report—and I failed. I won't fail again."

The men were close enough now Ravi caught the grimace the guard made in response before the man said, "I understand, holy brother, but no man can go on indefinitely without rest. You've investigated every tiny wisp of something strange for nearly three days straight. You won't be able to do much of anything if you pass out on your feet."

The brother did look pretty haggard. His eyes had that glassy, crazed look Ravi's had probably had when Daks had forced him to come to bed only a few days ago. He'd feel sorry for the brother if he wasn't in imminent danger of being discovered and possibly killed... or worse.

Making the sign of the Three yet one more time, Ravi closed his eyes.

I know most of the time I'm pleading with you to leave me alone, so this might sound a bit ungrateful, but please, please, *don't let them find me.*

Something stirred inside him, a tingling, and his stomach lurched.

Of course. He was cursed. For a second there, he'd forgotten.

Swearing internally, he scrabbled around until he found a thick branch on the forest floor. The brother gasped and pointed as the Vision erupted in Ravi's mind. But this time, instead of overwhelming him, it simply overlayed his reality. Like some sort of miracle, he still had use of his limbs and his wits.

Blinking away the disorientation of having two scenes atop each other, he rose and ran farther into the woods, away from the camp and more soldiers. He stumbled several times, trying to get used to differentiating between what appeared to be a Vision a few seconds in the future and reality.

When the Vision suddenly showed the brother turning and heading back toward the camp, Ravi stopped running, spun to face his pursuers, and shouted to get their attention. He was no match for a trained guard, but he'd be finished for sure if the brother brought more soldiers after him on horseback.

With courage only desperation and a grim sense of impending doom could muster, he lifted his branch and faced the two men.

"Put the branch down," the guard ordered, drawing his sword.

The voice in his Vision had barely faded before the real guard repeated the command. Ravi's heart thudded as his palms grew damp around his makeshift club.

He was so out of his depth it was laughable. What did he think he was doing? Daks might be able to fight his way out of a situation like this, but Ravi was not Daks.

Think!

In his Vision, the guard charged him, swinging to knock the weapon out of his hand, and Ravi had only a few seconds to decide what to do about it before the guard actually moved. Instead of trying to counter the strike, he lurched out of the way, managing to clip the guard on his unprotected side as he went. The Vision swirled, blurrier now, and Ravi danced backward, trying to make sense of it even as the guard growled and came after him again.

When Ravi ran toward the brother, hoping to maybe use the man as a shield, the sudden thunder of hooves radiated through his Vision, drawing him up short. The sound of actual hooves echoed through the woods a moment later, distracting the guard and the brother, and Ravi's eyes bugged out as a large white blur surged from between the trees.

"Horse?" he gasped, not quite believing his eyes.

Horse didn't stop. He bowled straight into the guard before spinning and charging the brother. The brother shrieked and ran, leaving his companion rolling on the ground moaning. Ravi didn't stop to wonder or marvel. He ran to Horse and leapt awkwardly onto his back. With no saddle to grab, Ravi had to practically drag himself up, using Horse's mane and the dangling reins, but Horse didn't buck him off.

"Sorry. Sorry," he gasped. "Gods, I can't believe you're here. How in the hells…?"

Horse took off running, leaving Ravi gasping and clinging to his neck.

At least Horse headed in the direction Ravi's gift had been pulling, so Ravi didn't have to try to figure out how to turn him. Horse didn't slow his headlong dash until they were far up the northwest road. When Ravi could finally relax a little and pry his cramped fingers loose from the reins, he made the sign of the Three to be on the safe side while searching the road behind him for the hundredth time.

"Not that I'm ungrateful," he huffed as he tried to catch his breath, "but if you were going to show, couldn't you have done it just a half hour earlier?"

Horse broke into another bone-jarring trot that left Ravi scrambling for a tighter grip on the reins again. He was cursing at every bounce of his ass against boney horse spine by the time the animal slowed to a stop once more. Knowing he'd probably regret it when it came time to remount, Ravi slid off Horse's back and staggered a few feet away. Much more of this and he'd be lucky if he could walk at all.

Once the worst of the pain and tingling in his extremities had subsided, Ravi limped to the river. The landscape around them had turned significantly wetter the farther west they went. They were headed back into the boglands, a thought that definitely did not bring him comfort. How soon before he needed to start looking for traps around every corner? Maybe he shouldn't be quite so thankful the weird Vision overlay had stopped after Horse's arrival.

The thought of riding even one more mile made a little whine escape from the back of his throat, but a glimpse of the sun sitting perilously close to the treetops had him limping back to Horse's side and leading the animal to the largest rock he could find to mount again. Gritting his teeth, he nudged Horse into another trot.

When he first spotted a single rider on a dappled brown horse in the distance, his heart lurched and he held his breath. At the sound of their approach, the rider turned, and even at that distance, Ravi knew it was Daks.

Oh, thank the gods.

Daks pulled his mount up short, allowing him to catch up, and Ravi felt like fainting with relief.

"Ravi? How—?"

"Never mind that now. We need to turn around and get out of here."

"Why?"

"I had a Vision. There's a Spawn out here."

Daks's eyes widened, which was good. But he still hadn't moved… which was not good.

"Come on!" Ravi cried.

"Wait a second," Daks said, infuriatingly calm as usual.

His eyes got that faraway look as his attention drew inward. When he focused on Ravi again, he was shaking his head.

"There's not a Spawn within miles of us. It's okay."

Ravi glanced at the lengthening shadows of the trees scattered around them. Almost dusk.

"It's not okay. I *saw* it."

"What did you see?"

"You, alone in the woods, facing off against a thing with glowing red eyes," Ravi shot back. "Now can we go, please?"

Daks nudged his mount closer, though the poor animal didn't seem to like the idea, because its eyes were wide and it kept sidestepping restlessly. "Do you know when this is supposed to happen?"

"At dusk. Like, now!"

Ravi squeezed the reins until his knuckles were white and clenched his teeth instead of wringing the man's neck and shouting obscenities at him.

"Do you know what day, though?" Daks asked calmly.

"It felt like today."

Daks raised an eyebrow, and Ravi wanted to smack him. When Ravi only glared back at him, Daks scratched one stubbled cheek and sighed.

"Ravi, I can't go back, not without Shura. It's almost dusk as it is. We won't be out of the trees before nightfall, even if we start now. And you're here with me, so I'm no longer alone." He dismounted in one fluid movement that made Ravi narrow his eyes in jealousy. He moved in close and took Ravi's hand. "I promise you, if a Spawn were that close to us, I know I would feel it. They light up like a bonfire to my gift. Please believe me. I'd *know*."

Ravi worried his lower lip, letting Daks's words sink in and trying to think rationally beyond the fear that had been riding him for hours. He was tired, every muscle in his body ached from trying to stay on Horse's back, and now that he'd stopped his headlong chase, his stomach reminded him he hadn't eaten since his meager breakfast.

After blowing out a long breath, he nodded and allowed Daks to help him off Horse's back. When Daks pulled him into a hug, Ravi melted against the man with a whimper of relief. Maybe Daks was right. Maybe he'd already changed things. Daks would have kept going at least another hour if Ravi hadn't stopped him. Was that enough?

His stomach didn't think so, but that could just be the hunger.

"You came to save me, huh?" Daks murmured.

Ravi could hear the stupid, smug grin in his voice, even if he couldn't see it, and he gave Daks a halfhearted shove. Daks's big body didn't move an inch. In fact, he tightened his grip and kissed the shell of Ravi's ear.

"You're amazing," he whispered, his lips brushing Ravi's skin, making him shiver.

"When I need to be," Ravi replied, borrowing a bit of Daks's bravado.

Daks chuckled, the sound vibrating through his thick chest and into Ravi's. He drew back enough to capture Ravi's lips, kissing until they both forgot about anything around them. Then Horse sidled into them, knocking them apart, and the spell was broken.

"You're going to have to tell me how in the Seven Hells you managed to get this brute back across with you without the ferry. Did you swim?"

"I'll tell you everything I know, but please tell *me* we can stop here for the night." He gave Daks his most pathetic expression. "I'm not sure I'll survive much more riding today."

Daks's lips split in a crooked smile. "Not even the good kind?"

Ravi's cock twitched at the huskiness in his voice, but he ignored it and narrowed his eyes. "I don't think you fully realize what I went through today to get here."

Daks just smiled and shrugged as he moved to take the reins of both horses. "We'll stop for the night and get a fire started, and then you can fill me in."

Chapter Fifteen

"You traded Horse?" Daks asked incredulously.

Ravi gave him a sour look. "I thought the risk worth it. Maybe I was wrong? Maybe I should have just left you to your fate?"

The fire he'd made burned cheerily against the cold and damp of their surroundings. In the flickering light, Ravi looked as lovely as ever, despite his current expression.

"I'm not saying that, but…." Daks left the wording hanging and had to hide a grin when Ravi huffed and his scowl deepened.

He wanted to be mad that Ravi had endangered himself like that—and perhaps he would be later—but right now he couldn't get past the giddy realization that Ravi had risked so much just for him. Other than Shura, he didn't think there was anyone in the world who cared that much. Unable to hide it anymore, his grin spread from ear to ear as he put his hands behind his head and stretched his boots toward the fire.

Ravi's eyes narrowed to slits as his cheeks darkened. "I could go back, you know. I could leave you here to get eaten by Spawn or cursed by a wizard or whatever."

"You wouldn't do that to me. You like me too much," Daks replied as he sat up and scooted until he was pressed to Ravi's side.

"I can't think why," Ravi replied, obviously fighting an exasperated smile.

"It's the sex," Daks deadpanned.

Instead of the punch to the arm Daks half expected, Ravi barked out a laugh, but his smile faded to something much more intense as Daks moved in for a kiss.

He sucked on Ravi's soft lips until Ravi opened and deepened their kiss. Ravi allowed Daks to push him to the ground. He draped himself over that lanky, perfect body as Ravi's arms wrapped around his shoulders, holding him close.

Daks was just wondering how much of that lovely skin Ravi might be willing to expose to the cold night air when Horse suddenly snorted and stomped the ground. Reluctantly lifting his head, Daks scanned the shadows beyond the firelight, but he saw nothing.

"What is it?"

Daks held up a finger and opened his other sense.

Seven Hells!

He rolled to his feet and rushed to where he'd left the sword he'd "borrowed," the same way he'd "borrowed" the other horse. Putting himself between the thing in the woods and Ravi, he widened his stance and lifted the sword.

"What's going on?" Ravi hissed.

"Spawn," Daks gritted out through clenched teeth.

The I-told-you-sos would be never-ending… if they lived that long.

Horse snorted again and moved to stand next to him, making Daks gape at the beast. As if he needed more proof Horse was not at all what he seemed. As soon as the dapple caught scent of the Spawn it screamed and lunged, trying to break the reins free of the branch Daks had tied them to, but Daks couldn't spare it more than a quick glance before riveting his gaze on the approaching red, glowing eyes.

Ravi fumbled at Daks's belt, and when Daks spared him a glance, Ravi held his dagger pointed at the Spawn, his amber eyes wide, his face pale.

"Stay back, Ravi. You're not trained for this," Daks ordered.

"And you are?"

He had a point. Daks had never been this close to a Spawn before in his life. He'd sensed them beyond the magic walls of Scholoveld. He'd tracked them for hunters who did this kind of thing all the time, but he'd never actually had to fight one himself. He had no wizard or bespelled sword. He had no wizard stone to catch the Wraith in, even if he *could* manage to kill it. The best he could hope was that the thing would get discouraged and find some easier prey to go after.

He shot another glance at the dappled horse still trying to break free of its bonds and winced. He hated to do it, but if the choice was between the horse and them, the horse would lose.

He was still trying to figure out how to make a sacrifice like that work when the Spawn finally stepped from the shadows and into the small circle of firelight, and Daks did a double take. Another stallion, as tall as Horse and as black as Horse was white, stood in the clearing, regarding them calmly. It didn't appear corrupted or vicious. Its sleek sides gleamed whole and healthy in the flickering orange light, and if anything, the creature looked bored. If not for the glowing red eyes, Daks would have thought his luck had improved ten-fold with another beautiful horse to add to their collection. For his part, Horse seemed curious but definitely not alarmed, and as Daks watched in stunned silence, Horse ambled across the clearing toward their visitor.

The Spawn's attention shifted to Horse and the thing started. It took a seemingly wary step back, and Horse stopped.

"What's going on?" Ravi whispered.

"Not a clue," Daks replied without taking his eyes off the two animals.

At least the dapple had stopped fretting, possibly sensing the change in the atmosphere as well.

While Daks was frantically searching for what the hells to do next, the Spawn horse wavered and shifted in front of his eyes. Before Daks or Ravi could do anything but yelp, a rather lovely young black-haired man stood where the Spawn had been, completely naked.

"What are you?" the Spawn-horse-man asked, his attention still riveted on Horse.

Horse snorted, lifted his head high, and pointedly turned his back on the creature. He ambled back to Daks's side and turned to face the Spawn again, his eyes placid and serene.

"Uh, I might ask you the same question," Daks said hesitantly.

He'd never felt so out of his depth in his life, and that was saying something.

The Spawn—or whatever the hells it was—turned his attention back to them, though he still shot wary glances at Horse from time to time.

"What I am is no concern of yours," it—*he*—said primly.

"I think it is," Ravi piped up behind him, and Daks winced.

If the thing was willing to talk reasonably and not murder them, Daks was just fine not knowing the particulars or antagonizing him.

The creature turned his unnatural gaze on Ravi, and Daks tensed, tightening his grip on the sword. His eyes stopped glowing as he studied Ravi briefly, and Daks hoped that was a good sign. Except, when the Spawn kept eyeing Ravi, as if he were mulling something over, Daks started to get nervous. On a man who hadn't just been a horse with glowing red eyes, Daks might have considered the look to be one of interest, possibly sexual, but that couldn't be right.

He stepped in front of Ravi, blocking the creature's view.

"What do you want?" Daks asked, not sure he wanted to hear the answer.

"I might ask the same question," the young man replied mockingly.

Okay, questions obviously weren't working, so how about answers.

"I'm looking for a friend of mine who may have traveled this way," Daks said, doing his best not to growl the words.

The Spawn turned his attention back to Horse. "And you?" he asked, eyeing the beast warily.

Silence hung heavy and uncomfortable in the clearing, but for the pop and crackle of the dying fire.

"Uh, that's my horse," Daks answered, when he couldn't take it anymore.

Horse snorted, and the Spawn gave Daks a withering look.

"Look," Daks pressed on, "we're sorry if we disturbed you or anything, but, uh, we're just looking for our friends. We'll be on our way tomorrow… or right now if you prefer. No time like the present, right?"

Daks shuffled closer to Horse's side but froze when the Spawn raised a hand.

"Do these friends of yours happen to be two women, one pale, one dark?" he asked, as if the question had to be dragged out of him.

Daks's chest tightened. "Yes," he replied breathlessly as Ravi gripped his arm.

The Spawn sighed and rolled his eyes. "Well, at least none of us will have to listen to the darker one rail at us anymore, while the little pale one coos and consoles. You are Daks, I presume."

He said the name as if it tasted foul, but Daks couldn't have cared less. His grin was wide as he asked, "Is she all right? Where is she?"

The Spawn man shrugged. "She is recovering well enough. I will take you to her, if only to cease her constant complaining."

"Where?" Daks repeated.

"At our encampment. I told you I would take you there."

Daks shot Ravi a hopeful, questioning look, but Ravi only shrugged.

"As usual, when it could be at all helpful, my curse is silent," Ravi whispered.

Daks gripped the hand on his sleeve and kissed Ravi's forehead. "It's okay. The encampment was where I was headed anyway. And honestly, if he wanted us dead, he wouldn't have to resort to trickery to make it happen."

The Spawn must've had good hearing, because when Daks turned his attention back to him, he was smiling… or baring his teeth, Daks couldn't decide which.

The Spawn turned and headed for the road, displaying his high, rounded bare ass in the process. Under any other circumstances, Daks might have done a bit of ogling, but he hadn't quite decided whether to piss himself in fear or relief yet. Spawn were the stuff of nightmares, corruption and evil made flesh, the cautionary tales told to scare children into obedience. You didn't lust after them... or at least he hadn't before.

"Daks," Ravi said, a warning in his tone.

"What?"

Ravi simply scowled at him as he pushed past him after the Spawn. "Hey! Hey you!"

Daks caught back of Ravi's cloak and pulled him up short. "What are you doing?"

"I'm tired. I'm sore. And now I'm just pissed off," Ravi huffed.

"Are you coming?" the Spawn called from the road.

"Can it wait until morning?" Ravi shouted back. "Unlike you, I'm guessing, some of us actually need to sleep. And who knows what we might blunder into in the dark? I really don't relish the thought of being hit by another trap, thank you very much."

While Daks looked on in dread, tightening his grip on the sword again, the Spawn studied Ravi for a few moments before a true smile spread across his somewhat disturbingly handsome face.

"There are no traps the way I will take you. I've destroyed any such things as I've come across them. You've had dealings with the bogfolk before, I take it."

"Enough," Ravi huffed, and the Spawn's smile widened.

After a few seconds of anxiety-producing silence, the Spawn nodded, as if he'd made his mind up. "Very well. You may sleep. I will return at dawn to guide you the rest of the way, for the sake of your friend, if nothing else. We owe her a debt." His face softened at the words, making him appear even more human... at least until he glanced in Horse's direction and his expression turned unreadable. "I will let them know you're coming."

One second, the Spawn man stood naked in the middle of the road, the next, the air was filled with the flapping of great black wings as a raven took off into the night sky and disappeared.

"Seven Hells," Daks whispered vehemently.

"Yeah," Ravi agreed, still staring where the thing had vanished.

After a few seconds, Daks blew out a breath, grabbed Ravi's shoulders, and gave him a little shake. "*We need our sleep, thank you very much?*" he repeated, huffing out an aggrieved laugh.

At least Ravi had the decency to blush. "I *am* tired. And who knew a Spawn could be so annoying."

"You kill me," he said with a half smile. "Come on. I have a feeling sleep isn't going to come so easy, but at least we can build up the fire and make ourselves comfortable. I managed to, uh, *borrow* a flask of something pretty potent from a guy passed out in the corner of the pub. I think I'm gonna need a snootful or two to relax. At least it's Shura getting us into trouble this time and not me."

While Ravi puttered with the fire, Daks checked on the dapple. The poor thing had calmed down considerably at least, though it had chafed the skin around its halter, trying to break free. Horse was, as always, serene and regal, and Daks eyed the animal with a new wariness.

After not sensing the Spawn until it was right on top of them, he began to question the limitations of his abilities a little. But if Horse was more than an exceptionally smart, loyal, resourceful animal, Daks still couldn't sense it.

"You stumped a Spawn, though, and I've never even heard of such a thing," Daks murmured to the beast as he held its pale blue gaze until he had to look away. "Whatever you are, I'm glad you're on our side," he finished, clapping Horse on the shoulder before carrying the flask and borrowed bedroll back to the fire.

"You came prepared," Ravi said wryly, eyeing the bedroll like it was the softest of featherbeds.

"You need but ask, and the gods shall provide," Daks intoned with a grin.

"Uh-huh."

Daks shrugged before shaking out the roll and spreading it over the ground. "The guards I borrowed this stuff from won't suffer… too much."

"Eh, they deserve it anyway."

"They do," Daks agreed.

He settled onto the bedroll after tossing a half-empty pack down for a pillow and opened his cloak in invitation. Ravi smiled sweetly and melted against his chest. Once they were cocooned together comfortably, Daks uncorked the flask and took a pull, hissing at the burn even as the fiery liquid settled warmly in his belly. He offered the flask to Ravi, but he waved it away sleepily.

"I learned my lesson. I don't know how you can drink that stuff. Wine, ale, and mead only for me."

He yawned and snuggled his face into Daks's neck. His nose and lips were cold, but Daks didn't mind. In fact, the world felt just about right in that moment. If only he knew for certain that Shura was safe, and they weren't in the middle of a hostile kingdom, relying on a Spawn to help them.

AFTER SPENDING the night with Ravi pressed against him, he woke up hard and horny. And thankfully, despite the chilly damp, their admittedly uncertain circumstances, and being out in the open, Ravi seemed perfectly amenable to ignore all that in favor of some fooling around. Slow, sleepy kisses built on one another until they were both panting into each other's mouths and groping through layers of clothing, trying to have as much skin-to-skin contact without actually undressing or exposing any sensitive bare flesh to the icy fog surrounding them.

They wrestled inside the warmth of Daks's heavy cloak like puppies under a blanket until they both broke out in breathless chuckles between kisses. Finally, Daks couldn't take it anymore and rolled Ravi onto his back beneath him. He shimmied down Ravi's body, ducking his head into the shadows of the cloak. He didn't need to see the ties of Ravi's breeches to get them undone.

He would have liked to see Ravi's face as he slid his mouth down Ravi's cock, but this time, he'd have to be content with the hot little noises his lover made and the convulsive clutching of Ravi's fingers in his hair. The poor man fought valiantly not to thrust up into

Daks's mouth as Daks teased and tormented his cock, bringing Ravi to the edge twice before taking pity on both of them.

Ravi let out a little mewl of protest when Daks drew off his cock, and Daks grinned.

"Go ahead, beautiful. Let go," Daks murmured before kissing Ravi's crown and sucking him to the back of his throat again.

To get his point across, Daks slid his hands around to grip Ravi's delectable ass, encouraging him to thrust. Ravi only hesitated a moment before flexing his hips experimentally. After another encouraging squeeze and a hum of approval from Daks, Ravi finally let go and fucked Daks's mouth, increasing in intensity and speed until he gasped and arched his back off the ground. He flooded Daks's throat with his release as Daks hung on, swallowing around his crown. At last Ravi collapsed onto the ground again, panting, and Daks quickly undid the ties on his own wool breeches, took himself in hand, and worked his shaft, lifting up to take in Ravi in all his flushed, sweaty, and spent glory.

After all the groping, kissing, and sucking, Daks's release didn't take long. He let out a happy groan as he came all over Ravi's spent cock, belly, and his own hand, while Ravi gazed up at him with dazed, sated amber eyes and flushed cheeks. All Daks wanted to do after that was collapse into his lover's arms, but Ravi's warm flush wouldn't last long, and the result of their combined releases would become very uncomfortable very quickly. Daks tucked his cock away and stretched to rifle through the pack. Once he'd found a scrap of clean flannel, he wiped the mess from Ravi's body and helped him put his clothes to rights.

Unwilling to get up quite yet, Daks settled next to him again and pulled him close. They lay like that in companionable silence for several minutes before Daks finally sighed and surrendered to the inevitable.

"The Spawn might come any minute, and we need to discuss some things."

Ravi yawned and nodded without lifting his head from Daks's chest.

"I'm a little torn right now, to be honest," Daks continued. "You present a bit of a problem."

Ravi stiffened, but Daks tightened his arm around him. "Don't get mad. Hear me out first." When Ravi relaxed again, Daks pressed on. "Now, I can't tell you how much it means to me that you would come charging to my rescue after everything you've already been through, but it changes my plan."

"Plan?" Ravi asked, with enough of a smile in his voice that Daks couldn't stop the rueful grin that split his lips.

"Okay, I'll give you that one. Planning may not be my strongest attribute, but we're going to have to make one now, or at least a choice, before that thing gets here."

"Do you trust it?"

"Hells no. But here's the thing. If I believe he's telling the truth, then Shura is safe and well taken care of, so I could take a few days to get you to safety and then come back for her. Or send her a message and wait for her to be well enough to come to us. If he's lying, Shura needs me now, but that would mean dragging you into an even more dangerous situation than you're already in, just being in Rassa." He growled and blew out a frustrated breath. "I should have asked the thing to bring me a message from her, something that would tell me she was all right, but I was too distracted to think clearly."

"I'm going with you," Ravi said calmly but firmly.

"Ravi—"

"No." Ravi sat up, allowing their cloak blanket to fall around his waist as he narrowed his eyes at Daks. "You're not going to waste several more days traipsing across Rassa because of me. My stupid curse has caused enough trouble. I won't be the one responsible if something happens to her and you're not there… not again."

"More than likely, the Spawn isn't lying," Daks argued. "Why would he bother? He could have just killed us outright."

"You don't know that. Horse seemed to spook him quite a bit. He wasn't like any Spawn I've ever heard of. Maybe we're wrong. Maybe he's something else and he means to lure us to the wizard or something."

"If that's true, it's the last place you should want to go."

"You shouldn't go *either*," Ravi huffed, "but I know you can't leave Shura, so we have no choice."

Warmth spread through Daks's chest at Ravi's continued use of "we" and "us."

"Besides," Ravi added sourly, "someone has to come along to keep you from doing something stupid."

Daks grinned. "You say the sweetest things."

Ravi narrowed his eyes and growled. It was adorable… and sexy as hells. Daks cocked an eyebrow and licked his lips. "Maybe we should stop the talking. We seem to get off track with the talking."

"Daks, will you be serious!"

"Sorry," he replied, trying to sound contrite and probably failing. "I am being serious when I say I don't want either you or Shura in danger, so this isn't easy for me."

"You told me to listen to my feelings. That's what I'm doing. When you walked away from me, my Vision sent me after you. To me, that means together is good, apart is bad."

"Was it only your Vision?"

The question slipped out of him before he could stop it, and it revealed a level of vulnerability Daks wasn't ready to contemplate, so he shook his head and waved a dismissive hand. "Forget it. I—"

Daks actually slumped in relief when Horse snorted out a warning, drawing their attention to the giant black bird as it swooped out the sky and transformed into the lithe dark-haired young man from the night before. His relief was short-lived, because watching that transformation was seriously unsettling. Color drained from Ravi's face, and Daks rolled to his feet and put himself between the Spawn and Ravi.

"You're not ready to go yet?" the Spawn asked peevishly.

THE JOURNEY to the barbarian encampment was about as pleasant as Daks expected. The boglands were as cheerful as ever, and both he and Ravi were tense with anxiety over what they might be walking into. Privately, Daks questioned his sanity, but he kept following the black stallion Spawn anyway as they trudged along in silence, his hand never leaving the pommel of his sword, should the creature make any sudden moves.

He would have liked to have Ravi on the same horse as he was for some companionship and physical reassurance, to hold him close and murmur stupid, inappropriate things in his ear to distract them both… plus, maybe a little groping. But they needed their mounts as fresh as possible, in case they had to cut and run.

Daks spotted the lookouts long before they broke from the cover of trees into a large, recently cleared area along a fork in the Bael river. He was actually astonished at the number of buildings the "barbarians" had managed to erect in such a short time. All the rumors they'd heard said the mountain tribesmen had only left their home and invaded Rassa a couple of months ago. But instead of the crude tent city Daks expected, several wood buildings and even one made of stone occupied the space.

Curious eyes followed them as the Spawn horse led the way straight into the newly made village. Very tall blond men, women, and children paused in their work to study the strangers, but Daks didn't sense any outright malice. He would have scanned the area with his gift as well as his other senses, but with the Spawn so close, he probably wouldn't be able to sense anything else.

Ravi had drawn the hood of his cloak up as they'd entered the village, and the more people who surrounded them, the more he shrunk into its shadows. Daks felt a pang of regret and sympathy for him. He'd almost forgotten, in their last few days of freedom in Samebar, just how much more open and happy Ravi had seemed. The contrast now was stark.

Daks's hand tightened on his sword, and he had to force himself to relax his grip and finally release it altogether. He couldn't fight his way out of this one. With a Spawn, a wizard, and a whole crowd of giant mountain fighters, he wouldn't stand a chance… and neither would Ravi.

"Daks! Oh, thank the gods!"

Daks started on Horse's back and swung around. Those tall mountain men parted like wheat before a scythe as tiny Fara sprinted toward them, her gold braid flying behind her. She swung wide around the Spawn horse and skidded to a halt next to him.

"Thank the gods," she repeated breathlessly as Daks's anxiety tripled. Any fatigue he might have felt evaporated, and he eyed the people around him warily.

"What's wrong? Where's Shura?"

"She won't listen to me," Fara cried, her eyes filling with unshed tears. "She won't let them help her. She's hurt, and she won't let them do anything. The tribesmen's herb woman is the only one she'll let close, but she needs more than that. You have to make her see reason!"

"Take me to her," Daks ordered as he swung off Horse's back, ignoring anyone or anything else around them except Ravi, who joined them a moment later.

"This way."

She took off at jog, and Daks took Ravi's hand and followed on her heels. When they entered the long log building, the smell hit him first, a combination of infection and medicinal herbs he wished he could say he didn't recognize.

Seven Hells!

Shura lay on a small bed nearby, gray and unmoving, and Daks's stomach flipped and his throat closed. He rushed over and knelt beside the bed, taking her hand in both of his.

"Shur?"

She cracked a glassy eye and smiled weakly. "Took you long enough," she whispered hoarsely.

Swallowing past the lump in his throat, Daks gave her a grin that probably looked more like a rictus and said, "I had a few complications."

She studied his face for a second, her smile fading to a frown. "You look like shit."

"So do you."

"Daks," Fara exclaimed, her voice tight with worry.

"What happened, Shur?" Daks said.

"Damned arrow… gut shot. Blighted cowards afraid to come out and fight like men."

"Fara says you won't let these good people help you. Why not?"

Daks thought he probably already knew the answer, but best to let her get her objections out of the way first so he knew what tack to take to change her mind.

Shura grimaced, and Fara let out a little mewl of concern as she rushed to hand Shura a cup of what Daks assumed was water.

"Don't know these people," Shura croaked after a quick sip that she obviously only took to appease Fara.

"And?" Daks prodded.

She scowled at him. "What and? Not going to let a wizard touch me without my partner here to check him out first, to make sure he doesn't do anything else to me. Rather be dead than cursed."

Daks's stomach twisted. Cigani were always suspicious of magic users and, well, anyone outside of their clans. She wasn't wrong. You never knew what a mage had up his or her sleeves. If he hadn't dicked around at the inn waiting for her to contact him, if he'd come straight over as soon as possible, she wouldn't be half as bad as she was now.

"Well, I'm here now." He lifted his gaze to Fara. "Get the wizard."

"I'll do it," a tall blond stranger said from the doorway. "Lyuc is out with some of the others, but Tas is here. He can help."

Daks had been so distracted, he hadn't heard the man enter, but he nodded and the stranger turned and left.

"Who's Tas?" Daks asked Fara.

"He's the rogue brother we heard about on our journey. He was a member of the Thirty-Six."

Daks grimaced as Ravi stiffened and sucked in a breath.

A pain priest? Great.

"You trust him?"

"They've all been kind to us. I believe he has reformed from what he was."

That wasn't exactly a stunning endorsement, but Shura was in a bad way, and he'd be present to make sure the guy didn't do anything shady. He could tell by the look on her face that she was working up the strength to argue, but he glared at her and shook his head.

"You can curse me and my lineage later. Right now, I don't give a damn about your Cigani pride or nobility, understand? You're gonna let this man heal you, and I'll be right here to make sure that's all he does."

She narrowed her eyes, but she wasn't in any shape to do much about it. She'd hate to be healed by magic torn from the pain of others, but when it came to the people he loved, he didn't give a damn about morality. If he had to pull rank in their dynamic and remind her of her oath, he'd do it so she could still be alive to hate him for years to come.

Movement by the door made them all turn. The lean dark-haired man who entered in front of the blond giant from earlier didn't look like much in his plain gray jerkin and trousers, but the rock around his neck sent out pulses of energy that throbbed against Daks's mental shields, so much so he was surprised he hadn't sensed the thing the second he entered the village.

"I'm Tas. Girik tells me our patient is finally willing to let us help her."

The man smiled disarmingly, and Daks felt his shoulders relax just a little. He didn't look like any pain priest Daks had ever seen.

"Where's your red robes, priest?" Daks asked, poking the bear to see what would happen.

"Daks!" Fara hissed.

The man's smile vanished, and the blond brute behind him glared and took a step forward, but the priest laid a hand on his arm, stopping him.

"It's all right, Girik. They don't know us yet, and the Thirty-Six have much to answer for. As for your question, Daks, I've left the Brotherhood for good. Therefore, I will never again wear the red."

"Good answer." He glanced at Shura's pinched expression and sighed. "Last question. Did the person who fueled your stone do so willingly?"

Tas's smile returned. "He's not really my stone anymore. Think of us as a partnership. And no one fueled him." Tas glanced at Girik, and the big man took his hand and gave him a loving smile. "I don't do that anymore. He fuels himself from the world around us now. No one should ever have to suffer that abomination again."

On the one hand, Tas's answers allayed at least some of Daks's concerns—and hopefully Shura's as well—provided he could believe them. On the other, the way he referred to the stone opened up a whole new set of questions and worries. What had they gotten themselves into now?

Shura shifted on the bed, and though she obviously tried to stifle it, a hiss of pain escaped her lips.

"Then work your magic, Pr—Tas. She won't object."

Daks held her gaze as he said it, and though he could tell she wasn't happy about it, she wouldn't fight him.

"Please," Fara added pointedly.

Her eyes were overflowing with a mixture of emotions when she turned her gaze back to Shura, and Shura's face softened as she reached for her. Fara rushed to the other side of the bed and clasped the hand.

"Stupid, stubborn woman," Fara huffed, though she was smiling.

Shura's lips curled at the corners until the priest approached. Daks made way for him, seeing how desperately Fara clutched at Shura's hand. He needed to be able to concentrate on his gift anyway. But something in the intensity of the two women's interactions made him glance at Ravi, who hovered nearby, pale and obviously frightened. He eyed the former priest like he had the Spawn, but Daks supposed they were both monsters in Ravi's world, so he couldn't blame him.

He moved to Ravi's side and wrapped an arm around his waist, drawing him closer. Though he remained silent, Ravi molded against him. Daks drew strength from their contact, because he *really* didn't want to open his shields. He'd never been this close to one of the holy relics before. Hells, even the Scholomagi kept their most ancient and powerful relics buried deep under the school, so no one could get this close to them. He'd be lucky if he didn't pass out altogether. But Shura needed him.

Drawing in a steadying breath, he opened his senses and swayed under the first onslaught of power. Ravi wrapped his arms around Daks's middle, shoring him up. After the shock of the initial wave, Daks found could tolerate the feeling, though every hair on his body stood on end and he'd have a massive headache later.

He opened his eyes in time to see Girik and Tas exchange a soft look before the big man swung a warning look in Daks's direction— not openly hostile, but promising trouble if Daks stepped out of line. The large, shaggy gold hound at Girik's heels also gave him the side-eye, and Daks lifted his hands in a placating gesture. Glancing at the two men once more, Daks smothered a knowing smile. Guess the priest had forsaken more than one of his vows to the Brotherhood because the looks they were giving each other were anything but chaste. Despite the vague threat posed by the priest's companions, the thought actually made Daks feel a little better. It made him more human somehow.

As everyone in the room seemed to hold their breath, Tas closed his eyes and lifted his hand above Shura's abdomen, drawing Daks's attention back to him. Energy flowed from the stone on his chest into him and out through his extended palm, concentrated solely on Shura's belly. Nothing about the magic felt wrong to Daks. In fact, the vibrations were vaguely familiar. They were different from anything he'd sensed from the wizards of Samebar, and nothing at all like the one time he'd felt a pain priest at work—from a very safe distance, of course. He'd met a visiting witch from Ghorazon once in Scholoveld. She'd done a demonstration at the school. That was probably the closest thing he could compare the feeling to.

Shura gasped, drawing his attention back to her. Fara leaned forward, still clutching Shura's hand, her eyes worried, but Daks could already tell the magic was having a positive effect. The deep lines etched into Shura's forehead had faded, and some of the color had returned to her skin. The energy traveling through her wasn't tainted and wasn't directed anywhere else. Daks would have to trust that was enough, because he didn't want the man to stop.

After what seemed like far too long, Tas blew out a breath and the energy coursing over Daks's skin ebbed. Shura sighed and closed her eyes as the rest of the lines of pain on her face eased.

"Shura?" Fara called, leaning forward anxiously.

"She's all right," Tas said. "She's just resting. She'll need it. The wound is healed, but she may still be fevered from the infection flowing through her body. I could only do so much. Perhaps Lyuc will be able to do more when he returns, but she is out of danger for now and will heal in time, even without further intervention. I promise."

"Thank you," Fara said before returning her attention fully to Shura again.

"Thanks," Daks added gruffly, and the former priest gave him a tired smile.

"I'm still learning to work with the magic as it is, not as it was, but Singer says she will heal quickly."

"Singer?"

Tas lifted a hand to his chest to indicate the stone. Daks shifted uneasily. He had so many questions he hardly knew where to start.

"I need a drink," he said, and Ravi snorted at his side despite how bowstring taut his body still was.

The big guy, Girik, smiled. "Tas, are you okay?"

"Yes. I could use a little food, though."

"Why don't we leave Shura to get that rest and I'll take all of you to get a good meal," Girik offered with a soft smile.

"The horses," Daks exclaimed, suddenly remembering he'd essentially abandoned them.

"We took care of that," Girik replied calmly. "If you want to see them, you can, but we've put them in the stables with the others. Karn is more used to goats, given that he lived his whole life in the mountains, but he's turned out to be an excellent stable master. He'll take good care of them. Come."

"I'm staying," Fara said, and Daks gave her a grateful smile.

If she hadn't been there, he wouldn't have been willing to leave Shura alone, even though both he and Ravi hadn't eaten all day.

"Lead the way," Daks said, and they trailed after the blond giant, keeping a safe distance between themselves and that monstrous hound.

As soon as they were outside, Girik's hound bounded away from them toward several others of the same size and coloring playing in the river with some children, and Girik watched him go with a fond smile. Daks had heard tales of the mountain clans' hounds before but never thought to see one. Now he was glad it had moved off.

Daks and Ravi each had a large tankard of some of the best mead Daks had ever tasted, plus a heaping bowl of mutton stew, and were following Girik and Tas to a rough plank table and benches in a green space at the center of the little village when a commotion near the tree line caught everyone's attention. Daks saw the great black stallion Spawn first and scowled, tensing in instinctive fear, but the man who followed it out of the woods quickly grabbed all of his attention. He was dressed in brightly colored patched robes that almost hurt the eye to look at. But despite the change in clothes, the stranger's bushy red beard sparked a memory, and Daks froze.

The red-beard who'd eyeballed Ravi in the market was the infamous mage who'd saved Traget from the flood?

Fuck me.

"Lyuc!"

Girik and Tas waved until they caught the man's attention, and the man and his companion strode toward them as, thankfully, the Spawn strolled off in the opposite direction. Daks was trying to decide whether to throw his delicious supper away and free his sword hand or not, when Ravi let out a strangled sound and the force of his impending Vision nearly knocked Daks off his feet.

Tossing his mead and stew aside, he lunged for Ravi, fighting through the storm of power rushing over him. As soon as Daks reached him, Ravi's back arched off the ground and his eyes shot open. They glowed silver under the setting sun, and Daks couldn't pretend it was a trick of the moonlight this time.

He heard the footsteps of people rushing toward them, but he didn't take his eyes off Ravi.

"Come on, sweetheart. Push it away. You know you can," Daks said hoarsely as he struggled to think past the waves of energy coursing through him. "I'm here, love. You're not alone."

"What's happening? What's wrong?" Daks heard someone, possibly Tas, ask, but he couldn't answer.

"To heal the wound, you will need the strength of all.

Twin roses of the winds, ever after entwined: the pillar and the shield.

Free the stones from Black Tower to Knowledge's heart.

Cleave to your own heart, your sight, and the bearer of your burden.

Gather the stone that sleeps, the three made one, the bridge, and the axe.

At the end and the beginning, the last will come to fulfill the promise and change his song forever."

Ravi's voice had that creepy, foreign overlay Daks had only heard once before, and he groaned. Gods, he hated prophecies, even more so for the toll they took on his Ravi. Feeling helpless, he clutched Ravi closer and rocked him in his arms, murmuring useless reassurances. He didn't give a damn about the prophecy, or if it was important. He just wanted it to stop.

Shadows loomed over them, and Daks had enough instinct for self-preservation to look up. Red-beard, his small companion, Tas, Girik, and others stood over them staring. But when Ravi turned his head, his otherworldly glowing gaze fixed on the bearded wizard, pinning him in place.

"But beware, Riftwielder, another has returned to finish what was started, and they will destroy all in the name of a new paradise."

The magic flooded out of Ravi as quickly as it had rushed in, leaving Daks reeling. He couldn't even imagine how Ravi must feel.

As soon as Ravi went limp, Daks gathered him into his lap, clutching him tight and protecting him as best he could from the crowd of gawkers. He wanted to lash out at all of them, chase them off like the flock of buzzards they were, but he would've had to put Ravi down to manage it.

"Back up, everyone. Give them some air," a new voice yelled.

When Daks glanced up, he saw the wizard's petite black-haired companion making shooing motions, and the crowd of mostly giants quickly dispersed under his orders.

Daks liked him already.

The red-beard stood frozen, staring at the two of them as if he thought he could will more information out of them, but Daks was done. Heedless of anyone else, he rose to his knees, hefted Ravi in his arms, and struggled to his feet. Girik lurched forward as if to help, but Daks simply growled at him until the man stepped back. Before anyone else could get in their way, Daks lumbered toward the building where Shura lay. He'd seen another small bed in there, and Shura and Fara were the only people here he trusted.

Chapter Sixteen

"What happened?" Fara asked as she made way for him and closed the door behind them.

"Vision," Daks grunted around the headache that threatened to gray out his world.

He laid Ravi carefully onto the empty bed and plopped onto the mattress next to him.

Fara worried her lower lip before looking over her shoulder the way they'd come. The door remained closed, though, no matter what went on outside, and that was all Daks cared about for now.

"Were they.... Was everyone, uh.... Is everything okay?" she asked.

"Don't know. Don't care. They've got a wizard, a rogue pain priest, and a Spawn, so I'm pretty sure having a Seer around shouldn't ruffle their feathers too much."

"You're going to stay here?"

"Yes."

She turned her gaze to Shura's sleeping form. "I don't want her to wake up alone."

Daks lifted his aching head and held her gaze as he said, "She's been my partner for close to ten years. I'll never leave her alone unless she tells me to."

A small smile crept over Fara's lips, and the worry lines on her brow faded. "Of course. I'll go see what's going on out there, then, try to calm things down if I have to. I'll be back soon."

Silence fell heavily in the small building once she'd left, and Daks blew out a long breath and rubbed his temples. If Ravi had to have a Vision anywhere in Rassa, this was the place. The Brotherhood might have scryers locked on the wizard's little town and Sensitives in Traget, but if they hadn't sent any brothers or guards after the magic users already, chances were, they wouldn't mount an offensive for one Seer.

"Daks?"

Some of the tightness in his chest eased at the sound of Shura's voice. He managed a weak grin and moved to the chair at her bedside that Fara had vacated.

"Feeling better, you stubborn old goat?" he asked.

She narrowed her eyes at him. "No more stubborn than you, idiot."

That was certainly true.

She frowned when she spotted Ravi. "Is everything all right? How long was I asleep?"

She tried to rise, but Daks put a hand to her shoulder to stop her. "He had a Vision, a prophecy. I have a feeling he'll be out for a while. I'll be joining him as soon as Fara comes back to report on the state of things out there."

She grimaced. "Gods, I hate prophecies."

Daks barked out a weak chuckle. "I've missed you."

When she turned back to him, her gaze was troubled. "When the flood hit, I saw the ferry go under, but there was nothing I could do. As soon as I realized the wizard was working against the flood, I went to his aid, hoping it would help you."

"And got yourself shot with an arrow," Daks finished, frowning at her.

"Nobody's perfect," she replied, giving him a wry smile he rarely saw when they were outside of Samebar.

"I try to tell you that all the time and you get mad at me."

Instead of laughing with him or giving him one of her stern, exasperated glares, her expression sobered. He squirmed under her continued study.

"What's wrong, Shur?"

"I've missed you, *Vaida*...."

"But?"

She dropped her gaze and fiddled with the edge of the blanket draped across her middle, making Daks's stomach twist. She was never shy. She never held back with him.

"Spit it out, Shur," he poked, and she threw him a glare.

After taking a deep breath, she said, "You will want to return to your home as soon as you can with him, yes?"

"Not until you're well enough to travel."

She shook her head impatiently. "I know that. I know you would not leave me… unless I asked you to."

That uneasy feeling in his stomach doubled. "Talk to me, Shur."

"I am… *conflicted*. For the first time in many years, I… I want something solely for myself."

"You know I'll give you anything you want. Don't be stupid."

She leveled her dark gaze at him. "I want some*one* for myself."

Daks followed her gaze past his shoulder, though no one was there. When he turned back to her, he was grinning. "Well, obviously, I can't you give you that. But I won't stand in your way. You know that. Go for it. What's stopping you? Gods, Shur, you had me worried for a sec—"

"Will you be quiet for a minute?"

He blinked at her but clamped his mouth shut.

"It isn't that simple anymore, *Vaida*," she continued, sounding tired but determined. "Fara will not be accompanying us to Samebar. She has found the answers she was seeking here. We talked a great deal before the fever got bad." She actually blushed, but cleared her throat and plowed on. "In Scholoveld, she would have to fight for information and deal and trade in foreign lands, the results of which are uncertain. While here, the brother and the wizard seem more than happy to share. Here, she has found possible allies for her cause and her people—much more than she would ever get coming with us—allies they'll need."

Conflicted, she'd said. His chest felt tight. He might be a little slow on the emotion front sometimes, but not that slow.

"Do you want to stay here with her?" he asked. "Is that what you're telling me?"

The Seer

She wouldn't meet his gaze. "I am sworn to you."

He sighed and took her hand. "That's not what I asked, and you know it."

Her hand tightened in his, and she met his gaze with tortured dark brown eyes. "I am oathbound."

The best Daks could manage was a sad twist of his lips. "You know I never asked for that. You're my partner. That's how I've always seen it. I respect the ways of your people and I honor the gift you gave me, but I would never hold you to that if it stood in the way of your happiness."

She stared unhappily back at him in silence until Daks squirmed under the weight of it. "You told me years ago, when I asked, that there was no way I could free you from your vow without bringing shame on you and your whole family, so I won't ask again," he continued soberly. "But is there a way I could, I don't know, *order* to you stay and make sweet sweet love to Fara for a decade or something?"

Shura snorted out a laugh, as he'd hoped she would.

"Idiot," she said as she pulled her hand out of his grip and slapped his arm.

"What? It's a valid question."

He glanced over at Ravi's sleeping form, and his expression turned wistful. It seemed he and Shura both wanted things they hadn't in a long time. Change wasn't necessarily a bad thing.

Shura gripped his wrist, drawing his attention back to her. "Daks—"

He held up a hand to silence her. "Let me do some thinking, okay? Just give me a little while. You know the thinking part is harder for me."

She rolled her eyes at him.

He rose and stretched stiffening muscles, trying to work the tension out of his neck. "Keep an eye on him. I'm not going far. I'll be able to see if anyone other than Fara heads your way."

"I will."

At the door, he paused and threw what he hoped was a comforting smile over his shoulder. "We'll figure something out. We always do."

Outside, he found the nearest tree and slumped against it with a gusty sigh. People eyed him curiously as they went about their work, but he didn't see anyone he knew, and almost everyone turned the other way under his forbidding glare, which was just fine with him. His head was throbbing, his skin felt too tight, and he needed time to think. Damn, he wished he still had some of that mead he'd dropped earlier, but he wasn't going to risk dealing with anyone new right now to get it.

AFTER A brief scan of the area outside the building where he'd awoken, Ravi spotted Daks's broad back leaning against a tree. He sat stiff and unnaturally still as strangers bustled around him, giving him a wide berth. That, combined with Shura's oddly guilty look, made Ravi's stomach churn even more than the Vision hangover.

"Daks?" he called, when he was within easy earshot.

Daks started, his face drawn and troubled when he met Ravi's gaze. "Oh, hey. Feeling better?"

"Not much, but getting there. What happened?"

"You gave us another prophecy."

He smiled gently and lifted his arm in invitation. Ravi should have been embarrassed at how quickly he rushed forward to accept it, but he was too tired for that. Daks's arms were strong, his chest broad, and his body warm as Ravi dropped to the ground at his side and buried his face against that scruffy neck.

"I'm sorry. I couldn't stop it," Ravi mumbled against his skin, and Daks's arms tightened.

"I felt it. Even a trained Seer wouldn't have been able to control that. I'm sorry you had to suffer through it. You probably wouldn't have had it at all if I hadn't dragged you here."

"You didn't drag me anywhere," Ravi said, pulling back and meeting his eyes. "I came to get you."

Daks grunted and fell silent.

"What's wrong?" Ravi prodded.

"Wrong?"

"Come on. You're out here alone, leaning on a tree, instead of either pumping the locals for information, conning them out of more food and drink, or being inside with us. I may not have known you as long as Shura has, but I know you well enough."

"I have a lot on my mind."

"Is it something I said in my Vision?"

Daks shook his head and kissed Ravi's forehead. "No. Nothing like that. To tell you the truth, I don't even remember what you said."

"Then what?"

"I think my Shura may have finally fallen in love."

Ravi drew back and gaped up at him, and Daks grinned. "I know. Crazy."

"Mistress Sabin?"

He nodded.

"That's good, right? I mean, I might still hold a little grudge over the drugging incident, but anything that softens her up is a good thing in my book."

With a chuckle, Daks released his hold, stood up, and dusted himself off. "I'm glad she's found someone. It's just… Fara isn't coming with us back to Samebar. She's found what she needs here, more than she would ever get at the Scholomagi. That leaves Shura and me torn as to what to do next."

Ravi bit his lip and stood too as his stomach twisted for an all new reason. "Shura wants to stay?"

"Yes."

"And you?"

Daks blew out a breath and stepped in close. He brushed a lock of hair from Ravi's forehead as he said, "It's a little more complicated than that. I was hoping I'd have more time before I had to make any life-altering choices."

"What kind of choices?" he managed to get out around the lump in his throat.

He sighed. "You know Shura and I are partners, but you don't know all of it. Remember when I told you about the time after I was sick and I lost Jos?"

Ravi nodded.

Daks's lips twisted in a wry smile. "If you think I'm a pain in the ass now, you haven't seen anything. I went a little crazy for a while. I searched Rassa for two years for any sign of him until the High Council finally recalled me, because I was making more problems than I was solving. They cut me loose, and I drank my way through several villages, moving farther south into the forests, avoiding returning home to my family hold in defeat. Until one night, I witnessed a mob forming to go after a clan of Cigani in one of those villages. A girl had been murdered, and they of course blamed the Cigani. Even drunk, I knew it wasn't right for a whole clan to pay for something probably only one of them did, so I snuck out of the village and warned them."

He grimaced uncomfortably and waved a hand in the air. "Anyway, some other stuff happened, and I was able to trace the magic used on the murdered girl back to a villager and not the Cigani at all, without much in the way of bloodshed, but the details aren't really important. The important part is, the Cigani decided they owed me a great debt. And no matter how hard I tried to tell them a simple thanks and maybe some of their famous wine was enough, they decided to bind Shura to me anyway. In case you don't know this, they take their oath-bindings very seriously. By that vow, she can't leave my side until her death without disgracing herself *and* her entire clan." He sighed and shook his head. "But that doesn't mean she stopped being human, that she doesn't have needs of her own. And if I force her to choose, it will tear her apart. She's my partner and my friend. I love her too much to do that to her. She's fought a fight that wasn't hers too long for my sake…. But I have needs too, needs I've successfully ignored up until recent events have made that next to impossible."

He met Ravi's concerned gaze, and his lips curved in the oddest little smile as he skimmed his thumb over Ravi's lower lip. A shiver ran through Ravi's entire body.

"I'm really hoping you're talking about me right now. Because if you aren't, this is going to be extremely humiliating," Ravi replied breathily.

With a chuckle, Daks moved closer. "I'm talking about you," he agreed before kissing him deeply.

When they finally pulled apart again, Ravi clutched the wool of Daks's cloak so he couldn't go too far and pressed their foreheads together.

"So, uh, you think you might just like me too much to leave me, then? Is that what you're trying to say?" Ravi asked, hesitantly, hopefully.

"I think I might have just fallen in love with you too much to leave you," Daks corrected far too calmly.

When Ravi jolted and stared at him, Daks grinned.

"You don't tiptoe around, do you? You always just wade right in," Ravi croaked.

"Part of my charm."

After sucking in a shaky breath, Ravi searched his face. "You mean it, though, right? You really love me?"

"I may be impulsive to a fault, but once I make up my mind about something, it's made." He trailed his fingers over Ravi's cheek. "You snuck up on me, but I'm not going to hide from it anymore. I can't."

He didn't exactly sound ecstatic about it, though, which put a damper on Ravi's joy.

"But?" Ravi prodded reluctantly.

"But the two people I love are pulling me in different directions, and I have to make a choice—"

"Excuse me."

Both of them swung angry looks at the newcomer. But though the young dark-haired man with startling blue eyes barely came up to their chins, he didn't flinch or back down under their glares.

"Forgive me," he continued in oddly accented trade speak. "I'm sorry to interrupt, but we would all really like to speak to you about what happened earlier, now that you're awake... particularly Lyuc. We've prepared a fresh meal for you in our home, since your last was interrupted... if you'd like to follow me."

He lifted an arm in invitation, but when neither of them moved, his pretty face hardened. "We really must insist on speaking with you, if you intend to stay in our town. I'm sorry, but you made quite an entrance, and people are understandably uneasy."

Ravi swallowed. The last thing he wanted to do was talk to a bunch of strangers, particularly when at least one of them had triggered that massive Vision he couldn't even remember. He wasn't sure he could handle another Vision so soon after that one. He still felt shaky all over, and Daks's confession hadn't helped.

He opened his mouth to argue, but stopped when Daks sighed and put a hand on his shoulder.

"Why don't you lay down for a little while, and I'll go see what they have to say?"

"I'm sorry," the stranger cut in again. "But we really need to talk to both of you. Fara has vouched for you, but we still need to ask you a few questions... please."

The "please" came out sounding more like a command than a request, and Ravi could see Daks getting his back up, so he stepped forward before Daks could do anything they'd regret. The stranger might be small, but he was dressed all in leathers with both a dagger and a short sword at his belt. Ravi had seen Mistress Sabin in action. He knew not to underestimate someone based solely on how they looked.

"Come on. The sooner we get it over with, the sooner we can get back to our conversation."

He held Daks's gaze until Daks grunted and nodded. When the stranger headed off toward the woods, away from town, Daks shrugged and followed, and Ravi took up the rear.

"I'm Yan, by the way," the man said over his shoulder with a small smile. "I should have introduced myself."

He didn't give a family name, and the spiral of stars family mark on his arm looked new for someone who had to be at least in his twenties.

Bet there's a story there.

"I'm Ravi," he replied to be polite, but didn't offer his family name either.

Yan threw another smile over his shoulder, this one warmer and filled with a hint of humor. "Fara told us. I'd say that the circumstances of your arrival were unusual, but things are always strange wherever Lyuc goes, to the point where I've begun to wonder if 'usual' or 'normal' actually exists at all, or if the words are just something people use to comfort each other."

Ravi was trying to come up with something to say to that when they stepped into a small clearing and he got his first look at the gaudiest, most brightly-colored cabin he'd ever seen in his life. Its shape was fairly ordinary, a simple rectangle made from scraped logs with a peaked wood-shingled roof, but the logs and shingles were painted in a dizzying array of colors and patterns. Odd crystals and strands of colorful glass beads numerous enough to make a kind of fringe hung from the eaves around the entire cabin and curtained the interiors of all the windows. The only thing that made it bearable to look at was that he was seeing it by torch and lantern light. At midday, he'd probably go blind, especially when coupled with what looked like an equally garish covered wagon tucked around the side.

"We're going in there?" Ravi asked before he could stop himself.

When he winced and cast a guilty glance at their host, Yan grinned back at him. "If I hadn't guessed from your accent, I'd have figured it out by your reaction alone. You're definitely Rassan."

Daks snorted, but Ravi couldn't decide if the joke was on him or Yan. The raised eyebrow Daks was giving the cabin made Ravi feel a little better, though. He wasn't the only one.

"You should have seen the look on Fara's face the first time she came. I thought she might faint," Yan said with a laugh.

Ravi hesitated to cross the last few yards, despite the warmth in Yan's demeanor.

"Who all will be at this meal?" Daks asked, pressing close to his back.

"Like I said, Lyuc is very keen to meet you, and Tas and Girik would like to know more, particularly after what happened when Lyuc arrived," Yan replied.

"And the Spawn?" Ravi asked nervously. He wasn't sure he could take such close quarters with a wizard, a former pain priest, and a Spawn all at the same time.

"No. Bryn tends to avoid anything boring, and a group of humans sitting around talking definitely fits that definition."

Something in their expressions must have told him just how crazy all of this sounded, because his smile turned sympathetic. "It's a lot to get used to. Believe me, I know. But I promise you, no one here means you harm, including Bryn. Bryn is unique among his/her kind and a bit of a cranky princess sometimes, but not an unreasoning monster. You don't have to worry."

Yan started walking again, and Ravi reluctantly followed. When they reached the cabin and he held the door open for them, they stepped inside.

Despite the assault on his eyes, warmth spilled from the interior, and Ravi moved toward it like a moth to a flame. He hated the cold, and yet he seemed to keep moving farther and farther north. What did that say about him?

If anything, the interior décor was even worse than he'd imagined. Multiple patterned rugs had been piled on top of one another over the floor, with piles of cushions scattered around to add to the chaos of colors. The crystals and beads in the windows caught the light of several lanterns and candles resting on shelves and ledges haphazardly mounted around the room, flashing even more colored patterns on the walls. Odd stones, large, glittering crystals as big as a man's fist, trinkets, carvings, and baubles filled nearly every flat surface, while colorful scarves, blankets, and more pillows draped most of the furniture. The sight was so overwhelming, the red-bearded man nearly blended into everything else in his brightly patched robes.

Mistress Sabin, in her plain gray travel costume, helped blot out some of the garish display around her, and Ravi hurried to her side for some soothing familiarity after Yan took their cloaks. They might not have been the best of friends on their journey, but she was the closest they had to an ally in this group and the most normal of all of them.

A large table, draped in more patterned cloth and filled with plates of food, dominated the open area in front of a stone hearth. The gaudy wizard sat at the head of the table in a pink-and-purple cushioned chair, while the priest from earlier and his blond friend sat on a bench along the far side. Their guide, Yan, moved to the wizard's side, bent, and kissed the man before taking a seat on the bench next to the others.

"Daks and Ravi, may I present Lyuc, the leader of our little group here and temporary town leader until a new Elder is chosen for the clan," Yan said.

"I'm glad to finally have a chance to meet the infamous Daks," Lyuc replied with a grin. "Your partner has made quite an impression on us."

Ravi followed Daks's gaze as he lifted his eyebrows at Mistress Sabin.

The mistress grimaced apologetically at the wizard. "Shura was rather, uh, *displeased* when she woke up to find she'd been carried away from Traget. She refused to rest or let anyone tend her until Lyuc and Tas graciously agreed to scry for you, to make sure you were all right."

"She wouldn't let anyone else rest either," Lyuc added wryly.

The familiar, proud, cheeky grin Daks threw at the wizard eased some of the tightness in Ravi's belly, and he found himself smiling too.

"You scryed us?" Ravi asked a little nervously, not quite knowing what that entailed.

The wizard's green eyes twinkled at Ravi.

"We did. I thought it an excellent opportunity for Tas to practice working with Singer... and without him. But don't worry.

We didn't give her details, only that the two of you were quite safe and, uh, *comfortable*."

Lyuc winked, and Ravi felt his face heat. Daks's grin faded as he scooted closer to Ravi.

"Why don't we all dig in?" Yan asked, breaking the awkward silence. "I'm sure our guests have to be starving after their long day. We'll talk when we're finished."

"I told Shura I wouldn't be gone long," Mistress Sabin said regretfully.

"We can fend for ourselves," Daks offered. "We'll fill you in later if you want to get back to her."

Daks said it with his usual confidence, and Mistress Sabin smiled gratefully at him. She gathered a heaping plate of food to take with her and hurried out the door, leaving Ravi and Daks alone with a group of strangers who were a lot stranger than most. Strangers he already resented for not even allowing him a minute to process the fact that Daks had told him he loved him.

Under the table, he sought out Daks's hand, and Daks immediately threaded their fingers together. When he looked up, he caught the wizard, Lyuc, watching them with a small smile on his face before he turned to glance at Yan, his smile warming.

Well, at least I shouldn't have to worry about any of them trying to poach Daks. They all seem pretty firmly paired up.

That probably should have been the least of his worries, with a pain priest sitting right across from him, but he'd take what he could get.

"Please, help yourselves," Yan said when no one moved after the mistress's departure.

Daks apparently didn't need to be told twice. He reached for a large pitcher on the table, filled his mug, and downed half the contents without putting the pitcher down. When he caught Ravi looking at him, he said, "I was thirsty. Want some?"

He poured for Ravi before topping his off again; then they both joined the others in filling their plates. Ravi wasn't particularly hungry. His Vision hangover hadn't subsided yet, and he had a lot to think about. But he knew better than to ever pass up a free meal. Who knew when the next would come. Plus, putting this conversation off as long as possible wasn't a bad thing, except that it meant he'd have to wait that much longer before he and Daks could finish their talk.

Their respite couldn't last for long, though, and sure enough, only about halfway through the meal, the strange red-bearded wizard in the garish, comically patched robes speared Ravi with his gaze. "You made quite an entrance earlier. Do that often, do you?"

The hum of murmured conversation between the others stopped dead, and Ravi caught Yan giving Lyuc an exasperated frown.

"Not really," Daks replied somewhat hostilely while Ravi struggled to swallow his bite of food.

Thankfully, Lyuc turned his intense gaze to Daks, because there was something off about that man, something in the depths of his eyes that made Ravi shiver. He really wished he hadn't allowed Yan to take his cloak now, so he could hide inside it.

"But it has happened before?" Lyuc pressed.

Daks pursed his lips as he leaned back in his chair and straightened his legs under the table. "Why don't we start by you all sharing a bit more information about yourselves before we get into any of that? Shura was hurt, and Fara was obviously distracted, so as far as we're concerned, you're all strangers, not even counting who and *what* you are. Why should we trust you?"

The former pain priest, Tas, narrowed his eyes. "If you recall, we've been taking quite good care of your friends for days. I healed Shura right in front of you, and Yan and Lyuc have opened their home to you—"

He stopped when the big blond man, Girik, put a hand on his arm, though not without a last disapproving harrumph that made Ravi's lips twitch. Maybe the Brotherhood wasn't so scary when you were up close and personal with them. They were just men, after all.

"We understand your reticence," Yan jumped in before anyone else could speak. "Meetings can be tense when all parties don't know where they stand. That's why I'd hoped we could relax over a good meal before easing into more serious topics."

He threw a look at Lyuc as he finished, and Ravi had to hide another smile. Despite the strangeness of their situation and the hard lessons life had taught him about trust, he thought he could learn to like these people. They hadn't shunned him or treated him like some alien thing to be ogled. They had gifts, just like him—or probably even stranger. He wasn't used to being on this side of the fence, but he liked to think he was a better man, more accepting of differences than his family and his fellow Rassans had been.

"It's okay, Daks," Ravi murmured, and Daks turned his stubborn glare away from the others to give him a searching look. "You said to follow my feelings. These people have been kind to Shura and the mistress, and they're showing kindness to us. We shouldn't insult their hospitality." He reluctantly turned back to Lyuc, though he kept his gaze trained somewhere in the vicinity of Lyuc's chin. "That's only the second time something like that has happened to me... that I know of anyway. But I do have other Visions and Dreams. I'm only here now because I saw your Spawn, uh, the horse, uh, *man*—"

"Bryn," Yan interjected.

"What?"

"Our *friend*, Brynthalon."

"Oh. Uh, okay. I saw Brynthalon in a Vision and feared for Daks's life. But since the prophecy happened the second I saw you, I suppose that means I was meant to come here."

Habit made him shoot nervous glances at everyone at the table, but their faces all remained purely curious, no judgment, no fear or disgust, and he relaxed a little more.

"And can you tell us anything about what it meant?" Lyuc asked.

Ravi grimaced, and Daks took his hand under the table again, giving it a squeeze. "I can't even tell you what I said. I don't remember any of it. Sorry."

He braved a glance upward to gauge Lyuc's response, but the man simply smiled knowingly. "I thought so. That's the way prophecies usually work for the poor soul burdened with giving them. That's all right. I just hoped it might be easier this time."

"You've heard prophecies before?" Ravi asked, curious enough to meet the man's gaze dead on.

Lyuc's green eyes crinkled at the corners, and his teeth gleamed behind the copper strands of his beard. "I've been around for a few in my time."

Yan snorted, but it must have been an inside joke, because Daks didn't seem to get it either.

"Do *you* know what it means?" Daks asked.

"I believe some, but not all," Lyuc replied enigmatically. He sat back in his chair and stretched his legs out, mirroring Daks's earlier pose.

A pipe appeared in his hands, and he lifted it to his lips and sucked as he pointed a finger at the bowl. The shredded dried leaves flared to smoky orange life without benefit of any flame, and Ravi gasped. To his surprise, Daks also tensed at his side.

"Show-off," Yan murmured under his breath, and that actually eased some of Ravi's fear.

"Who are you?" Daks asked baldly. "You're not of the Scholomagi. And you don't work magic like any witch, priest, or shaman I've ever seen. How is it I've never heard of you?"

"Oh, you've heard of me," Lyuc said, his wry grin widening behind his pipe.

Tas groaned, and Yan swatted Lyuc's arm gently before saying, "It's rude to tease a guest, oh great-and-powerful-one."

Yan's last words held enough gentle mocking that Ravi was torn between smiling and scooting closer to Daks.

"Mind enlightening us?" Daks asked with a hint of a growl behind his words, and Ravi clutched at his hand, hoping he'd get the hint that he needed to be careful.

"Sorry," Yan said, leaning forward with an apologetic grimace. "He can get a little puffed up from time to time. He was out in the wilds by himself too long."

Lyuc pulled his pipe away and stuck his tongue out at Yan, but Yan only smiled. "Suffice it to say, he's a lot older than he looks… *and* acts. But maybe tonight isn't the right time to get into all of that. You're both probably tired from your journey, and we've taken you away from your friends. I'm sure Fara can help fill you in on some of it later."

Daks pursed his lips as if he were weighing his options, but after a few beats and a quick glance at Ravi, he nodded.

"Maybe we should," he agreed. "But before we go, I'd like to know what your intentions are for us."

"Intentions?" Yan asked, looking reassuringly confused.

"Are we free to come and go as we please?" Daks clarified.

The strangers exchanged glances until Lyuc said, "As long as you pose no threat to anyone here, you may do whatever you wish. I would like to talk to you a little more about any other Visions you may have had lately, Ravi, but it isn't urgent."

"Did you discuss the prophecy at all with Fara?" Daks asked. "Does she know your thoughts on it?"

"No. I have not," Lyuc replied.

"Then will you share them with us so we might discuss it amongst ourselves?"

Everyone leaned forward, all eyes on the wizard.

"If you're sure you really want to get into this tonight," Lyuc murmured, quirking an eyebrow.

"I'm sure," Daks replied with his usual bluster.

"As you wish." He took another puff of his pipe and settled back in his chair. "Now the first thing you must know is almost all prophecies are vague enough to be open to interpretation. Like with the one heralding the coming of Rassa's *blessed* Harot." He grimaced. "I'd heard it secondhand from a passing merchant and believed it meant one thing, but what actually happened was nothing like what I expected. I might have done something to stop it otherwise."

Ravi frowned in confusion. The man spoke as if he'd been there in person when Harot had returned from the Riftlands and ascended to join the gods, but that couldn't be right.

"Lyuc," Yan murmured gently.

The wizard glanced at him and smiled. "Right. Getting off topic. What I meant is that you should take my interpretation with a grain of salt. So, there's the first lines: '*To heal the wound, you will need the strength of all. Twin roses of the winds, ever after entwined: the pillar and the shield.*'"

Ravi listened closely, since it was his first time hearing it, but it meant absolutely nothing to him.

"This may sound a bit conceited," Lyuc continued, throwing at smile at Yan, "but if I choose to believe the prophecy was meant for me—or *us*—I have to conclude the 'wound' is referring to the Rift. If that's the case, your prophecy could be very important indeed, particularly with regards to another prophecy I've only recently learned about." He turned his gaze toward Tas. "Did Singer have anything to say about it today?"

As Ravi gaped at Lyuc in growing fear and disbelief, Tas shook his head. "He asked to be alone with... his friends." Tas shot a meaningful glance in their direction before facing Lyuc again. "But that's where he prefers to be most of the time. If he had any thoughts, he kept them to himself."

"Stubborn rock," Lyuc grumbled. "But it's a fair guess that is what it's referring to."

"Closing the Rift," Ravi choked out. "Like, you're talking about *the* Rift, the hole in the world that monsters come through."

Yan stood up and came around the table, while Ravi was still shifting his gaze between each of them, trying to determine if this was all some kind of joke. After sitting down next to him, Yan gave him an understanding smile. "This is why I tried to save this conversation for later. It's a lot to take in all at once."

Ravi shifted backward, mostly on instinct. The last thing he wanted was another Vision involving these people, given what little he'd learned so far.

Daks squeezed his hand again to get his attention. "Do you want to go?" he asked, ignoring everyone else. "I can come back to get the rest, but I think we really need to know what's going on before we make any decisions."

Ravi shook his head. "No. I'll stay. I'm the one that spouted it, after all. I'm not going to be just some vessel for fate or the gods. I control my own life."

He spoke with more determination than he felt, but Daks's smile was proud as he placed his other hand over their joined ones.

"Good for you," Yan murmured encouragingly.

Lyuc cleared his throat, drawing everyone's attention back to him. "Shall I continue?"

At Ravi's nod, he explained, "So, as you all probably know, a rose of the winds is a compass rose, which could mean from every possible direction, or something more basic, like the rose itself, an eight-pointed star. The latter part of the prophecy makes me lean toward that, given it names eight things: three that we must 'cleave to,' four we must 'gather,' and one who will 'come.' That's eight. But the 'twin' part leads me to believe there must be two of them—'the pillar and the shield'—which would be sixteen and not eight." He grimaced and took another puff from his pipe, his attention drawn inward. "'*Free the stones from Black Tower to Knowledge's heart*' seems a bit more straightforward, but worrisome at the same time. Obviously, the Black Tower is in Blagos Keep. The Brotherhood built the keep around Ryarth's black tower almost five hundred years ago, and it's where the Thirty-Six go when they aren't out on missions. With what Singer told us of the other prophecy, we already know we must gather their stones, but 'Knowledge's heart' is something else altogether."

When Lyuc fell silent for several beats, frowning, Yan moved to his side again and placed a hand on his shoulder.

"Lyuc, what's wrong?"

"Something I thought was safely locked away and forgotten a long time ago. I don't like that someone or something remembers its existence." Lyuc looked at Ravi as he said it, and Ravi shivered and turned away.

"I don't know where the Visions come from or what they mean most of the time," he protested.

Daks tensed next to him, and Ravi allowed himself to be pulled against his broad chest for comfort. So much in his life had gotten so complicated. He was having a hard time keeping up.

"Right," Lyuc said a little more gently. "Anyway. We need to collect the stones and gather the points of the star or stars—who or whatever they are. That seems fairly clear and only marginally troubling. But that warning he gave at the end concerns me more. The Seer looked right at me when he said it, and he called me Riftwielder. There aren't any other Riftwielders in the three kingdoms... or there weren't. *Another has returned*,' he said." Lyuc paused and glanced at each of his companions. "Yan and I have told you about the magic-wielding Spawn we faced. And we all know what happened in the mountains last winter was no accident. Livestock missing or killed with no one knowing how. Food stores rotted inside their barrels and crates. Clan members disappearing, no matter how many shields or barriers we put up or how many times we tried to scry out the culprits... and the shaman and chief dying, of course." Lyuc turned back to Ravi and Daks, his eyes grave. "Your friend will fill you in on the details, but the gist of it is, Girik's clan was pushed out of the mountains by unseen forces, and other clans may have suffered similar fates. The energy contained beneath the Great Barrier Mountains is too strong and chaotic to get a good read on what was happening, or from where it originated. But the warning in the prophecy does not ease my mind on the subject, not after some of the things we've seen."

Ravi shivered, and Daks tightened his arms around him. "Sorry to be blunt," Daks cut in, "but I think we've heard all we need to. It sounds like this prophecy doesn't have much to do with us, even though Ravi had to be the one to deliver it. You all seem to have a lot to discuss, so, uh, we'll just go and leave you to it. Thanks for dinner and everything else."

Without waiting for a response, Daks rose to his feet and tugged Ravi with him, leaving his mostly full tankard on the table.

They'd only taken two steps toward the door when Lyuc spoke again, stopping them.

"You may have more of a part to play than you think."

Ravi winced, and Daks let out a pained groan as they both slowly turned to the wizard.

"Your Seer's prophecy said, '*Cleave to your heart, your sight, and the bearer of your burden,*'" Lyuc continued. "Now, my heart could simply be a metaphor for my feelings, and my sight a clarity of thought or vision, but the last part makes me think not. Ravi, you could have said 'cleave to my burden,' but you didn't. You said cleave to the *bearer* of my burden, which makes me think it's meant to be a person." He turned to look at Tas, who started, eyes widening. "We know what my burdens are. You are the bearer of one of them." He tipped his head back to gaze up at Yan, who still stood behind him with hands on his shoulders. "Following that logic, you know who my heart must be." They shared a sappy look before Lyuc leveled his gaze at Ravi again. "Who do you think my sight is, then? I tell you now, I have many talents, and power and knowledge no one else alive possesses, but the gift of Sight is not among them."

Ravi began to regret that stew he'd crammed down his throat. Daks stepped in close to his side, his body stiff.

"But as you said, you can't be sure of any interpretation of prophecy," he argued. "And Ravi isn't the only Seer in the world. The prophecy might not have even meant a Seer at all. 'Your sight' could be anything."

"But he *is* the Seer who brought us the prophecy, and he is the one standing here with us now," Lyuc countered.

"Exactly. He did his part. We'll leave you to do yours. We'll see ourselves out."

Daks covered the distance to the door in a couple of quick strides, grabbed their cloaks off the hooks, and lifted an arm to usher Ravi outside. Ravi stumbled into the dark in a daze, his mind awash with questions and anxieties. The comforting weight of the cloak Daks draped over his shoulders helped, but his head was spinning as they hurried to the cabin where Shura and Mistress Sabin waited, without a backward glance.

He didn't participate much in the conversation that followed, once they'd closed and bolted the door. He let the words wash over him as Daks explained what had happened, Shura and Mistress Sabin shared what they'd learned of their hosts, and all three of them argued possible interpretations of a prophecy Ravi couldn't even remember saying. He should have been listening closer, particularly given everything Lyuc had said—and not even counting his love of fantastic stories—but he was too tired to make sense of it. His thoughts wanted to go in too many directions at once.

The gods were making him regret all those times he'd wished and prayed to be in one of those tales from his childhood. He'd laugh if he wasn't worried he wouldn't be able to stop once he started. The Rift, Spawn, wizards, sacred stones, and cryptic prophecies? Not even counting the adventure he'd already had and the declaration of love he hadn't even had a chance to let sink in. He was no hero from a tale, no warrior or magic user. Whatever magic he had used him, not the other way around. Tales were for childish dreamers. He was supposed to have been a scribe, or a scholar, or teacher at the very most. He hadn't even been that much for the past ten years. What was he doing here?

Dragging a hand over his face, he sighed.

Tomorrow, he promised himself.

He'd try to make sense of this craziness tomorrow when he'd had a chance to catch his breath.

"Daks?"

Daks stopped midsentence and turned to him.

"Can we go to bed now? Please?"

Daks's eyebrows drew down for a second before his expression softened. "Sure. It's been a long day for all of us. We'll have clearer heads after some rest anyway. They shouldn't bother us again tonight, if they know what's good for them."

Despite looking drawn and pale, Shura quirked her lips slightly at the ridiculousness of his implied threat, given who and what was out there. She rose slowly from her spot at the end of the bed, and Mistress Sabin helped get her settled beneath the covers. Relieved everyone agreed, Ravi shuffled to the far side of the second bed, took off his boots, and stretched out beneath the blankets without bothering to undress any further.

Both beds in the cabin were quite narrow, but no one seemed to mind as Shura and Mistress Sabin cuddled up together in theirs and Daks put out the lamp and slid in next to him.

"Are you all right?" Daks murmured, tucking Ravi against his side and wrapping an arm around him to hold him close.

"I don't know," he answered honestly. "A lot has happened."

A breathy chuckle rumbled through Daks's chest. "You could say that again. But we'll figure it out."

Ravi smiled against Daks's chest. When had that overabundance of confidence become more charming than annoying? He chose not to question it or him and closed his eyes.

Chapter Seventeen

Ravi felt surprisingly good when he rolled out of bed the following morning. Even waking up entirely alone in a strange place didn't seem to bother him as much as he thought it would. Someone had left him a small tray of bread, butter, and some now cold honeyed tea, and he ate unhurriedly as he pondered his odd newfound calm, poking and prodding at it with a strange detachment.

He'd slept curled in Daks's arms all night long, pressed together not for sex, but for comfort and connection. That could definitely be one reason why he was no longer feeling overwhelmed and anxious.

He loves me.

He rolled that thought around in his mind, but he had a feeling it would take a while before it really sank in and took root. Slowly and deliberately, he changed into the set of freshly cleaned and mended clothing someone had kindly left folded in a neat pile at the end of the bed. Many thoughts fluttered at the back of his mind, not frantic, fearful, or loud, but soft, determined, and possibly even hopeful. He felt... settled, which was a sensation he hadn't experienced in a long time and seemed distinctly at odds with his current situation.

After pulling on his boots and cloak, he stepped out into the cool, mist-shrouded morning without bothering to draw up the hood. A soft breeze caressed his cheeks, and he smiled despite the chill. For some reason, the fog didn't seem anywhere near as unnerving or oppressive as it had the last time he'd been in the boglands.

He started walking toward the muffled sounds of the villagers going about their day, but not in any rush. He needed just a little more time for his thoughts to finish taking shape and to fully understand where this new feeling came from before he went in search of Daks.

With each welcoming or curious set of eyes he boldly met as he made his way through the village, his confidence grew. This might be Rassa, but he wasn't alone in his strangeness here. These people lived alongside men far stranger than himself. If he had a Vision, no one would call the Brotherhood, and he doubted anyone would shun him. Hells, they all had to know about his prophecy by now, and they still greeted him kindly. It was a revelation of sorts.

When he caught sight of Tas, the former pain priest, his newfound calm faltered a bit. Apparently, shoving aside a lifetime of fear wouldn't be quite as speedy a process as he might've hoped. But when Tas spotted him and changed direction, Ravi lifted his chin and didn't run away.

"Good morning," Tas greeted hesitantly.

"Good morning."

"I, uh, hope you're feeling better today, now that you've rested."

Tas's awkwardness did much to ease Ravi's fear of him—though the fact that he wasn't wearing red robes or his holy stone helped immensely. Tas was only a man, and one who seemed almost as troubled by Ravi as Ravi was by him.

"I am. This is all a bit much to take in, though."

Tas's smile was sympathetic. "It is. I would be lying if I didn't say I suffered through months of turmoil and uncertainty before wrapping my head around Singer, Lyuc, Bryn, and all the rest. I was very lucky to have Girik by my side, or I might have lost it altogether more than once, so I perfectly understand your feelings."

Ravi frowned. "You were a brother, though, a member of the holy Thirty-Six. I would've thought all this magic stuff wouldn't have come as that much of a surprise."

His words had come out a lot more accusatory than he'd intended, and Tas actually flinched and took a small step back. "As I said yesterday, the Brotherhood, and I, have much to answer for. I am not proud of some of the things I've done in their name. My only excuse is that I thought I was doing good at the time... or at least I was doing what was necessary for the good of all."

"But now you know differently?"

"I do. I learned the truth, which is why I will never wear the scarlet again. I also learned just how much I didn't know about magic and the world we live in." His lips twisted wryly. "Last winter in the mountains was very enlightening, and I've had months to work my way through it all, so don't feel bad for being confused or overwhelmed, believe me."

The self-deprecating smile and openness with which he'd spoken called forth a flood of questions that burned on the tip of Ravi's tongue, but he bit them back. He had more important things to deal with first, before satisfying any insatiable familial curiosity. His mind was already full enough. Besides, open and friendly or not, Tas still made him uncomfortable and probably would for some time to come. He'd drag whatever details he could out of Mistress Sabin and Shura first before risking a lengthy conversation with this man, no matter how much the storyteller inside him whined with impatience to hear his tale.

Still, he did have one question niggling at him that might have great bearing on his immediate future.

"Why did you come back?"

"What?"

"Why did you come back? Lyuc said the barb—the, uh, clan was pushed out of the mountains by something, but why here? Surely Ghorazon or Samebar would have been safer for you to settle in. You'd just gotten away from the Brotherhood. Why come back?"

"I left Rassa only for some breathing room and time to train. I never intended to stay away. Rassa is my home. I dedicated my entire life to protecting its people. Even if the means to that end was a lie and wrong, who I am and what I want for my kingdom hasn't changed. I believe in fighting for it."

Tas had puffed up as he spoke. The fire of his conviction lit his eyes, and he shed the penitent villager-next-door persona like a cloak. It was Ravi's turn to take a step back. He could see the brother Tas used to be now, and it made him wary, even as Tas's words struck a chord.

Last night—and honestly for the last several years—he'd spent a lot of time concentrating on all the things he wasn't. How long had he trudged along, hiding and mourning the life he'd left behind, running away from everything instead of running *toward* something else?

If what he'd learned so far was true, Tas's entire world had been turned upside down too. But even through a complete upheaval of his life, he'd still figured out who he was and who he wanted to be. It was time for Ravi to do the same.

"Thank you for being honest with me."

Tas blinked at him, seeming a little nonplussed, but then he offered a hesitant smile. "Of course. As I said not so long ago, I was as overwhelmed as you must be now. If there is anything I can do to help you, I will." His smile turned rueful. "In that vein, I should warn you now that Lyuc usually gets what he wants. No matter how infuriating he can be, he is a force to be reckoned with, and he isn't wrong often."

When Ravi grimaced, Tas rushed to add, "But of course he won't force you to do anything you don't want. He's a good man. He cares about people and all of Kita. I'll let him tell you his story. It's not my place. But you'll understand when you hear it. He only wants what's best for everyone."

"I'll have to take your word for that," Ravi hedged. "Our plans aren't settled yet, obviously, but I'm sure we'll at least be willing to hear him out. I should, uh, probably find my friends now, though."

"Of course. I understand. I believe I saw Shura and Fara headed toward the stableyard, but I'm afraid I haven't seen Daks."

"I'll find him. Thank you."

"Come find us when you want to talk."

Ravi gave a noncommittal nod, and Tas headed off in the direction he'd been going earlier.

Ravi's feet led him down toward the river without any real intention, but he wasn't surprised when he spotted Daks sitting alone on the rocky bank, obviously deep in thought by the frown on his face. Ravi's heart swelled along with his smile.

He loves me. He accepts me for who and what I am. I can be myself with him. And maybe now I know who I want that to be.

What a wondrous thought.

"Hey! Don't strain too hard, you might break something," he called.

Daks started and jerked his head up, but his confused frown soon twisted into a smile. "Don't worry about me." He tapped his forehead with his knuckles. "Hard as a rock. Won't break as easily as that."

"Everyone was gone when I woke up," Ravi complained as he sat down beside him.

"Sorry. I had some thinking to do. I didn't realize Shura would be able to be up and about so soon. She was still there when I left."

"You don't sound very happy about that."

Daks grimaced. "Of course I'm happy she's feeling better. But if I don't have concern for her welfare and ability to travel to use as an excuse anymore, I can't really put off making a decision much longer."

He picked up a small rock and tossed it in the flowing water, staring after it broodingly.

Yesterday, that statement would have made Ravi's gut twist with anxiety, but not today. With his newfound preternatural calm had come a bit of clarity.

"I might be able to help you out there, if you'll let me," he offered hesitantly.

Daks's confused frown returned as he turned back to him, but Ravi took a breath and plowed on. "You see, I've been thinking through everything you've told me, and the whole situation we're in, and I've come to the conclusion that this isn't really your decision to make, or even Shura's. It's mine."

Daks opened his mouth, but Ravi held up a hand. "Just hear me out, okay? You told me Mistress Sabin needs to stay here. For her family, her friends, and her cause, this is the best place for her to be. You told me Shura's fallen in love and has to choose between her honor and following her heart." He ticked off the first two points on his fingers before pausing and slowly lifting a third. "Then, you told me you loved me." He paused when Daks's sexy grin came out from behind the clouds of worry. "*But* you also love Shura and want her to be happy, because you're a good man who has a soft heart under all that bluster and surliness."

Daks snorted and cocked an eyebrow at him, but Ravi turned his gaze to the river before he could get distracted.

After clearing his throat and straightening his shoulders, he said, "So, the way I see it, each of you seems to be faced with an impossible choice. Therefore, logic dictates that the only one who should be making the decision is the one whose choice is *not* impossible… and that's me." He rushed his next words so he could get them all out before he lost his nerve. "You see, my choice is to either stay in my home country, where I might be able to do some good and possibly find a home for my friends, or to force you and someone you love to drag me all the way up to some town I've never been to, in a kingdom I don't know, so I can learn to use a gift you yourself told me no one has ever managed to control completely. I mean, hardly sounds like a choice at all, when you think about it, right?"

He snuck at look at Daks and found the man watching him with the softest expression he'd ever seen.

"You know, you're making it really hard for me not to want to kiss the hells out of you right now," Daks murmured. "But it isn't as simple as that, and you know it."

"Seems pretty simple to me."

Daks sighed and scooted close enough their thighs touched before cupping Ravi's jaw and forcing him to meet his gaze. "Rassa is on the verge of civil war. This quiet little town they've created will be under siege at some point. They've poked the Brotherhood in the eye, and the Brotherhood has no option but to respond or lose their hold on Rassa. And in case you didn't notice last night, the village's all-powerful wizard seems to have other things on his mind. Scholoveld may be strange to you, and the other Seers might not be able to teach you complete control, but you'd be safe behind the walls of the city. You'd have a home and training, a place you belong and are valued. I can't ask you to give all that up to fight for a cause that isn't yours, just for me. I've done it for far too long with Shura. And I wouldn't be able to live with myself if you got hurt or killed because I couldn't protect you... I can't go through that again. I'm not strong enough."

Daks whispered the last so quietly, Ravi could feel how much it cost him to admit.

"Maybe it is my cause," Ravi murmured, wrapping a hand around the back of Daks's neck and squeezing. "Listen. Since the first day I met you, you've called my Visions a gift. Maybe it's time I start believing you."

"You remember what happened in Urmat? What you had to do in that alley to save Shura and how you felt afterward? You're not a fighter, Rav, and that's perfectly okay. If you stay here, you'll probably have to do much worse. You realize that, don't you?"

Ravi's stomach twisted, but he lifted his chin. "If Lyuc is right, this could mean a chance to *heal the entire world*. If that is me in the prophecy, am I dooming the world if I don't at least try? Could I live with myself? What kind of hero would I be in that story?"

Daks shook his head. "You can't take that kind of weight on your shoulders. You're one man—a pretty amazing man and quite irresistible," Daks added, his grin returning, "but still only one man. The thing about heroes in history is a lot of them end up dead, and you don't have a magic sword or wizard at your beck and call to help."

"I have my gift and my wits, and I can learn the rest. Plus, I have you, don't I? What could possibly stop us?"

Daks rolled his eyes and let out a weak chuckle.

"Daks, do you love me?" Ravi asked.

"I told you I do," he replied, frowning slightly.

"Well, good. Because I love you too, and I'm done running away. So listen up, you big, irritating, stubborn blowhard of a—"

Daks tackled him to the rocky bank, which was a little on the painful side, but Ravi soon forgot about it under an onslaught of hot, wet kisses and urgent fumbling hands finding their way beneath his layers of clothing. Daks only pulled back to grin down at him when Ravi was about to pass out from lack of air.

"We're staying," Ravi gasped out firmly between breaths.

"We'll talk about it," Daks replied just as breathlessly.

Ravi frowned up at him, but Daks's habitual grin was infectious, and he couldn't hold his glare for long.

"Say it again," Daks ordered as he bent and braced his elbows on either side of Ravi's head before bussing their noses together.

"We're staying?" he replied with a grin.

Daks growled. "No, the other part."

Ravi was going to make him work for it, but something in Daks's dark blue eyes changed his mind.

"I love you."

"Okay, then that's settled. We'll stay here for a little while, if that's what you want. But if things start getting dangerous, prophecy or no prophecy, I'm taking all of you out of here, even if I have to tie you to Horse's saddle and walk you out through the mountains myself. Got it?"

"I guess we'll see," Ravi shot back, knowing about how much Daks's bluster was worth. "Where *is* Horse, by the way?"

Daks shrugged. "He went with that sorrel I stole to what passes for their stables here. I'm not worried, though. He never goes far. I'll check in on him later." He bent and kissed Ravi roughly, with lots of tongue. "Much later."

"Can we find somewhere a little more comfortable for the rest of this discussion?" Ravi asked, even as his body argued the river stones digging into his back weren't that bad.

Daks pulled back and gave Ravi that cocky grin of his. "You got it, beautiful."

Epilogue

Brynthalon followed the white stallion out of town, across the chest-deep river, and into a clearing on the other side before he shifted back to human form and announced his presence.

"Where are you going?"

The stallion stopped and gave him a regal glance over its shoulder but didn't answer.

He stepped closer and glared. "I may not know exactly what you are, but I know you understand me, and *you* know I can keep following you, so you might as well cut the crap and talk to me."

The horse eyed him for a few more moments before it shimmered and took the form of a hawk-nosed young man with curly sun-kissed brown hair and olive skin. It wore a simple pair of brown trousers and a soft umber linen shirt, but it was barefoot in the damp spring grass.

Bryn hissed and took a step back, his fingers elongating into claws. "What are you?"

"I think you know," it responded in a soft baritone.

"If I knew, I wouldn't have asked," Bryn growled back. "Tell me."

"Ah, the young, so impatient, so passionate. I can't tell you how much I've missed this, being out and about in the world, interacting with people again."

"I'm not young. I wasn't young when I came to this plane, and I've been here for over a thousand years. I have never met one that feels like you. You feel… like me, but not."

He cocked his head to the side, trying to sift through the swirling energy that surrounded the other, but it was muted somehow.

It grinned. "I *am* like you… but not."

Bryn hissed and took a step forward, but the other held up a hand. "You don't want to do that. Believe me. I was not created to be a fighter. It isn't in my makeup. But there are other ways to win a battle, and I'm old enough to know most of them."

Bryn narrowed his eyes but didn't attack. He wasn't an impetuous human to be easily goaded into making a rash mistake when he did not know what he faced. Instead of rushing the creature, he took one deliberate step forward, and for the briefest moment, the power around the other pulsed stronger.

"I know your scent, your vibration," Bryn said, only just realizing it. "Yesterday, when the Seer collapsed with his prophecy, the feeling was the same."

The other actually flushed, its grin widening. "I'm not usually so obvious, but desperate times and all that."

"The priest, Tas, says prophecies come from the gods, but Lyuc does not believe in gods. Which is it? Are you a god, or was it some kind of trick?"

The other grinned wider. "Both."

As if it were enjoying itself, the other dropped to the ground and folded its legs under it, still grinning up at Bryn like a mischievous child. With an irritated sigh, Bryn moved closer and sat on the ground across from it.

"You speak in riddles."

"Not riddles, exactly, but I can't make it too easy. Where would be the fun in that?"

"Are we having fun?"

"I am."

"The prophecy was yours, so you know what it means."

"No and yes."

Bryn clenched his teeth. The last time he'd met another being similar to himself and sentient enough to talk, he'd had to help Lyuc destroy it. He kind of wanted to learn a bit more this time, but he didn't like being toyed with.

"No, the prophecy isn't yours, but yes, you know what it means?"

After casting a glance over its shoulder, the other's smile gentled. "I'd like to play with you longer, but I haven't much time, so I'll try to be as helpful as my nature will allow. I should have said the prophecy isn't solely mine. Seers sense the patterns of the world around them but aren't advanced enough to take it all in, so they get flashes of the most probable events. I just helped him along a little."

"By making him spout a riddle?" Bryn huffed.

"As I said, it is as much as my nature will allow. They would have sent someone else, but *their* natures don't allow for quite as much interference in the world of men as mine does. My sole purpose for existing on this plane is to stir the pot, you see." He stood up with a grin and spun in a little circle with his arms outstretched. "I am mischief made flesh… or made thought anyway. That's how the humans summoned and molded me, with their prayers and their belief. Thousands of them over hundreds of years, they brought me forth from the void. I've changed a little over the intervening millennia, and there's still a core that is me as I was before, like there is still a core to you, but in this plane, I cannot exist as other than what I am."

Bryn jolted and stared at it. "So you are Spawn? You came from the void, the between?"

"Like you, but not," it agreed. "I was summoned. I was called forth by the creatures that belong to this world. You tripped and fell through the tear, as it were. Whole different bargain. In some ways, you have more freedom than I. But you don't truly belong here. You are tethered, for now, but when that tether breaks…."

If Bryn could feel fear, that's what he would call the odd sensation that moved through his chest. But he didn't have emotions like that. He was above such things.

"Explain," Bryn demanded, but the other grinned and shook its head, making its floppy brown curls bounce.

"I told you. I can't make it that easy."

"You're lying," Bryn countered. "You helped the warrior and his Seer. The one they call Mistress Sabin spoke of what you did for them on their journey, how you helped. I saw it myself. You stayed with those two, tagging along like a puppy, doing their bidding, letting them *ride* you, yet you won't help me now?" Bryn let his lip curl, showing his disgust, but the other only laughed.

"More like a herd dog than a puppy. Although I may have overdone it here and there. I'd forgotten how fragile humans are. I nearly broke the Seer when I first came upon him by not shielding my power enough. Oops, my bad. Luckily, he was drugged at the time and I reacted quickly, so no real harm was done."

It giggled, but Bryn continued to scowl.

"Obviously, I am not so particular as you," it continued with an indulgent smile and a shrug. "I am worshipped, but not in the way others of my kind are. I am worshipped more in deed and consequence than thought, and so I grow fond of my most faithful acolytes. Wherever mischief goes, so does my heart, even if my devotees do not know whom they serve. Besides, all the portents said they must remain on the path or the worst will happen. Who cares if I had to help them along a little."

It sounded a little defensive now, as if it were talking to someone else. Bryn sat silently for a moment, trying to puzzle through all it had said until an unpleasant thought occurred to him.

"But if you revel in discord, shouldn't you want the opposite of the prophecy? I mean, wouldn't you be rooting for the other side? Unless you're already helping them too."

Its answering smile wasn't particularly comforting, but it said, "I'm the god of mischief, just a little harmless fun. I'm not the god of chaos and destruction. Humans didn't create that in its elemental sense. Chaos is an unstoppable law of the universe that humans constantly strive against, not a god they can summon through thought and deed. I'm just here to make it a little more interesting." Its smile fell away and it leaned forward. "If the other side wins, there will be no more harmless fun, the game will be over, and I can't allow that."

"So why are you leaving now?"

"I told you. I can't make it too easy. That would be cheating."

Before Bryn could come up with anything else to say, the other simply vanished. Bryn searched the ground for any living creature it could have turned into but found nothing. Even the strange scent of it had disappeared.

"I have more questions," Bryn yelled. Nothing but a slight breeze tousled his dark hair in answer.

Rowan McAllister is an unapologetically romantic jack-of-all-trades and a sucker for good food, good cocktails, rich fibers, a great beat, and anything else that indulges the senses. In addition to a continuing love affair with words, she likes to play with textiles, metal, wood, stone, and whatever other interesting scraps of life she can get her hands on. She lives in the woods on the very edge of suburbia—where civilization drops off and nature takes over—sharing her home with her patient, loving, and grounded husband, her three rescues, and a whole lot of books, booze, and fabric. Her chosen family is made up of a madcap collection of people as diverse as her interests, all of whom act as her muses in so many ways, and she would be lost without them. Whether her stories have a historical, fantasy, or contemporary setting, they always feature characters who still believe in true love, happy endings, and the oft-underappreciated value of sarcasm.

Email: rowanmcallister10@gmail.com
Facebook: www.facebook.com/rowanmcallister10
Twitter: @RowanMcallister

The Wanderer
Rowan McAllister

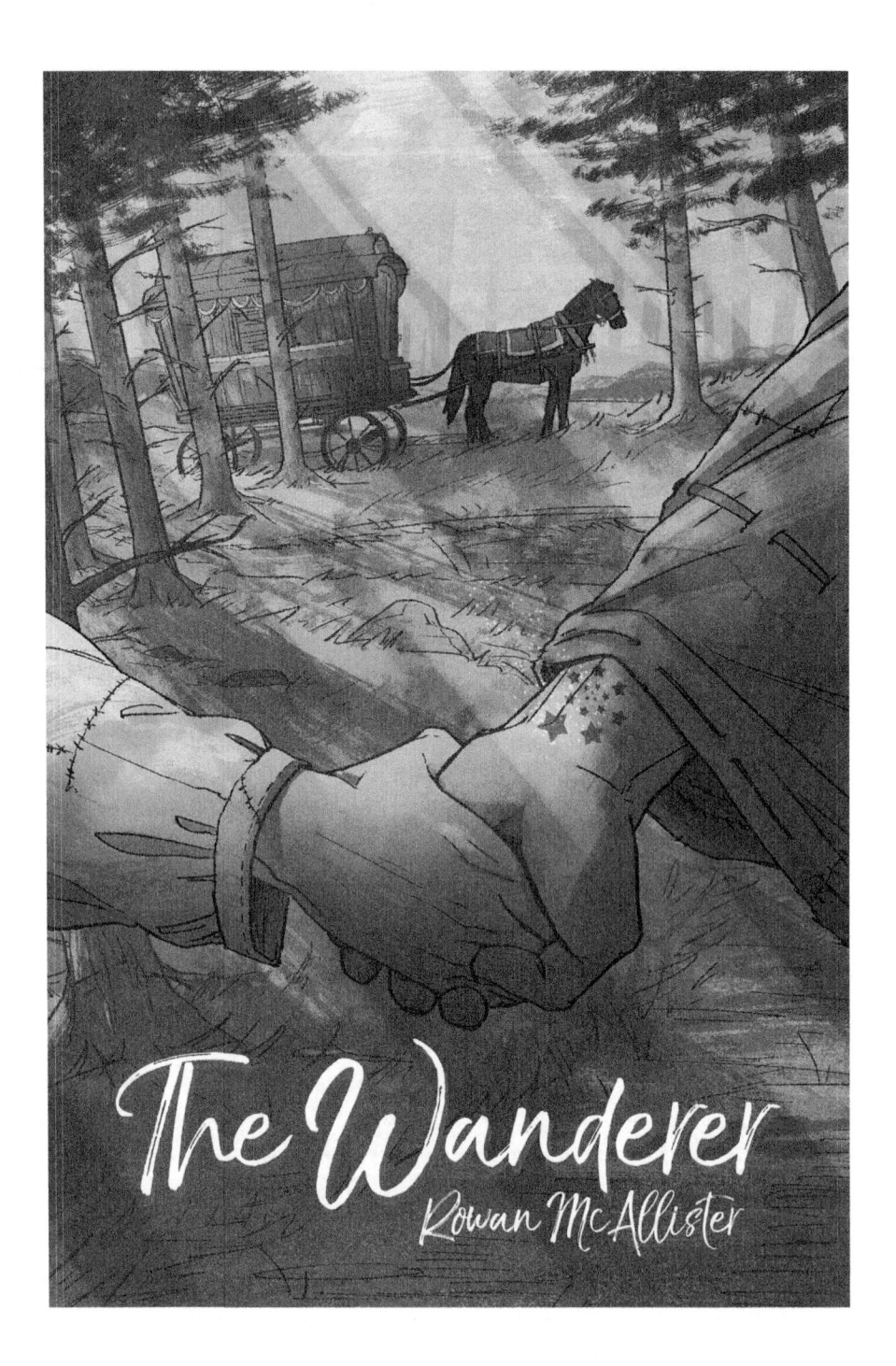

Chronicles of the Riftlands: Book One

After centuries of traveling the continent of Kita and fighting the extradimensional monsters known as Riftspawn, mage Lyuc is tired and ready to back away from the concerns of humanity.

But the world isn't done with him yet.

While traveling with a merchant caravan, Lyuc encounters Yan, an Unnamed, the lowest caste in society. Though Yan has nothing but his determination and spirit, he reminds Lyuc what passion and desire feel like. While wild magic, a snarky, shapeshifting, genderfluid companion, and the plots of men and monsters seem determined to keep Lyuc from laying down his burden, only Yan's inimitable spirit tempts him to hang on for another lifetime or so.

All Yan wants is to earn the sponsorship of a guild so he can rise above his station, claim a place in society, and build the family he never had.

After hundreds of years of self-imposed penance, all Lyuc wants is Yan.

If they can survive prejudice, bandits, mercenaries, monsters, and nature itself, they might both get their wish… and maybe even their happily ever after.

www.dreamspinnerpress.com

The Priest

Rowan McAllister

Chronicles of the Riftlands: Book Two

Brother Tasnerek, one of the infamous Thirty-Six stone bearers, is facing a dangerous crisis of faith after uncovering a secret that could shake the foundations of the Brotherhood of Harot. When Tas is sent to protect a tiny village on the edge of Rassa's borders from Riftspawn, he struggles to resume his duties, risking his life and the lives of those around him.

Girik has always been an outsider, but to help his sick mother, he agrees to be the village's offering in a painful ritual deemed necessary by the Brotherhood. But when the priest has a crisis of conscience, Girik offers his help to untangle a web of lies—even if it means getting closer than he ever imagined and committing sacrilege in the process.

With a monster lurking in the forest, a wandering mage mysteriously appearing, and more secrets awakening to unravel the truths of their world, Tas and Girik must make grave decisions. A life without danger seems a far-off hope, but love just might be theirs… if they survive.

www.dreamspinnerpress.com

Danny Doormat

ROWAN MCALLISTER

It's time to wipe his feet of the idea that he's not good enough to be loved.

Danny Dorfmann is dependable, no matter what's going on in his own life. So when widower Asa needs a sitter for his dog, Minion, Danny is the natural choice. Besides, Danny's had a crush on Asa—a hot architect who's way out of his league—for years.

Asa is just climbing out of his grief over the loss of his husband and trying to reclaim his life. Love and dating aren't on his radar, but as one favor turns into another and he spends more time with Danny, romance sneaks up on them.

Friendly adventures gradually turn into something deeper, but a manipulative roommate and interfering family and friends want to douse the slow burn building between Danny and Asa. To keep the chances of a happily ever after going, Danny will have to take a stand—and to hold on to the man of his dreams, he'll have to stop letting everybody walk all over him.

www.dreamspinnerpress.com

ROWAN McALLISTER

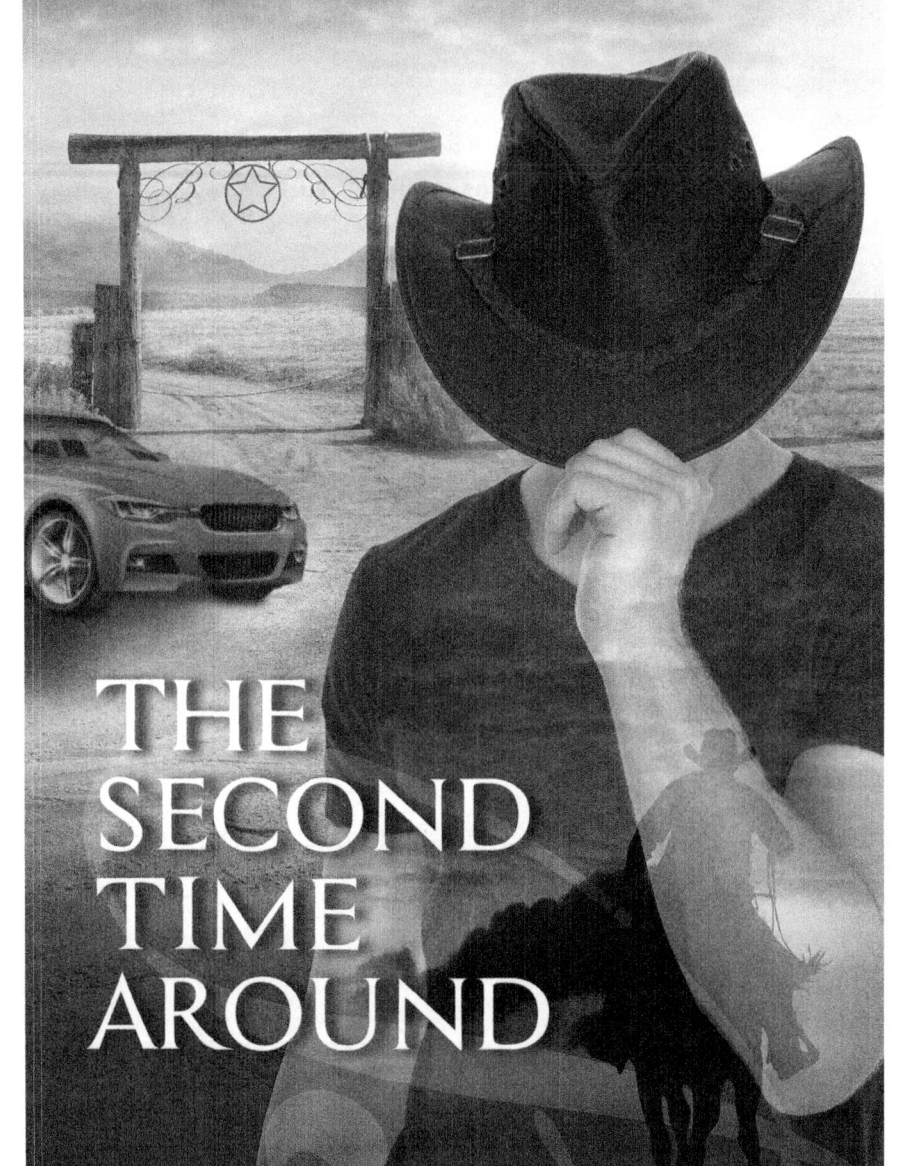

THE SECOND TIME AROUND

Though born into wealth and privilege, Jordan Thorndike can't keep pretending. He's never going to become the lawyer his parents hope for… or provide the daughter-in-law and two-point-four grandkids they expect. Faced with an ultimatum—carry on living the lie or get out—Jordan leaves with only what he can pack in his BMW.

Homeless, jobless, directionless, Jordan heads to one of his mother's pet charities: Better the Second Time Around Rescue ranch. With his family name and charm, he has the staff eating out of his hand in no time—except for one man.

Russ has never been handed anything, and he resents the spoiled rich brat using the ranch to live out a fantasy. Though Jordan is determined to prove himself to Russ through hard work, family and old wounds complicate matters. Will Jordan realize that what he sees as an escape is real life for most people? And can Russ accept that Jordan can grow—and that he wants him?

www.dreamspinnerpress.com

WE MET IN DREAMS

ROWAN MCALLISTER

In Victorian London, during a prolonged and pernicious fog, fantasy and reality are about to collide—at least in one man's troubled mind.

A childhood fever left Arthur Middleton, Viscount Campden, seeing and hearing things no one else does, afraid of the world outside, and unable to function as a true peer of the realm. To protect him from himself—and to protect others from him—he spends his days heavily medicated and locked in his rooms, and his nights in darkness and solitude, tormented by visions, until a stranger appears.

This apparition is different. Fox says he's a thief and not an entirely good sort of man, yet he returns night after night to ease Arthur's loneliness without asking for anything in return. Fox might be the key that sets Arthur free, or he might deliver the final blow to Arthur's tenuous grasp on sanity. Either way, real or imaginary, Arthur needs him too much to care.

Fox is only one of the many secrets and specters haunting Campden House, and Arthur will have to face them all in order to live the life of his dreams.

www.dreamspinnerpress.com

FOR MORE OF THE BEST GAY ROMANCE

DREAMSPINNER PRESS

dreamspinnerpress.com

Printed in Great Britain
by Amazon